THE
NEVER ENDING
GAME

RAYMOND HICKMAN

Printed in the United States of America
Library of Congress Control Number: 2024923321
ISBN: Softcover   979-8-89518-445-5
              e-Book   979-8-89518-446-2
Published by: WP Lighthouse
Publication Date: 10/24/2024

To buy a copy of this book, please contact:
WP Lighthouse
Phone: +1-888-668-2459
support@wplighthouse.com
wplighthouse.com

TABLE OF CONTENTS

This book is dedicated to Astasha, my beautiful wife

Prologue

Amir looked around his small bedroom watching the elongated shadows disappear as dawn touched the horizon. He still seethed in anger as he thought about his uncle, Slim, passing him what he had thought was marijuana; the rolled up cigarette had actually been hash-laced with P.C.P. Amir had been imagining seeing demons ever since, and he cringed as he thought about the strawberry milk Slim had forced him to drink; his uncle had claimed that the milk would help him come down from his high, but all it seemed to do so far was make his stomach feel queasy. Amir had never felt this way before and he couldn't understand why people choose certain types of drugs to indulge in. Amir remembered losing it in the party-thinking that people were out to get him; he had later kissed on a stranger's breasts before vomiting all over her and running out of the house naked. The next thing he remembered was Slim and his play brother, Los, forcing him inside of a vehicle, wrapping him in a blanket, and forcing milk down his unwilling throat.

Amir glanced down at the roaches devouring something on the floor next to his bed, wishing that he had money to purchase his mother a home in the suburbs of Kansas City, Kansas. Amir was tall, dark, and handsome; he was only fifteen years old, but he had already lived the life of someone many years older. He wished he could shake off the drug so that he and Los could proceed with their hustling plans for later in the morning. The number one rule for the two friends was to get money: by any means necessary.

Amir stood up from the bed and looked down at his feet-noticing that the new Air Jordan's that he had been wearing the night before were gone. He was also still naked from the waist down.

"I'm telling momma! You're nasty!" His little sister, Loren, had her hands covering her eyes, as she walked backward out of his room. Everyone called her Lo-Lo, and she was a handful.

Amir yelled at his little sister. "What did I tell you about coming in my room without asking? I'm going to beat your butt!" He heard his sister informing to their mother as he attempted to shake off the dizziness in his head as he strolled toward the shower.

He finished bathing and pulled on his silk boxer shorts; he lightly applied some cologne-laced lotion to his flesh before heading toward his small family. Amir could hear his mother scolding Loren in the kitchen for entering his room unannounced.

"I don't care what he does in his room! If you wouldn't have gone in there, like he's told you many times, you wouldn't have seen him naked! I don't want to have to tell you again, little girl. You respect your brother and knock before you walk into his room; do you understand me?"

Amir could hear his little sister sobbing softly before responding.

"Yes ma'am."

Candace redirected her wrath toward her son.

"Amir Wilson! When you get dressed, I need to talk to you!"

He knew his mother wanted to scold him about being high and arriving home wrapped in a blanket. Candace Wilson had been a widow for four years. Amir's father, Malik, had died in a car accident with his brother, Slim, at the wheel. Candace had never forgiven Slim for it, and she didn't appreciate Amir associating with him in any way. Although Amir loved and respected his mother, he needed Slim for things that his mother would never understand. Slim and Malik had always hustled together, and Amir had personally witnessed Slim's dark side on numerous occasions. His uncle was a stone-cold killer, and his name was well known in the streets. With his backing Amir and Los were able to hustle in locations that would have been otherwise impossible. They also needed Slim to transport them to and from locations throughout the city. Neither Amir nor Los could drive well.

Amir entered the kitchen where his sister was enjoying her daily dose of Lucky Charms.

"Swine eater!"

Amir often taunted his sister about her marshmallow-based cereal; he had grown up as a Muslim, but his sister knew almost nothing about the religion. It seemed that Candace had chosen her new boyfriend, Mike, because he was the exact opposite of how his father had been. Malik had been tall, dark, and dangerous. Mike was a short, mulatto player hater. He had attempted to play father to Amir and Lo-Lo, until Slim had pulled him to the side to have a serious talk with him-laced with venom.

Lo-Lo complained about Amir's name calling as usual as their mother entered the room, and Candace glared at her son with amused scorn, shaking her head. She looked him over, noticing the expensive jogging suit, shoes, and jewelry. Amir's outfit was complemented with his usual "fitted" Kansas City Chiefs headwear.

Candace glared at him before speaking.

"Amir, where are you getting money to purchase all of these things?" She stood over him, obviously waiting for a response.

He responded with a shake of his head. "Momma, I told you so many times, I be cutting grass for Mike, and you know I be saving my chips. Dang momma, chill out!"

Candace playfully punched him.

"I'm not stupid, boy! I know how much you make cutting grass. By the way, I saw how you came in here last night and I know that you weren't acting like that off liquor and weed. Do you want to become a wet-head like Slim, or do you want to accidentally kill your sister like he did his own brother? I've told him too many times to stay away from you and Loren. The next time I'm going to get my gun and blow his brains out. I don't care how crazy he thinks he is; I'll leave him lying there and call the police myself! Now, you tell him I said to stay away, and I'm not playing. Do you hear me, Amir?"

"Yes ma'am." He knew not to argue. Candace was like a female bear protecting her cubs, and Amir knew that she wasn't bluffing. Lo-Lo giggled and pointed a finger at him like she was shooting a gun, and he simply shook his head and sampled the hamburger gravy his mother had prepared. Candace still didn't eat pork from living with a Muslim for so long. She was a Christian, but she lived her life based on the old-testament; there were few religious arguments between her and her son.

Amir heard the lock disengage on the front door, and he knew who it was immediately. Candace and Mike had split up about a month before and she had forced him to give up access to their home. Lo-Lo raced to the door and Amir could hear his little sister's young voice yelling.

"I give, Los! Stop tickling…..me!" She sprinted back into the kitchen with Los slowly stalking her with his fingers flexing as if he couldn't wait to get his hands on her.

"Who's your master? Who…is…in…con…trol?!" Los grabbed Lo-Lo and lifted her above his head as she screamed with glee. The two had been keeping up this routine since Lo-Lo was a small child, and it seemed that they would continue for as long as Amir's play-brother was around.

"How are you doing, Mrs. Wilson?" Los already had a smirk on his face; he knew how his god-mother would react.

Candace turned to Los with a frown.

"Boy, if you keep it up, I'm going to beat your ass, do you hear me? I'm *Mrs.* nobody to you! You're my son, and you call me by my first name, or call me momma. I thought you looked at Amir as a brother."

Los grinned. "He is my brother: blood brother." Amir cringed, knowing what was coming. About a year ago, he and Los were in the backyard slicing open their palms with a knife, grasping hands in a ghetto blood-pact. Candace had walked out of the door and lost it; Amir couldn't believe Los was reminding his mother once again. His friend often tormented people, and he couldn't seem to help it. Los walked over and stood over Amir and stared him down-attempting to get a reaction out of him.

Just as Amir's lips turned up into a smile, Candace walked up to her son and stared directly into his face.

"Go ahead and laugh, Amir! I will slap the shit out of you! Stupid-ass niggas cutting on yourselves like fools! Get out of my sight, both of you!"

Los grabbed Amir and pulled him outside. Slim was waiting next to his Audi; he knew not to approach the house. Los was still laughing, and Amir turned to him.

" Nigga, you need to gone with that bull-shit! I gotta be here and listen to this shit. Stop bringing that shit up, fool!

They walked toward the vehicle and Amir's neighbor, Ashley, approached them. She had grown up next door for as long as Amir could remember, and she had always had a crush on Los.

"Where y'all going?" Amir attempted to hide his smile as he responded. "We're going over to Los's house to meet up with some fine-ass chicks we met yesterday. We'll be back later; don't wait up!" The color drained from Los's face as Ashley stood staring. She suddenly screamed and rushed up to attempt to claw Los's face.

Los yelled. "Ashley! He just bull-shitting, baby!"

Amir climbed into Slim's vehicle and yelled out of the window.

"No I aint, nigga! Ashley's my friend, and you aint playin' her like a fool no more! Don't worry about him, Ashley; he aint nothin' but a trick-ass nigga. Los, let's go!"

Los climbed into Slim's vehicle complaining and watching Ashley stomp back into her house; they both knew she wouldn't be speaking to Los for a while.

Los shook his head. "Nigga, you aint shit!"

Amir smiled. "Eye for eye, my nig."

Slim glared at the two teenagers as he shook his head.

"You boys need to grow the fuck up. We don't have time to be playin' games. I'm gonna pick up your punk-ass homeboys, and you're on your own after that. I got business to take care of, so you no-driving niggas is taking my van. You wreck it, you buy it, or I beat the black off y'all asses. You little niggas feel me?"

Amir just sat back and didn't say anything; he was already plotting on how he would manipulate the kids they had chosen to steal for them at the Oak Park Mall in Johnson County, right outside of Kansas City, Kansas. Slim pulled up to one of his "spots" and they watched him step out and begin arguing with one of his workers. The man was about twenty years old, and he had been working for Slim since he was a young boy. The two had been arguing about money a lot lately, and each time the talk became much more animated. Tony had always been like a son to Slim, but Los had never liked him.

Los nudged his best friend. "Meer, I bet that nigga's stealin'! I don't know how Slim fucks with that nigga." Amir glanced over in time to see Tony punch Slim, and his uncle immediately pulled his pistol and started blasting as the man attempted to flee. Tony dodged bullets for a couple of seconds, but just as he made it to the corner blood sprayed out of his chest as he was hit in the back. Tony fell to his knees and eventually dropped onto his face and lay still.

Slim ran to the van and tossed his keys inside.

"Meer, y'all gotta get little, and I mean right now! That bitch-ass nigga stole from me, and the fool decided to get violent with a playa that been down since the first day! I'll talk to y'all later. Take my van to the house when you finish handling your business. Go!"

Amir slid over into the driver's seat and they sped off past Tony's body and heard Slim barking orders as he climbed into a GMC Yukon with one of his women. Amir had heard stories about his uncle, but it was different seeing it with his own young eyes. Tony was dead! He wasn't a friend, but he had always been friendly with Amir. When Tony fell, Amir knew he was gone forever. He thought about Tony's family in Kansas City, Missouri, and realized that the feud that had been waged for as long as he could remember would soon get much worse. Amir didn't know exactly what had happened, but he was afraid for his uncle- and anyone that crossed him.

Reese, Flip, Pete, Tracy, and Arthur were in the back of the van listening intently to Amir's instructions while they passed a marijuana "blunt" around.

"Remember Pete and Tracy, you two have to distract for each other and get the big plastic bags. Don't worry about the small ones. At Dillard's stores they got security that pretend to be customers, so stay on your damn toes. Reese, you and Flip go to each counter and stack the shirts and pants in piles of ten. Don't make them any bigger than that because people might notice, just make more piles. Arthur, you go through with me and Los once we get the bags. Don't look around and worry about nothin'! Just fill your bag up and walk out to the van fast. Stay there and wait for everybody to jump in. Y'all feel me?"

Everyone nodded in unison as Los grinned and looked each youngster in the eyes.

"The first nigga that makes it to the van gets an extra twenty, and I got a fine-ass bitch that's gonna suck yo' little-ass dick. We all getting' pussy, don't worry, but bitches always do something special for fools that get that money." Most of the younger boys wore embarrassed looks on their faces; Flip and Reese looked greedy and lustful as they stared at Los in awe. It was time for the group to get down to business.

Things went on without any complications until a security guard grabbed little Arthur and put him in a headlock.

"You think you can steal from me, boy? You're going to jail today!" Arthur struggled, but he was small, and he was no match for the man's strength. The security guard pulled the boy's hands behind his back as if he was trying to break them, and Arthur let out a blood-curdling scream. The man smiled in satisfaction as he continued his assault on the boy. He didn't see Los come out of the store with his bag and hand it to Tracy before pulling a small switchblade from his rear pocket.

The security guard pulled a pair of handcuffs out of a small pouch at his waist as Los struck. He repeatedly stuck the knife into the man's back viciously.

"Bitch-ass-nigga!-Wanna-be fuckin'pig!" The man screamed as he attempted to grab Los's hand, but all everyone could see was a blur as the boy continued to strike; the security guard's hands and limbs now seemed to be the target.

Everyone climbed into the van as Amir grabbed his friend and pulled him away from the moaning man now lying on the pavement. Blood was dripping off Los's knife and murder was in his eyes. Los was usually the comedian, but his ties to his dangerous father gave him a very aggressive side. Los was half-Mexican and half African-American. His father was a member of the Border Brothers gang based on the west-coast. Los's pretty-boy looks, long wavy hair, and playful nature often caused people to assume that he was just another potential victim; Los was an aggressive agitator who welcomed violence.

The boys made it to the Argentine District in Kansas City, Kansas, and they entered Los's cousins' house to see a living room full of naked women gyrating to music and snorting cocaine out of a large mound on a glass table. Los's uncle, Chino, approached them with his shirt off, sporting a large tattoo of a darkened letter "B" on each shoulder. He began conversing with Los in Spanish. "Pequeno primo lleva estas rucas para astras……." Amir understood the Spanish, and he cringed at the disrespect aimed toward them because of the color of their skin. Chino referenced the Border Brothers as if they were strangers to the boys. Los had never gotten along with his cousins because of the African blood coursing through his veins. He didn't appreciate Chino reverting to Spanish and talking about him and his friends as if they were fools.

Los responded to his cousin in English. "Man, women love us because of our big dicks, homeboy. I know they get tired of getting by on y'all little-ass shit. I know what's up with the Border Brothers because my dad runs that shit down this way! We the black version over here, cousin, and we're eventually going to take this shit to another level. The Black Border Brothers are gonna take over and you mothafuckas aint gonna have no choice but to accept it and fall the fuck in line!" Chino smiled without responding and motioned the group of boys and the handful of beautiful women to the rear of the house.

Reese, Flip, Pete, and Tracy glared at Chino as if he were their worst enemy. Arthur had already left. He had gotten the extra twenty dollars for making it out first, but he had been in pain from the security guard's assault on his underdeveloped arms. The other boys had gotten their money also, but it was chump change compared to what Amir and Los would have once they sold their merchandise-even at half price. The two would be making a very nice amount for their fifteen minutes inside the mall. Amir and Los devised schemes like this all over both Kansas Cities, and they had many young hoodlums that were willing to assist them for some quick, reliable cash.

Amir's ambition was to get his family out of the dire circumstances they were faced with; Los's misguided motivations were to become a ghetto celebrity.

They all went into the back room with the women and were taught new, exciting things by the escorts. They were still only boys, but they were greedy and anxious to learn. There was no embarrassment etched on their young faces. The women were performing tricks and begging for the drugs that were unlimited whenever Los was around.

They spent most of the night there before going to Amir's house to shower and sleep off the liquor and marijuana.

"Where is he, Candace? He has gone too far this time!" Amir watched Los climb off the floor and look around in dismay. His father, Carlos Sr., was banging on the door, yelling obscenities, and demanding to be let into the room. When Los opened the door, he was snatched off his feet by his father.

"Boy, what the fuck is wrong with you? You know that I have drugs all around my house, and now you're getting caught on tape stabbing a man! I don't know what petty shit you've been into, but you won't be getting me a life sentence! You're going to turn yourself in, do your petty time, and we're moving to Missouri. Candace, I don't want Los and Amir to turn out like me and Malik. I've told them too many times, but this was the last straw!"

Candace nodded her understanding and watched Amir closely. There were problems between Kansas City, Kansas, and Kansas City, Missouri, but she knew that the border was not enough to stop her sons from connecting with the bond they had formed: with blood.

CHAPTER 1

"Ah! Ah! Mmm! It's big, Los! Hurt me, please! You're touching it, baby!" Ashely and Los were on the balcony of her condominium, and she was bent over the ledge with her skirt hiked up around her waist. She was staring down at the street far below while Los had her hands handcuffed behind her back, penetrating her dripping vagina as deep as he could. He suddenly pulled out, spread her cheeks apart, and he plunged into her anus savagely.

Los began pounding furiously at Ashely's flesh while she screamed.

"No, Los! Please, stop! I don't do that! Stop!!" Los began trembling as he ejaculated into her, and Ashely's screams became moans of ecstasy. The two lovers performed the rape scene often, but this time Ashely didn't want the typical blindfold that they usually used so that it would be more exciting looking far down to the street. Facing death turned her on, and she often begged for more punishment. Los spent himself completely before pulling out, making sure to spread the excess semen onto her lower back. He took his key and freed her from the handcuffs, and Ashely immediately forced him into a chair and began licking on his manhood, sucking the remaining sperm out and twirling it around her fingers like it was a string. Ashely was in love with Los, and she would do anything for him: even murder. Los had already used her to set up a couple of horny drug dealers, and she was willing to do much more; Los was her man, and he controlled her mind.

Los moaned and shook his head as he grinned.

"Oh, baby! I love when you do that shit! But, damn, that shit makes my dick sensitive as fuck!"

Los had remained incarcerated inside the Youth Center at Topeka until adulthood, and he was eventually sent to the Lansing Correctional Facility in Lansing, Kansas, to serve a short sentence. When he was released, Los moved to Kansas City, Missouri, with his parents. It wasn't long before he was out of his parents' home and living in the inner city. Ashely had become an attorney, and she made a living defending Los's Border Brother relatives. They were illegal immigrants, drug traffickers, and murderers. Ashely, Amir, and Los's parents had been the only ones to hear from Los during the years of his incarceration. As soon as he was released, Amir and Ashely were outside with his new Audi sedan and plenty of cash to get him started. They soon formed the Black Border Brothers, and Los's family ties elevated them to becoming one of the more powerful organizations in the twin cities (Kansas City, Kansas, and Kansas City, Missouri). There had been a deadly feud waged between the cities, and Amir and Los were often forced to meet on neutral ground to handle their illegal business in the drug trade. The "Bottoms" area was controlled by the Italians, and these men were careful in not allowing illegal drugs to affect their prostitution business in the area. Los had no problem paying a toll to avoid unwanted consequences, but he hated dealing with the racist organization.

Los finished getting himself cleaned up and turned to Ashely.

"I'll be back tomorrow; There's some cash under the bed, and I need you to take it to Amir. Tell him to have Slim call me at my momma's house."

Los had received information that Tony (who Slim had killed years ago) had a brother that had just been released after serving fifteen years in Jefferson City, Missouri. Oscar had made a vow to avenge his brother's death. Los didn't know what the man looked like, or anything else about him, but he knew that he had to find out. In the meantime, Los wanted Slim to be aware of the man's interest in him.

Los had been pondering death a lot lately, and this latest information seemed like a premonition of an approaching catastrophe. He pulled Ashely's Range Rover into his mother's driveway and smiled as he noticed the neighbors staring at the new rims he had installed onto her vehicle. Los had also painted it "candy" white, installed two flat-screens behind her head rests, and oiled up her white leather seats.

Carlos Sr. had berated his son several times about drawing attention to himself, but Los felt that he deserved to be noticed after being invisible for the years of his incarceration. Carlos Sr. also had expensive tastes, but they were not as noticeable to casual observers. The interior of his home was decorated with white marble and black leather, and his Lincoln Mark LT truck, Cadillac CTS, and Audi Q7 were flashy enough without the accessories. It often angered Los to think about how hypocritical people could be, but he tried to keep in mind that his father's legitimate businesses helped shield his illegal activities.

He glanced at his parents' manicured lawn and headed into the house, eager to get back to the Chouteau Village Apartments in Kansas City, Missouri, where he lived. Los didn't have a desire to leave his neighborhood; Amir had been practically begging him to go into real estate with him and move inside a suburban gated community somewhere. Amir owned a detail shop and a Laundromat, but Los was too busy selling drugs and living the fast life to comprehend the importance of having a legitimate income.

He used his key to enter the house and was surprised to see his older sister, Mona, lounging in the living room. His sister always reminded him of Pocahontas, especially when she wore her hair in two long plaits as they were now. Mona was three years older than Los, but he had often fought with friends and associates when someone had pursued her when they were in school. Mona worked as a veterinarian, and she was currently engaged to be married to a doctor from Africa. Los had been relieved when she had moved to Florida to live with their aunt while he was incarcerated. His father's lifestyle often made him fear for her and his mother's lives. Mona frowned.

"Carlos Jr., I heard you before you even got close to this house. Do you just want to announce to the police that you're a drug dealer, carnal?"

His sister often switched between English and Spanish because they spoke both languages so frequently. Los preferred English most of the time, so he replied with a mean glare.

"They have to catch me to prosecute, and I've told you a thousand times, little girl, that if you talk to me don't mix it up. Either use English or Spanish, not both. Didn't you learn anything from all those years in school? What are you doing here, anyway? I thought you was following that punk-ass nigga to Africa?"

Los didn't like Mona's fiancé; he felt that most Africans looked down on African-Americans, and Los being half Mexican really made him confrontational when dealing with certain people.

Mona glared at her brother. "I had too much work to do, so I'll go next time. We're planning to make a move to North Kansas City this month, and I'm decorating myself. By the way, when are you going to stop living in that hell-hole neighborhood in Chouteau?" Mona hated inner-city life, and she couldn't understand why people cherished it. Los realized how his sister felt, but he stayed silent because he didn't want to ruin her visit with an argument; he didn't see Mona very often.

She stared at him for a moment before returning to the sofa to finish watching the local news. She glanced at Los with a frown.

"Did you hear about those boys from Kansas that were killed last night? They were mutilated and pieces of their bodies were missing; why would people do something like that to other human beings?"

Los shook his head and walked into the kitchen to make a call; he cursed inwardly as he thought about Reese. The situation Mona described sounded like something that Reese was supposed to take care of. Los had specifically given him instructions to discard the bodies on the Missouri side of the border- in the same location that they had decided to hustle in Black Border Brother territory. He wanted to send a clear message to everyone: respect or die. They had gagged and tortured the men unmercifully at Quindaro Park late into the night. They began by pulling off finger and toe nails, and they poured salt on the wounds before smashing the fingers and toes with hammers. They eventually doused the captives' hair with lighter fluid and let it burn until they passed out from the pain. They awoke to Amir shattering their kneecaps and elbows with a sledgehammer, and Reese sliced off their ears, noses, and what remained of their fingers and toes. Amir showed the men mercy by slitting their throats, but Los was so upset about the men's disrespect that he cut both of their penises off and stuffed them into each other's mouths. Los was furious as he spoke to his friend through the receiver.

"Reese, what the fuck is wrong with you, man? I told you how I wanted the shit done and where I wanted the niggas to be left! Did you think I was just talking to hear myself?"

Reese gripped his cell-phone tight as he pushed the woman off his chest and came wide awake. He responded respectfully.

"Bro, them M.O.P. niggas was too thick on the block for it to happen like that. They had the whole street sowed up and they didn't move! When they saw me, they started getting off shots on me, my nig. They know I'm a Black Border Brother, so it must be static between us on sight."

They had been having problems with another local clique called M.O.P. (Money Over Pussy) and they were beginning to be a problem, especially for the Brothers on the Missouri side. It wasn't a coincidence that Oscar's son was the leader of the clique. Los couldn't believe that they were bold enough to come after a Black Border Brother as if there would be no consequences.

Los asked, "Did you leave the message, Reese?"

His friend didn't hesitate. "Yeah, man. I cut a fat B in both of them two niggas' ass cheeks. If I could have done it exactly like you said it would have been done, my nig. You know that. I gotta deal with this female, bro, but I'll be over to talk to you in person tomorrow. Border!"

Los smiled. "Border! We gonna find that bitch-ass nigga Paris and send his ass home to hell; make sure to be at the spot early." He ended the call and looked up to see his sister glaring at him, shaking her head.

"Did you have something to do with those killings, Los? That word border you're using is exactly what the police say they're investigating. They gave information about some letters carved into the bodies. What are you doing, Carlos Jr.?"

He was irritated by Mona's obvious eavesdropping, but he answered her.

"Mona, I aint killed no damn body. The Black Border Brothers organization is just part of my life. I take the good with the bad. Would you rather it be me or Amir stretched out?" She shook her head again.

"Los, you just don't get it, do you? I love you, brother, but I hate your evil ways. I want to witness you strive for more than controlling a drug-dealing gang. Papa and his gang is why you started out in those streets in the first place- acting as if you're some god or something. Do you want the same thing for your son?"

Los stared defiantly at her, but Mona simply turned and walked into the other room; she knew that he wouldn't listen.

CHAPTER 2

Slim walked into his house, deactivated the home security system, but he still checked every corner of each room that could conceal someone. He felt that the spirits of the people that he had killed were making him paranoid and fearful for his life. The P.C.P. and heroin that he indulged in only made matters worse. He motioned to Monica, who was sitting in his truck outside, and Slim smiled when she entered the house and he saw the surprise on her face as she looked around the luxurious living room. Slim only dealt with women nearly half his age; the women were always impressed: most young men their ages couldn't see past what was inside their candy-painted vehicles. Slim lived in Olathe, Kansas, and he had to deal with occasional racism, but he loved the suburban area, and he couldn't find an excuse not to reside in one of the wealthiest counties in the United States. He watched the young beauty walk around his home, marveling at the expensive paintings, exotic fish, and the thick carpet that ran through her pretty, perfectly shaped toes. Monica knew that Slim always ordered people to leave their shoes at the door, so she kicked hers off without him having to ask. Slim picked up her heels as he watched her; he imagined having the shoes in the bedroom for some fun.

Monica was wearing a skirt that barely covered her shaved vagina, and it hugged her large, perfect backside like a pair of yoga pants. Slim stared into her pretty face and melted, hoping she was as good as she appeared. Slim had reached middle age, and he was tired of living the street life; he was anxious to settle down with a nice young woman. The only problem was the demons of his past coming back to haunt him.

There were plenty of people that wanted him dead, and they would go through anyone to achieve their goal. If he married this beautiful woman and someone hurt her to get him, he would murder their entire families and everyone they knew or associated with.

He looked at her with her legs spread, lying back on the couch fondling her wet vagina and swollen nipples. Slim motioned for her to wait and watched her pout; Monica had heard rumors that he was well endowed, and she could imagine the older man tearing her apart.

Slim had remembered the call from Ashely and knew he had to call Los. He listened to a few rings and cringed when Vonda (Los's mother) answered the telephone with scorn in her voice, obviously having recognized his number on the caller I.D.

"What are you calling here for, Slim? Who are you planning to kill now? Why involve my son and Amir? Don't answer! Here's Los." Slim heard Los and his mother arguing and waited with a detached look on his face. He knew what he represented to Vonda, and he couldn't blame her. He realized that she also blamed him for his brother's death (Vonda's secret lover).

Los spoke in a frustrated voice. "Sorry about that, Playa. You know how it is with her. I just wanted to let you know that Tony's brother just got out of the joint, and he's telling mothafuckas that he gonna kill you. I know you can handle yo' business, but I wanted you to know, anyway. You do remember the bitch-nigga you killed in front of us, right?"

Slim sadly couldn't remember at first, but when he did, he felt a regret that had never been there before. He silently wished that he had allowed Tony to live instead of shooting him down in the street, but his younger age and false pride would not allow it at the time. He thanked Los for the information and reprimanded him for speaking so freely about murder over the telephone lines. He also instructed him to get as much information about the man as he could. He looked down to see Monica on her knees in front of him, unbuttoning the slacks to his tailored Armani suit.

CHAPTER 3

Monica pulled Slim's boxer shorts around his ankles and began licking around the tip of his penis, playing with the small hole with her tongue while massaging his scrotum softly with her oiled hands. When she took him into her mouth, Slim ended the call with Los and grabbed her by the hair and pulled her down on his shaft until she began gagging from his length. She sucked until his toes began to curl and he was approaching his climax; she retreated and laid back, sliding her bikini panties off and freeing her medium-sized breasts from her bra. Slim looked in fascination at her young, tight, beautiful body, and glanced down at his manhood jerking in anticipation.

Monica began rubbing her clitoris and tasting herself. When she started concentrating on her breasts, Slim knelt and sucked the juices off her thighs, marveling at the strawberry smell that seemed to leak from her pores. Slim could not detect a scent from her vagina; Monica was nice and clean. When he began parting the lips between her legs with his tongue and sucking on her clitoris, Slim began to hear her moan as she pulled his face into her sex as if she wanted to suffocate him with her most intimate treasure. They performed foreplay for some time, and when Slim finally entered her, Monica couldn't help but to scream. Slim was the first man to give her oral sex; none of her past boyfriends had been concerned with her needs. That was the reason that Monica preferred older men, but they had to be handsome and take care of their bodies. She looked down at Slim's muscular frame as he continued to plunge into her body, and she clenched her vaginal muscles around his large shaft. She had already climaxed twice, and Slim didn't appear to be slowing. When she finally climbed on top of him to control how much length came into her she was already sore and throbbing, but she was still greedy-urging him into her creamy vagina. When she pulled him forward to suck on her nipples, she began licking the top of his bald head. Monica could feel his manhood swelling inside of her and knew what was coming. She immediately felt him ejaculating into her; it seemed that each time he squirted a large load she shivered another strong climax. Monica felt like Slim had loaded a pint of sperm into her before he also shivered out his orgasm as she collapsed on top of him, licking on his lips and professing her love.

In the middle of the night, Slim gently pushed her off his chest and showered in the downstairs restroom so that he wouldn't wake her. He was headed to meet Amir at his home in Kansas City, Kansas. They had many things to discuss about the escalating feud between the Black Border Brothers and the M.O.P. Things were bad enough with the Kansas against Missouri strife, but now they had to worry about a clique that was not afraid to travel to either side of the border in pursuit of them.

M.O.P.'s leader, Paris, was young, but he had plenty of cash. He was connected to the Jamaicans, and his drug connections put him on a level close to theirs. Paris's problem was that he felt that he had something to prove because of his youth. He was originally from Columbia, Missouri, and he often feuded with other Missouri "blocks". He was now in a battle with a dangerous foe, and Slim knew that the M.O.P. couldn't win, but Paris couldn't retreat; at this point there was no turning back.

CHAPTER 4

Lo-Lo woke up to see Mike staring into her bedroom door, watching her sleep and obviously hoping to see an exposed area of flesh. Loren was seventeen years old now and her body had developed so much that the sports bras her mother purchased for her couldn't hide much. Mike had returned to live with Candace, and Lo-Lo couldn't believe how blind her mother was to something so obvious. Mike had walked into the bathroom on her twice, and she had complained to her mother a few times about the grown man wrestling around with her. One day Mike had pulled her onto his lap, and Lo-Lo had been surprised to feel something hard jamming into her backside. When she looked back, she could see the outline of Mike's penis standing straight up as he stared at her with lust in his eyes. Lo-Lo made sure to cover all areas of her body when Mike was in her vicinity.

Lo-Lo walked over and slammed her bedroom door in his face, not hiding her disgusted expression. She smiled when she thought about how stupid he looked standing in the hallway like a stray dog, but she also felt a tinge of fear when she realized how bold the man was getting. She didn't hear him walk away for a long time; Mike stood there in the dark doing whatever his sick mind instructed.

Lo-Lo returned to her bed and sat back thinking about a boy she had met at her school. *Keith is so cute!* He was always real polite and considerate of her wants and needs. He carried her books, waited with her for Candace to arrive to take her home, and he even helped her when she needed tutoring. Keith was extremely intelligent. Lo-Lo had French-kissed him on the back stairs of the school, but when his hands began exploring her body, she held him off and told him that she wouldn't give more than a kiss. Lo-Lo wanted to save all of that for the man she married, and Keith said he respected that; Lo-Lo hoped that he was the one. But, as perfect as Keith seemed, she had to be sure.

What Lo-Lo didn't know was that Keith was Tony's son. He was a year younger than his father had been when her uncle Slim had shot him down in the street. Keith hated pretending to like Lo-Lo, and her being cute did not matter to him. He planned on using her to set Slim up for his uncle, Oscar, who had been released from prison and had revenge on his mind.

CHAPTER 5

Amir was on his knees turning his head first to his right shoulder, then to the left, and finishing his salat (prayer) with a warm feeling inside.

"As-Salamu-Alaikum, As-Salamu-Alaikum wa ramatullah!"

He began visiting the mosque regularly on Fridays, but observing the prayers at home had been a challenge. The negativity in his life had a lot to do with it, but Amir tried to observe his personal prayers when he remembered them.

He walked into his game room to see Carlos Sr. at the bar being served drinks by one of the women Amir often hired to entertain when he and Carlos Sr. met. The women provided everything from cooking to sex; the beauties did everything extremely well.

Carlos Sr. was ogling the young Japanese/African-American bombshell when Amir approached.

"When did you get here, Papi?"

Carlos Sr. turned around with a huge smile on his face.

"Meer! I just got here, man! I need this woman; do you hear me? I mean, I need her!" Amir laughed and glanced at the beauty his godfather was referring to. She was the best of both worlds. She had a beautiful china-doll face with an even more beautiful, well proportioned body with no noticeable flaws.

"She's all yours, sir, but we have business to discuss first. Where are Tracy and Arthur? I thought I heard them come in."

Carlos Sr. reluctantly released China's hand and followed Amir to his study. "They went to pick up a few things for me at Quick Trip, son; I need apple juice for my cognac, and I refuse to smoke my marijuana out of those cigars you have all over the house. And you know I need some condoms." He nudged Amir playfully and listened to his son come down the winding staircase with the other women who were laughing at the jokes he often told.

When he saw his father, Los straightened up immediately and sat down in the leather sectional across the room. The women noticed the mood in the room, and they retreated upstairs to wait until business was concluded.

Carlos Sr. glanced around Amir's home with approval and silently wished that his son would be more responsible and stop returning to the inner-city to invite trouble into his life. Amir lived in Kansas City, Kansas, in a large house on the border of Lansing, Kansas. Amir didn't want to leave Wyandotte County, Carlos Sr. pondered, but at least he had the sense to purchase a property on a few acres of plush lawn. It was not a mansion by any stretch of the imagination, but it was a home that was worth at least five hundred thousand dollars. Amir was modest considering the amount of money he made, and he took care of both Candace and Loren to the best of his ability. Candace had not accepted Carlos Sr.'s help when Malik had died, and she had moved her family deep inside of the inner-city because of her pride.

As soon as Amir was old enough, Carlos Sr. pulled him under his wing and gave him an offer that he couldn't refuse, and they took the organization to another level with Amir's ties to the African-American community.

Carlos Sr. hadn't liked the idea of the "Black" Border Brothers at first, but in time he took the title as a compliment, especially when the money started piling up.

Tracy and Arthur came down the stairs followed by Slim.

Amir asked, "Where's everyone else?" Tracy shrugged as if he could care less, and Arthur pulled out his cell-phone and attempted to call Pete and Flip. He didn't bother calling Reese; he was known for showing up whenever he felt like it. Amir hoped that Reese hadn't had a confrontation with a clique from Missouri that he had been feuding with. Reese had been involved with one of the females from his enemies' neighborhood. He seemed to enjoy testing them by going to Missouri to take her out to shop in public. Reese reminded Amir so much of Slim that it was scary at times; the young man looked for trouble. Amir shook his head and tried to prepare for the meeting with his godfather.

CHAPTER 6

Carlos Sr. had waited long enough. "Los and Meer, whatever the others need to know, you two or Slim can tell them- whenever they decide to show up. The first thing we need to talk about is the ongoing feud you dumb mothafuckas have going with these fools over in Missouri, for no apparent reason. We have enough to worry about with this Kansas against Missouri bull-shit that's been going on for as long as I can remember. We already are forced to go through the damn Bottoms and pay these greedy-ass Italians and the bitch-ass police, but now do we have to worry about those punk ass bastards also? You boys need to handle your business and get this foolishness over with! My Border Brothers won't have anything to do with your mess. You have a lot of manpower and resources at your disposal; finish this shit before it affects our business. Is that understood?" Everyone nodded in unison and Carlos Sr. turned to Slim.

"Brother, whatever you can do to help with this situation will be appreciated. I know that you've been trying to lay back and enjoy your money, but we need the old Slim, at least for a little while. That person would have had this shit over with a year ago. I don't want anything to happen to anyone's family, but when these situations continue for too long, innocents often suffer the consequences."

Ashely came down the stairs and all eyes were glued onto her. She wore a silk, form-fitting dress with her hair cascading down her back with it cut across her eyebrows in the front as Asian women often styled their hair. She was a caramel-complexion beauty with deep dimples and beautiful light-brown eyes. How she made it down the winding staircase in the stilettos was a mystery, but everyone appreciated the view, especially her shaved mound that could be seen plainly from the bottom of the staircase where they all gawked at it with approval. After staring for a few seconds, Los responded to his father.

"Pops, we don't need Slim to help us with those fools; we already snatched a couple of them up and tor…."

Carlos Sr. cut his son off with a dismissive motion of his hand, signaling silence.

"I don't know how you and your little friends handle business, but it has obviously been the wrong way!"

He suddenly turned to Ashely. "Young lady, would you leave the room, please?" She stood and glared at the older man with hate in her eyes while thinking: *He wouldn't have a problem if I was in here fucking and sucking his old ass!*

She angrily strolled out of the room without a word, and Carlos Sr. stared hard at his son.

"I don't talk business around women and all of you know it! Unfortunately, if you keep rolling the dice, you'll find out why the hard way. I don't want to have to tell you hard-headed mothafuckas again. Keep your bitches out of my business; is that clear?" Carlos Sr. was not having it.

"Yes sir".

Los acknowledged the respect he had for his father, as did everyone else, but he felt that he must speak on Ashely's behalf.

"Pops, that woman is a straight killer. She aint your average bitch, and she been in love with me since…"

Los was cut off again by his father. "Is that clear?" They all nodded, knowing how Carlos Sr. was. He was from the old school and didn't feel women should be trusted because of their emotions. Amir silently agreed even though he knew of Ashely's deadly ways, but she was and would always be a vindictive female, and he felt Los should know that from the way she had behaved with jealousy when they were younger.

Slim stood and approached Carlos Sr. "Carlos, I'll do what I can to get the bull-shit over with as fast as I can, but these cats need to learn how to end their confrontations on their own." He turned to his nephew.

"Meer, you and Los don't have no damn excuses. Do your homework and find these niggas and kill them like they're out here tryin' to kill you! I'm not talking about a couple niggas; I'm talking about overkill on their whole family if that's what needs to be done. If you niggas want me to hold your hands and show you how to do it, so be it, but my lessons are expensive." Amir had heard enough.

"Uncle Slim, why are you coming at us as if you don't know how we get down on that killing shit? We've simply been trying to get this money, so we haven't had time to think about anything else, but those fools killed Pookie last night. Every one of those mothafuckas are going to die a horrible death, and that's my word. Slim, we know how you get down, but you're going to have to pass the torch, man; it's my turn to handle the situation how I see fit. Do you feel me?" He stared at Slim with the eyes of a killer, and Slim recognized it immediately from his lengthy time in the streets. He stared right back into Amir's eyes before smiling and slowly nodding his head in agreement. He knew that Amir would spill blood: he didn't have a choice. Tracy and Arthur stayed silent- they were anxious for any situation to arise. The two men were never consciously into the meetings, and they were anticipating mingling with the women and dealing with their enemies later. Arthur attempted to call Pete and Flip again, but their telephones were still going directly to their voicemails which was strange for the two men, especially on the day when they all were supposed to meet.

When Carlos Sr. was done speaking, Ashely and the other women in the house walked into the room, as if on cue. Tracy headed toward China, but he stopped when Carlos Sr. pulled her into his lap. The old man always got the first choice of the women; Amir and Los made sure his personal rule was followed. When Tracy looked at the other women in the room, though, he shrugged and grinned at Arthur; the women were all very beautiful. They each chose a female and headed to the bar for drinks and later smoked blunts on the patio and ended up surrounded by the women in various beds throughout the house.

CHAPTER 7

Pete exited on the Prospect exit in Kansas City, Missouri, and shook his head when he thought about Reese's call to him: *"Blood, y'all gotta come get me quick! My girl picked me up from my apartment earlier and brought me over her house. She caint take me back, my nig; she and that bitch nigga layin' here dead!"*

Pete tried to stay within the posted speed limit because he and Flip both had handguns and an AR-15 assault rifle. He glanced over at Flip loading two fifty round magazines with a handkerchief, dreading what could possibly be waiting for them on the Missouri side. They eventually turned the power off on their cell-phones because Reese wouldn't stop calling, babbling as if he was "shermed out" on P.C.P.

Flip said, "This nigga gonna end up gettin' us locked up or killed with this wet-head shit! The next time we gonna leave his ass over here since he like Missouri so damn much!"

Pete didn't comment because he realized Flip was just venting his frustrations. They were used to Reese and his die-hard ways. It was worth dealing with these situations from time to time because their friend had always been loyal to them, no matter what. When they pulled in front of Imani's house everything appeared to be normal, but when they noticed her boyfriend Dre's S.U.V. idling on the side of the house they knew something was very wrong. Pete turned his music off because he didn't want to bring unwanted attention to their presence. The neighbors who were outside were already looking at his new Porsche; it was equipped with a set of shiny rims, and the people stared with hate-filled eyes. They were also paying close attention to the Kansas license plate on the rear of the vehicle.

Flip turned to Pete. "Hurry up, man, you know they're going to call hella niggas now that they've seen us over here. It's late, but niggas gonna get out of bed for a nice lick. That was good thinking bringin' this flashy-ass car, my nig!"

Pete smiled, grabbed his pistol, and motioned Flip to follow him toward the front porch of Imani's house with the AR-15 in tow. When they made it to the steps, they could already detect the unmistakable smell of blood, urine, and feces that was always present when they crossed paths with death. They could also smell the chemical scent of P.C.P. in the air, and they hoped Reese wasn't in the house "stuck" and out of commission. They needed to return to Kansas fast, so that they could attend the meeting at Amir's home.

Flip stepped onto the porch first and glanced at Pete with a frown.

"That nigga Dre is on the porch, P, and that mothafucka Reese must have a damn shotgun or something. Half this nigga's head is gone and one of his damn arms is lying next to him!"

When Pete saw the body, he quickly covered his mouth and nose with his handkerchief; the smell was sickening, and the sight was horrid. When he entered the front door of the house, he knew that Reese had completely lost his mind.

Imani's two children were lying across the doorway, and the adolescent girl's head was tilted at an unnatural angle while the small boy's body lying next to her had his eyes open, but lifeless. The little girl's tongue was hanging from her mouth with teeth marks evident, and blood had congealed at the wounds.

Reese was sitting on the couch smoking a "wet stick" with Imani's corpse lying across his lap; her throat was slit, and her nipples were cut from her breasts. There was blood evident between her bare thighs and Pete was sickened to see blood on the open crotch of Reese's jeans. There was also dried blood around his lips, and Pete didn't want to think about where the blood came from: but he already knew. On closer inspection, where Imani's nipples had been were rips in the flesh, not cuts. Reese looked up and began to slur.

"I tol tha bitch, don…fu…wit…meee!" Pete attempted to grab the bottle of P.C.P. that was on a table alongside a fresh red pack of More cigarettes, but Reese clamped his hand on his arm like a vise. It always amazed Pete how strong people could be when they were under the influence of the drug, and he understood why the police were fast on the draw when dealing with these individuals: fear.

Pete attempted to talk to Reese while Flip removed the guns, knives, and other potential evidence that was strewn throughout the small house. When Pete finally got Reese onto his feet and steered him toward the front door, vehicles began screeching to a stop in the street out front. Flip dropped the bag of evidence and started gunning for the men with the AR-15; men were running and ducking for cover behind their vehicles or any other shelter they could find. Flip was not firing erratically or rushing, he was taking careful aim and it wasn't long before Reese and Pete had joined the gunfight. One of the men made it to the fence and his face disappeared in a shower of crimson as his body slumped to the ground.

Reese yelled, "Kansas, nigga! Killer Kansas!" He yelled this repeatedly while he fired.

People started pulling away from the house when they realized that they were outgunned, so Pete, Reese, and Flip took it as an opportunity to jump into Pete's vehicle and speed away from the area; sirens were approaching rapidly. They headed toward 12th street and began crossing the bridge toward Kansas. When they were crossing the Missouri River, Pete stopped and allowed Flip to climb out of the Porsche with the bag of evidence. He tossed it into the river to be lost forever.

Pete returned to the road and observed the speed limits as he headed up I-70 West to 75th street on the Kansas side of the border, and he headed toward Leavenworth Road. Once he made it to within a block of Amir's home, he turned his music off completely, pulled out his cellphone, and called the house.

CHAPTER 8

"Salaam." Pete smiled when he heard his friend's voice, but he could also hear the irritation over the phone lines. Pete responded.

"Bro, we been in some shit! It's me, Reese, and Flip. Is everything cool?"

Amir instructed him to pull up to the privacy fence, and before long it slid open and they noticed that the garage door was already raised- he pulled inside. Reese was stretched across the backseat and refused to move until Amir's voice boomed around the garage.

"Park and get in the damn house, man! Reese, what are you laying there for?" Pete knew that Amir was upset because Reese was reeking of P.C.P. He was completely against anything that altered someone's thinking processes. Amir had told his friends about using the drug without knowing it when they were younger, and he had explained how he lost control of himself. He vowed to never use the drug again, and he didn't like associating with anyone who indulged. Reese looked up to Amir as an older brother or father, and he was the only one who could instruct him to do anything. Reese was a stone-cold killer, but he had gotten his schooling from Amir and Los; he had never adopted Amir's casual attitude toward adversity.

Amir rushed Reese straight to the kitchen and forced him to drink a half gallon of chocolate milk. Pete and Flip headed to the game room to wait.

The room had just enough light to see Los and Ashely on the sofa. Los was stretched out on his back while Ashely slowly gave him fellatio with her eyes locked directly onto Pete and Flip. While they watched, she rose up and positioned herself above Los's manhood, and she slowly lowered herself onto him with a sigh. Ashely didn't show any embarrassment as Los began frantically pounding into her body, and she softly moaned and called out his name as if they were in the room alone. Los glanced over at them briefly, knowing they would never approach Ashely, under any circumstances. The rule they all followed was to stay clear of each other's women, no matter the situation. Tricks that they tossed up were different. Baby's mothers, wives, and longtime girlfriends were avoided at all costs. They felt that if you wanted something that belonged to your brother, you were jealous of him, and jealous men were extremely dangerous and unpredictable. There were many women to choose from, so they left each others' ladies alone.

Flip and Pete stayed and watched the performance until Los lowered himself to his knees and pounded Ashely from behind until they both reached a loud, screaming climax. Ashely pulled herself off Los's glistening shaft, and she turned around and kissed him passionately. She gathered her clothing and walked past them with a wink. Pete watched her leave in amazement, marveling at her stunning profile and amazing figure; she was the type of woman that made men lose their minds, but she eventually handed them over to Los to be robbed, or took care of them herself. Pete shuddered when he had this last thought, and Flip grinned, misunderstanding his friend's action. Los pulled on his clothes.

"Where you fools been? I hope you horny niggas enjoyed yourselves while we been in this bitch having to deal with pops. That young piece of meat just might have his old-ass sleep right now, but next time I'm sickin' Ashely on his ass to see how tough he is with a pretty pussy in his face.

They all laughed, knowing how Carlos Sr. was attracted to young, black women, but Pete felt that Los was underestimating his father; Carlos Sr. was well on top of his game.

Amir, Tracy, and Arthur entered the room followed by Reese, who had a small bucket in one hand, and a half-gallon of 2% milk in the other. He had a sick look on his face, but it appeared that the milk was doing its job against the P.C.P. He looked more aware of his surroundings. Carlos Sr. was obviously still occupied with China, and Ashely was still getting cleaned up. Slim walked in with a young woman holding onto his arm, but when he saw that everyone was in the room, he said something to her, and she retreated from the room with a frown. Flip began stating the details of the situation that had occurred earlier in Missouri, and everyone swung their heads toward Reese with mean stares when Flip started detailing the deaths of the children and Imani's mutilation.

CHAPTER 9

Amir sat Reese down. "Man, why in the fuck did you trip out like that?" Reese hung his head but not one person in the room believed that his remorseful look was authentic.

"Meer, I was in the bathroom and I heard the bitch whispering on the phone with that nigga, Dre; she was telling the bitch-ass nigga that I was in the bathroom and for his ass to hurry up and get over there! I smoked a stick while I waited for the nigga to show up. When he got there, I grabbed my Mossburg and caught the fool creeping up to the front door like a bitch! I didn't want to hurt the little kids, but they wouldn't stop screaming, Meer. That was they damn daddy that I had blasted, and they wouldn't shut the fuck up! When they started talkin' bout telling on me I didn't have a damn choice. I did it quick so they wouldn't feel too much, but I did that nothin' ass bitch real slow, just like she was tryin' to play me. The bitch was happy that I couldn't get my dick hard, but her butcher knife got some of that funky-ass pussy, don't trip!"

Amir stared at his friend in disgust before asking Reese a question. "Was this shit worth it, my nig? We've all told you many times to leave that bitch alone, but you had to keep throwing the shit in those Missouri niggas' faces! I'm not falling for the act, homeboy, I know you enjoyed killing those little kids and that tramp! You shouldn't have no problem finding those M.O.P. mothafuckas and dealing with them. You could've got Pete and Flip caught up right along with your crazy ass! Man, go clean yourself up!"

Slim shook his head as Reese stumbled out of the room.

"That nigga is scary as fuck, nephew. He's on that sick shit."

Amir nodded. "We're going to use that sick shit to get at our enemies, and later we're going to have a serious talk about Reese. I don't trust that fool no more, and I definitely don't fuck with no cannibal-ass niggas."

Everyone nodded and struggled with their individual inner thoughts, knowing that Reese had crossed the line in a major way.

CHAPTER 10

Detective Richard Davis had been on the Kansas City, Missouri Homicide Squad, The Gang Unit, and the Narcotics Division, but none of that had prepared him for a situation like this. *Little babies!* He walked out of the house and allowed forensics to do their sick job; he had seen enough of the mutilation. He decided to closely scrutinize the scene after the bodies had been removed; he couldn't think with the little boy's eyes staring lifeless, yet accusatory. He thought about his own children and remembered when they were in their pre-teens: beautiful and full of questions. Dick was a giant of a man, with dirty blond hair and skin so pale that it seemed translucent.

"Are you alright, Dick?" His partner, Susan Mendez, was looking at him with sympathy in her eyes; she knew how he felt about children from being around him for the past ten years, and she was suffering also. Susan was a dark-skinned beauty from Puerto Rico, and the woman reminded most people of the models that were on display in hip-hop videos.

Dick nodded. "Yeah, Sue, I just can't believe the things people do in this damn city, and the one across there is not much different." Dick motioned west, toward Kansas City, Kansas, and Susan simply nodded her understanding. She knew both cities well, and nothing surprised her anymore.

"Look what I found, Sue. Why do you think they did this?" Dick was holding up a filter that had been removed from a brown cigarette.

Susan nodded. "P.C.P. Where did you find that?"

Dick dropped two more filters into a plastic bag with a pair of tweezers before responding.

"One was in the bathroom, and two of them were on the couch where the woman was found- right under her head. It's like he, or they, sat back and got stoned to celebrate these killings. I can't wait to catch these fucks and put them on death row!" Susan nodded and motioned Richard toward the vehicle that they often shared.

"As soon as they remove the bodies, we're going through this house thoroughly. If the murderers were comfortable enough to sit here and get stoned, they were not strangers. Catch your breath and keep your cool, man, it's going to be a long night."

They sat in the vehicle for hours, smoking and drinking coffee, until eventually the bodies were removed, and the medical examiner gave them permission to enter the murder scene.

The man leaned forward and spoke to them through the window.

"We'll be performing the autopsies immediately. If either of you have any questions, you know where I'll be all night."

Dick nodded and stepped out of the vehicle followed by his partner. He noticed people sitting on the porch next door, and he made a mental note that they would be first in line to question about the murders. They were lounging outside very early in the morning as if this was a nightly occurrence, and it would be interesting to receive some valuable information from them, but he wouldn't count on it. People in the area harbored a mistrust of law enforcement, and none of them wanted the label of a "snitch", which could mean certain death.

They began their investigation at the fence and slowly moved onto the porch, being careful not to leave footprints in the huge pool of congealing blood. When they entered the house, Dick concentrated on the couch where the woman had been found, and Susan inspected the area surrounding the front entrance where the two children had been brutally murdered. Susan went into the bedroom and as soon as Dick found a matchbook and began scrutinizing it, he heard his partner say something in the next room.

"Son of a bitch!"

He hurried into the cluttered bedroom and saw Susan standing there and shaking her head.

"This woman was playing a deadly game." She showed Dick a secret compartment in the floor of the bedroom closet. There were naked pictures of several different men, camcorder tapes, sex toys, currency, and two prepaid cell-phones embedded in the floor under what Dick assumed were her boyfriend's assortment of Nike shoes. One individual was depicted much more than the others, and there were some photos with him and the victim engaging in several positions during sex. The man was a brown-skinned African-American with a slightly muscular build. He was handsome with cornrow braids hanging well past his shoulders. In a couple of the pictures his gold and diamond teeth were on display, glistening from whatever light source was being used to take the photograph. Dick realized that the teeth could be removable, but he felt something that expensive would be worn frequently, nonetheless. The man also had tattoos that stood out; there was a large letter "B" on each side of his chest. There was also another letter that matched them in the center of his neck. Dick kept this information stored in his memory.

Susan retrieved a picture from a bedside table and compared the men.

"This man is clearly not the woman's boyfriend, and none of the others are either. There are a lot of photos of this man; there may have been some bad blood between him and her boyfriend, or whoever the other man is in the picture on the table next to the bed. What is your opinion, Dick?" He nodded approvingly.

"I think we should discover the identity of the man that was killed on the porch first; there wasn't enough of his face left to identify him. We'll complete our search and head down to meet with the medical examiner. Good work, Sue!"

Susan smiled and continued looking for clues. She felt good about the crucial evidence they had uncovered so far. Dick was pondering on the body that was located at the fence-line, and the assortment of spent shell-casings in the street, all over the yard, and on the porch. He knew that someone had seen something, and next door would be the ideal location to begin his questioning. There was no chance all of this went on without them hearing and seeing everything. It would be a challenge piecing the puzzle together, but that was the one thing he still loved about being a detective. He smiled to himself and followed his partner into the living room.

CHAPTER 11

Keith walked Lo-Lo to the concession stand when their first movie ended and carefully concealed the frown on his face as she began talking about her brother.

"I want you to meet Amir; he's so cool and laid back. I just hate that he stays so busy doing God knows what! I know he's the reason for what we have, but I'd rather him give everything up and simply be my brother. You know what I'm saying, Keith? Are you even listening?"

Keith quickly recovered. "Oh yeah, Loren, but your brother must have a good reason for what he's doing. Trust me, he must have a reason. Now, we need to talk about our relationship for a few minutes."

He was tired of hearing about her precious brother, especially knowing that her uncle, Slim, had killed his father. Keith didn't have anything personal against Amir, but he didn't want to meet him, and Lo-Lo's precious brother would probably have to die also if he interfered in any way.

"Oh, does my baby feel neglected? I wouldn't do that to you, Keith. You know that I'm very interested in you." She gave him a light squeeze on his backside which irritated him even more.

"Loren! I told you not to do that, girl! Men don't like that funny-ass shit! At least real men don't!" Lo-Lo just smiled and ordered her favorite nachos and popcorn along with the Mike and Ike's soft candies that she knew Keith loved. They had already watched the latest Taraji P. Henson movie, and the whole theater had been emotional watching her unique acting skills. Keith felt that those types of movies are best viewed alone, unless you were married or in a real relationship. He thought: *That will never happen to me!* He watched Lo-Lo licking the cheese off a nacho chip and couldn't help but admire her shapely legs and round backside. Keith had to admit, Lo-Lo was beautiful, and under different circumstances he would be in love with her. He couldn't help himself when he walked up and rubbed his stiff manhood against her soft body as he hugged her from behind.

"Oh! Boy, stop! You're not even slick, Keith! Come on, we still have one more movie to watch before you have to take me home."

Keith sat and drifted in and out of sleep while Lo-Lo attempted to force him to watch the newest animated movie.

She complained. "Keith, you slept through the whole movie." He watched her smile as he simply turned and ran his tongue across her lips while apologizing.

When he finally walked Lo-Lo to her front door, he could tell that he was making progress.

She asked, "Where are you going when you leave here? You're not going over some tramp's house, are you?" Keith smiled and pulled her into his arms.

"Now, why are you worried? If you do your job as my woman you wouldn't have to worry about any other females. What, are you ready to give me some loving?" She playfully punched him.

"No, Keith! I've already told you many times that this down here is for my husband." She pointed toward her crotch as Keith looked at her in lustful amazement.

Lo-Lo looked at him somberly. "You need to call me tonight, okay? We may be able to come to some type of compromise." She giggled as Keith began to grind sexually against the porch banister.

"Boy, you're so nasty! You need to leave before my mother sees you and comes out here to put you in check." Keith walked up and kissed her passionately to end the discussion.

"I'll call you when I get home. Keep it warm for daddy, beautiful." He drove away in his mother's new convertible Mustang and smiled as several women he passed ogled him at stop signs, tossed their telephone numbers, and asked where he was going. Keith was light-skinned with alluring green eyes, had natural curly hair cut into a short taper, and he dressed very casually for his age. Women loved him, and he smiled when he thought to himself: *I don't blame them.*

CHAPTER 12

Keith smiled as he pulled into the driveway of Paris's "spot" in Kansas City, Missouri. Paris was his cousin, and he had formed the M.O.P. click on the streets that his father, Oscar, had formed inside of a Missouri prison. Paris had made connections with his father's suppliers and he had access to all of his Missouri clientele that weren't afraid to travel to the Kansas side of the border.

Keith climbed out of his vehicle and jumped in surprise as his uncle, Oscar, walked out of the shadows of the house like a ghost.

"You breakin' that bitch down yet, little nigga? You gonna end up havin' to lick that little pussy to get things done! You aint got enough game to fuck that bitch, and you a damn pretty nigga?"

Keith seethed in anger, but he knew that he should stay silent. Oscar was clearly drunk, and he was extremely unpredictable when provoked. Oscar was a remorseless killer, and Keith didn't believe he would be above murdering a member of his own family.

"Oh, you mad, bitch?" Oscar pulled a large revolver from his waistband and hung it at his side. "I don't know what the fuck Tony was doing to have a little pretty, faggot lookin' mothafucka like you out his damn nuts!"

The garage door suddenly rose, and a Jamaican man Keith knew as Peter walked out onto the driveway.

"Oscar! What gwon boi?"

Paris appeared behind him. "Daddy! What the fuck are you doing? Put that damn gun up; that's your damn nephew right there!" Oscar's whole attitude changed; he looked like a little boy caught stealing as he slipped the weapon into his back pocket.

Keith frowned. "I'm not doing this anymore, Paris! Set them up yourself. I have to worry about my own uncle more than any of them!"

Oscar glared at him as he walked past and entered the house, but he didn't say a word. He had been this way toward Keith ever since he was released. He often tried to compare him to the way Keith's father, Tony, had been, and he refused to accept the results.

Paris turned toward Oscar.

"Daddy, this is my house, and that's my damn cousin who you fuckin' with. He aint Tony, and he can't help the way he looks! You should be trippin' about Tony; He's the one that couldn't stand being away from an Italian bitch. The boy is still a kid, man, and he'll come along at his own pace. You need to apologize to that little nigga or you gonna fuck up our chances at really getting' at those Black Border Brother niggas. Did you hear how they did my boys?"

Oscar nodded in silence and headed into the house to try to talk to his nephew while thinking to himself: *He aint nothin' but a cryin' ass bitch!*

CHAPTER 13

Mike silently watched Lo-Lo and Keith outside. He was relieved that Candace was called to work early. He seethed in anger as he watched how his step-daughter flirted and teased. He felt that she had been doing the same to him for years. She walked around partially clothed, and one night he had imagined Lo-Lo smiling at him crookedly, and the same night leaving her bedroom door open for him to see inside. He thought: *She had had the nerve to slam the door in his face when she knew perfectly well what she was doing!* He could barely restrain himself when he saw Keith grinding on the banister, and Mike seethed in anger and lust when Lo-Lo walked up and kissed the boy passionately on the lips. He decided that this would be the night that the teasing would stop. He thought: **She's going to at least give me some head and let me get a taste of that pussy.**

When Keith pulled away from the house, Lo-Lo looked down the street after him for a while, and Mike sat back on the couch masturbating, getting ready.

When Lo-Lo came into the house, Mike asked, "Are you fucking that mothafucka?"

Loren got angry and flicked on the light to tell him to mind his business, but she realized what he had been doing, and she cringed in disgust and fear.

40

She yelled. "Mike, put your clothes on! What's wrong with you?"

Mike stood up and pulled up his shorts. "I saw you out there acting like a damn whore! Don't come in here trying to play innocent. Come here!"

Lo-Lo already had her cell phone out of her pocket, and as Mike grabbed for her, she pushed the button to put Amir on speed dial. Just as Mike grabbed her around the neck, she heard her brother yelling her name into the phone, but all she could do was scream as she was forced onto the living room floor. Mike was a small man, but he was much stronger than her, and when he slapped her, she attempted to shake off the dizziness. Lo-Lo knew that she couldn't lose consciousness.

When Mike roughly snatched her skirt off, she began kicking frantically and delivered a glancing blow to his groin. When he doubled over and grabbed himself Lo-Lo attempted to sprint into her room and lock the door, but Mike met her there and blocked the door with his arm. He pulled her into the room, tossed her onto her bed, and ripped her panties from her body with a mean, satisfied look on his face. Lo-Lo gagged as he tried to kiss her with his foul breath, and the sweet smell of the Crown Royal he drank was on his shirt. When Mike pulled up her shirt and began sucking on her small breasts, Lo-Lo began kicking again, but this time Mike squeezed her neck until she saw stars and froze in pain and fear. Her step-father was beyond being rational; Mike believed in his sick mind that Lo-Lo secretly welcomed the perverted brutality that he was displaying.

CHAPTER 14

Keith was on his way back to Kansas in his mother's vehicle. Lo-Lo had left her backpack in the vehicle, and he knew how much she liked to complete her homework as soon as she made it home. He was surprised that she hadn't called him by now; he had been gone long enough for her to realize that she didn't have it. He thought about Oscar and gripped the small pistol that Peter had shoved into his hand. He had struggled to understand what Peter had said to him.

"Don't let no mon take ya life, brudda. If he gwon do you, you gwon do him, ya hear?"

Keith had nodded and accepted the weapon, and when Oscar stopped him in the hallway to give an unconvincing apology Keith silently gripped the weapon in his pocket. He had been hoping that he wouldn't have to use it, but he knew that he would if he was forced to.

He attempted to call Lo-Lo, but the line was busy. When he pulled up to the house the front door was open, and he immediately felt that something was wrong. When he climbed out of the convertible and approached the front door, he could hear a man yelling.

"Open your legs up some more! Don't make me slap the shit out of you again!" Keith heard Lo-Lo cry out.

"Mike stop! You're my momma's man, and you know that Amir's going to kill you if you do this! Please stop, Mike!" The man was beyond hearing anything; lust and greed had taken control of his mind.

Keith ran into Lo-Lo's room and was enraged when he saw Mike with his hands around her neck while he was attempting to push his manhood inside her virginal vagina. Keith already had the pistol in his hand.

"Hey, you bitch-ass pervert! You better get the fuck off my girl, nigga!"

Mike hastily pulled his pants up and made the mistake of reaching for his shirt that was on the floor next to the bed. Keith fired three rounds thinking that Mike had been reaching for a weapon. He didn't hesitate to pull the trigger.

Mike clutched his shoulder initially, and he attempted to reach back to where a bullet had stung him in the back. Before Lo-Lo could stop Keith, there was another blast. Mike clutched at his face with a horrified expression as he rose to his feet and ran out of the room with Keith soon following, making sure that Lo-Lo was alright. The small gun was not very loud, so she didn't think that anyone had heard the shots, but when Keith came back inside, she took the gun and hid it inside her closet. She hugged and kissed Keith all over his face for saving her from the rape. She had completely forgotten about Amir.

CHAPTER 15

When Amir heard his sister screaming his body had turned cold. He grabbed his .40 caliber Beretta as well as his .45 caliber Smith and Wesson and headed to the driveway while yelling Slim's name. He climbed into his Dodge Viper for speed and Slim rushed out of the front door carrying his AR-15 assault rifle.

"What's up, Meer?" Amir explained to his uncle what he had heard on the telephone, and Slim's mind went from relative, to business associate, to stone-cold killer in the blink of an eye. He felt protective of his only niece since he didn't get to see her very often because of Candace and the hate she had for him.

Slim was forced to grip the dashboard as Amir gunned the customized vehicle away from the house. When he reached Parallel Parkway, it wasn't long before they screeched to a stop in front of his mother's home on 75th street. Slim climbed out of the vehicle and followed Amir into his mother's house, noticing blood on the floor trailing to his niece's bedroom.

When they entered the room, Amir yelled, "Nigga, get your hands off my damn sister!"

Slim moved into position for a clear shot, but Lo-Lo was blocking Keith's body with hers. When Lo-Lo explained the situation, Slim ran out in search of Mike, and Amir pushed Keith out of the way and embraced his sister, relieved that she was not seriously injured. He covered her with a blanket as she began to speak.

"Meer, Keith shot Mike at least three times when he caught him trying to rape me! I saw blood come out of his face! You're not going to let them take him to jail, are you? He's my boyfriend!"

"Hold on, Lo-Lo, tell me everything that happened; everything." She explained the details of the entire incident and Amir could hardly contain the rage he felt toward Mike; the man had been around his family for years.

When Lo-Lo made it to the part where Keith appeared inside of her room, Amir was stunned. He noticed how young and innocent the boy looked and was reminded how much looks could be deceiving. Keith was far from your average pretty-boy, and it seemed that he had been shooting to kill from his sister's description of the events. He turned to Keith.

"My man, I owe you for saving my little sister. I love you for that, bro, and it's always salaam when you see me from here on out."

He shook Keith's hand firmly and pulled him into his arms for a fierce embrace. It was obvious that the police weren't called, but Amir still put Lo-Lo to work cleaning up the blood and disarray while he gave Keith his business card.

"Call when you need me, you hear? I don't care what it's about. I got love for you, bro." He watched Keith climb into his mother's vehicle and felt relief that his little sister had the sense to associate with good people.

Slim walked back into the house shaking his head, and Amir gave him the keys to the Dodge Viper so that he could make his exit before his mother arrived. Candace still hated Slim, and Amir didn't want to stress her any more than she would be when she received the news: *her longtime boyfriend was going to die a slow, excruciating death.*

CHAPTER 16

Ashely walked out of the courtroom in frustration, furious that Los had sent one of his "boys" to the courthouse for her to represent. She thought to herself: *The fool can't keep his damn mouth shut*! The young boy didn't know anything about how the system worked and blurted out accusations about the police department, the judge- anyone who could ultimately send him to prison for life and damage her reputation. When she pushed the button on the elevator, she immediately kicked off her high-heels and began massaging her sore feet before the doors even closed. She ignored the lustful stares at her backside. She had gotten used to it, and she used it to her and Los's advantage. Unfortunately for the men, the only ones she allowed into her space were people connected to the streets; they could provide what Ashely needed.

When she made it to her pigeon-blood red Infiniti, there was a security guard leaning against her vehicle as if he owned it."

She said, "Excuse me, but why are you disrespecting my property like this? I don't think sitting on top of my car goes along with that fake-ass badge! ''

When Marlon smiled, Ashely was blinded by the large diamonds and rubies glistening from the sunshine.

''Damn, baby, you the one got me hooked up with this punk-ass job. Now you wanna talk to me like I'm a flashlight cop? Come here, baby! ''Ashely smiled and sashayed into the man's arms. She did not even protest when Marlon squeezed her backside and ran his hands under her skirt in public.

She stared at him. "Marlon, you're the one that has to participate in community service." She looked him over before continuing. "By the way, you need to stop allowing everyone to see all of them damn jewels in your mouth! You can only keep the feds off you for so long when you advertise." Ashely couldn't care less about his situation, but she intended to lower his defenses completely. Marlon had already begun taking her to his main stash house to retrieve stacks of currency; it was time to collect.

He said, "I hear you baby, but you're the only one that can make me smile like this. I don't even talk to mothafuckas, so not many people have seen my teeth."

Ashely deactivated her alarm and climbed into her vehicle, locking her doors before Marlon could react. She lowered her window.

"That's for freaking me in public, nigga."

He playfully rocked her Infiniti back and forth. "Oh, it's like that? I can't touch you now?" Ashely smiled as she started her Infiniti.

"You *are* still taking me out, right? You can do all the touching, sucking, licking, and rubbing you want later, but right now I need to go home and clean myself up. I don't feel right having you all up on me when I'm all sweaty, now go try to arrest somebody with your flashlight!" Marlon smiled as she pulled out of the parking lot, laughing.

When Ashely turned the corner, her expression changed to one of disgust; she couldn't stomach too much more of the man disrespecting her. She had allowed Marlon to perform oral sex on her the last time they had met, and she smiled when she thought about him ejaculating into his pants like a virgin. This time Marlon was going to wine and dine her, take her to a club in Lawrence, Kansas, and retire to his home for the sex she had promised him. She pondered this last thought: *sorry mothafucka!* Ashely's sex came at a very expensive price.

She laughed to herself when she thought of Los and Amir. They often joked that she had a "recession proof" vagina between her legs, but they just didn't know how right they were. She had always been able to get what she wanted and needed from men. She had started using sex when she was twelve years old, by first performing fellatio on her stepfather, and eventually allowing him to take her virginity, always for a price. Sometimes the lights and gas in her home were disconnected, but she always had plenty of money to take care of herself proficiently. If she wanted to sleep in a motel, he provided that while her mother was left in the dark, figuratively and literally. Her stepfather didn't realize she had been doing the same thing with his friends, until he caught her over one of their homes, but what could he say? She learned the methods to save her cash; she couldn't believe her mother had attempted to question her about the situation. She had a thought: *and the bitch was fucking and sucking for free!* Ashely pulled up to her condominium on Ward Parkway in Kansas City, Missouri, and she smiled in satisfaction as she already felt the security and comfort that she deserved.

Ashely didn't have to worry about much in her gated, security patrolled community, except racism. The white women were mostly middle aged or older, and their husbands and boyfriends couldn't help but stare in fascination when Ashely had moved in. She looked like a caramel completed Halle Berry, but with a body like the actress, Lisa Raye, that debuted her acting career in the movie, "The Player's Club." It didn't matter if the wives and girlfriends were around or not; the pathetic men couldn't help but stare and hope for just a whiff of her expensive perfume. So, the women were jealous, and Ashely's skin color only made them more disrespectful. If the women knew who they were dealing with they wouldn't call the police every time Los and Amir came by, destroy her mail, leave black dolls hanging from nooses around her property. If they knew how many people she had set up, or personally killed, they would only smile and wave as they departed her presence.

When Ashely entered her residence, she headed directly to the bathroom to fill her large tub with oils and sweet scents so she could soak her body in peace.

After taking a long bath, she picked out a silk dress, diamond earrings, heels, matching thong and bra, and put everything to the side while she applied lotion to her body and made sure her hair was styled to perfection. Just when she was getting dressed, her special "trick phone" rang and she smiled, staring at Marlon's number on the screen. She thought to herself: *The fool can't wait to get played!* She pushed send on her cell-phone.

"Hey, baby! You're early, and I'm not even dressed yet." She could hear his music in the background playing too loud, and this irritated her.

Marlon responded. "I'm trying to come pick you up early so I can stop by my spot to drop something off; what's your address?"

Ashely froze. She had never allowed anyone to know where she lived, but she couldn't ruin her chances with Marlon by being obvious. She responded without further hesitation.

"Baby! I'm not ready yet, and my parents are here. I'm not ready for them to meet you yet! How about I meet you at the restaurant? You said Bristol Grill in Missouri, right?" Marlon turned his music off completely after her last words.

"You want me to meet your parents? Is someone starting to catch feelings on the sly?"

"You're easy to get along with, baby."

Marlon was quiet for a moment.

"No, babygirl, just meet me at Harpo's in Westport at seven, okay? We gonna have a couple light drinks and talk for a minute; our reservation's not till eight. I'll just do my drop off after we leave the restaurant. Have you been to any clubs over there?" Ashely stopped jumping around long enough to respond.

"No, you know I don't get out much, Marlon, but I'll see you at seven, baby. I have to get dressed."

When she ended the call, Ashely called Los and Amir with the news. Los was excited, but Amir stayed silent and unreadable. The two men were best friends with totally different mentalities. She placed her phone on her bed and shook her head, watching the clock as she dressed.

CHAPTER 17

Amir was at the Kansas Speedway silently watching his beautiful woman jumping up and down, cheering for one of the race cars that rarely housed a female driver. He couldn't understand the excitement of watching these vehicles racing around in seemingly endless circles, and he could hardly bear the noise. He would rather have been at home watching a Kansas City Chiefs game, but he pretended to enjoy himself. He always gave his girlfriend, Mecca, everything that she wanted. She looked up into Amir's eyes and kissed him on the chin.

''I won a thousand dollars!''

Now he understood her excitement. Money made anything exciting as far as he was concerned. He met his woman in Olathe, Kansas, inside of a local grocery store. He had been rushing because he was on his way to bond Arthur out of jail before they sent him to an alternate jail in Gardner, Kansas. The bonding company wouldn't accept cash, so he had dodged past Mecca to get in line for a money order, not realizing that she had been doing the same thing. He remembered the scene fondly.

Mecca had tapped him on the shoulder, and he turned around to see a spitting image of Alicia Keys.

''Are you always this rude toward women? You're simply going to race me to the line? Are you from the hooood!?''

He laughed and apologized, explaining the situation to the stunning beauty. He watched her study him from head to toe, and she quickly realized that he was far from the "hood" with his Armani suit, and his light, but expensive jewelry. He asked for her cell-phone number and they had dated for nine months before he met her parents, and three more months before she finally gave herself to him. They had been together for two years, and none of his friends or family knew about her, not even his mother.

He looked down at the small bulge in her stomach and knew that he couldn't keep her a secret any longer. Mecca gripped his hand and pulled him close.

"As a Muslim, don't you think you should be asking me something?" She smiled and he melted inside, he had loved her since the day they met, but he felt he should keep her away for now; these were dangerous times.

"Yes, baby, do you eat pork?"

She punched him and he smiled crookedly. He turned serious.

"I'm just teasing, momma, but don't you think it would be better if I made the decision on my own? That way you'll know it comes from the heart." Mecca shook her head in frustration.

"I don't care how it happens, Amir, I just want to live the right way, and I want what's best for our daughter."

Amir smiled. "You're not slick; you're trying to control everything already, Mecca. We're having a daughter?" It was her turn to be serious.

"Baby, your name means prince, or ruler. When this baby is born, he or she will take that place and you will be king over me and everything connected to me, but only if I'm your wife. The queen supports the king, but she is also his equal with different responsibilities. Baby, you are the one in control, but you don't seem to know it."

Amir was stunned into silence for a moment.

"Baby, have you been reading up on my religion?"

Mecca nodded. "Yes, but it was not for you, Amir. I want to know as much about you as I can because we're a family now. I know about drugs and the violence; I have eyes and ears. I just want to know the *real* you! When are you going to let that life go like you promised and learn something about me?"

Amir shook his head in amazement and stared at his beautiful, intelligent, religious counterpart. He wanted to give Mecca the world, but he honestly couldn't answer her question. He pulled her into an embrace and held her tight, but he didn't notice the disappointment etched on her lovely face.

CHAPTER 18

Los and Amir stood on the Kansas side of the bridge, across the Missouri River, watching the Italians blocking the streets with stretch limousines. One thing they could count on, Los mused, was that they would not have to worry about a robbery attempt in the "Bottoms". There was no threat from law enforcement or anyone else; everything was taken care of by the Italians. Los and his Border Brother family members simply had to compensate them for their services.

Los turned to Amir. "What's up with these bitches and they damn limos? What do they think this shit is, The Sopranos? I know they run this shit down here, but they don't have to advertise their shit." Amir smiled.

"Don't worry about it, Los, let's just get our shit and get away from here. You need to make sure your Mexican homeboys don't come rolling up in some damn low-riders." Los laughed and shook his head.

Amir looked at his friends and associates in various positions around the long street, waiting on instructions for when the shipment arrived. They would assist in packaging, concealment, and the delivery of the various drugs that would be available for distribution. He scrutinized the vehicle that Reese and Flip were in, making sure that they were staying alert and were not being careless. Arthur and Tracy were stationed on a side street with Rag and Looney all the way on the other end keeping watch.

Reese, Rag, and Looney had grown up as Bloods, but they didn't associate with their cronies much since they became members of the Black Border Brothers; Amir and Los would not allow it. The only reason Amir had considered any of them was because of his cousin, Mate. He was the heart of the aggression Reese and the others exhibited. Regardless of Amir being a relative of this man, he still wouldn't have dealt with him if he wasn't a hustler and family man. His relative being a Muslim sealed the deal, though, but they hadn't associated on that level much because of the evil paths they were traveling down at a rapid pace.

At least twenty Black Border Brother members, from Kansas and Missouri, were strewn around the neighborhood where they awaited instructions. Amir was proud to see that both sides of the border could come together and put their differences aside for a common goal; *getting to the currency.*

As Los and Amir watched, they noticed two old trucks arrive- so rusted that they couldn't tell what color they had been. There were also three small vehicles behind them with what appeared to be families inside.

Los turned to Amir. "My cousins know what the fuck they doing, but I wouldn't bring kids to be meeting mothafuckas for dope. Only damn Mexicans do shit like this."

Amir nodded and watched the small convoy heading over the bridge toward them before putting his walkie-talkie to his mouth and barking instructions.

"As soon as the cars pull into the building, follow me across. When I park, make sure that we have people directly behind each one of their cars. If me or Los are not outside within thirty minutes, leave all these mothafuckas stinking, do you feel me?

Over twenty short responses came over the airwaves and Amir climbed into the van they had rented and made their way across the bridge while being scrutinized by everyone present. Amir could care less how the Italians or the Mexican Border Brothers felt about them or their movements. Business was business, and Amir personally loved being able to care for his family in any way he saw fit. This made him feel that he had a purpose in what he was trying to accomplish in the wicked streets.

Amir parked, and as they climbed out of the vehicle, a small group of men approached.

"So, who's gonna be the next Gotti?"

Amir shook the older Italian man's hand who had spoken.

"Frank, how have you been, sir? We hope to be out of your way real soon. There's no John Gotti impersonator here, Frank, we're all equal."

Frank was normally the person they dealt with when taking care of business at the border. He didn't seem to be concerned about the color of their skin like most of the Italians.

They entered a large warehouse and they all watched the drugs being extracted from concealment throughout the vehicles that had arrived. Los casually strolled to the other side of the room to have a conversation with one of his cousins.

Once the drugs were separated, Amir spoke into his radio and informed his people that the transaction was nearing its conclusion. The meeting was not always about acquiring the drugs or cash; sometimes they met to send products away or make a payment for the next shipment. Amir barked instructions into his radio.

"Reese, you and Flip follow the first car all the way to the spot. Arthur, you make sure you're behind the last car. If the police get behind you, pull them away from the rest of us any way you can. You got me?" There was an affirmative response and he nodded in silence. He then gave instructions to the people that were on the scene; they were there to secure the safe transport and delivery of the product.

Amir and Los eventually headed to a hotel room they had rented, anticipating Ashely's call.

CHAPTER 19

Ashely arrived at the bar in the Westport neighborhood and was surprised to see Marlon casually leaning on the front of a H2 Hummer stretch limousine with what appeared to be a dozen roses in his hand. She paused, but Ashely didn't reveal the disgust and revulsion she felt by altering her expression; she smiled and stared at the man with imitation affection.

"What is all of this for, Marlon?"

He smiled and Ashely was amazed by the diamonds glistening from his mouth in the moonlight. She had to admit that the man looked good in his suit and ostrich skin shoes.

Marlon responded. "Baby-girl, I wanted to take you out in style because you're worth that shit. Come sit in the car with me; we have our own bar, so we don't have to go up in there." He motioned to the bar where he had recommended her to meet him for their "date".

As soon as Ashely entered the vehicle, her eyes scanned the interior like a hawk, spotting the large duffel bag as she tried not to grin wickedly.

Marlon misunderstood the look on her beautiful face.

"Yeah, baby, we gonna have some fun up in here. After this we going to the house and I'm gonna eat you for dessert."

Ashely smiled again as she thought to herself: *Nigga, you the dessert! A trick-ass nigga that's sweet as pie.*

They eventually traveled to the high-class restaurant, Bristol Grill, in Kansas City, Missouri, and they didn't have to be concerned with parking. The driver gave Marlon his business card for him to call when they were finished with dinner. They didn't have to use a valet although it was available.

When Ashely was seated, Marlon immediately went down on one knee and pulled a ring from his pocket that had a diamond larger than any she had ever seen. When Marlon began proposing, Ashely felt the first pangs of regret; she realized that Los would never ask her to be his wife.

Marlon looked concerned after asking the most important question in a man's life. "Ashely, are you alright?"

She quickly wiped the tears from her eyes and wrapped her arms around his neck, letting him know softly in his ear what he should expect from her when they arrived at their destination.

Marlon asked, "What is your answer?"

"Yes."

Ashely excused herself to go to the restroom to call Los; she had been instructed to let him know when they were leaving the restaurant and were on their way to Marlon's "spot."

When she emerged from the restroom, Marlon stood watching her silently, and Ashely paused again, seeing the love and affection on the man's face.

They climbed into the limousine and Ashely roughly pulled Marlon's pants down, and she gave him fellatio until Marlon climaxed inside her mouth; she continued to lick, pull, and suck on his manhood until he became limp in her mouth and began inching away from her. When they arrived at his residence, Marlon turned to her. "I have a surprise for you."

He deactivated the alarm and held the door wide for her to enter, and she began getting irritated by his chivalry; Ashely was already feeling regret by what she knew would transpire later.

Marlon led her down into the basement and moved a table that concealed a trapdoor that was embedded into the floor. Ashely figured that he was usually alone for this. She watched him remove six wrapped packages that she assumed were filled with cocaine or heroin and place them on top of others in the now open bag that had been in the limousine. The bag appeared to hold at least ten more packages.

When he finished, Ashely followed Marlon upstairs to the dining room, and he carefully moved a china cabinet to reveal a large wall safe filled with stacks of currency and other valuables. She was stunned; Marlon appeared to be on a more advanced level in the streets than she had thought.

He pulled his duffel bag over and began stacking the items inside the safe. He turned to her.

"Baby, this is for our future and my exit from this madness in the streets. I want you to be my wife, and I also want you to be my partner in moving forward in some legal shit."

Ashely closed the safe herself and tugged Marlon into his bedroom while they discarded their clothing along the way. When she slipped out of her dress and removed her bra and panties, Marlon stared at the beauty in stunned fascination. He had never seen Ashely completely naked, and her slim waist, firm breasts, and perfectly proportioned backside caused pre-cum to escape into his boxer shorts.

Ashely noticed the stain and asked, "Does your friend want my pussy that bad?"

Marlon answered by pulling his underwear down and Ashely watched his manhood point toward her and jerk in anticipation.

She relaxed on the bed and accepted Marlon inside her without foreplay and willingly gave her body to him as if she was his woman.

CHAPTER 20

Later that night, Ashely called both Los and Amir from Marlon's kitchen while he slept, and she unlocked the back door after making sure that the alarm was still deactivated. She had shown Los the location of the house after the first time that Marlon had taken her there, but they had delayed their plans until after Ashely knew where the stashes were located.

She reentered the room and calmly lay back in the bed, irritated by Marlon's arms relentlessly encircling her waist; his lips were resting on her neck. She felt his penis begin to stiffen against her back, and Marlon began to gyrate; They both froze when they heard a sound.

"Isn't this sweet? You niggas all hugged up like you in love. Ashely, have you changed your mind about me?"

She immediately climbed out of the bed and rushed into Los's arms, planting wet kisses all over his face.

"Bitch, go brush yo' damn teeth! I don't need you breathin' this nigga's nuts all over me, move!"

Ashely looked hurt as she retrieved her clothes and purse from the floor, but she calmly walked to the other side of the bed and grabbed the 9mm Ruger that Marlon was quietly reaching for.

"Sorry baby, but I can't have you hurting my man." Marlon looked incredulous. "Bitch, yo' funky-ass on some set-up shit? After how real I've been with you? I hope you choke off that nut I made you swallow, you a raggedy ass bitch!" Ashely looked at him with contempt.

"Nigga, it was all part of the trick game. I'll do anything for my man, but he doesn't have to pay for it. If it takes sucking off a pencil-dick trick like you, so be it; I hope you tasted enough pussy, bitch, because you'll definitely never taste it again."

Amir walked out of the shadows.

"That's enough talking. Ashely, go and get your things together. Los, make this nigga right.

He tossed Los a roll of duct tape and a small ball they used to muffle screams. After he was bound, Marlon yelled in frustration.

"You niggas is dead, cuz! As soon as my niggas find you, it's over! Let me go now, and it's cool, you hear me?"

They ignored him, and Los even pulled a cigarette from his pocket and silently watched Marlon as he lit up and smoked. Marlon couldn't contain his anger any longer.

"Alright, cuz! Y'all niggas and that funky bitch is hit! It's Crips on mine you slob-ass niggas!"

Los shook his head. "We Black Border Brothers, homie, we're not Bloods. But my boy here might take offense; don't you know his cousin, Mate?"

Marlon smiled at this. "Yeah, every time that nigga went to prison I was putting my dick down his bitch's long-ass throat. Ask that nigga how my dick taste."

As Marlon laughed, Ashely returned to the room and Amir instructed her to gag the man so that there would be no more interruptions. Amir slapped him hard in the face and ignored the look of hatred in his eyes.

"Man, I don't care what you did to that bitch, and my cousin definitely don't either. He knew what he was getting himself into when he chose that tramp. Besides, you're a stranger and that bitch was fair game. Who hasn't made bad decisions about women? How do you think we knew so much about you? Yeah, my nig, your bitch told me about you speaking about my cousin, but you didn't have the heart to cross him; you know you would have been erased! I'm not a gang-banger, and my brother here isn't either, but when a nigga starts asking questions and he's from a different clique, we investigate. That bitch you were creeping with was your downfall, not his. What about that tramp with the strawberries on her ass, though? Yeah, she told Mate everything we needed to know, and all you got was some stank, worn out pussy! Laugh now, nigga. Yeah, I got a taste of that fruit."

Marlon's demeanor completely changed when a feature from his woman's body was vocalized. He looked confused initially, and then he was angry, then afraid. He froze in shock when Reese dragged his stunning girlfriend, Carla, into the room by her long Cuban locks. She had nothing on her voluptuous body except her own blood.

Marlon whimpered and immediately looked down between the beautiful woman's legs.

Los laughed. "Don't worry about that shit, nigga, we don't get off on fuckin' other niggas bitches against they will. She already gave it up to Amir and his cousin enough for all of us anyway."

Everyone laughed while Marlon attempted to speak through the gag; he also attempted to rise and come to his woman's aid. Amir held him down.

"We're going to give you a chance to save yourself, player, and all you have to do is give us permission to kill this funky-ass bitch right here."

Carla screamed and attempted to run, but Reese savagely kicked her in the back of her legs, and there was a sickening sound from one of them breaking.

She screamed in agony and fear. "You promised that you wouldn't hurt us! Why are you doing this to me? Marlon was the one that was doing things!"

Los sneered. "You see, nigga? Fine bitches like this aint shit, are they? She offered to fuck all of us to save her life, but she didn't say shit about you."

Reese gagged her and she calmed down, knowing that she would only choke on her own saliva if she continued attempting to speak, but the pain from her wounds caused her to whimper softly.

Amir calmly asked Marlon a pointed question. "What's the combination? Be careful, my nig; each time it doesn't open you're going to listen to her scream. Do you understand me?"

Marlon nodded, but as soon as the gag was removed for him to give the combination, he began to yell.

"Help! Please, somebody help me!"

Los approached the bed and pointed his pistol at his face, and he quieted immediately. Marlon mumbled some numbers to Amir, and he disappeared into the dining room where Ashely was waiting in front of the safe.

CHAPTER 21

Amir recited the numbers. "24, 16, 10!" Ashely worked the combination, but after the third failed attempt Amir simply nodded at her.

She grabbed her purse from the floor and re-entered the bedroom followed by a stone-faced Amir. Ashely stood looking down at Carla with a blank expression, but when the injured woman looked up at her, she pulled a small hammer from her purse and smashed her nose flat. Marlon saw the blood spray onto Ashely's dress and cried.

"Please, don't hurt her no more! She didn't do anything to none of y'all! I'll tell you the combination, just let my girl go!"

Amir nodded to Ashely again and she smashed the hammer into the knee of Carla's uninjured leg. The sound was sickening, but the keening sound escaping from the woman's lips sounded like it was coming from a wounded animal.

Marlon began reciting a number to them while Carla balled up to attempt to protect herself while Ashely kicked and spit on her while screaming obscenities. She was complaining about the new dress that had been destroyed by all of Carla's blood.

Los shook his head in exasperation.

"Ashely, shut that bitch the fuck up! She makin' too much damn noise!"

Ashely produced a small handgun and shot Carla twice in her neck, and she finished the evil deed by emptying a round into each of her lifeless eyes. Before Marlon could say anything, he was gagged and dragged into the dining room to either give the correct combination, or to be tortured until he complied with their demands.

This time when Ashely tried the combination the door opened with a small metallic sound. Los reached around her from behind and gave her breasts a soft squeeze.

"That's my baby-girl! Take everything out of there after you show us where the rest of the shit is."

She nodded and led them downstairs to do what she had been instructed while Marlon's eyes locked onto her with a mixture of hatred and disgust. She immediately made her way back upstairs to handle her business.

Amir approached and patted Marlon on his shoulder.

"You see, that's how women will do you, dawg, but you thought that pussy was strictly for you. Unfortunately, we can't let you go, banger, but we're going to send you on your way with dignity and respect- with a bad bitch at your knees."

Los yelled. "Ashely, come down here!"

She appeared again with a confused look on her face, but when Amir whispered something into her ear, she smiled wickedly. She strolled over to where Marlon was sitting and expertly removed his boxer shorts. She began licking and sucking his manhood while slowly rubbing on his chest lovingly.

After a couple of minutes when his penis was still flaccid, Ashely turned to Los.

"This bitch is too scared to get hard."

Marlon was sweating profusely and continued to stare down at Ashely in fear and hatred. She ignored him and began pulling and sucking again, and out of nowhere she produced a knife and swiftly severed his uncooperative penis.

Marlon attempted to scream out in agony and surprise, but the gag muffled and choked the sounds off in his throat. Blood sprayed and Ashely discarded the limp flesh before plunging the knife repeatedly into Marlon's face and stomach. When the deed was done, she picked up the penis and placed it inside the man's still open mouth and carved three letters into his back, signifying their organization. Reese grabbed the drugs and weapons while they collected the cash and jewelry from the home and wiped the house down with soapy water. They could do nothing about Ashely's DNA, but she was not registered in any database that would match her profile.

They eventually climbed into the stolen van that Reese, Amir, and Los had arrived in with Carla in tow, bound and gagged. They were all silent as Ashely pulled away from the double murder scene; Amir pondered the fact that there would be plenty of bloodshed in the future. Marlon had been a Crip, but he was also a key figure in the deadly M.O.P. clique.

CHAPTER 22

Slim casually hung his arm out of the car window while Flip explained to him what he had been hearing about Reese in the streets. They were headed to a new "spot" they had opened in Grandview, Missouri.

"Man, that nigga be hittin' the pipe now-with wet on it too! I know that nigga down and everything, but I caint trust a nigga that be killin' kids and fuckin' with dead bodies."

They stopped in front of a restaurant on Troost because there was a party going on at a nightclub nearby. People were out in droves "ghost walking" the intersection. Slim pulled a machine gun from under the seat when people began getting too close to his window.

Flip turned to him. "This shit is crazy as fuck! Somebody gonna end up getting killed at this mothafucka with this bull….."

Shots rang out and Slim was sprayed with Flip's brains, bone fragments, and blood while what remained of his young friend's head slumped over onto his lap. He ducked down and snatched his weapon off the floorboard where it had fallen, while he reached for his door handle with the other hand. He ducked again as windows shattered and slugs tore up the dash as they buzzed over his head. He could hear shouted orders coming from the other side of the vehicle and knew he had to get out of there before the vehicle was surrounded and the chances for escape were eliminated.

When he opened the door, someone yelled.

"M.O.P. nigga!" He felt a bullet rip into the flesh of his right arm and heard bullets whine around his head while striking the door panel and window frame. He looked around the parking lot and realized his only chance for escape was directly behind the vehicle. Everywhere else would leave him exposed; he would have to make it to the houses nearby. He spotted one of the shooters wearing a dark-colored ski-mask, wielding what looked like a Kalashnikov assault rifle that he fired in his direction. Slim fired his weapon and heard curses as the man hit the ground from being hit by rounds.

Another man attempted to cut off his escape route by cutting across the parking lot, but he made an easy target for Slim. The man tried to shoot it out with him, but he was not an experienced shooter; Slim smiled as he saw blood geyser out of the man's back as he rolled on the ground, attempting to hold his hand over the wound in his chest.

Slim felt a sting in his side and dove behind the vehicle, and he looked down to see blood all over his shirt and pants, and a gaping wound in his side. Someone yelled again.

"Slim, that was my brother you killed! Bitch nigga, you won't be getting out of this one, mothafucka! They then fucked up released the mothafuckin' beast!"

People ran out of the parking lot as rounds from automatic gunfire shredded vehicles and ricocheted off the asphalt. Slim spotted a youngster hiding in the rear of a new Cadillac Escalade and silently suggested with the barrel of his weapon that the young man should assist him in escaping. The man immediately handed Slim his keys and ran behind another vehicle. He realized that he had to have as much space as possible away from Slim who was clearly the target.

Slim opened the door to the Cadillac, but when he attempted to climb inside a bullet smashed into his shoulder- knocking him to the ground. He could feel his flesh stinging from the other two wounds, but he struggled to ignore the pain; he knew that if he didn't, certain death would not be far away. He was able to climb inside and got the engine started. As he pushed the gas pedal to the floor, bullets immediately began shattering windows and ricocheting off the Cadillac while Oscar yelled Slim's name from across the parking lot.

He put the vehicle in reverse and smashed into an SUV to make room. He drove straight toward two more men wearing masks, attempting to take his life. They both leaped clear of the large vehicle's path, and someone ran from the side, shooting a shotgun while he ran.

Slim felt a sting on the side of his face and knew he had been hit by shotgun pellets; he crashed through two more vehicles at the intersection and sped down Prospect Avenue toward the highway so that he could reach the Kansas side of the border.

CHAPTER 23

Slim could hear sirens approaching and slowed down to the posted speed limit, wondering who would help him in treating his wounds. The hospital was not an option.

When he arrived at the exit to the highway ramp, he pulled his cellphone from his pocket and called Amir.

"Nephew, be on your toes, for real! Flip is dead, Meer. I'm on my way, so make sure you can get somebody to help me with these bullet holes. I'll be there soon if I don't run into no laws. Border!"

He turned onto I-70 going west and cringed when he noticed the pool of blood soaking the seat beneath him, knowing he had to hurry. He was beginning to feel exhausted and drowsy. Slim replayed the events of the night in his head as he drove, and he recognized Oscar's voice from the incident.

He had gotten the message from Los, but he had not believed that Oscar was really in the streets. He cursed himself for letting money cause him to become so careless; he knew Kansas and Missouri had a high rate of success on appeals to the court. Oscar had been a friend in the earlier days, but now Slim knew that the man had to die for his clumsy attempt at taking his life. Slim should have known that he would be faced with Tony's death eventually, and he knew that he had better locate and deal with Oscar soon. He and the man had done dirty deeds together, and Slim knew that Oscar was a relentless killer, who wouldn't stop until one of them was dead.

His vision blurred as he tried to focus on the next exit, but before he made it, he was forced to pull onto the shoulder to rest his eyes. Within minutes, Slim was asleep behind the wheel about a mile from the 57th street exit in Kansas City, Kansas.

CHAPTER 24

Amir hung up the telephone and turned to Mecca and Lo-Lo.

"There's a problem, and I have to get things ready for someone to show up. Mecca, I need you to take Loren home for me and I'll call you later. As a matter of fact, make sure you call me as soon as you make it home."

Mecca looked concerned, but she began preparing to follow her man's instructions. She could tell that Amir meant business, so she knew not to argue.

Lo-Lo looked on in fascination; she admired Mecca, but she looked at her brother as though he were a King. She couldn't wait for them to get married, and she was also anticipating Mecca giving birth to her niece/nephew.

Mecca was the type of woman that Lo-Lo wanted to emulate, and she watched in silence and noted that Mecca didn't question or argue with her man. She was very demure and intelligent about the situation.

Lo-Lo made it a point to remind Amir that they were supposed to double date on the weekend at the Dave and Buster's at the Legends Shopping Center near his home. Keith had spoken with Amir a few times, but Lo-Lo wanted her boyfriend to see how Amir and Mecca interacted with each other; she wanted him to know how she expected him to treat her.

Amir pulled Mecca to him and kissed her long and hard, and Lo-Lo stamped her foot impatiently, feeling a small pang of jealousy. She tried not to think about boys too much because she wanted to finish school and meet the right man for marriage, but lately she had been yearning for a man's touch.

Amir walked them to Mecca's Audi convertible and placed her in the driver's seat gently before turning to Lo-Lo.

"Start paying close attention to your surroundings, and make sure to be around groups of people; do you understand?" She nodded and climbed into the vehicle, immediately loading a Keyshia Cole disc into the system, and they blasted the music as they headed down the street.

Amir shook his head as they pulled away, listening to male bashing at its finest, bobbing their heads in agreement to the lyrics. He grabbed his cell-phone and dialed Arthur's number.

"Art, something bad happened to Slim and Flip. Get your nurse girlfriend over here as soon as you can. I don't know where they are, but it sounds like something really bad went down."

He disconnected and called his workers and friends from the Kansas side so that they could prepare for what needed to be done.

Chapter 25

People started showing up in droves, and Amir had to constantly remind them not to play their music loud outside his home; his neighbors were nosy and were already suspicious of the flashy vehicles and expensive diamond jewelry that they wore.

Amir spotted Reese walking into the garage with a pistol hanging out of each pocket, and he also noticed the glassy look in his eyes as well as the hard look on his face. Amir decided to wait until everyone was settled to confront him about his nonchalant attitude, which was very dangerous in the "business" they were all involved in.

Carlos Sr. walked toward the house and Amir noticed how slow he was moving. The man was getting old, but he tried to mask his limited mobility by adapting an old-school pimp step. He was still a force to be reckoned with in Amir's eyes, and he had molded himself off Carlos Sr. and his late father, Malik's, characteristics: calm authority. Amir entered the house and directed everyone to his study where they usually met for their meetings. Reese was on the couch, sprawled out and asleep, snoring loudly with saliva running down the corner of his cracked lips. Amir kicked the couch: hard.

"Nigga, get yo' dope fiend ass off my couch! What's wrong with you, Reese, do you think it's a game with me now? Or do you think you can disrespect me in my own home? After this meeting we're going to be having a serious conversation about you and your fucked up ways! Too much is going on for us to be high and tripping out. Sit up on my couch like a fucking man!"

Reese rose to his feet and stared defiantly at Amir, causing Los to grip his weapon in anticipation, preparing to kill Reese without hesitation. Los loved Reese just like he knew Amir did, but if Reese made the wrong move it wouldn't matter; he would be shot down like any other stranger in the inner-city. In fact, it seemed that Reese was becoming more and more like a stranger each day. Los was going to make sure that neither him nor his brother took anything for granted where unstable men were concerned.

Ashely and Tracy walked into the room laughing and joking, and the mood in the room improved. Carlos Sr. walked in followed by Arthur and everyone else, and the first situation for them to discuss was financial. Carlos Sr. spoke sternly to the small gathering of loyalists.

"Until you men handle whatever has people out here dying, we're going to have to cut back on our shipments; my brothers in California have been hearing about the murders and the increase of law enforcement because of it. Also, the Italians are skeptical about dealing with drugs as it is and they're feeling heat on their other business ventures because of the situation." He mentioned their problems with the drug trade, and everyone reached an understanding: they would lose money if things were not taken care of soon.

Amir had told him about the call from Slim, and Carlos Sr. had shaken his head in sadness, hoping that Slim would make it home safe. He and Slim had been close for years- even before Carlos Sr. and Slim's brother, Malik, had gotten acquainted.

Amir rose to his feet and walked to the front of the room.

"We have to hit these niggas hard! We're making sure this thing is done as soon and as bloody as possible. I don't know why a lot of you are with us, but I'm in this game for the money, and these niggas are not going to fuck that up!"

Everyone suddenly looked up because there was screaming and cursing coming from upstairs.

Amir and Los grabbed their weapons and started up the winding staircase to see Slim being pushed into the guest bedroom by Arthur's girlfriend, Shonda, with blood all over him- from head to toe. Slim was arguing about getting a drink from the bar, but Shonda didn't play any games when it came to physical health. As a nurse, she realized that his wounds were more serious than he probably thought. She barked instructions to another woman that often assisted her, and she grabbed her duffel bag that she used to carry her medical instruments. She spoke to Amir through gritted teeth.

"The fool has a bullet in his hip somewhere, so you can't talk to him until we're finished!"

She slammed the door in his face and Amir smiled and looked at Arthur, who shrugged and walked over and handed him a bottle of Moet.

"Don't trip, Meer, I go through that shit daily, but Shonda only acts that way when somebody gets hurt; it's like she takes it personal." Amir didn't even pretend to understand, but he admired the woman nonetheless, and he knew, beyond a doubt, that his uncle was in very good hands.

CHAPTER 26

Reese came up the stairs, and Amir motioned for his friend to join him in conversation. He walked into the kitchen, grabbed two large wine glasses, and popped the cork loudly, pouring both glasses to the rim.

Amir spoke sternly. "Is there something I need to know, dawg? You know I don't like to be around people on that magic, and now I'm hearing that you be going out all the way with that glass dick. You're a different person than I knew, Reese, and I can't trust you."

Reese sat his drink on the counter and looked at his friend with scorn.

"You believe I'm smoking a fuckin' pipe? After all these years and you still don't know a nigga like me? I do be smoking wet, my nig, and I know I need to stop that shit, but I don't smoke *no* kind of dick, Meer; glass, metal, or any other kind. Jealous niggas will say anything, fool!" Amir studied his friend with a blank expression on his face, waiting to hear things from the horse's mouth. Reese took a long drink from his glass and sat down.

"I been going through some shit lately that I tried to deal with, but all that shit went wrong. Somebody killed my momma and my little sister, dawg! I know it was them niggas! They stuffed some one dollar bills inside them to send me a message. Can you imagine a nigga doing some shit like that to your mother? What about your sister? Mine's was seven years old and niggas fucked around between her damn legs! When I heard that bitch on the phone with that nigga and saw a picture in her bedroom earlier with the nigga in it, I snapped the fuck out! I saw M.O.P. tatted on the nigga's stomach and lost it! If I could go back in time, my nig, I would be as brutal as the first time, maybe even worse. I'm gonna slow up on the wet-sticks man; you're like a big brother to me and I respect you, but I'm going on overkill on those M.O.P. niggas! They took my will to live, and I'm taking theirs. I live an eye for a fucking eye!"

Amir was stunned into silence. He had known Reese's mother as well as his little sister, and he couldn't blame him for his rage: he just wished Reese would have told him so that he could have at least tried to talk to him.

Amir embraced his friend before speaking.

"Bro, if there is absolutely anything I can do, just say the word and it's done. I can't imagine what you're going through, but I'm here for you and yours." Reese shook his head sadly.

"All I want you to do is to point me toward these niggas and they gonna get mutilated, blood! I won't stop till everybody they know is layin' on a damn slab! They won't be able to tag their toes because they won't have any of those mothafuckas! Just call when you need me, relative. Border!"

Amir wrapped his arms around him again.

"Border, dawg! You're not alone; we're going to get these cowards for what they did. Get you another drink and we're going to put something together tonight. It's hot outside, but I'm planning to cross the border and put some of those bitches on ice. Do you feel me?"

Reese nodded while wiping tears from his eyes. He picked up his signature AP9 from the counter and walked silently out of the room.

Amir stood for a moment, contemplating their predicament, knowing that he had a dangerous and loyal ally, for life.

CHAPTER 27

Detective Richard Davis stared at the small diamond the medical examiner had in his hand and listened to what he had to say.

"The man started out sucking on each nipple according to the amount of blood and saliva evident at both exits wounds, as well as the redness around the areola. There's no evidence of vaginal or anal penetration: other than what was done with the kitchen knife. The man on the porch was killed immediately from the wound to his chest. The sawing on the face was post mortem and was most likely done to send a message. The man at the fence was taken down by a .223 round to the head and after the body was down, it was hit six more times after the man was deceased. There were twenty nine spent shell casings recovered from the porch, and there were some 9mm rounds, and a lone 12 gauge shotgun shell that delivered a large slug into the man's chest. There were 7.62mm casings as well and some .45 caliber shells at the fence-line. There was a shoot-out detective, and the ones at the fence were obviously not expecting what came at them. You said one of your witnesses had Kansas tags? Well, these murders were very personal, in my opinion, and whatever those three letters Bs mean that was carved into the corpses is an obvious signature of one of the groups that you should be concerned with. We have seen this signature on both sides of the river, but this is the second time in a week I've seen it in Missouri. In my opinion, there is something going on between the states, but much more than the rivalry we have grown accustomed to. I'm going to get with Mr. Alan Hancock, the coroner in Kansas City, Kansas, and try to see if I can find any similarities between these latest murders on his side of the border."

The thorough medical examiner handed over a small plastic bag with the diamond inside to Detective Davis (it was found on Imani's stomach amongst the clotted blood).

The medical examiner began speaking again, snapping Dick out of his reverie.

"Detective, these individuals are brutal, and they are mutilating people, not just killing them. To have the time and confidence to take this long to murder someone, and in this way, usually means financial stability. Money is the root of all evil, so look for the heavy hitters and work your way down to the goons who await their instructions."

Dick shook his head and slowly walked through the double doors, pulling his cell-phone out of his breast pocket.

"Sue, I think we need to get ready to stake out some of these night clubs that you were mentioning. There seems to be popular clubs on both sides of the border that people from both cities enjoy wasting their time in. Let's see if our man shows up; we need to be at one of these locations each night. Contact Kansas City, Kansas, homicide and find any similarities to these killings and get back with me, pronto. I know a homicide detective over there; mention my name and you may get more cooperation. Call me when you're done and try contacting the club owners so that we can be amongst the security team if necessary. Get to work!"

Dick knew that Sue would do everything he needed her to do while he found out what the carved letters meant from the gang unit. These murders made Dick feel very uneasy, and the death of the Kansas City, Kansas, Highway Patrol officer sent shivers down his spine. The murder rang of *overkill*. This seemed to be the way people were being murdered lately. These black men killing each other didn't bother Dick, but he knew by the death of the officer that the situation had begun to touch his world. Killing a police officer was unacceptable, and he would look for these people until he caught them. Prosecution would be sweet and justified, but Dick wanted them dead.

CHAPTER 28

Lo-Lo walked with Keith through the Power and Light District in Kansas City, Missouri, and marveled at the sophisticated establishments to serve the public's need to be entertained. They had just finished watching a pre-season N.B.A. exhibition, and Lo-Lo was surprised to be interested in the sport at all. She guessed it was because she was in good company; Keith was someone who would explain things to her patiently.

"Keith, where are you going?" Her boyfriend glanced in her direction, but he continued walking.

He eventually turned around.

"We're going to a new restaurant down the street, baby, and we're going to a hotel as soon as I can get someone to rent us a room. Are you still cool with everything?"

She smiled. "Yes, Keith, don't worry, I think you deserve something special for being a good boyfriend."

Keith and Lo-Lo had been talking about sex lately, and it was agreed that the time had come for them to take things to another level, or Keith would leave the relationship. Lo-Lo thought back to the time that he had saved her from being assaulted and how he didn't hesitate to pull the trigger in his rage to prevent her from being deflowered.

She gripped Keith's arm and held on to him tight, not noticing Oscar and Paris across the street stalking them patiently and waiting on an opportunity to abduct her.

Lo-Lo sat down at the edge of a fountain, complaining.

"Baby, my feet hurt! Will you rub them for me?"

Keith bent down and removed her sandals and began massaging her feet. He had totally disregarded his uncle's instructions regarding Lo-Lo and her uncle, Slim; her beauty and sweet nature made it impossible for him to hurt her in any way.

Suddenly Keith was grabbed in a headlock and lifted to his feet.

"I knew you was a bitch, nigga! You ain't my fuckin' nephew! "

Paris snatched Lo-Lo off her feet and rushed her to a van across the street to be gagged and subdued.

They forced her to swallow the "date rape drug" and Oscar pulled Keith along, throwing him inside of the van beside her, shouting curses and threats.

Paris growled orders to the other two men in the van.

"Drive them to the spot over on Benton Street and take her in the damn basement. It's already set up for her down there. One more thing: don't touch her in the wrong way. This shit ain't about her; she's just bait."

Keith began to struggle with his uncle, until Oscar pulled his weapon out and leveled it at his face.

"Nigga, you can die with these bitch-ass mothafuckas. Is that what the fuck you want, little nigga?"

Keith slowly shook his head, staring at Oscar with hatred in his eyes.

Paris eyed his father. "Daddy, you need to leave that boy alone. He'll be straight once we get to the house; he just likes the damn girl. Can you blame him?"

Oscar turned and stared at the beautiful young girl lying unconscious on the floor of the van and began massaging the hardness in his jeans as evil thoughts invaded his consciousness.

CHAPTER 29

Tracy sat in his vehicle as he waited for his girlfriend to leave the hotel room with the overnight bag she had mistakenly left under the bed. The Residence Inn was somewhere he usually took Donna because it was not in the inner-city, and it was not very expensive to afford a room.

He sat listening to the latest Messy Marv album, bobbing his head to the music, and impatiently waiting for Donna to return to the vehicle. He didn't see the stolen Dodge Charger slowly creeping alongside him until he saw a clown mask and what looked like a Thompson submachine gun.

Tracy attempted to fire with his pistol, but his efforts were to no avail. The first slug entered his neck, and the second took away part of his scalp. He didn't know about the rest because he was dead. The two killers still ran up to the car and unloaded dozens of rounds into the man's corpse. A curtain moved to the side high up in the hotel, and Donna clutched the cell-phone in her hands tightly; she had used it to call Paris to inform him that she was out of harm's way.

The men stared up at her briefly, but they decided to get her on the next trip; her death would guarantee full payment of the contract, but sirens could already be heard approaching.

CHAPTER 30

Slim woke up to see Amir and Los smiling down at him with a beautiful young woman reading a book in the corner. She was ignoring them completely.

"'We saw the punk-ass bikini panties you had on. What's up? Are you one of those faggot-ass stripper mothafuckas now, Slim?"

Los seemed to be back to his old self, making light of even the grievous circumstances that they were faced with. Slim lifted himself up on one elbow and nodded toward the woman; it was obvious that he needed to tell them something.

Amir said, "Shonda, we need to talk about some things; will you excuse us for a few?" Amir noticed she was reading Quentin Carter's book, Hoodwinked, and he smiled his approval- giving her a wink as she silently walked out of the room.

Slim asked, "Did they find that highway patrolman yet?" Amir was stunned. He had heard about the police officer getting killed, but he didn't know his uncle was the culprit.

Los asked, "What the fuck happened that you had to kill a damn police officer?" Slim leaned back and shook his head sadly.

"Los, I had been in the car with bullet holes and blood all over it, and I had a gun on me that niggas got killed with. Do I need to remind you that I'm a convicted felon? When I woke up to see the mothafucka talking on his radio, I snapped. I unloaded the whole clip and stuffed his punk ass in the back of the Escalade I was in. I called that nigga Arthur because he lives right off parallel, and him and that fine ass nurse came to pick me up on the highway. ''

Amir sobered up immediately.

"Things are getting out of hand. When you killed that damn policeman things went to another level, and Flip is dead on top of that! I didn't want to tell you this, but you need to know, uncle Slim. Tracy got killed, and Lo-Lo never came home today. She didn't call and I'm worried about her. The people at the hotel where Tracy was killed said that the woman that was with Tracy left him in the car and went back inside about ten minutes before he got chopped up, and I mean chopped. I need to spread my wings and find that bitch and the fools that killed my nig. I just hope my little sister is on some bull-shit, because if these niggas have her, I'm trying to go to hell, because I'm mass murdering mothafuckers!"

Slim didn't see Amir exhibit his emotions often, and this certainly supported the fact that things were out of hand. Their enemies were playing for keeps, and Slim couldn't help but feel responsible for what was occurring. The M.O.P. was influenced by Oscar, and there was nothing Slim could do about it except hope for the best; he was out of commission. His ribs were wrapped, but he didn't know if they were bruised or broken; he couldn't take a breath without feeling excruciating pain. He also had an IV hooked into his hand and was wearing a sling on the other arm. He felt helpless, but he knew that he would be back in the thick of things soon. The old ''Player Slim'' would eventually be reminding the fools about who they had crossed, and how stupid they were to engage them in conflict.

Los walked up to the bed. "You get well, old man. We're gonna get out here and wet up these streets. We're all getting together to pop bottles and mourn later, but right now we don't have time for no long-ass faces. I'm gonna smile while I'm killin' these fools, and when I'm finished I'm pissin' in their damn faces." He walked out of the door and Amir sat down next to his uncle with his head in his hands. He eventually looked Slim directly in his eyes.

"Remember Lo-Lo's boyfriend that shot that nigga Mike that night? I found out that he's Tony's son. All the love I've been showing that little dude, and now I find out he was snaking me. I know his mother from when I took him home a few times. If they hurt my sister, I'm going to rip that bitch into pieces. I didn't know who the boy was for sure at first because she lives on the Missouri side, but I saw a picture of Tony holding a little boy and it had his name on it. I don't think his mother knows what's going on, but it won't matter if something happens to my sister. I'm going to tell you one more thing; that woman hates that nigga Oscar you used to do dirt with. She said that he tried to rape her; his own brother's wife!" Slim didn't say anything because he was not surprised at the information. Oscar was one of the grimiest individuals Slim had ever met. Slim knew that if he didn't tend to Oscar soon there would be plenty more bloodshed. Slim looked at Amir sternly.

"Amir, you have to do whatever needs to be done right now. I'll be back on my feet soon, but until then you need to get vicious with these fools. Go out there with Los and your other homeboys- strap up and go find these niggas! There's something else you need to know, though. Candace sneaks off to meet that nigga Mike whenever she gets a chance. I didn't step to him because of how she feels about me, but you need to handle that business, nephew."

This information was almost more than Amir was prepared to deal with, but he already visualized how he would handle things as he shook his uncle's hand and walked out of the door.

CHAPTER 31

Donna sat back in the chair and spread her legs wide as the male stripper played with her clitoris, and her friends screamed with excitement and pleasure. She lived in a house that Tracy had purchased for them in the small city of Basehor, Kansas, so that she didn't have to worry about inquisitive neighbors complaining about her loud stereo system. She was drunk from cognac, and she had already taken three ecstasy pills, so her usual shyness had disappeared. Paris had given her money to set her longtime boyfriend up to be killed, and just two days after the funeral she had already forgotten him. Her girlfriends thought of her as a victim and wanted to take her mind off Tracy by hiring the four strippers that were performing.

Arelia, Donna's best friend, pulled her away from the man kneeling between her legs and guided her toward the front door.

''A woman is waiting for you outside. I told her to come in, but she said she would wait for you to come out because she wasn't invited. She's in that cute little Porsche out there. Tell her to come in and let me get a taste, she's fine!''

Arelia was a bi-sexual female that was open about her preferences. She had looked Ashely over provocatively and was given a wink in return, which she took as a promise that she would see her again that night. Donna didn't know who was in the vehicle, but she felt it had to be

94

someone that she considered a friend for her to know where she lived. The drugs and alcohol were affecting her vision, but when she walked out and looked into the vehicle to see Ashely smiling at her, her body went cold.

She attempted to mask her feelings with a large smile as she opened the passenger-side door, and she tried not to wet herself in fear. She had seen Ashely kill before and knew how unpredictable and ruthless she could be.

She climbed into the vehicle, and as soon as she closed the door Ashely turned to her with a smile that did not reach her eyes.

"You're having a party already, girl? Don't you feel pain over seeing Tracy die like that?"

Donna felt relieved. "It wasn't me, Ashely. My friends threw me a surprise party to try to lift my spirits because I was so depressed."

A male voice came from the floor of the backseat. "It looks like they did a good job, bitch! You in there lettin' niggas lick yo' funky pussy, and it aint been a damn week since my nig's funeral. I got a question, Donna. Will you fuck for a buck? Or would you rather keep settin' niggas up for death like you did Tracy? That nigga cherished the ground your funky feet walked on."

Los sat up in the seat behind Donna, and when she turned to face him, he had tears in his eyes.

Donna began to plead. "Car…."

He yelled. "Shut up, bitch! You ain't getting' out of this shit! "

Tracy had been like a little brother to Los, and he took the way he died personally.

Ashely asked, "Why didn't you tell us before that you seen him die? You said that you were in the hotel and didn't see anything."

Donna started crying hysterically and Ashely put her arms around her as if to give comfort. When she wrapped her arms around her shoulders, she jammed a chloroform-laced handkerchief into Donna's face and watched her lose consciousness. Los nodded to her and they drove down a gravel road that eventually turned onto a path leading to a lake.

Los climbed out and approached the unconscious woman; he lifted her and carried her over his shoulder to the bank of the lake and watched Ashely strip her out of her clothes and pin her to the ground with stakes. She also covered Donna's mouth with duct tape, and she placed a blindfold over her eyes.

Donna came awake to the smell of burning, and she attempted to look around, but couldn't see anything. Just as she recognized the smell of hair, the lighter fluid burned off and she felt the most excruciating pain she had experienced in her life. She attempted to scream, but the duct tape only allowed a small squeal to escape her lips.

After her hair burned off completely and the fire extinguished itself, Los spoke.

"Bitch, you look like a plucked chicken! I was gonna fuck you, but I know Tracy wouldn't want that. What do you think? It don't matter, though; Ashely has a present for you."

Without warning Ashely tossed a bucket of salt water onto Donna's head and watched her attempt to scream and writhe in pain. Los walked off and ignored the sounds he was hearing behind him. He knew Ashely would soon become weary of the torture and begin mutilating the girl for killing her cousin. Los had heard about the contract on Donna, but he didn't want the killers to collect. The situation had gotten very personal, and he wanted to be sure that he saw it through to the end.

He heard two small explosions and knew that Ashely was done with her personal vendetta. She eventually approached the vehicle with blood spatter on her clothes. Los was relieved that she was on his side, because Ashely was a remorseless killer.

Chapter 32

Lo-Lo looked around at the dark, dirty basement as the events of the day slowly came back to her. When she realized that Keith knew the people that had kidnapped her, she felt sickened. Every few hours Keith would come down the stairs and attempt to talk to her, but she would just ignore him and stare at the ceiling.

She could now hear the locks clicking on the door and began getting angry again, especially when Keith tiptoed down the stairs like a burglar.

She refused to look up at first, but when she did her blood ran cold. Oscar was staring down at her wearing nothing but boxer-shorts on his large frame. The underwear clearly showed a large bulge inside the crotch. He calmly stroked himself and watched her as she squirmed and made whimpering noises, unable to escape the bonds or the dirty gag they had stuffed into her mouth. She was tied down to each bed post, so she couldn't even close her legs as he roughly rubbed along her inner thighs, then without warning, he palmed her vagina and bent down to suck on her breasts that he had freed with his other hand.

Lo-Lo attempted to yell and squirm away, but there was no escaping from what he was doing in her vulnerable position.

Just as he pulled her panties to the side and she felt pressure on her vagina from his fingers, she heard someone yell.

"What the fuck? Daddy, you need to gone with this bull-shit, man! We're not doing this shit to rape no little girls. Get the fuck away from her!"

Paris roughly pushed his father away from Lo-Lo and covered her body with a large blanket while she watched him, silently blinking away the tears that flowed from her eyes. Oscar didn't even look embarrassed, he simply began ascending the staircase, silently eyeing Keith who was now standing next to Paris; he walked upstairs with a grin slowly spreading across his face.

Keith said, "P, you're going to have to get her out of here, man. That nigga is going to hurt her- with his rapist ass! The niggas can be taken care of without having her all tied up and shit; she won't even eat."

Paris walked over and slapped Lo-Lo hard in the face.

"Don't get shit twisted, little cuz! I don't give a fuck about this bitch. I just ain't with being around no rape shit! If she don't make it any easier for us to get them, she's in the way and she gotta be dealt with!" Keith looked at his girlfriend sobbing silently into her gag and refused to leave the side of the bed where she lay.

When Paris finally walked upstairs Keith looked down at his girlfriend.

"Lo-Lo, I'm getting you out of here, do you hear me? Before I really got to know you I was helping them because Slim killed my dad, but, baby, I love you to death, and they'll have to kill me if they try to do something to you."

He could still see the anger in Lo-Lo's eyes, but he could also see a flicker of hope and the trust that she used to have in him.

"You're going to have to eat, baby, and do exactly what I tell you. I don't know if you hate me or not, but you need to pretend that you do hate me so that they won't get suspicious." He pulled her hair to the side and gently planted kisses all over her face, whispering his love for her over and over. When Lo-Lo felt Keith's tears on her face she knew he was sincere, and this made her weep again, but this time from joy. She didn't know how Keith got involved in the situation, but it didn't matter; Lo-Lo loved him and knew he felt the same way about her. She hoped that Keith could get her out of danger; she had no doubt that Oscar would try to rape her again.

CHAPTER 33

Mecca lay back on the bed at St. Joseph's Medical Center in Kansas City, Missouri, as jelly was rubbed onto her abdomen for the sonogram procedure. She watched Amir nervously looking out of the hospital window and smiled, knowing he would be a good father. She knew Amir didn't want to know the baby's gender, but she wanted to be content that her baby was developing properly.

She said, "Baby, come over here! You don't have to know what the baby is to give me some affection."

Amir grudgingly strolled across the room and massaged Mecca's shoulders, refusing to look up or even acknowledge the staff until the procedure was over.

"How do you feel, Mecca; do you need anything, lady?"

Mecca shook her head. "Amir, I'm only five months along, baby, don't start worrying until I need help moving around and my feet start swelling. Right now I'm just happy you took the time to come with me, but we need to let these people finish their job; we can talk later."

Amir spoke with the female doctor about the baby's progress, and he walked into the hallway and sidled over to the waiting room to watch the tropical fish in the large aquarium embedded into the wall. He pulled a small box from his pocket and opened it to stare at the large diamonds in the ring he was offering to his future wife. He was going to kneel by her bedside when she called him over initially, but he decided against it because of the procedure they were performing on her that morning. Amir had a problem with knowing about the gender of his child before the birth, he wanted to realize it when he reached down to cut the umbilical cord. He sat for what seemed like hours before he felt a hand on his shoulder, and he looked at the doctor smiling down at him.

"Everything is fine, Mr. Wilson, would you like to come back to the room with me to see Mecca? Are you sure you don't want to know about the procedure?"

Amir shook his head. "No, doctor, I'd rather know about that after the labor, ma'am. Is everything going alright with my baby?"

She explained everything to him with patience, expertly detailing what was going on with Mecca's body and the baby's health.

When they entered the room, Mecca was fully dressed and looking beautiful in her pregnancy. Before the nurses and doctors could leave, Amir kneeled and produced the ring in silence.

Mecca didn't understand what he was doing at first, but when it dawned on her tears began flowing freely down her face. The doctor and nurses behaved like any other women in the world; they cried and gave Mecca hugs and words of encouragement, looking at Amir as if he were an African prince. Mecca grabbed Amir around his neck and pulled him tightly to her.

Amir asked, "Mecca, will you be my wife? I love you more than life itself, and I want you to be in my life for the rest of my days on this earth."

Mecca attempted to blink away the tears as she mumbled.

"Yes sir, I love you too. I'm yours!"

Amir nodded and said his goodbyes as he made his way out of the hospital; he was on his way to handle his business in the streets. He knew about the rendezvous his mother was having with, Mike, the man that had attempted to rape his own step-daughter, going so far as touching her vagina with his penis. Amir didn't know what was going on with his mother, but Mike was about to pay the piper, regardless.

CHAPTER 34

Reese was at the carwash in his pigeon-blood red Lincoln MKZ getting his wheels ready for the club. E-40 was supposed to perform at a Kansas City, Kansas, venue that night, and he was also supposed to appear at The Wax Factory music store on Parallel Parkway to sign autographs. Reese had already met the K.C. legend, Rich The Factor, and many other rappers in the town, but there was something about E-40 that Reese liked; he could relate to the struggles that the man had overcome. Reese knew that if Mate wasn't in prison, he would be right there with him. E-40 had a song called "Checkmate" that always made his boy feel himself.

He watched a young woman washing her Chrysler 300 in the next stall and gave her eye contact to see if she was interested. When she boldly stared back at him, he smiled and strolled over, knowing that he would be taking her somewhere to eat, and most likely to a hotel later that night.

"What's your name, baby-girl? "

He noticed how she watched his mouth as he spoke; women were usually fixated on his diamonds when he conversed with them.

"Alexis."

He spoke with her for almost an hour, noticing that she was very articulate and intelligent. He gave her his number and told her what time he would be at the club later, hoping that she would show up. Her white spandex pants accentuated her curves and he could plainly see the slit in her vagina and the peaks of her breasts through the sheer material. She was focused on the swelling at his crotch as he talked, and Reese was sure it would be an interesting night if she felt as good as she looked. He watched her leave and strolled toward the machines to get change for his car wash. Shots rang out and shattered the silence.

He dived behind a dumpster and listened to shells ricochet off the metal, sounding like hail. He looked longingly over at his vehicle, but he realized that he had no chance of getting there to retrieve one of his weapons. He cursed himself for spending so much time talking to the woman out in the open, knowing he was at war in the streets.

He peeked around the corner of the dumpster to see two SUVs blocking the entrance with Missouri plates and stickers in the rear windows: boldly announcing where they were from. They were concentrating on where Reese was hiding even though there were expensive vehicles abandoned from when the shooting had begun, so he knew they were there strictly for him.

When three men began approaching the dumpster, squad cars began pulling into the parking lot. The gunners didn't hesitate to turn their attention toward the police. They began firing on the police officers immediately, and the few onlookers were stunned.

The police were outgunned, and Reese saw at least two go down after taking hits, but he was relieved when the men climbed into their vehicles and exited the carwash with the police right at their bumpers. The highway was a quarter of a mile up the street, so Reese knew they were going to make a run back to the Missouri side of the border.

Reese ran to his Lincoln and called Amir as he pulled away from the carwash, telling him about the clumsy attempt on his life. He didn't know if this was a Black Border Brother situation, or something to do with the family he had killed in Missouri. He turned his music to full volume and smiled as heads turned in his direction, surprised by the deep bass shaking the pavement. He wasn't far from the Wax Factory, so he decided to go mingle with the women, but this time he would be ready. Reese didn't care about the attempt on his life, and he was accustomed to brushes with death. The men had attempted to take his life in a cowardly way. He would go and meet one of his favorite rappers, check on the three spots he was in control of, and head to the club to enjoy the show.

He also hoped that Alexis would make an appearance in order to help him relieve some stress.

CHAPTER 35

Amir listened intently to Keith on the telephone explaining the situation with Lo-Lo, and he was saying that he would bring her home to safety. After he hung up, Amir mulled over the situation, having noticed that Keith refused to tell him where Lo-Lo was being kept. Even though Keith had had a change of heart about the kidnapping, he still had love for someone that had orchestrated the kidnapping; he clearly didn't want to bring them harm.

Amir glanced at his watch as he climbed into his Range Rover, knowing that his mother would be meeting with Mike at his job soon. Amir could have gotten to the man sooner, but he wanted his mother to witness the abduction, so she would know that what Lo-Lo claimed was true; the man had attempted to rape her only daughter. Amir knew from experience that when a woman was in love, she would try to believe her man, no matter if it was an obvious lie or not.

He called Los and Arthur, making sure that they were already present in the parking lot of Mike's job. He explained to them that he was on the highway and would be there within minutes.

When he pulled into the parking lot of the establishment, he immediately located his mother's vehicle without her in it, and he noticed that the van that his boys were in was directly behind it.

He parked in a location across the street, secured his weapons to his body, and approached the van- making sure that they saw him coming. The side door slid open and Los sat there with a huge grin on his face, and he motioned to the back of the van where Mike lay wrapped like a mummy, complete with a fresh gash in his forehead and urine staining his pants.

Arthur announced, "We grabbed this trick-ass nigga before your mother showed up. She went into the building about five minutes ago to look for him; are you sure you want her to see this shit?"

Amir slammed the door shut without saying anything and stood over his stepfather in silence before viciously kicking him in the face.

''Yeah, she's going to see this shit! My mother's not going to be caught up behind a trick nigga like him. She needs to see what happens to anyone that crosses the line; that's my sister he fucked with! ''

Los moved to the back of the van and kicked Mike in his scrotum. It didn't matter that the man had been with the woman he considered a mother for years; Mike made it clear that he had no morals, and Los considered him an enemy. He pointed his weapon at Mike's manhood to stop his moaning as they watched Candace step out of the building and walk over to stand beside her vehicle, gazing around the parking lot in confusion.

Amir pulled Mike to the sliding door of the van and removed the tape from his mouth before opening the door. When his mother heard the door opening, she reached in her purse for what Amir assumed was mace, and she quickly backed away from the van.

She didn't recognize Mike at first, but when she did, she began to sob in anguish.

''Meer, Carlos, what are you doing? This man helped raise both of you! He sacrificed and helped me to care for both of you when you were little boys!''

Amir slid the door shut and stepped out so that Mike's condition would not be observed by any good Samaritans.

''Momma, he changed Lo-Lo's diapers too, and the way you're acting you wouldn't have known if he did something to her or not. Come over here and get in the van, momma.''

Candace complied with tears roaming freely down her cheeks, and as soon as she saw Mike she attempted to reach out and comfort him.

Los gently grabbed her hand.

"Momma, this nigga ain't shit, so why are you letting him do this to you? Didn't Lo-Lo tell you what this nigga did?"

Candace nodded. ''Yes, she told me something, but she never liked Mike! He said none of what she said was true!'' Amir squatted over Mike, who was curled up in a ball.

"And you believed this bitch over your own kids? Is he worth that much to you?"

Without warning, Amir pulled out a small blade and stabbed Mike in his right eye. A geyser of blood and puss shot out onto him, and even with the gag the noise Mike made was deafening inside the van.

Amir calmly spoke. ''Tell her what you did, fool, or I'm going for the other one. You have five seconds.Mike immediately stopped wailing and admitted to Candace exactly what he had attempted to do that night. He used him being drunk that day as an excuse and begged her for mercy.

Candace looked stunned and sickened after having defended him so passionately.

"How could you, Mike? How could you? She's still a child!" She said this repeatedly as if in a trance.

Los gently pulled Candace from the van and walked her away. She looked up at her two sons and asked with a forlorn frown.

"Do you have to kill him? I don't want you boys killing people."

Amir walked up and kissed his mother on the cheek.

"I considered this man to be my family, but Mike was a fraud, and he violated everything we've worked and bled for. The people in my life must be trusted, or they will be eradicated. Mike violated in the worst way, and he should have known what the consequences would be by attacking his own step-daughter. I'll call you later, momma. I found out where Loren is; don't waste your love on a corpse; Mike is a dead man."

He re-entered the van behind Los and Arthur and silently watched his mother sob as she pulled away, but he refused to comfort her. This was the life he chose, and he made sure his emotions didn't get in the way of what needed to be done, no matter what.

CHAPTER 36

Detective Galubski walked past the barricade that the D.E.A and A.T.F had set up around the house on 34th street. He had been a homicide detective for the past twenty years with the Kansas City, Kansas, Police Department, and he had always hated dealing with Federal agencies in the city. Galubski had wanted to get a warrant and kick the door in as soon as detective Mendes called him, but the Federal Marshalls were already inside of the home and he was ordered to stand aside. When Susan first explained about tattoos on the man's body, he immediately thought about Robert Adams who was doing life at Hutchinson Correctional Facility. The detective was aware of the Black Border Brothers and how they marked their enemies' bodies. Robert had been in and out of the county jail for years, and the money he was connected to usually was a huge help to him. The attorneys he could afford often destroyed the cases within months.

His last run-in was the murder of a rival drug dealer and his girlfriend. He and his partner in crime, Reese, were charged, the witness was intimidated, and the case was dismissed.

Detective Galubski knew that Reese was the man in the picture Sue described, but he couldn't approach the youngster directly; he was too intelligent for that. What he needed was someone who needed law enforcement assistance and had weaknesses, and this drug raid was the perfect opportunity.

Pete and his friends had gotten caught with assault rifles, bullet-proof vests, and several kilograms of cocaine that had already been converted to crack with baking soda. The A.T.F. had already left with the weapons, but the officers searching the home were still finding drugs hidden throughout the house, and they had uncovered over a quarter of a million dollars inside a safe in the basement.

He watched the men being taken to the vehicles to be transported to the detention centers and was surprised to see a female sitting in one of the vehicles.

Galubski walked over to the vehicle and addressed an agent that was standing there. "What's the deal with her?" The man grinned before responding.

"I don't know; she won't even talk to us. Do you want her to give you a call from the jail? You like that dark meat, right, detective?"

Galubski scowled and looked closely at the woman for a minute before walking away. It was a known fact that Galubski mingled with people from the inner city, particularly young African-American girls and women. If the females committed a crime, he would make the evidence disappear, or he would destroy the files for sexual favors. If the women needed money, it was all part of the "game". Galubski even had a daughter by a woman he often "tricked" with, and there were always more options around. He was a homicide detective, and the women were valuable assets against their men; he used them as pawns. The women thought of him as a "trick", but he was staining their sheets, getting information about their people, and he would likely spend the little money he gave them anyway; most of the time the cash was taken from one of the fools he had arrested for their crimes anyway.

The detective was still smirking at him as he walked away, not knowing that he already knew the woman, and she wouldn't talk. He had met her when he first started investigating the Black Border Brothers, and she was not a weak female that would turn on her own.

She also didn't associate with white men, no matter the price. Reese took good care of Keisha and used her as a mule to move the drugs, and the home was owned by her.

Galubski headed to the federal building downtown in order to talk to one of his informants; he needed more information about Reese. He headed directly to a Marshall he knew well.

''I already cleared things with your department, and I believe this man is connected to a person that killed another man, his girlfriend, two small children, and possibly one more man in the yard coming to their aid. All this occurred on the Missouri side. We stood aside until you made your arrest, but now I need to see if I can shake him up while he's in this situation. Don't tell him anything about me; he knows me well, so just put me in a room with him so that we can work out a deal. These murders are connected to these men and he has access to information we need to stop these killings, and their drug organization.''

The agent sat back as if deep in thought before he responded.

"What organization are we talking about, and what will our department get out of handing this man over to you?''

Detective Galubski sat down.

''They call themselves the Black Border Brothers, and they are not your typical Bloods and Crips. They have ties to the original Mexican Border Brothers from California through a man we've already been watching. The fool you have in custody is not considered small time, but he's nothing compared to the men he works for, and the killings won't stop until we get a break, and this could be it. ''

The Marshall silently left the room and didn't come back for about thirty minutes, but he had Pete in tow, shackled by his arms and legs. When he sat down, Pete lowered his head to the table, knowing that it was over for him. The Marshal left the room, and Detective Galubski stood over by the door, watching the man sweat. Galubski eventually pulled up a chair and placed it right next to the young man before sitting.

''You know the least you're looking at is life in a Federal prison, right? We're not going to beat around the bush with this shit. I want you to help the Marshals with Amir and Los. You also should tell me what I need to know about your boy, Reese. I know it was him who killed those little kids; were you with them that night?''

Pete began hesitating about his involvement at first, but he slowly began getting comfortable being a snitch. He was thinking about never being able to live a free life again, and he was soft. Pete told him about Reese's red Lincoln and about a couple of his women, but he didn't know where Reese or any of his family lived. Pete was not trusted as much as the detective at first believed. He was informed about a shootout earlier that day that Galubski had wondered about. He also stated that Reese was planning to attend the club scene later that night.

The detective stored the information in his memory and used his cell-phone to call the Missouri detectives so that they could collaborate on the story so that they could put the final nail in Pete's coffin.

Detective Galubski knocked on the door for the agent to re-enter, but before he took Pete away, he loomed over him with a mean glare.

"Pete, if you fuck with me, you're dead, one way or another! Either I tell your boys about you or I shoot you down like a runaway slave; are we understood?"

Pete stared daggers at detective Galubski, but he didn't say a word; he had already said enough.

CHAPTER 37

Lo-Lo stared at the filthy floor, hoping that what Keith said was true. He claimed that there would only be two people there to watch her that night, and that he had a plan to get her out of the house. The basement was filthy, and rats had been present each night; the rodents were getting bolder each day. At first the pests would simply fight over food she threw against the wall. Now they would boldly approach the bed where she lay captive.

Keith came by the night before, but she didn't tell him about Oscar forcing her to play with his uncircumcised penis. He had expelled a load of sperm all over her face and hair as he held a gun to her head. Lo-Lo figured that the next time Oscar would force his body between her legs and take her virginity like some savage beast.

She shuddered when she thought about the older man; when he was around she was more afraid than she had been in her life. He always seemed to be either slightly intoxicated or stone-cold drunk, and he always had something negative to say or do. He talked about her uncle, Slim, as if he was determined to murder him, and Oscar claimed they had been friends when they were younger. She hated the man with a passion and hoped that Amir would kick the door in and end her misery.

She heard the locks rattling on the door and felt a tinge of fear as heavy footsteps began to descend the long staircase. She let out a squeal as someone clamped their hand over her mouth, but when she heard

Keith talking softly into her ear she relaxed and allowed him to work on her bonds.

"Lo-Lo, you need to do whatever I tell you, baby, no bull-shitting! These dudes are not just going to let us walk out of here; my cousin Paris will kill them. They won't hesitate to kill us; do you understand?"

Lo-Lo nodded and when Keith released her arms, she put her arms around his neck and applied pressure.

"I could kill you for what I'm going through, but I feel sorry for you because of your father. Keith, please get me out of here! I know you love me, so I don't care about the past!"

Keith grabbed her clothes from a shelf and tossed them to her while he made sure that he had the large gun that he had stolen from Paris; he needed more firepower than the small handgun he had been carrying.

After she had gotten dressed, Keith gripped her hand and led her up the staircase. After they had gone through the basement door, Keith pushed her into a closet in the vacant house.

A man he knew as Monster approached with a quizzical frown on his face.

"What the fuck was you down there doing that long? You was supposed to feed the bitch and come back up here. I didn't see you take no food down there." Keith shook his head sadly.

"She wouldn't even eat, man, and I don't think she's feeling well."

Monster grabbed his crotch and opened the basement door.

117

''I got something yo' little bitch might wanna suck on to help her appetite. All that little bitch need is a man. You too gay to fuck her, so move!''

Keith moved out the way, and when he heard Monster reach the bottom of the staircase, he locked him inside with the dead-bolt key Paris had given him. When Monster began yelling and pounding on the door, Keith pulled the gun from his waistband and cocked it, knowing that Monster might be coming through the door soon. Red suddenly entered the hallway with a shotgun in his hand and started pulling on the door to open it for his partner while Keith ran and hid in the next room. When the door did not open, he looked around and opened the closet door for some reason, and Red was surprised to see Lo-Lo standing there shaking in fear. Just as Red began raising his weapon toward her, Keith started unloading his clip, spraying Lo-Lo with blood and brains. Monster stopped banging on the door and Keith approached it with murder in his eyes.

''Do you still want out of there? I'll open the door if that's what you want.''

Lo-Lo didn't recognize the cold look on Keith's face or the eerie sound of his voice. He had killed a man and he would be changed forever because of it. Lo-Lo grabbed his arm to pull him out of the house, but she shuddered when he looked in her direction but didn't focus on her.

She said, ''Keith, baby, we need to get out of here! Those shots were loud, and I can hear sirens. Please don't be like them; you had no choice, so come on!''

The body had already voided its bladder and colon, so it didn't take any more convincing to get Keith out of there. Before they left, Keith grabbed a gas can that they had planned to use on Lo-Lo after the deed was done, and he splashed it all over the rooms, paying special attention to the basement door. He pulled off one of his socks and used some matches out of the makeshift living room, put flame to the sock, and tossed it into the curtains.

He grabbed Lo-Lo by the hand and pulled her out of the back door while Monster screamed, smelling the gas and smoke. Keith had become stoic and dispassionate; recent circumstances were forcing his hand. He had wanted to avoid things like this all of his life, especially considering what had happened to his father. Now he actually was enjoying the thought of killing a man. He could still see the damage he had caused in his mind, and he could feel the power from the hot gun in his pocket.

He and Lo-Lo walked out of the back door, and they ran into the alley where his mother's car waited. Lo-Lo glanced at him, taken aback by his drastic change in demeanor. Lo-Lo was excited by him, but she was afraid of him at the same time. Keith placed her in the passenger seat and even made sure that her seat belt was fastened before driving off into the night, not knowing where to go.

CHAPTER 38

Paris turned onto Benton Street and could see fire trucks, ambulances, and squad cars in front of the vacant house where they were holding the girl captive. He couldn't believe his eyes; he had given instructions for the girl to be killed and burned after she served her purpose, not before. His father, Oscar, sat next to him and stared at the house, knowing the girl was a special link in his chain to getting Slim. Paris turned around and headed back to the Blue Hills Apartments where they had left Keith earlier, telling him not to go and visit the girl that day. They said they didn't want him in the way, but truthfully, Paris didn't want him to be around when the girl died.

Oscar said, ''I been trying to call Monster and Red for a minute. Something ain't right with this shit!'' Paris pulled his new Chevy Tahoe into the parking lot and hurried up the stairs, entering the apartment in a rush. His girlfriend, Sheila, had a concerned look on her face. "What's wrong, Paris?" He stared at her hard.

''Have you seen my little cousin, baby?'' She nodded, still confused. ''Yes, he was here with his little girlfriend for a little while. He packed up the rest of his clothes and stuff. He was acting real mean and protective of her like she would break; is something wrong?''

Paris turned around to see Oscar glaring at him with a gleam in his eyes. ''I told you that little nigga was a pussy! We should've never took him to that house; I know he didn't get her out his damn self!''

Paris wasn't listening; he was picturing seeing a covered body being brought out of the burned house, and he was wondering what had happened. He dialed Keith's number and listened to it go straight to his voice mail.

Paris turned to look at Oscar. "Let's go, daddy." He kissed his girlfriend on the cheek and told her he would talk to her later; he had to see about his wife soon and make sure that she was out of harm's way amidst the drama. His girlfriend stayed on his heels all the way to his vehicle, telling him not to use her house for trouble and complaining about him leaving her to see his wife.

Shots rang out from behind a parked minivan and Sheila's body was ripped apart from her head to her waist. Paris saw it was too late to help the woman and hit the ground in a crouch. He was suddenly hit through the right side of his chest by a ricochet and dropped to his stomach with a groan.

Oscar went down to hits in both of his legs and pulled his son as far underneath the SUV as he could. He began shooting toward the muzzle flashes he saw coming from across the parking lot. He knew he had to do something fast when two masked men came out into the open. One was holding an assault rifle, and the other man held a shotgun. Softball sized holes came completely through the vehicle, and Paris could see the slugs embedding into the brick apartments. When the assault rifle began firing and the metal frame of the vehicle caused the bullets to flip, Oscar pulled Paris to his feet and they both sought shelter beneath Sheila's Honda Passport. Oscar fired toward where the men were now hiding behind a BMW on the opposite side of the lot. Vehicles suddenly began appearing in front of the apartment, and Oscar was relieved to see Jamaican Peter's Lexus and members of Paris's M.O.P click jump out of a Ford Excursion, unloading on the two men.

"M.O.P! M.O.P, nigga! Yeah! This is what you need!"

The men who had killed Sheila jumped into their vehicle, and the passenger leaned out of his window, still firing, hitting one of the Jamaicans in the shoulder. The power of the 7.62mm round left the man's arm dangling by tendons as he screamed in agony and frustration.

Oscar yelled, "Call a damn ambulance, fools! Paris don't look too good! I got hit in my legs, but I'm straight!"

Jamaican Peter said, "You got holes in your leg, boi, what you talking bout! I'll take you if they don't show up quick, ya hear?"

Everyone made a dash to stash weapons and drugs before the inevitable police arrival. Oscar leaned back against the Honda.

"They gonna come at us hard now. I don't know what they been doing, but niggas better stay on they fuckin' toes. We got lucky this time, but we caint wait for them to come the next time, or we're all dead. Soon as I get patched up we going to the Kansas side. Them bitch-ass niggas shot my son!"

Oscar looked down at Paris; he was writhing in pain as he held his chest. He wasn't panicking or bleeding excessively, but Oscar was still relieved to see the ambulance pull into the parking lot.

Oscar turned toward Jamaican Peter. "As soon as I can get on my feet, we're going to find these niggas and end this shit! If you see that little-faggot ass nigga, Keith, don't worry about him being my nephew. Take his bitch-ass out the game! Slim is probably laying up healing from the holes we put in his ass, but I followed Keith to that little bitch's house one night. It ain't over!"

Peter nodded and moved out of the ambulance workers' way and contemplated leaving the city altogether. He knew from his days living in Kingston, Jamaica, when to judge that things were out of control. When you began involving families in feuds, you also had to prepare for people to attack yours. Peter knew that Oscar was totally out of control and it was too late to back out of the situation; too many lives had been lost. The money was the reason he was associated with Paris. The M.O.P. moved the kilos he supplied like it was nothing, but he didn't want to lose his life because of a personal vendetta. He also knew of the Black Border Brothers and the small army of men that Amir had amassed. It was time to use his brains, because if he didn't, he had no doubt they would eventually be splattered on the streets.

The Black Border Brothers had too much money and influence to take lightly, and he knew eventually they would meet. Like them, the Black Border Brothers played for keeps.

CHAPTER 39

Amir pulled off his ski mask and watched Los pacing the floor with an Ak-47 still gripped in his hands.

"We had that bitch-ass nigga, Meer! I told you Ashely be on point with her damn info; that bitch Sheila was fucking that nigga, Paris, and was meeting with him at that spot every chance she got. I didn't mean to hit her, but she shoulda known the game when she started fucking with the bitch nigga!"

Amir didn't like the idea that killing innocent women was justified, but he couldn't bring Sheila back, so he let the matter rest.

"Los, we know how Oscar looks now and I know that nigga Paris got hit pretty good. We can use the other information Ashely got from her home-girl and go after the Jamaicans. Those M.O.P. niggas need money to do what they gotta do; niggas need to have money to fund every war, or they will definitely get fucked off. My cousin, Country, just got here from Wichita, and we're getting him hooked up with Looney and Rag. Tell Ashely I need to see her so that she can get us into the next spot we're hitting up, and we need her to find out where Keith is with my sister. I'm going to pay his mother a visit if I don't hear from Lo-Lo by tonight, so get ready to have a house ready for us to keep someone."

Los smiled. "I'll do all that, carnal, but I got a funeral to go to before that happens."

Amir looked confused until Los finished.

"I know them niggas that got burned up in that house in Missouri. They was that nigga Marlon's boys; the nigga had to be trying to set Ashely up the whole time. I'm just glad we got to his bitch-ass first, cause' he must've already known that she was with us. The niggas that got burned up was Paris's little flunkies, and the police found leather straps burned in the basement that might be where they were keeping Lo-Lo. I'm gonna let them niggas know that it *aint* no rest in peace when you fuck with the niggas from the border!"

Amir stared hard at Los before responding.

"I don't care what you do to them dead niggas, Los, but it's the ones that are still breathing that we should worry about. Do what you feel, man, but be careful. Don't waste time sending a message to niggas that don't matter."

Los had already started pacing again, but this time with a huge smile on his face. Amir shook his head, thinking how crazy and unpredictable his best friend had become. But one thing had never changed: Los's loyalty to the blood pact they had formed years ago in his mother's backyard. Amir would always be Los's keeper, and nothing about his best friend's ways would ever change that. He picked up his Holy Qur'an and retreated to his study to ask for forgiveness and to search for answers. He thought of Mecca and his baby growing in her body; Amir had no doubt that he must do something drastic about the situation they were in- he was yearning for a normal life. He didn't want to repeat the footsteps of his deceased father by dying young or living a life surrounded by violence; he would not neglect the things that he knew were very important to a child.

He shut the door and rolled his prayer rug out to begin his last prayer of the night, and he would pray to hear from his sister soon. If he didn't, Satan would win, because he had evil things planned for the M.O.P. and anyone associated with them.

CHAPTER 40

Detective Richard Davis stood outside of the nightclub at the Kansas/Missouri border, anticipating the arrival of Reese, their number one suspect in the murder of five people. He had murdered two men, a woman, and two small children at a house in Kansas City, Missouri. The call they had received from Detective Galubski had confirmed their suspicions that the matchbook they had found in the house belonged to the killer, and that he must attend the nightclub, at least occasionally. Sue was on the other side of the street controlling the constant flow of vehicles that were arriving. She was scrutinizing each one closely, and at one point she noticed a gleaming red Impala. It was filled with females that were eager to find a place to park, so she ignored them and continued looking closely at all new arrivals. She winked at her partner even though she knew he couldn't see her eyes from that distance in the night. She went about her business while Dick pretended to be one of the security crew for the club that night. Some rapper was in town, and from the size of the crowds it was obvious that he was popular. The steady throb of the music and the frequent need to control the crowd made Dick appreciate his home on the outskirts of the inner-city. The security detail had already broken up two separate fights between women, and a man had been arrested for disturbing the peace. Dick was beginning to give up hope when Sue's voice came through his headset.

''Is that a Red Lincoln, Dick?'' He glanced over to the area where Sue was indicating on the corner, and he noticed the vehicle parked alongside a white Chrysler. Two people stood outside of the two vehicles deep in conversation. The man wore an expensive suit, and his diamonds could be seen shining out of his mouth and all over his wrists and neck. From the way people gave him space, the man was well known to them as well as respected. Dick crossed the barrier and nodded to the plainclothes officers from Missouri that were there to make the arrest.

It appeared that the woman had gotten into her vehicle and the man that they now believed was Reese appeared to be texting with his back turned.

Sue was approaching from the other side of the street with her weapon drawn; suddenly the man backed off and ran behind a building, noticing her clumsy approach. Dick ordered one of the officers to question the woman in the Chrysler while he, Sue, and another officer pursued the murder suspect. Reese ran behind one of the buildings; it was often used for a haunted house in October, but it was now vacant and eerily dark inside. The clap of Reese's dress shoes could be heard as he ran down an alleyway, and Dick took off in pursuit of him with Sue right in front of him.

Sue yelled, "Stop right there, Reese! "

The man was pulling on a door to one of the buildings, not realizing that they had been so close behind him. Reese pulled out what appeared to be a .40 caliber Glock and began firing, and they leapt behind the corner of a building, returning fire. When Dick saw the man ejecting his magazine, he sprang from where he had been taking shelter and placed two well-placed rounds into Reese's body. The young man fell onto his back and they could hear his weapon as it fell to the pavement.

Sue began approaching the man slowly; Dick noticed that her weapon was pointed in the killer's general direction very loosely. Just as

Dick began yelling for her to stop, Reese climbed up off the ground with a chrome revolver and began shooting Sue at close range.

Dick yelled, ''No! Sue! ''

Reese disappeared inside of the building as the young officer followed while reporting the incident on the radio that he was carrying. Dick rushed to his partner and dropped to his knees, applying pressure to the wounds in Sue's neck as blood oozed through his fingers. He looked down at the bullet-proof vest that his partner was wearing, noticing that slugs were mushroomed on it without penetrating; the bullet-proof vest didn't stop the slugs from entering her neck and lower stomach.

Sue was whispering something incoherent and the officer was now off the radio, carefully entering the building in pursuit of Reese. Dick knew that he should assist the man, but he couldn't leave his friend alone in the dark.

He heard the officer yell, ''Drop your weapon and place your hands on your head!''

The building was suddenly illuminated by gunfire as Dick looked up in horror. He gripped his weapon after he heard a window shatter above his head; the young officer came hurtling out, screaming until he hit pavement far below. The silence was pierced by a laugh coming out of the building; Dick overheard the sound of footsteps retreating and continued to hear them diminish as the killer fled. The wailing sirens were very close now, but Dick knew it was too late for them to stop Reese from making his escape.

He looked down at Sue staring vacantly into the night, and he realized that it was too late for her also.

CHAPTER 41

Candace sat in the lobby of the morgue holding her head in her hands, still disbelieving the sight of Mike's body. She had secretly married the man years ago, and she had never informed her children, knowing that they would have never approved. She only recognized Mike because of a birthmark on his temple and a couple of freckles on what was left of his face. She had identified Mike for the detectives before vomiting all over the floor next to the table he was on. She had known that Amir and Los would kill if provoked; they had no other alternative in the life that they lived. Regardless, Candace hadn't expected the viciousness of the torture that her husband had undergone. Amir very seldom showed his anger and frustration, but he was very stern and calculating, just as his father had been.

Candace's cell-phone vibrated in her pocket and she reluctantly answered.

''Yes? Oh my god! Lo-Lo, are you alright? Where are you?''

She hadn't heard anything from her daughter or Keith in two days, and the boy's mother didn't seem to have a clue where either of them had been. The way Amir clammed up and was silent, she knew something was wrong, but her son had refused to tell her anything.

Lo-Lo told her where she was and Candace rushed out of the building, refusing to end the call. Lo-Lo sounded afraid, and she was alone, saying something about Keith not wanting to be seen by Amir. Candace was puzzled by this last admission, but she disregarded it because she was relieved to have her daughter back. She was afraid of her own son, but she called him to let him know about his sister. His questions kept focusing on Keith so she knew that something was wrong, but Candace would not let anything happen to Keith, no matter what. She told Amir to be at her house later so that he could find out what was going on with Lo-Lo; she was determined to find some things out for herself.

When she pulled up to Lo-Lo's school and saw her daughter with dried blood on her face and bruises under her eyes, Candace couldn't hold in her grief any longer. She totally broke down and Lo-Lo was relieved that the school was closed, because if someone would have seen her mother, they would have thought that she had gone crazy. Lo-Lo comforted Candace as best as she could, but she ended up having to place her mother in the passenger seat and drive her home. Candace blocked out the world and imagined beautiful things that she could handle. She fell into a catatonic state, completely ignoring the hard world she could never grow accustomed to. She thought about Amir and the boy he had been, and she realized that she should have known what he was becoming: another inner-city hoodlum.

CHAPTER 42

Rag had just finished recording in his underground studio. Amir called and told him about the instructions he had for him and Looney to follow. Everything sounded good until Amir mentioned his cousin, Country, and the fact that he would be riding with them. Country was trustworthy, but he was also very unpredictable and violent. The man was like having three Reese's wrapped up in one. Rag was aware that he and Looney had killed with the best of them, but it didn't take much to set Country off, and they didn't need to be facing criminal charges behind his craziness. Rag realized that there was no use complaining about the situation; the man was Amir's family, and Rag knew he didn't have to worry about Country's loyalty. He was an authentic street warrior, and Rag simply had traveled to the Missouri airport as instructed.

He turned east on Parallel Parkway and headed for the highway; he was making the trip to the K.C.I Airport in Missouri. He raised his top in his Cadillac and concentrated while Looney rolled the "blunt" and dipped it into the bottle of P.C.P. When they pulled in front of the hotel near the airport people couldn't help but stare in their direction.

Rag's Cadillac CTS had oversized 26 inch rims, and he had a chameleon paint job that looked like it was wet, changing colors frequently before their eyes. Young women in the inner city tended to love this combination, and the two men boldly stared at them and smiled, showing the diamonds in their mouths when the opportunity presented itself. Rich the Factor was playing extremely loud in the aftermarket system announcing ghetto tales all around the parking lot: *Now I'm at the spot doing thangs to tha rocks; I'm a G, I put those thangs in a pot. Watch it lock up to a brick and a half; turn my kitchens to labs. Only Pyrex utensils be in my cabinets…*

They both loved and were loyal to their local rappers and anyone associated with their cities. Houston, Texas, the bay area in California, New Orleans, Louisiana, and various locations in Kansas and Missouri were all welcome if they came with respect. Some people assumed that it was slow in Kansas City, and they often received a rude awakening for their ignorance.

Rag and Looney could see Country walking across the parking lot toward them and groups of people were parting like the Red Sea. Country did not drive down from Wichita, Kansas, as they had expected. He had flown in from Oakland, California, where he had been visiting with family.

Country was built like a football player, and he possessed an imposing gold-toothed smile that reminded Looney of a shark's evil grin. Rag considered taking Country to add jewels to his grill, but the man wasn't having it. He was satisfied simply having "gold slugs" and not getting caught up in trends from another city.

When Country spotted them, he started smiling his signature smile.

"What's down, my nigs?" He had already adapted to the Kansas City, Kansas, slang used by Looney and his associates from being around them so much, and they had adapted to some of the Wichita Ebonics.

Looney asked, "Are you ready to get at these fools? That nigga Checkmate locked up again, but Amir still holla when he needs us, regardless. Them bitch-ass M.O.P. niggas killed Flip and Tracy already and they tried to get at Slim. We hookin' up with them Black Border Brother niggas on the Missouri side so they can show us where them niggas be at. They're Crips, but them fools is bool as fuck, and they about that business. Amir don't play that gang banging shit anyway. We put that shit to the side for the Border. What's up with you? I thought you was through with the twin cities?"

Rag opened the trunk of his vehicle and Country tossed his suitcase inside.

Country smiled. "When my relatives need me, I'm here. Anyway, I love it down here, playa, and niggas from the Dub K fit right in. Nigga, I had to come back and meet some more K.C. women!"

Looney laughed and opened the door for him while handing him the "lovely" P.C.P. blunt, and he also tossed him a .45 caliber handgun that Amir had provided for him. They headed toward a Black Border Brother house in Missouri on 59th and Jackson to meet up with Lunatic, one of Los's henchmen. This was going to take patience; the three of them were Bloods, but they were dealing with a house full of Crips. They all knew that Lunatic was about his money, but they also realized that some of his friends lacked direction and were seeking a reputation in the streets.

They stopped at Tony's Liquor Store on 31st street to get some vodka to drink; a small group of youngsters kept walking around the vehicle observing Rag's rims, seeming to peer closely at the Kansas license plates in the rear.

Country stepped out of the store with the liquor, and the teens hesitated, not just from the fact that Country was built like a tank, but his pistol was hanging from his pocket like it was legal. One of the youngsters was bold, though.

"What up, cuz? Why you niggas on this side of the water? This Hoover hood over here; are you niggas lost?"

Looney stepped out of the vehicle and smiled, hoping that something was going to happen. Rag just continued to puff on his cigarette, watching the group's women as if the men weren't there. Country walked up to the teen and stared at him with contempt.

"If you don't get the fuck out of my face, you aint gonna leave this parking lot, little nigga. I'm not from either side. I'm from Wichita, but it's Black Border Brother with me, playa, so what you wanna do?"

The youngster was looking back at his friends for help; he was not trying to get embarrassed in front of the females. If he made a move, Rag and Looney knew that Country was going to light up the parking lot.

Looney walked away from the vehicle with a huge smile.

"Don't bitch out now, nigga! Represent this raggedy ass parking lot and die. You niggas don't want nothing with mothafuckas like us; we should just mash ya'll out and take the bitches. I know they wanna go, anyway."

The women quietly stared at Looney as he spoke, and they were ultimately the ones who defused the situation. They walked between Country and the frightened teen, and they pulled him and his three friends back to their vehicles.

Country nodded before speaking. "I talked too much to those fools. Next time I'm just blowing a niggas noodles back, you feel me?" Rag shook his head.

''Blood, we up here on business, and nothing else. You know Amir called you up here on some real shit, so we don't got time to get locked up for killing one of these hoe-ass niggas over some bullshit. Let's go.''

Rag pulled out of the parking lot, noticing that some of the women were still there, opting not to leave with the youngsters.

He winked at the women, but Rag knew to leave it at that; he wouldn't put himself in a position to be set up by any of the unloyal females in the streets.

CHAPTER 43

When they were within three blocks of the house, they could already smell the P.C.P. lacing the air in the neighborhood. The house they were approaching was a major supplier for both cities, and the strong chemical smell often permeated the air in the neighborhood. They parked in front of the house, and they saw a sea of blue everywhere, but they also saw that the men were stenciled with the same tattoos as they wore on their torsos and necks.

The ones stationed on the roof of the house already had their rifles pointed in their direction, and one individual was talking into a cell-phone, no doubt announcing their arrival.

As they parked, Rag watched Lunatic walk out of the house smiling, but with no humor touching his eyes.

''My nigga, Rag. What's up with you, cousin?'' Rag smiled.

"Nothing much, relative; we're just bickin' back, and being bool.''

They laughed and embraced; everyone relaxed, knowing there would not be a confrontation. Lunatic gestured to his people and everyone went back to whatever business they had been conducting before they had arrived.

Lunatic looked Looney over.

''You look like you're going to a Valentine's party. You think you got on enough red, homeboy? Don't just come over here throwing it in my boys' faces next time, do you feel me?''

Looney nodded and followed Lunatic toward the house while people eyed Country suspiciously, noticing the pistol that was stuffed into his waistband. When Lunatic found out who Country was, he shook his hand and stared him directly in his eyes before speaking.

"That nigga Amir is a mothafucka I would do damn near anything for, cause I know he would do the same for me. He told me about you and how you get down in the streets; we know where some of these cats are hiding out. As soon as I finish popping off these last gallons of piss for Amir we gonna suit up.''

Lunatic walked off and they were ushered into a bedroom to have drinks; Lunatic even had monitors set up so they could watch different locations throughout the house and outside. Looney rolled up another blunt without the P.C.P. and they sat back and waited for Lunatic to conduct his business so they could handle theirs. They were just getting comfortable when one of the men, Blue, who had been in front of the house when they arrived, brought in some gloves, ski masks, and other items that they would need.

Rag noticed that the youngster donned a pair of gloves himself.

''What's up, home-boy? You riding out with us?'' The young man shook his head.

"Naw man, I'm just showing you where the fools is at. Amir said if something jumps off to be ready, but this is you niggas thing, man; they won't know what hit em', trust me."

Country stood and glared at the youngster.

"Nigga, I don't trust no mothafucka. Just show us where they at and get the fuck out of the way. The only reason I'm fucking with you rip niggas is because of my people; We don't need you to do shit else!"

Looney noticed that the youngster had put his hands in his pockets and prepared for trouble, but the man simply pulled out a pack of cigarettes and stared Country down.

"Cuz, I don't give a fuck what you think, or where you from either. Us being Black Border Brothers is the only reason you up in here. If you want to get up on some bullshit gangbanging, you can get handled, cuz; Crip gang run this shit over here."

Country smiled and nodded respectfully; he liked testing people and he was impressed by the young man- he showed no fear.

Lunatic walked into the room wearing all black and carrying an army duffle bag filled with weapons. Looney grabbed the bag and began pulling the weapons out, laying them out on the floor with a smile. He looked up at Lunatic and grinned.

"I like your taste, dawg, but when are we gonna roll on these niggas?"

Lunatic picked up an AK-47 from a table.

"As soon as my niggas get back with some tilted cars, my boy Blue is going to show us the shack where the niggas be, and the rooms where they be handling they business at. One of the fools be fucking his baby momma there, and her and the dude got into it recently. He started running his mouth to her about Amir's little sister and talking shit about our click. Because his girl is down with Crips, he didn't think she was down with the Border; he gonna find out tonight, though."

Looney looked up. "Are we pulling a kick door?"

Lunatic shook his head. "Naw, man, we got a key to the back door. The nigga's chick had one of her home-girls get a copy made of his keys while he was sleep. We know where they chill out at, where they keep the money, and where the dope is at. It's a stash house for that nigga, Paris."

Rag, Looney, and Country took off their red shirts and Lunatic noticed that they all had on black underneath. The three of them also handed around latex gloves and grabbed ski masks from the things Blue had brought in.

One of Lunatic's henchmen came into the room and gave him a nod, and he motioned to them that everything was ready. There were two minivans sitting across the street from the house; Lunatic climbed into one of them with Blue before calling them over.

"Ya'll follow us; we going to the house in one of these rides; the other one gonna be around the corner just in case it get ugly and somebody notices this van. They're hot-wired; do ya'll know how to fuck wit em?"

Looney nodded and headed to the van with his weapons, and after Lunatic gave them the rest of his instructions, they all prepared to hunt men in the inner-city.

CHAPTER 44

"Keith, what is going on? What do you mean you have to go? You're only seventeen years old; you can't be out in the streets without a place to go! If Oscar comes around here I'm calling the police, so unpack those bags and let me try to call Paris."

Keith had attempted to explain to his mother what was going on, and why he should leave before things progressed any further. He left out the fact that he had taken lives, but he told her about the kidnapping, and about Oscar's plans for revenge in retaliation for his father's death. Now he regretted telling his mother anything and having her worried about him. At the time it seemed like the right thing to do, but things had changed. Keith had extended family in Oklahoma, but he knew he had to stay away from them, as well as his family in the surrounding Kansas City area until things simmered down.

His grandmother lived in Port Saint Lucie, Florida, but he didn't know her well and he also didn't want to intrude into her life. He felt that the only option he had was to go underground in the streets and distance the precarious situation as far from his mother as he could; he had no doubt that Oscar would come knocking with evil intentions.

Paris was his favorite cousin, but Keith felt that he could not put him in a position to oppose his father. They would most likely end up in some type of confrontation, and Keith knew he would shoulder the blame for the entire situation.

Lo-Lo had stated that Amir would appreciate Keith protecting her and getting her out of danger, but he wasn't so naïve as to believe that. Keith was a large part of the reason that the kidnapping of Lo-Lo had been possible, and he didn't think his change of heart would negate the fact that he had been a pawn to ensure that Lo-Lo's kidnapping was successful.

Keith had asked Lo-Lo to find out if she could steal money or drugs from her brother if it was possible, and they could relocate temporarily, get married, and eventually begin a new life. Lo-Lo had remained silent on the issue. She had called him earlier to inform him that she was waiting on Amir to arrive, but Keith wanted to be clear of the house in case the man sent some goons to pay him a visit.

While his mother was on the telephone attempting to locate Paris, Keith tossed two suitcases full of clothes out of his bedroom window, left a note for her, and climbed out silently; he wanted to take any rash decisions out of his mother's hands. He already had the keys to the Dodge Intrepid that she had practically given to him, anyway. So, he at least had transportation while he figured out what he needed to do.

He called Lo-Lo and was relieved that Amir was bringing her money, but her mother was still not responding to her; Candace was lost in her own private world.

Keith instructed Lo-Lo to give him a call after Amir left so that he would feel comfortable picking up the money that she had for him. He felt confident that they could find someone to rent them an apartment.

In the meantime, he headed to Lawrence, Kansas, to talk to his friend, Steven, who had recently graduated from high school and began attending the University of Kansas. Keith explained the situation as best as he could over the telephone, but he decided to travel to Steven's campus in order to see what he had to say about the situation in person. Keith also wanted to know if Steven could help them in any way.

He looked down at his telephone vibrating on the seat next to him and reluctantly answered.

''Hello, who's calling?'' A woman named Ashely was on the telephone saying that Paris had been injured in a gun-fight, and that Keith should come to her house to visit him in Leawood, Kansas. He had been considering it until he realized that Paris hardly knew anyone in Kansas, and Keith recalled Lo-Lo mentioning a very dangerous woman with the same name. Lo-Lo had claimed that the woman would do anything for the Black Border Brothers organization, and that Ashely was laced with poison.

Keith listened to her sultry voice calmly attempting to draw him in, but when she realized that he was not responding the way she had planned, she turned nasty.

"We're going to get your little ass, and you can believe that! I know Lo-Lo cares about you, but she's letting her little pussy think for her. Me, I'll cut your little dick off and make you eat it for fucking with my little sister. I don't care about that fake-ass shit you did for her!''

Keith turned his telephone off, knowing that Amir had instructed her to call. There would be no more doubting Amir's intentions for Keith, regardless of what Lo-Lo thought.

CHAPTER 45

Ashely stared at the telephone with a smile on her face and looked over at Amir.

"That little nigga hung up on me! He's not stupid enough to fall for something so obvious, Meer."

Amir stood silently, contemplating his next move. He should have known not to allow Ashley to make the call- her temper was too potent. He grabbed Ashley's drink from the bar, straightened his tailored suit with his other hand, and strolled over to where she stood.

"I'm not going to harm that boy. He killed his own people to save my sister."

Ashley grabbed the drink and sat at the foot of her staircase before responding to his comment.

"Meer, you can never trust that boy; he agreed to set us up for them. He changed his mind once, and he's sure to do it again. Why would you take a chance on him?"

She watched her long-time friend stare up at the ceiling.

"That boy loves Lo-Lo. I've seen it with my own eyes, Ashely. That's the second time he put his life on the line to save her. Those M.O.P. niggas simply played him because of his age and the fact that Slim killed his father. He showed what he's really about, eventually."

He walked around the living room, admiring Ashely's paintings and the expensive layout of her country home. He had visited her parents' home in Missouri, but her house in Kansas was beautifully built. Ashley had erected a mixture of African heritage and femininity into the décor, providing a stunning atmosphere.

He glanced at Ashley and shook his head, silently reminding himself of her ferocity. She was like a female lion; she would hunt and pursue her prey until she took the life and anticipated where to find her next victim. She had been this way since they were young; Amir knew that something had to have made her so heartless.

He strolled over to her plate-glass window and stared at the wild scenery.

''My cousin, Country, is in town. We need to end this feuding situation real soon; we're meeting in the West Bottoms again this weekend, and we can't have the Italians back out of our deal. Forget Keith for now; I need you and Country to go after these M.O.P niggas. You know how ruthless Country is, but we need more than that. We need you to get him close enough to the Jamaicans to shut M.O.P.'s money down for good. Get in them niggas heads, pants, and do whatever needs to be done.''

Ashley smiled, and she walked over and kissed Amir full on the lips.

''You're the only one, other than Los, that I'll do anything for. Do you know that, Amir? If it was up to me, you'd be fucking me by now. If you ever change your mind all you have to do is order me."

Amir walked over to where Ashley stood and grabbed her by her neck, slapping her viciously.

"Bitch, don't you ever talk to me like that again, do you understand? Los isn't my home-boy; that's my brother! I don't fuck with disloyal niggas *or* bitches. If you want to get in someone's head, you had better try someone else; that bullshit doesn't work over this way. I'm going to let you tell Los what happened here today. Don't downplay or try to twist the shit either. If you do that, I'm going to make you regret ever crossing me."

Amir finally released his hold on her, and tears streamed down Ashely's face in shame. She had attempted to find a weakness in Amir, but she had chosen the wrong route. Acquiring women had never been a problem for him, and none of them had been successful in turning him against someone that he loved and respected. Amir sleeping with Ashley behind Los's back would be disrespectful and cowardly; he was the leader of the Black Border Brothers for a reason, and he didn't take short cuts. He would severely punish anyone that did not respect the type of man that he was.

CHAPTER 46

Detective Davis stood in the back of the cemetery, unable to join the huge group of mourners at his partner's funeral. Sue was pronounced dead at the scene of the crime, but the reality of the situation didn't hit Dick until he viewed the body prone in the casket. He had been reliving the scene of her demise over and over in his dreams, and he felt an uncontrollable rage building to a crescendo. Reese had killed Sue as if she was nothing, had mortally wounded the other young officer, and had laughed mockingly as he made his escape. Reese clearly thought of the situation as some dangerous, sick game.

Blake, Sue's husband, looked Dick in his eyes earlier and gave him a silent nod and a reassuring smile, knowing what was going through his mind. Dick had been around their family for many years, and everyone understood how Dick felt about cop-killers, especially where his partners were concerned. He wasn't concerned with the law at this point; he would search for the man, only using the law to locate him. Dick often daydreamed of shooting Reese in the *medulla oblongata*.

He walked through the crowd and watched the casket being lowered into the ground alongside the family. Frank Mendez, Sue's father, stared at Dick as if he wanted to kill him. He didn't hide the fact that he blamed him for putting his daughter's life in danger, and Dick wasn't sure if he disagreed with the way the man felt.

He didn't attempt to comfort Frank because he felt that it would cause a scene. He simply tossed his handful of roses into the hole and walked away before the officers gave their salute, not wanting to hear the blasts from the weapons. He planned on making his own blasts sooner rather than later.

CHAPTER 47

Rag, Looney, and Country sat in the "tilt" after receiving the keys to the back door of the house from Blue. They were waiting for Lunatic and Blue to park one of the vans around the corner so that they could handle their business. A handful of women arrived at the house minutes ago, and it seemed that the men inside had already decided to shut down business for the night. The lights were dimmed, and they could see outlines of people partying throughout the house, with no one on sentry duty.

Lunatic appeared, walking up the sidewalk on the opposite side of the street. He motioned them out into the street.

When Country grabbed his gun and began getting out of the vehicle, Rag stopped him.

"Country, we're here to handle business, so don't go in this house just killing fools. We need to find out where these niggas are laying; we have to get them to talk, do you feel me?" Country smiled mockingly.

"Rag, why you on me about some bullshit? I know we gotta get these niggas to talk. I aint about to trip out like that." Rag pulled his ski mask over his head and watched Looney, Lunatic, and Country follow suit.

The residents of the nearby homes didn't own dogs, so it wasn't a problem getting to the house undetected. There was a lone security camera at the "spot", but it only viewed the front porch and part of the yard.

Once they made it to the side of the house they simply peeked in the windows to pinpoint how many people were inside and where they were located. Looney tapped Rag on the shoulder, and when he looked up Looney pointed to a back window where Country was crouching. He was staring into the window while fondling himself. As they got closer to him, they could hear the grunts and moans of sex coming out of the open window. Rag roughly pushed Country away from the window and they made their way to the back door where Lunatic was waiting with the key already inserted.

Rag whispered to Lunatic. "Did you see which rooms they was in on this side of the house?"

Lunatic stared at him hard. "All ya'll gotta do is go to the spots we already saw; there's only one room on the other side, and some dumbass nigga is counting money while all this shit is going on in the house. Go straight to the rooms we already peeped; we taking everybody in the basement, ya'll ready?"

Looney smiled as he quietly opened the door, taking the decision out of their hands."

He and Rag went into the first room where the couple were having sex, and Lunatic headed to the opposite side of the house where the man was counting cash. Country entered the room next door and was surprised that there was a three-way sexual episode occurring. He smiled as he closed the door behind him.

The couple in the next room were so into each other that they didn't realize someone was in the room until Rag grabbed one of the woman's bouncing breasts and twisted her nipple savagely. "Ow! Stop!"

She had been on top of the man with her back to him, so the man had assumed that she was reacting to his sex.

"Bitch, don't act like you cain't take this dick now, we not stopping shit!"

He began pounding into her harder, until he felt Looney's 9mm press into his face.

"Nigga, no means no, don't you know that? If you move to even take your dick outta this bitch, yo' noodles gonna be all over the wall, understand?"

The man nodded and Rag grabbed the woman by her hair and pulled her off the bed while she screamed. Rag placed his hand over her mouth and whispered into her ear.

"We don't need *nothing* from you, so you're in the way. If you make another noise we gonna kill you right in this funky room. Damn, you got some stank pussy, bitch!"

He pulled duct tape out of his jacket and bound her arms, and he covered her mouth with a strap while Looney allowed the man to slide on his boxer shorts before binding him also.

Looney watched the couple closely while Rag went to the next room to make sure Country had his room secure. As soon as he opened the door, Rag knew that something was wrong. There was the unmistakable coppery smell of blood in the air, and the room was so dark he could hardly make out Country thrusting frantically into a young woman from behind while she made muffled screams through her gag. Rag could see two bodies beside the bed, and when he turned on the light, he saw that the two men were disemboweled. A huge knife was lying in a pool of blood next to them. When Country turned and noticed Rag, his face showed his irritation. He finished raping the woman, ignoring her cries and pleadings.

Rag pointed his pistol at Country's head. ''Nigga, what kind of sick shit are you on? What the fuck is wrong with you?''

Country shook and shuddered as he climaxed, and when he finished, he pulled his manhood out-covered with blood and feces.

The woman cried softly while she bled excessively, and she eventually yelled at Country.

''Why did you kill them, and why did you hurt me?'' She asked the question over and over through the dirty sock that was in her mouth. Country ignored Rag and approached the woman.

''Bitch! Put your damn panties on and shut the fuck up! Them niggas shouldn't have been looking at me like they was going to do something!''

He grabbed her by her arm and began dragging her to the doorway, holding her hands together behind her back. Rag walked over and yanked the woman away from him.

"Nigga, you already did enough; go grab Looney and head downstairs to the damn basement!"

Country glanced at the weapon that Rag was holding, as well as the look in his eyes. He turned and walked out of the room in silence. Rag bound the woman and headed to the other side of the house to find Lunatic.

He heard shots echoing through the house and readied his pistol as he pulled the woman down to the floor.

He heard Lunatic yell. ''You niggas can't fuck with me, cuz! Black Border Brother on mine!''

Rag taped the woman's ankles together and cautiously peeked into the room, seeing Lunatic standing over a man with blood oozing out of a large hole in his face. Lunatic looked up and smiled.

"The dumb-ass nigga didn't want to give up the money.". He thought I was robbin' his ass at first, but now I know where the Jamaicans are at. Another dude and his bitch in the bathroom tied up, but the police gonna be here soon after all this shit!''

They went into the basement where Country and Looney waited. Rag made eye contact with Looney, silently sealing the captives' fate.

Looney walked over to the group and shot them each in the middle of their foreheads, not hesitating on the females. Country stood over the bodies, pulled his penis out, and urinated on them while cursing and threatening their families- as if they could hear him. He then pulled out his .44 caliber Desert Eagle handgun and headed toward the woman that he had raped; Looney shot her himself before turning his weapon toward Country's head.

"Man, let's go! I had enough of this sick bullshit! I'm telling Amir to send you back to damn Wichita; I told him you were too damn crazy to handle shit like this! Now, grab yo' shit and let's go! Lunatic! You and Rag grab the money and meet us at the van. Spark this bitch before you leave, though; we don't need the police to have nothing to work with."

He headed up the stairs behind Country, still holding his weapon on the unpredictable man. Rag and Lunatic rushed to the bedroom and stuffed money into a pillowcase before setting each room on fire by using the cheap curtains to start the blaze. They retrieved lighter fluid from the back porch to make sure that the fire didn't neglect the bodies in the finished basement. They drenched all of the corpses before dashing out of the house. When they reached the van, the door was already open for them to climb inside. They switched vans on the next block and Blue drove them back to Lunatic's house to call Amir. Rag couldn't wait to get away from Country. He didn't want to be around the maniac any longer than was necessary.

CHAPTER 48

Carlos Sr. gave up the keys to his vehicle and watched as the valet attendant pulled his Lincoln Mark LT around the corner of the building to be parked. He waited until one of the younger Italians exited the five-star restaurant, shook his hand respectfully, and led him into the building to meet Manny Macon: the boss. There was a question of whether the Italians would continue to allow meetings and drop-offs in the West Bottoms. They had been in touch with Carlos Sr.'s people in California, but Manny wanted to know about what the Black Border Brothers were doing in the streets, and how it could possibly benefit the Italians.

Carlos Sr. could already see Manny sitting in the rear of the establishment in a section reserved for him. In fact, everything was reserved for Manny Macon; he was the sole owner. Carlos Sr. noticed that the exits were casually covered, and he observed that there was a man directly at the table behind where Manny was sitting. There was also an individual watching closely from two tables over. The man's hands were out of sight. Carlos Sr. also noticed that Frank wasn't around; there would be no friendliness or beating around the bush on this occasion. The young Italian that had escorted him to the table pulled a chair out for Carlos Sr. and silently walked away.

"Carlos, how are you doing, my friend? It is a good thing that you could make it!" Carlos Sr. waived away the waiter that approached their table carrying a menu. He concentrated on Manny.

"With all due respect, I'm not here for dinner or idle talk, and I know that you're not either, so why don't we just leave the small talk for the ones that don't know any better?" Manny stared at Carlos Sr. intently while lighting his Cuban cigar, and he took a small sip from his wine glass before speaking.

"What is going on with these niggers that you have me involved with, Carlos? It was bad enough having to deal with your so-called Mexican organization, but now I am associated with former-slaves that pretend to rule the very streets that are keeping them in bondage."

Carlos Sr.'s face screwed up in anger, but he knew better than to express his feelings aggressively.

"Manny, my son is one of these people you're referring to, and I would appreciate you keeping that in mind just as I consider your family when I have to deal with the European trash in your organization. My boys are involved in a feud that they are not responsible for, and they have been forced to deal with the situation in order to stay alive. These things have absolutely nothing to do with the business we have together, and it never will. We appreciate doing business with you, Manny; if it weren't for you, we would have to deal with the Kansas against Missouri bullshit. I realize that this situation must be dealt with immediately so that things can go back to normal."

Manny stood and paced the floor while responding. "I understand that when people intend to take your life you have to do them the same favor. The problem I have with the situation is that someone's been leaving clues carved into the bodies, and there was also a female officer killed by someone in the Bottoms connected to the killings. The police are not blind, and they seem to know too much about what is going on with this situation. I feel that our meetings and transactions are going to cost us far more than the petty cash that we are receiving from you. We will meet this weekend as planned, but after that you must handle your business in the streets before we can meet again, no matter what. I have no problem with you or the blacks in this community, but I distance myself from unnecessary trouble, and the niggers and wet-backs seem to be motivated by senseless conflict. My price has increased five thousand dollars; when things go back to normal the price will return also. Do you have a problem with anything I have said?"

There was no hesitation. "No, Manny, there is no problem, but you also must keep in mind who you're dealing with, with all due respect." Carlos Sr. stood and extended his hand to his business associate; he was eager to leave the restaurant.

By the time his vehicle was brought to the front of the building, Carlos Sr. could make out outlines of men lingering in the shadows. If he had taken longer than thirty minutes the Italians would have had a war on their hands. Manny Macon would have been forced to deal with those former slaves that he had verbalized so much contempt for.

Chapter 49

When Amir saw that Carlos Sr. was safe, he radioed to his men that there would be no need for action. He watched Carlos Sr. climb into his vehicle and exit the area before flashing his light for Los to follow him to his mother's house to see about Lo-Lo.

On the way, though, he had a stop to make at one of their houses to handle some business. Money had been coming up short at this location, and he had been hearing stories about his worker, Maniac, having wild parties and consuming the product that he was supposed to be selling. This was not the first time that Amir had had reservations about Maniac and the men around him, but he had been too busy with other things to deal with the situation.

He made it back to Kansas and got off on the 75th street exit, watching all the Black Border Brothers pass by, flickering lights, but continuing to their own destinations inside both cities; everyone but Los, of course. His friend trailed him patiently even though he already knew where Amir was headed. This house dealt in weight, so Amir had to be careful how he handled things. This was not the inner-city, and the neighbors in the area were extremely inquisitive.

Amir stopped at a full-service car wash to have them clean the exterior of the vehicle. He noticed a young employee at the carwash staring at the rims on the late model vehicle like he was in a trance. Amir remembered himself at that age and hoped the boy continued working hard in acquiring his dreams through hard labor. He walked inside and waited for Los to finish talking to another attendant, and they both stood in front of a large Plexiglass window to watch their vehicles move by as they were cleaned.

Los eventually focused on Amir. "Are we going to holla at that nigga Maniac, or what? I saw him at the club the other night doing lines with some bitches, tricking off like he was a fuckin' Don. I didn't even holla at the nigga about the money. I knew you wasn't gonna forget about that fool and let him disrespect."

Amir looked steadily at his friend. "Los, we're not going off hearsay on this one. Allow the man to defend himself; that's only fair. I'll tell you one thing, though, if he lies to me or tries to play me after I been there for him and his family, he'll never do it to anyone else."

Los moved closer and told Amir the plan he had for when they arrived to meet with Maniac, and Amir nodded and strolled out to his Volvo that was being wiped down. Their vehicles looked like they were coated with lip-gloss, gleaming in the sun. He handed the young car-wash employee a small stack of currency and his business card; Amir was always attempting to hire valuable employees at his detail shop, and the young man seemed to value his work.

Amir trailed Los this time, knowing that his friend would stop at the Go Chicken Go restaurant around the corner. No matter how much money they made, it seemed Los would still be attached to the small chicken business as well as the famous Gates B.B.Q. Amir also went inside and ordered gizzards and a box of wings, watching one of the women studying him and Los, nudging her friend in the side to get her attention. It was evident that the men represented money, and Amir's dark good looks and Los's Spanish/African-American heritage often garnered interest from the opposite sex. They had gotten used to the attention, and they handled the flirting with modest smiles. Los walked up to the window and boldly looked in and admired one of the women's curves, causing her to perform an unconvincing blush on her gorgeous face. It wasn't long before the woman was hastily passing her telephone number out of the serving window along with their order- with the promise of submission in her green eyes. Amir watched his friend retrieve the number from the counter, but Los tossed it into the wind when they were outside.

"I just performed a good deed. That'll save her from having an abortion. I know I wasn't wearing a rubber fucking that fine-ass bitch!"

Amir smiled until he climbed into his vehicle; he was all business as he thought about Maniac. He pulled his Calico M960 submachine gun from under the seat and screwed on his silencer before placing it in a duffel bag; He trailed Los once again. They both decided to park around the corner and walk to the house.

When they arrived, Amir noticed that something was wrong. There were several vehicles parked outside of the house as if there was a party occurring inside. He noticed Los adjust his weapon before following him to the house. Reese's, A.P.9., rode in Los's waistband, and he stopped and attempted to conceal it better with his shirt once he realized how he must look before they hurried to the house.

Before Amir could get his foot on the porch the door swung open and a woman stared at him accusingly.

"Did you call before you came over here? The next time you ain't getting served! Maniac!"

She opened the door wide and they could see activity all throughout the house. Los pushed past the woman with murder in his eyes, and when he spotted Maniac, he began the test he told Amir about.

When Maniac noticed them, Amir saw that the smile that had been plastered on his face moments before had disappeared. It was clear from the confused look on the woman's face that she had no idea who they were.

Amir grabbed her by the hand, noticing the way she kept twisting her mouth and wiping her nose.

"Do you know me, baby-girl?" From the way she stared at Amir, she was slowly realizing that something wasn't quite right.

Two other men walked into the room and simply sat on the couch with their drinks; security seemed to be nonexistent in the house, and there was the unmistakable aroma of cocaine in the room.

Los glared at Maniac. "Your so-called friends told us about the side hustle you got going on, homeboy. What's wrong? We're not paying you enough?" Los told this lie with a straight face. Maniac glanced around nervously; he looked like a cornered animal.

Maniac finally spoke to the people in the room. "Ya'll gotta burn out for awhile. I got business to handle." The woman hesitated to abandon him, but the men were finally realizing that something was amiss. When one of them sat his drink down and stood as if to confront them, Amir pulled his machine gun out and leveled it at his head while Los covered the other man with the AP9 and roughly shoved him into a corner.

Maniac stammered fearfully. "Ron! Hold up man, that's Amir and Los!" When the man heard the two names his face sagged, and his body posture slouched submissively. He blustered fearfully in response.

"I didn't know, man, I thought ya'll was on some robbery shit!"

Amir frowned. "It doesn't matter, just sit back down and shut up."

The other man attempted to break free, but Los forced him back onto the couch. From the tears flowing down the woman's face, and the evident concern for Maniac, Amir felt that there was some emotional attachment. The man wasn't stupid enough to come to her aid, though, as Los was silently wishing for. They eventually herded all of them into the kitchen and sat them down.

The cocaine that had been sent to the house was being cooked in large quantities over the stove, and the cook was being watched closely by two other men. Poonk's brother, Donald, was holding a 9mm in his hand and another youngster was helping himself to some lines of the uncooked drug on the kitchen table.

When Donald saw who had walked in, he started backing away from the table. He felt the need to distance himself from what he had been doing. Amir shook his head sadly.

"No, little man, go ahead and indulge. If it's alright with Maniac, it's alright with me. Do you want to take a bag with you for later?" Donald shook his head, but he didn't say anything; the drug had obviously begun taking effect from the glazed look in his eyes.

Maniac said, "My brother don't have nothin' to do with this, Meer. He was just chillin' for a minute.

Los savagely pushed the woman into the kitchen wall. They all watched her hit the floor, and Los leveled the A.P.9 at Donald. When the man dropped the pistol, Amir calmly strolled over and picked it up, ordering everyone to sit on the kitchen floor.

He asked patiently, "How much of my damn money have you been putting up your big-ass nose and tricking with on these bitches? We've been noticing the money coming up short, but I wanted to give you a chance to pay me. Dope-fiends always think they're nickel slick until they get caught red handed."

He reached into a kitchen drawer and picked up a carving knife. He savagely grabbed Poonk's hand before plunging the knife through it and impaling it into the floor. Poonk let out a blood-curdling scream.

''Ahhh!'' He attempted to kick out at Amir's legs, but instead he received four rounds from the Calico. The woman screamed and the men attempted to rise from the floor in an attempt to save their lives, but Los unloaded the AP9's extended magazine into all of them.

They left some of the cash and retrieved the rest of the drugs from a large floor safe, knowing that Ashley's mother would be receiving a call about the murders that had occurred inside of the house that she had been renting to Maniac.

Amir had left some drugs and cash on purpose. He wanted it to appear that a robbery had occurred, especially when the authorities found the open safe in one of the bedrooms.

They left the house and casually walked around the corner. When they climbed into their vehicles they slowly pulled away. It was time to make sure that Amir's family was safe.

CHAPTER 50

As soon as Lo-Lo saw Amir's vehicle she rushed out of the house in her bathrobe, not concerned with the way she was dressed or if she was seen. Amir jumped out of the vehicle and lifted his little sister off her feet; as soon as he placed her on the ground, he turned serious.

"Let's go inside; things are going to get heated around here."

Los arrived and Amir led his sister toward the driveway and climbed into his vehicle; he opened the garage door so that they could have their vehicles off the street just in case they had been noticed near the murder scene. He climbed out of his car and entered the house through the garage; he could hear his mother laughing.

"Malik, you're so crazy, why did you do Slim like that? He's your brother!"

Los entered and stood next to Amir, looking at Candace with confusion. "Who the hell is Malik?"

Amir's heart dropped. "She's talking about my father; he's been dead since we were kids, Los."

Candace behaved as if she couldn't see any of them, and Lo-Lo was now sitting on the bed with her head in her hands; she did not want to look at her mother; the woman had clearly lost her mind.

Los approached his god-mother. "Momma, what's wrong? Candace! Who are you talking to?"

Lo-Lo finally stood with tears in her eyes. "She's not going to answer you, Carlos. I've been trying for hours. Until she finishes whatever she thinks she's getting dressed for she won't talk. When she saw me with these bruises, she lost it. I feel like all of this is my fault!"

Amir grabbed his mother roughly by her arm as if he was demanding her sanity.

"Momma! Stop bullshitting! I need to talk to you!"

Candace finally focused on her son and spoke to him in an eerie voice.

"If Malik see's you with your hands on me, you're dead. Why don't you just leave me alone while you still have a chance?" Candace was still very beautiful, and she was obviously living out a scene involving one of the many men who had pursued her in the past.

Amir looked at Lo-Lo, noticing the bruises on her face and welts on her arms.

"Did those fools hurt you?" Lo-Lo knew that he was referring to rape, and she shook her head.

"One man tried, but Keith was always there to protect me."

Los walked over and continued to attempt to talk to Candace, and Amir used the opportunity to pull his sister into the living room to get details of what had occurred inside the house where she had been held captive. After she had told him everything, all the way up to when Keith set the house on fire, Amir stopped her.

"Where is Keith now? Why isn't he with you?"

Lo-Lo stared daggers at her older brother.

"Meer, you're not going to hurt him, are you? I'll never forgive you if you do, I swear!"

He smiled. "No, baby-girl, I'm not going to harm him, but I do need his help finding these fools, so this won't happen again. I need to find a place for both of you to stay while we end this beef. I'm going to have to call momma some help, though. She definitely can't be alone right now."

Lo-Lo nodded and tears began streaming down her face in torrents. So much had happened to her in so short a time, grief was the only way to deal with her mixed emotions.

"I don't know where Keith is; he won't tell me, but I know he's coming for me soon. He's not going to trust you to come around and I don't blame him. When he gets settled we're moving into an apartment together." Amir realized that this was coming.

Los came out of the room shaking his head sadly, and Amir gave Lo-Lo instructions to call around to find his mother some professional assistance. He placed ten thousand dollars on the table next to the telephone, knowing that the cash would eventually land in Keith's hand at some point. He would let the subject drop for the time being, but he felt that Keith was the key to finding Oscar and Paris.

He turned to Los. "I need you to have someone stay with them while we meet with Rag. He said that he knows where the Jamaicans spot is and how they're getting their drugs into the city. I know something else happened because he keeps telling me we need to talk about my cousin, Country; I know the fool must have done something stupid."

Los grinned. "Yeah, that crazy nigga probably did some Hannibal the Cannibal type shit! I don't know why you sent for him when you know he's fucked up in the damn head."

Amir nodded. "We need someone like him around; he doesn't hesitate to get down and dirty, and you know that he keeps his mouth shut. Reese should be coming through here also, so tell them to make sure he doesn't leave; He's wanted for killing that female police officer and that family in Missouri. I'm thinking about sending him to Wichita with Country or to my people's house in Bossier City, Louisiana, but that might be too tempting for him. Them niggas in Louisiana get down worse than us, and there's no telling what Country will be up to once they get to the Dub. Los, make that call to your family so that we can get back on track after we take care of these local jokers and the Jamaicans, do you feel me?"

Los frowned at Amir before responding.

"Sangr'e por Sangr'e" (Blood for Blood). You know how we live; we don't stop till our caskets drop, or we're as good as dead. After this bullshit is over, we're going on a vacation at my family's farm in Monterrey, Mexico, and that's where we're retiring." Los made the call and told Amir that he would have someone at the house soon. They both spent time there while making sure that Lo-Lo would be alright dealing with Candace's situation. Los looked at his cell-phone and turned to Amir.

"We can leave."

Amir nodded and they both walked out to the garage; he was headed to Lunatic's house in Kansas City, Missouri. Amir passed Ashely as he pulled away from his home, acknowledging her with a nod of his head, content that Los had indeed chosen the right individual to protect his family at all costs.

CHAPTER 51

Mecca sat in the waiting room at her doctor's office reading Sister Soulja's, *The Coldest Winter Ever,* massaging her swollen stomach. A large white man entered the room and seemed to study her face before taking a seat across from her, occasionally glancing in her direction. The nurse stepped inside the room and asked Mecca a few questions about her health. When the nurse left the room, the man walked over and took a seat right next to her.

He finally spoke. "Pregnant women are the most beautiful creatures in the world; do you know that? You carry your pregnancy like a goddess, and your weight is distributed throughout your body perfectly. Can I fuck you?"

The smile that Mecca had worn moments ago disappeared, and she now wore a shocked and angry expression. "Excuse me, what did you say?"

Dick snorted. "Bitch, you heard me! Amir and his gang of fools took something from my heart. I thought I may as well fuck the nice piece of ass he's been hiding. I will pay, though; will twenty dollars suffice?"

Mecca struggled to get out of her seat and the detective leaned forward and gripped her arm in a vice-like grip.

"Tell Amir that if he doesn't give up Reese, I'm fucking you in your pretty ass and carving that bastard out of your stomach! Do you understand me, you nigger bitch?"

Mecca nodded quickly, but when Dick released her, she screamed for help at the top of her lungs; she felt that the man would eventually harm her in the empty waiting room. Dick tossed a business card at her feet.

"Keep this to yourself because things can get much worse than this, trust me on that. Besides, you're the one that decided to sell yourself to a drug dealer."

Mecca looked up at the man and was surprised to see him holding a badge with a photo of him next to it. When the nurse returned to the room, Mecca pretended to be having complications with her pregnancy, and the detective played the role of a concerned citizen. Mecca was placed in a wheelchair, and as she was wheeled out of the room Dick picked up the card and placed it in her hand.

"Don't forget to give this to your fool, and you should tell him that I need to hear from his sorry ass immediately. Take care of yourself, Mecca." The nurse looked at him and walked away with a frown, wondering about his words and what he wanted with Mecca. She hoped it wasn't anything to do with the woman's boyfriend at a time like this, but she wouldn't doubt it. Amir's authority was evident, and he seemed to have plenty of money to spend for Mecca's physical health. The attractive nurse shook her head as she pondered finding a man like the confident Amir. She would welcome any number of complications for a dark, successful man like him. She looked closely at Mecca and could see real fear in her eyes. She hoped that the woman would be alright, but she would happily take her place. She set the room up for the next checkup while watching Mecca type furiously on her cellular phone, no doubt calling her man. The young nurse couldn't wait to see him again.

CHAPTER 52

Reese stood silently in the attic of Arthur's house, being driven crazy by the itching from the insulation. At one point the police were dangerously close to his hiding place during the execution of their search warrant. Reese had gripped his weapon, preparing himself to go out in a blaze of gunfire. He could hear Arthur's girlfriend, Shonda, arguing with the officers and ordering them out of her closets, knowing that there were stacks of currency hidden there.

Reese seethed when he thought about the search; an informant had notified the authorities about the safe house that had been under the radar for years.

Both Arthur and his woman, Shonda, had been working at Providence Medical Center for years, and they both made enough money to live beyond the modest way they chose to live.

Reese was convinced that there was a rat that needed to be dealt with. He had been simply stopping at the house to retrieve enough cash to last him for the time he would be in hiding, possibly somewhere in Mexico. He realized that he should have called first, but he was leery of using anyone's phone line. There was a manhunt underway, and his face had been displayed across the screen almost constantly. He had made a bad decision about visiting the home of someone who was a known Black Border Brother. He could hear the officers asking about the tattoos on Arthur's torso and arms, wanting to know what they meant. Reese assumed that the police had already been supplied with the information, but he also knew that Arthur would remain silent, regardless. He continued to hear things broken as both Arthur and Shonda complained. The house was eventually eerily silent, and he wondered if the officers had found some type of damning evidence. When he heard five short taps on the floor, he knew the police had left and the coast was clear, at least for the time being.

Reese climbed out of the small hole in the ceiling, itching from the insulation, but knowing that he had to get out of the house as soon as possible. Arthur walked out of the bedroom with a large shrink-wrapped bundle of cash under one armpit, and a suitcase in the opposite hand.

"They're still outside, so you might as well shower and get comfortable. My girl had one of her friends get you some clothes already, so you don't have to stress on that too much. I didn't know your exact size, but you won't be in skinny jeans or nothing like that." Reese laughed, still scratching the areas on his body that had been touched by the insulation.

"Yeah, I do appreciate that, my nig; I'll never get down with this new funny-ass shit. For real though, man, I need to get out of here as soon as possible; they ain't giving up about me smokin' that police bitch. Tell Amir I'll call him from time to time to make sure everything's straight with this drama. If shit get too thick, though, a nigga like me coming right back, you feel me?"

Shonda walked into the room carrying towels and other accessories for a shower.

"No, Reese, you're not coming back! These people are not trying to lock your dumb-ass up; they're talking about killing you! That detective from Missouri said that the woman that you killed was his partner. Don't you even wonder what he's doing over here in Kansas where he has no jurisdiction? You need to get away from here and stay away; do you hear me?" Reese simply smiled, and Shonda shook her head as she glared at Arthur as he shrugged.

"What can I do? You know this hard-headed nigga won't listen." Shonda tossed the items that she had been bringing for Reese onto the table and stormed out of the room while Reese laughed and shook his head.

"Man, she's still crazy as fuck, do you know that? I know she's just looking out for me, but why does she always think she can order people the fuck around? She was like that in school, on the block, and now up in yo' damn house. Be a man, nigga, and wear the pants up in here!"

Arthur smiled and attempted to take a playful swing at Reese, but he had already grabbed his things and headed to the guest bedroom to shower and prepare to leave. Reese wasn't sure if he would go far away at all; he realized that he would be hunted everywhere he went. He would get away from his friend's family, though; he didn't want to bring pain to them like the misery he was experiencing after the rapes and brutal deaths of his family members.

Reese also realized that Shonda was not from the inner-city, and he wouldn't bring the woman harm by bringing unfamiliar consequences her way. Los had family in the Argentine District that were Mexican Border Brothers, and that was a place where he could lay low for awhile. The police would not expect black people to be hiding in this area. Reese would have the Border Brothers send Amir a message; it would be impossible to attempt visiting his friend with all of the heat in the city.

Reese finished his shower, strapped on his bullet-proof vest, and he made sure that his spare magazines were full of 9mm rounds.

CHAPTER 53

"Amir's not here." Shonda stood in the doorway and Ashely studied her in exasperation before shoving past her and entering the house.

"Woman, you better stop acting like you're security or something; what is wrong with you?" Shonda was insecure about Ashely being in Arthur's vicinity, and she was intimidated by the rumors she had heard about Ashely's thirst for violence.

Shonda finally spoke. "I just figured that you wanted Amir. This is his home, you know."

Ashely frowned. "Just take me to Slim and don't hang around to try to eavesdrop. I don't know why Arthur puts up with your bossy ass!" Ashely then studied the young woman's figure with a leering expression before continuing. "I guess he has his reasons."

Shonda stared at her icily and led her to the bedroom where Slim was recuperating from his wounds. Shonda had heard that Ashely was bi-sexual, but this was the first time that she had given any indication that the stories were true. She knocked on the door and Slim yelled in response.

"Come on in, pretty girl!" Shonda opened the door and smiled when she saw Slim walking around the room without the aid of his crutches, and he even wore two ankle weights to further assist in gaining his strength. When Slim saw Ashely, he smiled and waved for her to enter. Shonda silently retreated from the room and closed the door.

Slim limped to the Jacuzzi inside the bedroom and dropped his robe to the floor; he then lowered his naked body into the steaming water.

"I see that you're still as nasty as ever, Slim; you could have warned me, though. I didn't realize that you were packing so much meat." She sat in a chair and crossed her long legs suggestively, allowing Slim a glimpse of her expertly trimmed crotch.

Slim looked at her and laughed.

"Woman, gone with that bull-shit! That dick teasin' don't work with a playa like me. I've been around you long enough to know that you aint givin' that pussy up to no man but Los around here, so miss me with the fake shit, okay?"

Ashely suddenly turned serious.

"Where in the world are Los and Meer? I've been trying to call them all day; I know them niggas are not ignoring my calls! A detective came by the courthouse today from Missouri talking about a drug conspiracy, and he even mentioned the Rico Act specifically."

Slim looked up at her knowingly.

"That's something we all should have been prepared for, baby-girl. I haven't heard from those two niggas since yesterday, though; what exactly was this pig saying?

Ashely was now all business. "They pulled out a picture of Reese at first, showing all of his tattoos. Next, they pulled out photos of Los and his Mexican cousins, and he even pulled out coroner photos of the bodies that were found at Swope Park. They showed pictures of the couple and the little girls that Reese killed, and pictures of that trick Marlon. They also had photos of one of Marlon's friends that the police found on the Kansas side last month. The last picture he showed was his female partner that Reese's crazy-ass killed the other night. They didn't have any pictures of Amir, but they kept referring to a handsome man that wore expensive suits that was orchestrating everything. You know that they were referring to Meer."

Slim stared hard at Ashely, and when he finally spoke, she knew that things had gone to another level.

"Give me one more week to lick my wounds; we're going out there to kill Paris and whoever else is connected to him. Get one of those white girls that be always sniffin' around for you and use them for more than just fucking lollipops! Don't think I'm fuckin' around, woman, by next week I'm puttin' Paris and the rest of those M.O.P. niggas' brains on the pavement, do you understand me?"

Ashely nodded respectfully. She often teased and joked around with Slim, but she knew better than to forget that he was a stone-cold killer. Amir and Los had gotten their aggressiveness from observing Slim, and although she could tell that he desired a normal life, she was convinced that he wanted revenge for what the M.O.P. had done.

Ashely pulled a bottle of Moet from an ice bucket next to the Jacuzzi and poured them both a glass. She walked over and handed him his drink.

"I have the perfect woman to put on the detective. She hasn't done anything serious for me yet, but I know how to put her in a position where she has no choice."

Ashely suddenly sat down on the floor and propped one of her legs up onto the side of the Jacuzzi, telling Slim her plan while he pretended not to notice her exposed vagina and her beautiful legs in the tight skirt she wore. Slim leaned forward and splashed her with water and was amused by her frantic rush to get away.

"I already told you, woman, that shit don't work on a nigga like me, but that was a nice try. I'll tell my nephews to give you a call as soon as I talk to them; get ready to help us turn these streets red."

He pulled himself from the water and ignored Ashely as she gazed at his nakedness, seeing his penis hanging freely.

"Woman, I know you aint scared of no dick! That might be what you need to help you loosen up from that tight-ass attitude, though." They both looked over as Shonda entered the room, staring in shock at the scene before her. Ashely grinned. "Slim, get dressed before this girl cream down her panties; she's already trying to pretend that she didn't check everything out." They both laughed when Shonda hurried out of the room, and Ashely blew Slim a kiss with the promise in her eyes that they would take the situation to the next level.

She walked out of the bedroom door knowing that Slim's eyes were locked onto her swinging hips. He couldn't fool her: he was still a man.

CHAPTER 54

Amir sat in his vehicle outside of Lunatic's house, and he stared in anger at the text message from Mecca. Los had seen the look on his friend's face when he attempted to joke with him, so he stayed silent in order to allow him to finish his conversation as he stepped out and walked up to the house. Amir could see Country, Rag, Pete, and Looney talking to Los on the porch, but he was too busy responding to his woman's message to acknowledge their stares in his direction.

When Amir finally climbed out of his vehicle, he headed toward his friends and family to find out what had happened with their home invasion and to give further instructions. Los turned without a word and entered the house. Lunatic shook Amir's hand.

"I know where those bitch-ass Jamaicans are, home-boy, but I don't know if I wanna use the same people on this one; shit gotta be more organized if we want to live to talk about it later. Your relative Country is on that sick-ass Brotha Lynch shit, and we don't have time for a nigga to lose his head. We can't be watching him while we're tryin' to handle business."

Amir looked over at Country and knew that he had done something bad from his non-reaction. He continued to stare him down, waiting for some type of excuse. Country became animated as he yelled.

"Fuck these niggas, relative! They just mad cause I fucked one of those fine-ass bitches and killed those niggas for disrepectin' me! It seems like these faggot-ass niggas was worried more about me fuckin' than finding out where those niggas was at! I found out what we needed to know just by fuckin'; believe that shit!"

Amir knew right then that Country was even worse than he had been years before when he had brought him into Kansas City, Kansas. He also realized that he had to obtain some level of control over his cousin before it was too late. Amir spoke in a calm, measured tone.

"Country, you're my cousin and I love you to death, but we don't have time for your personal bull-shit. My money is at stake, and I wouldn't allow my *momma* to get in the way of my damn money. I love you as my family, but you will not be the reason for my downfall. If you can't keep your black-ass dick in your pants or keep your attitude in check, let me know; if there's a next time with this bull-shit I won't waste my time, breath, or energy talking; do you understand me, *relative?*"

Country glared at Amir, but he nodded respectfully; he knew that Amir meant every word, and he did not allow his cousin's calm demeanor to fool him into challenging him.

Looney approached his friend.

"I want to put this next hit down, Amir. We should've been in and out of that last house a lot quicker; the whole thing was fuckin' sloppy." Lunatic began to protest, but Amir silenced him with a wave of his hand.

"Looney, I'm going to back you up on this, but I have to tell you and Rag something, and I'm not fucking around. Don't tell your Blood home-boys anything about our business, not even my cousin Mate. We live by a code, and if anyone violates it, they're as good as dead. I know you feel that your Bloods are loyal and I'm sure Lunatic feels the same way about his Crip partners, but if the Black Border Brothers catch heat because of loose lips, from anyone, we're going to war with every one of you gang-banging mothafuckas. Trust me, if that happens you won't win." He paused. "You're definitely going to need more people this time because the Jamaicans have numbers, so I'm sending Arthur and Pete with you. Whoever you feel like you need is fine with me, trust me, we can handle whatever those Jamaicans have on deck."

Pete stood off to the side, listening intently to his friend telling them what needed to be done, wishing that he could have been left out of the hit. He felt genuine love for Amir, but he felt obligated to cooperate with the authorities because he didn't want to spend his life inside of a Federal Correctional Institution. He also didn't want to get caught up in these murders; Pete didn't feel that he possessed enough information to be exonerated of the crimes that Amir was planning.

Lunatic occasionally glanced over at Pete with suspicion, and Amir noticed, turning his way. He addressed his longtime friend.

"Pete, what's up, playa? Don't you want to be a part of this shit? We need to get this out of the way and get back to business; we have to meet with the Italians soon and they're already asking a lot of questions."

Everyone turned to see Los walking out of the house with a scowl on his face and blood all over his hands.

"Cuz, what the fuck happened to you, Los?" Lunatic rushed toward him, but he stopped in his tracks when Los pulled his 9mm Ruger from his waistband and leveled it at his head.

Los turned to Amir while still holding his weapon on Lunatic, who looked angry and stunned.

"Meer, I caught one of Lunatic's homeboys watching and listening to everything y'all was talking about out here. He had a monitor on, and a little recorder was running next to the speakers. When he saw me, he tried to rush me; I bashed that little nigga's noodles in with my pistol." They all looked at the pistol in his hand, appearing to be smeared with hair and blood. Los continued while eyeing Lunatic.

"The nigga had a gallon of your wet in one of the cabinets too. We need to run a check on every nigga in this house. That's why I don't like fuckin' with this wet shit! I'll handle the coke and the K-town weed from now on, my nig."

Lunatic suddenly rushed into the house and Amir followed, after instructing Pete to take Los to get himself cleaned up. When they made it to one of the bedrooms, they saw blood splattered everywhere, and they could tell by the condition of the body that Los had shown no mercy. The man's head looked like a smashed cantaloupe; hair and bone fragments also littered the floor. They scrutinized the monitor that was still trained on the location where they had been conversing outside.

Lunatic had already begun stretching plastic across the floor for the removal of the corpse. Calling an ambulance about the situation was not an option, even if the man were still alive. Amir gathered everyone into a room and shut down operations until they found out exactly what was going on inside the house. All of Lunatic's people were forced out of their clothes and checked for recording devices, and everyone closely connected to the dead youngster was questioned. Before the body was removed, Amir sent everyone from the house except for County, Los, Lunatic and Looney.

Amir turned to stare at Lunatic. "We're burning this house to the ground and opening up somewhere else. Only Black Border Brothers will be allowed to work for us. None of your gang-banger homeboys, and not

181

any of your funky hoes either. I don't know who that little nigga was that was watching and listening to us, or who the fuck he was working for, but I'm glad my brother caught him and beat his fucking head in! You all know what needs to be done with the Jamaicans; I'll get with Arthur and tell him to give you a call tonight. If you niggas can't handle it, give me a call. Me and Los are not above being there to handle this business with you, but we have other things to take care of that will benefit us all."

Country walked over to Amir.

"Relative, I don't give a fuck about what these niggas do, I'm killing those hoe-ass Jamaicans and takin' they dope, money, and I know they got some bad ass bitches." He stopped and grinned before continuing. "I'm going back to Wichita with my pockets swollen, regardless. We know where these niggas are, so let's stop this beatin' around the bush shit!"

Amir nodded at his crazy cousin.

"I agree, cuz, but we're not going in there blind either. They're just like the Latinos and Africans; they have lookouts where you'll never see them, so don't take anything for granted-you'll just get yourself killed."

Los suddenly appeared inside the room.

"Meeting's over, my nigs. I gotta take a bath and get this snitch-ass nigga's stink off me. Lunatic, no more of your Crip homeboys are welcome around anywhere we do business. Nobody but Black Border Brothers work for us, so if you want another of your niggas to die, try me."

Because of Amir's strong leadership abilities, people often forgot that Los was his equal partner, maybe even the senior partner because of his family connections to the Mexican Border Brothers. At times like this people were reminded of his presence, and there was no doubt that he was in control of the situation alongside Amir.

Lunatic and Looney were already huddled in a corner planning how the "hit" would be enacted against the Jamaicans that were supplying their enemies with resources. Amir eventually headed to his vehicle, calling Arthur on his way to meet Mecca at her home in the suburbs of Johnson County. He was still fuming from what his fiance had told him about the Missouri detective's visit to her doctor's office.

CHAPTER 55

Rico stood over Paris's bed and strained to hear what he had to say; he hated to see his friend in this condition, and he couldn't wait to see him back on his feet. He shook his head before speaking.

"I know you care about your family, Paris, but your little cousin killed my brother and I can't let niggas get away with that shit, man! Fuck that other stupid mothafucka that got burned up in that house, but my little brother is going to get his payback!"

Since his brother, Red, had been found inside of the house where Lo-Lo had been held, Rico had been out asking questions about Keith, trying to find out where he was hiding so he could murder him.

Paris whispered painfully. "We don't know what happened in that house, homie, and you know Keith aint that type of nigga. Do you think he could kill and handle clean-up business like that?" Rico shook his head and sat down in the chair next to the bed, staring Paris directly in his eyes.

"Paris, I know we gotta get on this money like you said, but those fools are not gonna stop comin' at us, so we need to get at em' first! That little nigga Keith is just part of the deal. Those Black Border Brother niggas gonna die, you feel me?"

The door opened and Rico watched Oscar limp into the room with a cane in his right hand and murder in his eyes.

He stared at them. "Rico, we goin' over that little bitch house tonight, so get ready, but let me talk to my son for a minute." Rico smiled and exited the room, knowing that there wasn't much time left before they were going to head out, and it was a relief knowing that Oscar felt the same way that he did.

After Rico closed the door, Oscar turned to Paris.

"I'm gonna handle that little bitch and make her tell me where that little faggot ass nigga is at; do you understand me?"

Paris nodded and whispered to his father.

"I know that you're gonna go no matter what I say, pops, but I just wish I could be there to make sure you don't hurt my little cousin. I'm finished with surgery now, so I'll be back around in a couple weeks; just save some for me, cool?"

Oscar nodded. "I got you. After this we going right at Amir and that pretty-boy fool that's helpin' bitch-ass Slim. That nigga shoulda knew better than to fuck with my family. That little bitch aint the bait no more, she dinner."

Paris laughed this time before wincing and clutching his side in pain.

Oscar said, "Take it easy and get yourself together, son; them niggas is gonna pay for layin' you up like this, and that's a promise."

He hugged Paris, being careful not to rub against the stitches and staples that were temporarily mending his wounds. Oscar realized that he had started the entire situation with his vendetta against Slim, and he was determined to end it, no matter the cost.

CHAPTER 56

Arthur ended his call with Amir and headed to pick Shonda up to take her home. He realized that things would get worse once the Jamaicans were involved, and he didn't want her inside Amir's home if the location was found out by the opposition. He had been contemplating the last conversation he and Pete had, and he wondered what was going on with the man he had been practically raised with. Pete was sounding nervous, and fear was evident in his voice when they began discussing the possible consequences of their actions. Arthur felt that this was something that all men in the "game" should expect, if not embrace. Pete had started stuttering and seemed nervous when Arthur brought up the raid on Pete's house a week ago. He denied that drugs had been found, but Arthur knew that the authorities had found drugs and much more. When Arthur mentioned the murders that Reese had committed on the Missouri side, it seemed that Pete was willing to send their friend to the wolves. Arthur had never suspected that Pete was weak, but he began to moan about his family and cry about not wanting to be away from his woman. These things made Arthur wonder about his friend and hope that he was simply imagining things. Regardless, he would watch Pete as if he were his worst enemy; there was no telling what some men would do to save themselves from personal responsibility.

He pulled up to Amir's house and casually glanced around at the surrounding area. Ashely pulled out of the driveway with her pressed hair hanging freely, looking like the model, Ester Baxter, with her beautiful caramel skin-tone and slanted eyes. She smiled, winked, and blasted

Messy Marv as she accelerated her new Cadillac DTS into the distance. Arthur smiled when he saw Shonda step out of the house and admired her slim curves. He was amazed at how he could see details of Shonda's figure even when she was wearing loose-fitting hospital scrubs. When he parked and stepped out of his vehicle, Shonda ran up and flung herself into his arms.

"Baby, you have to get me away from these crazy people, I've had enough! Ashely is a psychopathic homosexual and Slim is nothing but an old-ass pervert. They need to find another nurse to deal with this mess; I can't handle it anymore. Where have you been, baby? Did you miss me?"

Arthur laughed. "Slow down, baby, damn! Don't worry, I'm taking you home to rub your feet and pamper you as much as you can stand, momma. I just have to talk to Slim for a second, okay?"

Shonda nodded and immediately followed her man into the house-heading to the kitchen while Arthur handled his business. She was relaxed now that she was near her best friend; she was confident that her man would do what was right for them.

Arthur walked into the bedroom and watched Slim slowly running on Amir's treadmill with headphones covering his ears and sweat glistening on his muscled frame. It always amazed Arthur how Slim seemed to have the physique of a boxer-in-training at his seasoned age, especially considering the lifestyle that the man lived.

Arthur walked up behind the man and placed his index finger on the back of his head as if it was a gun; he noticed that Slim didn't even flinch or break stride in the pace he had set.

He walked around and noticed Slim's dilated eyes; they looked like shiny black marbles. He turned his head and glanced at Arthur while still running.

"Boy, that shit don't work with me. If it's gonna happen, so be it. Being scared won't change a damn thing, and it may even get you killed sooner. What the fuck do you want, homeboy?"

Arthur strolled over to the window and stared out at Amir's swimming pool in the backyard. "We're supposed to hit the Jamaicans soon, but I wanted you to help me find the niggas that killed Tracy. I know it was a contract and the niggas don't have nothin' to do with our beef with M.O.P., but I aint for letting them niggas just walk away after killing my man. I know where that dyke Arelia live that used to kick it with Donna, and I heard she be fuckin' one of those M.O.P. niggas on the low. She had to be the one that hooked the shit up; Tracy kept a short leash on that trick bitch Donna, and Arelia was always with one of our girls. We would've found out if Donna was directly doing some bull-shit."

Slim turned the treadmill off and removed his headphones, listening silently to what Arthur had to say. Tracy had been like a younger version of Amir to Slim, and he had taken his death personally. He walked over and picked up a small bottle of liquid off the table. Arthur now realized why the man's eyes looked so strange.

Slim noticed Arthur studying him.

"Don't tell Meer; you know he hate for me to get watered out. Anyway, I was just talking to Ashely about those dyke bitches she be suckin' and fake fuckin'. She said that she was ready to put them to work; this might be the perfect test. Just go home and chill with your lady for now, and don't get at the Rastas till you hear from me. This might be the perfect time for those niggas to find out that they fucked up when they didn't kill me! I want to be right there to show you niggas who *really* started this shit!"

Arthur strolled toward Slim with a smile on his face.

"That's what's up, dawg! I knew you'd be back in the mix, just give me a holla. Make sure I have some quality time with my woman, though; daddy's been away for awhile. I can't forget about home; do you feel me?"

Slim nodded, secretly envying Arthur for having the life he desired. He was happy for Arthur, but he wished that he could have met a woman as good as Shonda, or half as beautiful. Slim walked them to the door and watched the two drive away while puffing on his "wet" and contemplating on what his next move would be. He took a little trip into what he called the "Matrix". He was the king and ruler of this land, and he didn't have anything to worry about while he was indulging in the hallucinogenic drug.

CHAPTER 57

Keith stood inside an apartment complex in Leavenworth, Kansas, observing drugs being sold at the housing projects that were called "The Ghetto". The apartments had central air-conditioning, manicured lawns, and were coated with fresh paint; they looked like luxury apartments out of a magazine, and Keith wondered how they came to be labeled with such a title. When he thought about the different "hoods" in Kansas City, all he could do was smile and be grateful for the opportunity to pursue drug-dealing that seemed reserved for people that were not hardened by inner-city life.

He stared at a group that seemed to be in control of a section of the complex, noticing how young and inexperienced they seemed to be. The young men did not have anyone looking out for the police, and they appeared to "serve" anyone who pulled into their section of the complex; they didn't even attempt to conceal what they were doing. Keith planned to use a portion of the money that Lo-Lo had given him to get with his friend, Steven, who claimed to be able to garner a promising drug deal. Keith had informed Lo-Lo that she needed to leave her home also, but she refused to leave until her mother was taken to the hospital.

Keith had enrolled in a technical school in Lawrence, Kansas, and he also found a part-time job near the University of Kansas campus; he wanted to have balance in his life, and he refused to be devoured by the "game". He was confident that he could be a successful drug dealer in the small town. He assumed that he could take care of himself and Lo-

Lo without too many problems. Keith hated the precarious position he was in, but he refused to cower without a fight.

He climbed back into his mother's vehicle just as he noticed a squad car moving very slowly between two apartments in the direction of the young dealers he had been watching; he was headed to meet with Lo-Lo in Wyandotte County (Kansas, City, Kansas). He had instructed her to sneak away from her house to meet with him on Parallel Parkway with the cash Amir had given her, and he promised her that he would come for her as soon as they were both ready.

He pulled away from the "Ghetto", watching the dealers running in different directions, laughing at the policeman's clumsy attempt at catching any of the young African-Americans in a foot chase.

Leavenworth was not very advanced, but for what Keith planned on doing he realized he still must be extremely careful. He was not inclined to be some flunky or a low-level drug dealer for life; he planned on using the drugs to deposit funds into his bank account, which would eventually garner him the capital it would take in order to take over a small apartment building in the city.

Oscar had been calling relentlessly, and the man had been leaving threatening messages on his answering service when Keith ignored the calls. This had been going on since he left Kansas City, so he realized that he had to be prepared to deal with the drama that would be constantly at his heels.

Keith felt his cell-phone vibrate in his pocket, knowing that it was Lo-Lo rushing him to the city. He answered with a sigh.

"What do you want now, princess?"

There was a pause, but his blood boiled when she spoke.

"Keith, Ashely's over here, and I don't think I can sneak away while she's here. She's crazy!" Keith cursed inwardly but made sure to remain calm and neutral.

"Baby, don't worry about it right now. When I give you a call, you'll know that I'm right around the corner. Let's worry about this when the time comes; are you still ready to run far away with me, baby? There's no going back when you're finally with me; when we live together there's no more holding back my love. You remember your promise, right?"

She giggled. "Boy, you're nasty. Is this pretty little thing between my legs all you can think about after all we've been through? I have your back, though, and you don't have to worry about anything where I'm concerned, but just keep in mind that I'm a virgin and we must use protection, okay?"

Keith nodded silently before responding.

"Okay, Lo-Lo. Just be cool until I get there. Maybe it's good that Ashely's there with you. I've heard that she really knows how to handle herself. I'll be there pretty soon, so don't do anything to make her suspicious, and make sure she doesn't leave you alone until I get there." He ended the call and loaded one of his favorite rappers into the You-tube app on his cell-phone. He listened to The Jacka's smooth Islamic rhymes and imagined a modest street prophet as he listened to the passionate words, hoping that he could get his life back on track. He hated that the man had been murdered.

Keith looked around at the small town he was driving through, knowing that plenty of funds were available on the streets, and feeling like it was his time to shine.

CHAPTER 58

Amir pulled up in front of his home in Olathe, Kansas, knowing that he would be having a major discussion with his woman. He felt bad about how she was feeling, but he needed to find out how the racist detective had discovered her existence.

When Amir pulled onto the street where he and Mecca lived, he noticed a vehicle parked in front of the privacy fence of their home. Amir approached the vehicle with his weapon brandished. As he reached the driver's side window, it slowly lowered, and he stared into the face of a chubby-cheeked white man.

"How are you doing, Mr. Wilson? You have a great woman in there, but you must have told her not to talk to strangers. You need to be a smart boy, though, and instruct her that the rule doesn't apply to law enforcement officers."

Amir leveled his pistol at the man's left eye.

"Is that what you are? Maybe you should follow procedure and get a warrant before bothering and harassing an innocent pregnant woman at her home. Speak with me directly the next time you want to talk, or you will get dealt with like anyone else who acts without considering the consequences."

When Detective Galubski stepped out of his vehicle, Amir recognized him immediately; the man removed his sunglasses and his fat belly hung over his belt. The detective looked down at the .45 caliber Glock in Amir's hand and smiled.

"Do you have a license to carry that weapon, Meer? That filthy money that you make does not transcend you above the law."

Amir cringed at the casual use of his nickname, but he placed his weapon into his shoulder harness inside his suit jacket.

"I actually can carry concealed or any other way I choose. What do you want, detective; don't you know better than to harass someone's woman? Surely you pay those project-living hoes enough; they will do anything for a few bucks, right? I won't warn you or that other cracker that disrespected my woman a second time; do not approach Mecca again, in any way. As a matter of fact, I don't want to see either one of you swine mothafuckas within a hundred feet of her. Consider this as a restraining order that I will enforce personally." Amir smiled when Galubski displayed his first signs of anger, screwing his beet-red face up in anger and blinking rapidly. He regained his composure in record time, though, before he spoke.

"I don't give a fuck about any restraining order from you or the courts, *boy*. If you want your people to be left alone, get your soft-ass out of my city. You and your Black Border *sisters* are on our shit list now, and you will fall hard once we get to you. How you handle these niggers out in the streets doesn't concern me, but when you kill a white female police officer, you should know that it's over for you. All I like about you black mothafuckas is those big booty bitches that you breed, and I'm getting tired of them because they're lazy just like you fools. I can't stand a lazy ass bitch!"

Amir didn't show any concern for the man's disrespectful utterances; he simply stood there and listened to Galubski's hateful words, not giving him the satisfaction of displaying his displeasure.

Without warning, Amir walked up and put his face within inches of the detective's forehead.

"Let's stop fucking around, man; I have more important things to do. Do you think I don't know anything important about you, Mr. Galubski? I've seen you with that funky black bitch and that Mulatto mutt you call a daughter. What is she, twenty years old now? Yeah, she does have a fat ass, just like you said. How about I send a couple of my, what did you call them, border girlies? How about I have a few of them drag her into a dark room and show the little bitch just how feminine they are? Is that what you want? Well, that's what you'll get if you fuck with my lady or harass any of my people. I don't know who that other pig was that left his card with my woman, but I'm leaving you and your little girl responsible for his actions until I find out more about him. Do you have anything else to say, cracker?"

Just as Galubski raised his arm to take a swing, they both watched an Olathe, Kansas, squad car approach with the dome lights flashing.

A young black officer stepped from the vehicle and turned his attention toward Detective Galubski.

"Is there a problem here, sir? We received a call that there was a weapon drawn on this street." He turned toward Amir. "Is there a problem here, Mr. Wilson? Do you have business with this man?"

Amir smiled, knowing that Detective Galubski was fuming, being ignored by the officer that was well below his rank. The man being young and African-American seemed to redden Galubski's cheeks even more.

Amir responded with a smile. "Thank you, officer, but there is no problem. This man is my insurance agent; he was just explaining to me how beneficial his life insurance premiums are." The officer gazed suspiciously at Detective Galubski, but he eventually climbed into his vehicle and pulled away to leave the two men to stare into each other's eyes. The detective broke the silence.

"I'm going to try to forget that you trained your weapon on me and insulted my daughter; just know that there are no second chances. I don't know who you think you are, but you're still the same wanna-be gangster that you've been your whole life. Turn Reese in and maybe we can speak numbers for us taking a step back. Until then you're in our sights, nigger!"

With his last words he climbed into the Crown Victoria he was driving and burned rubber up the street, burning marks on the smooth pavement, and leaving Amir coughing from the black smoke.

CHAPTER 59

The fence slowly opened, and Amir pulled into the garage to see Mecca standing next to her vehicle with one hand cradling her stomach and the other on her hip. The beautiful woman spoke through tight lips.

"This is the situation I've been told to avoid for a lifetime, Amir. That detective scared me the other day, and I know if I would have been in a secluded place, he would have hurt me. I met you out here because if you don't tell me the right things, I'm getting in my car and leaving, and you can believe that I won't come back just because you don't like it. You promised that you would leave this game that you're playing; baby, this game will never end. I should have given you time to do what needed to be done before I started seeing you because the fast money can't be easy to leave behind. Things are different between us now, Amir, and it happened when your life in the streets interfered with mine. Now, what are we going to do? Do not forget the other person that will be affected by your answer." She pointed at her swollen abdomen and Amir's love instantly grew for her, and his hate also blossomed for the man that had had the nerve to approach her. He walked up and wrapped his arms around his lady, noticing her hesitation.

"Mecca, you're absolutely right about the fact that I can't just suddenly leave the game as if I'm skipping school; I have too many loose ends to tie up for that. You and my beautiful child mean more to me than any of that, so I'm going to make a drastic decision right now. Get enough clothes to last you for a couple of weeks; I'm getting you and the baby a place where you can kick your feet up until I can get us a new house. I'm putting this house on the market as soon as possible. This will be my first step in protecting my family. Trust me for now, but if anything at all happens like this again, leave me and don't look back. I will handle my business as a man and earn the right to have a beautiful family by my side. I would rather cut off my own head than to lose my family, so you can believe that I'll be extra careful about what I do from this moment to the time I leave these funky-ass streets behind. Is it a deal, or what, baby?"

Mecca stepped out of his arms and eyed him closely.

"You are my best friend as well as my man, but if anything happens like this again, I promise you will never find me."

After Mecca finished her sentence, she turned and walked into the house without looking back. Amir smiled to himself, noticing that Mecca didn't question him about what was going on, or attempt to question him about his business. She was the type of woman he had been hoping to find for years. She was secure and didn't haul around insecurities as a handicap.

He walked into his home and began removing his clothing and discarding them haphazardly all the way to the bedroom he and Mecca shared. This was the part of the arguments that, in his opinion, made relationships sweet. Make-up sex from a fine, independent woman with a steamy pregnant vagina was all he envisioned as he stepped into the shower.

Chapter 60

Los sat back with his eyes closed, listening to Rag rap along with an old song he had recorded with Lil Flip from Houston, Texas, and Rag's cousin, B-Rich. He was allowing the marijuana to soothe him while he was pleased by what he heard; Los didn't realize at first that Rag was a rapper, and he was very good at it. One side of the double disk had features from Tech N9ine, Boy Big, and other local rappers and singers, as well as artists from different areas around the states. The other disk seemed to be aimed at individuals who Rag had been at odds with in the inner city. Los pondered the fact that Rag had sat through two trials for murder already.

Los nodded his head to the explicit lyrics. "This shit is tight as a mothafucka, my nig, but don't you think that this type of shit can make it worse for you if one of these weak-ass niggas try to bring another case against you?"

Rag smiled. "The bitch niggas tried to snitch on me when I was givin' them what they asked for. I'm just exposing those snitches to the niggas and bitches that think they're on some gangster shit."

Lunatic laughed as he entered the room.

"Nigga, you aint foolin' no damn body! You just like talkin' shit on them bitch-ass niggas."

Rag nodded and went back to concentrating on his verses while they prepared to hit the Jamaicans. Looney and Arthur were busy in the next room loading magazines into the various weapons they would use. Country and two other Black Border Brothers, K.B. and Lil G, was making sure that they all had enough masks, bandannas, and gloves to assist in concealing their identities. In the basement, Malik and K-Mack were maintaining contact with the people that were watching the Jamaicans' movements. They were also being informed as to how many people came and went from the apartment that they were in. Amir would not be present during this excursion, but Los insisted on being a part of the hit. Rag had mentioned that there would be a surprise addition to the team, and most of them figured it would be Ashely because she hadn't been seen in awhile. When the doorbell rang, though, and they saw who came through the door, everyone knew that things would be interesting.

"What's wrong with you niggas?" Slim had a cane in one hand and a large automatic handgun in the other. He was dressed in one of his signature expensive suits and a pair of alligator-skin shoes that matched the color of his shirt. He pointed his cane at Country who had entered the room carrying some hockey masks.

"Boy, you're my brother's son, but if you start that crazy shit, you don't have to worry about the dreads, I'm gonna bust yo' ass my damn self! I don't give a fuck what you do to niggas after you handle our business, but don't fuck up what we got going on; do you understand me, little big nigga?"

Country nodded respectfully, knowing that Slim was serious, and he knew that it was not an idle threat. After Country finished nodding, though, his gold teeth gleamed as he smiled. He rushed over and embraced his favorite uncle, and everyone else followed suit. They had all been together for years and they still looked up to Slim the same as they did when they were teenagers.

Slim smiled as he received the love.

"Alright, niggas, but don't be lookin' at me like you done seen a ghost. You all know I'm hard to kill in these streets. Anyway, how are we going to handle this?" Looney and Rag walked over, and Looney spoke.

"Me and one of my people got niggas watching the apartment right now, Slim. I know just how to hit those nappy-headed Jamaicans before they know what's happening. I know you aint new to this shit, but Amir left me in charge of this one. Trust me, I aint new to this shit either, gangster. Lloyd!"

A youngster walked into the room with dreadlocks hanging down his back. When he started talking in his Jamaican dialect, Slim smiled. Looney nodded toward the newcomer.

"Lloyd's been living in Kansas for about fifteen years, but he was born in Jamaica. He's gonna be our ticket inside the house so we can *really* touch those fools. He already been buying work from that Jamaican nigga, Peter, but there's always two carloads full of his homeboys around when they handle business. They want him to go with them to some Jamaican bar on the Missouri side to drink and shoot pool; we'll hit these niggas as soon as they get comfortable at the spot and start rollin' they damn blunts." Slim nodded his assent, enjoying the plan that Looney had devised, using all available resources. He asked Looney a serious question.

"What do you think about sending Ashely over there with him? Do you think she'll be good enough to distract those fools? She'll be callin' me later, so you can talk to her about it when we hook up." Looney smiled.

"Yeah, that'll be real cool, playa. I still love the shit outta that woman; tell her fine-ass to hurry the fuck up!"

Los pretended to stare him down in anger and they all started laughing, knowing that all of them used to take turns trying to pull Ashely into their web at one time or another since they were pre-teens. Los headed to the side door where the garage was located.

"I'll be back in a couple of hours; I gotta go meet Meer and handle some business. Tell Ashely to call me after y'all finish telling her what's up, and make sure no business is handled at this house until this shit is over. Lunatic, make sure your people get the tilts for us to roll out in; all they need to know is that you need them, and nothing else."

Lunatic nodded and walked to the other side of the room to make calls while everyone else got back to business. Slim followed Los through the door to the garage. When they were outside, Los turned to Slim.

"Unk, are you sure that you're ready to be out here like this? It aint like we can't handle this shit ourselves. You know me and Meer have plenty of people to roll on those dread niggas."

Slim pulled a red pack of cigarettes from his pocket along with a small glass vial with yellowish fluid inside.

"Little nigga, I'm ready for whatever. I can't sit back no longer and watch people going out to handle our damn business. I'm gonna sit out here and get high and mind my business; just get back over here so we can slump these fools to the pavement. And don't go runnin' your mouth to Ashely and Meer about my drug of choice-just know that my mind will already be concentrating on death."

Los laughed. "I know it will, playa, just don't do too much of that shit and get stuck; I'll see you in a few."

Los strolled into the garage and climbed into his vehicle, pulling off as Slim began dipping his first cigarette into the chemical fluid that Los knew was P.C.P. The killer blew smoke into the air while he watched Los leave and waited on his opportunity to meet death once again.

CHAPTER 61

Reese stared out of Chino's guest bedroom window, looking at little kids playing and scrutinizing one of the children. Another little boy approached the child and began bragging about the boy's father and Reese already knew who he was. Miguel was Los's son, and he looked like a miniature version of his father; he also possessed Los's dark sense of humor. Miguel had sabotaged the other children's water guns and poured vinegar into the water balloons they were using. He had giggled when the house eventually stank of the putrid liquid. The boy's mother was a very beautiful Brazilian woman who obviously had a problem with street drugs and alcoholic beverages. She had propositioned Reese multiple times before he eventually explained to her that he would not even *consider* sleeping with any of his friends' conquests, former or present. When he had watched her casually approach the next man, he realized that he had other reasons for hesitating. The woman was out there too frequently running the streets for sex with her to be safe.

Little Miguel ran up to the open window and made a funny face at Reese, and he smiled in return, planning on giving the boy's grandparents money for Miguel, if they needed it or not. Reese already knew not to hand the boy's mother any cash although it seemed that the woman dressed her son well and kept him clean. Miguel seemed to be taken care of amiably from what Reese had observed.

After the children were put to bed, the kegs of Corona were going to be brought out, and the adults were planning to host a block party. Some of the Mexican Border Brothers were in Kansas for a family reunion, and Reese saw it as an opportunity to leave for a larger city. California was huge, and it would be easier hiding there than where people were in much closer proximity to one another. He also felt that he could talk to Carlos Sr. about cutting the Italians out of their business; he felt that he had a better way to get the drugs into the twin Kansas Cities. He had already met some of the younger men in the Border Brothers organization, but he wanted to meet the ones who were retired from the streets.

"Ah! Stop it, Miguel! I'm going to whip your butt!" Reese smiled. Los's son had not fallen far from the tree. He had run up behind his mother and drenched her from head to toe with a bucket of water, and he was giggling gleefully as she chased him around the yard. Reese suddenly thought about his little sister that had been raped and murdered and he felt a familiar pang of anger. He knew that the longer he stayed in Kansas City the greater the chance that he would make more hits on the M.O.P., and Reese realized that he would eventually die or go to prison for life.

He entered the restroom and cleaned himself up to await the arrival of the fine Latina women that were sure to arrive. When he eventually walked outside, he could see that the street was already being cordoned off for the block party, and the kegs of Corona were being placed strategically along the sidewalks. He watched as the women began exiting vehicles, but what caught his attention was the stretch Ford Excursion limousine that pulled directly in front of the house. He was not surprised to see Carlos Sr. emerge from the vehicle followed by his brother, Jorge. These were the two men who controlled the drugs that fed their families and that made it possible for them to live in relative luxury.

Reese straightened his Kansas City Chiefs jersey and strolled onto the front lawn, knowing that all eyes were on him. It was not only because he was the only black face, he was also the only one with diamonds glistening from his wrist, neck, mouth, as well as both earlobes. His hair was also pressed straight and pulled into a ponytail that hung to the middle of his back, causing curious stares to be directed at him, especially from the women.

Some of the younger men screwed their faces up after seeing him, but when Chino pulled them to the side and spoke with them quietly, recognition and respect was etched on their faces. Everyone had heard about "Killer Reese", and they knew better than to take his pretty-boy looks as any form of weakness. Carlos Sr. stared at Reese with a mixture of anger and concern. He said something to Jorge before walking over to Reese.

"I need to speak with you. Come inside as soon as you're done talking to Jorge; he's waiting for you." Reese nodded and noticed that Carlos Sr. was all business; there would be no more joking around. When Reese walked over to Jorge, the man simply motioned toward the limousine and waited for Reese to walk around before entering the vehicle. As soon as he was seated, Jorge began instructing him after being sure that the driver had exited the vehicle.

"You are to stay at this house for one week, and after that you will travel with two of my nieces to Los Angeles. You have brought unnecessary heat to our organization as well as your own. I don't know why you have committed the crimes you are accused of, and I do not care. Eventually we're going to get you into Mexico where you can become invisible. Do you understand and agree?"

Reese leaned forward and grabbed a bottle of Remy Martin XO from the bar and poured two stiff drinks. He handed Jorge one of the glasses and sat back and stared through the sunroof while he sipped his cognac. When he sat his drink down, Reese stared intently at the older man.

"Jorge, I appreciate everything you and your people are doing for me, but nobody orders me to do anything. I think what you're sayin' makes sense, but I don't know about going to no damn Mexico; what's the reason for that?"

Jorge smiled. "What we need to do there is to make sure our drugs move across the border. The D.E.A., border patrol, renegade cartels, all have been a problem for our organization, as well as for yours. We need someone who will enforce order when necessary; we need these people put down if they get in the way of our money. We will not accept anything else. This is not an order that I'm giving you, but it is a request that I take very seriously. If you do not accept this arrangement, you can take your chances on your own. I'll give you one month before you're dead or doing life inside one of the many prisons in this country. Would you choose Lansing, or would you rather go to Hutchinson, Kansas? What is it called, Gladiator School?" Reese grinned before leaning forward and shaking the man's outstretched hand.

"I agree, as long as you listen to my ideas and stop going through the Italians to get the dope into Kansas City; I have a better way."

Jorge poured himself another drink and sat back, patiently listening to an idea to get the drugs into the two cities that had never occurred to him. When Reese was done speaking, Jorge responded.

"All of the time we have been moving our products and this has never crossed my mind, and I feel so stupid. We will use this method on the next shipment, but we have to make sure that we are careful!"

They shook hands, and Jorge opened the limousine door yelling female names; Reese watched several young women emerge from the crowd and they piled into the vehicle with hardly anything on their young bodies. The women didn't hesitate to move in on Reese, and if it wasn't for Carlos Sr.'s request, he would have stayed.

Instead he shook his head. "Sorry, ladies, but I have to catch up with you later; I have to prepare for something."

Jorge smiled and nodded his approval as the women pretended to pout. It was just for show; they knew that Reese would be there for the entire night.

Reese exchanged a few more words with Jorge before exiting the vehicle and making his way to the house to speak with Carlos Sr.

CHAPTER 62

When he walked into the house, Reese saw Miguel sitting on Carlos Sr. 's lap, listening to him singing a song in Spanish with relish; the little monster that Miguel had been earlier had vanished. When Carlos Sr. finished with the song, he received a kiss on the cheek, and Miguel rushed out of the room to find more mischief to get into. Carlos Sr. noticed Reese standing there.

"I love that little boy more than I love myself. Reese; how could you have murdered children?"

Reese attempted to explain, but it sounded lame even to his own ears. He went on to inform the man what had happened to his mother and little sister, and the man nodded grudgingly.

"I don't know what I would do if someone harmed my daughter or my wife, but your killing of that family and the female police officer has led to the end of your own life. How you live out the remainder of your days is up to you, but if you stay true to my sons, we will help you as much as we possibly can. Now, I know there are a lot of women around here that you have your eyes on, so go out and have a good time with my family-we'll talk later."

Carlos Sr. stepped outside to be greeted by yells of enthusiasm. Reese stared around the yard for awhile; he eventually seemed to snap out of a trance. He felt no remorse for the position he was faced with, and he would agree to the Border Brothers' terms, but not before he finished his revenge in the streets and made sure that he left something for people to remember him by.

CHAPTER 63

Lo-Lo heard a vehicle pull into the driveway and she was relieved to see Ashely grab her purse as if she was leaving. The woman walked up with a smile plastered on her beautiful face.

"Pete will be here with you until Amir gets back; make sure you let him answer the telephone so that people know that a male is in here, okay?"

Lo-Lo nodded and kissed Ashely on her cheek. She loved the woman even though she didn't agree with the lifestyle she lived; Ashely had been in her life since she was a child.

Ashely paused. "Mark Lockett, a counselor I know from Wyandotte Mental Health, is coming by to speak with Candace. If he feels that she needs to be treated, I don't want you causing problems for him. He knows what he's doing, so just allow him to help her."

She walked out of the door, and Lo-Lo watched her and Pete stand in the driveway conversing; Lo-Lo used the opportunity to run out of the back door. She looked around the side of the house and watched Pete lean into Ashely's car window to retrieve a handgun from the seat, and he walked into the house calling her name.

She sprinted to the rear privacy fence and rushed through the neighboring yards until she came to a side street a block away. She dialed the house telephone and hoped that Pete answered before he realized that she was gone; she didn't want him calling Ashely or Amir.

Pete picked up on the second ring.

"Pete, I walked over to my friend's house to get something for my face. I'm just two houses over, and I'll be right back."

She knew that when she mentioned her condition Pete would feel sympathy for her. He responded that he would go door to door to find her if she did not return soon. When Lo-Lo mentioned her mother's condition, though, Pete simply urged her to hurry back before Amir called or arrived at the house.

She ended the call with Pete and called Keith; she was relieved when he said that he was just a block away. She decided that they should meet at an apartment complex up the street, and she anticipated seeing him soon.

She waited on the steps of one of the apartment buildings, trying to conceal her black eye and the other bruises that were evident from her kidnapping. People had already begun staring at her, probably thinking that she was a victim of domestic abuse, so she kept her head down. She looked suspiciously at a tan Volvo that was idling on the other end of the parking lot. She had remembered seeing the same vehicle on the street behind Amir's house, and she had noticed it again a street over from the apartment complex. No matter how hard she tried, though, she couldn't tell if anyone was inside the vehicle through the heavily tinted windows.

When Lo-Lo's telephone rang she looked and recognized Keith's number; she stood up and walked to the curb, noticing that the Volvo still hadn't moved. Keith said that he was coming up the street and she recognized his mother's vehicle and waved her hands over her head so that he could see her. She smiled when she saw him turn on his turn signal, and as soon as Keith parked, she rushed to the vehicle. Just when he smiled up at her all hell broke loose.

CHAPTER 64

Oscar leaned back in the passenger side of the Volvo and handed Rico the blunt as he stared hard at Lo-Lo sitting on the steps of the apartment building. They had been watching Amir's house hoping that Slim or Keith would show their faces, but Ashely eventually pulled in front of the house. When they saw her leaving and noticed Lo-Lo peeking around the side of the house, Oscar knew that she was going to meet his nephew. They both noticed her staring at the vehicle they were sitting in, but they were confident that the five percent tint on the widows would be impossible to see through from that distance.

When Lo-Lo stood up and put her cell-phone to her ear as she walked to the curb, Oscar and Rico clutched their weapons and made sure that the chambers were loaded. Oscar watched as Lo-Lo waved her arms over her head, and he knew it was Keith arriving as soon as he saw his sister in law's convertible pull into the parking lot.

As soon as the vehicle came to a halt, Oscar announced that it was time to move. They pulled on their masks and jumped out of the Volvo, raining havoc on the parking lot. Oscar aimed for the windshield and saw Keith disappear in a shower of red, and he noticed Lo-Lo clutching her side from a bullet from Rico's weapon. She climbed into the backseat of the vehicle. Oscar saw the slugs from their weapons peeling the car like a can opener, but he knew he had to make sure the two of them were dead before they fled the scene.

He yelled for Rico to go around to the rear of the vehicle and was surprised when the vehicle reversed into the street and slammed into the median in the center of the road. Vehicles came to a halt and people rushed the vehicle to help, not fully understanding what was occuring. Oscar let off more rounds and smiled as a man was hit with heavy slugs that left an arm drenched in blood. He and Rico both replaced their magazines with fresh ones and prepared to go in for the kill.

When Rico approached the vehicle, though, Oscar heard a loud report from a weapon. Rico's upper body disappeared in a shower of blood, bone, and entrails. Oscar jumped behind one of the vehicles nearby and watched a man approach cautiously with a shotgun in tow and body armor around his torso and legs as he screamed for Lo-Lo to stay down in the seat.

Sirens were approaching and Oscar knew that he must make a swift decision. He slid from behind the vehicle and began to shoot toward the man, knowing that the armor that he wore could not stop the rounds that he was firing. He smiled as he saw the man fall to his knees as he dropped the shotgun, but Oscar didn't expect what happened next.

CHAPTER 65

Pete snatched the telephone out of the cradle in irritation, hoping that Lo-Lo was on her way back-he knew that someone would be calling to check on her. When he heard Lo-Lo's voice screaming through the telephone and the evident gunshots in the background his blood turned cold. He calmed her down enough to find out exactly where she was located, and he rushed to pull on his Kevlar body suit that was in the trunk of his vehicle; he gripped his semi-automatic shotgun from where it was stashed. Pete made sure that the house was locked and jumped into his vehicle, peeling out of the driveway in a cloud of smoke.

When he turned onto the next street and saw the smoke and the wrecked vehicle, he didn't hesitate to grab his weapon and stuffed the 9mm pistol that Ashely had left him into the small of his back. He pulled onto the curb and approached the scene cautiously, seeing the two men fire on the vehicle that he knew Lo-Lo was inside.

Just as one of the men noticed his presence and began turning his weapon in Pete's direction, his head was nearly taken off his shoulders with a well-placed slug from the shotgun. When Pete turned toward the other gunner, the man leapt behind a vehicle and disappeared. Pete decided to check on Lo-Lo instead of trying to locate the man. He began approaching the vehicle and was surprised to hear the unmistakable sound of an assault weapon firing. Slugs began to slam into his Kevlar suit feeling like hammers, and he soon felt a warm feeling on his back; there was no doubt that some of the bullets had penetrated his unique protection. He hit the ground hard as he dropped the shotgun as bullets went by where he had been moments ago.

He heard a blood-curdling scream and looked over to see Ashely crossing the street with the Calico machine gun he had seen on her backseat before she had left Amir's house. Pete saw the shooter grip his stomach and noticed blood spraying out of his back. Before Ashely could finish him, he climbed to his feet and limped to a vehicle in the apartment complex nearby, trailing blood.

As Oscar climbed into the vehicle, Ashely crossed the street, and Pete could see her ripping the car up with slugs, shattering the windows and flattening two tires as the vehicle limped away from the complex.

Ashely rushed over to Pete and attempted to get him to his feet, and he tried to help, but he was mostly dead weight. She decided to retrieve the gun from the small of his back and unloaded the magazine into the already slow-moving vehicle that was attempting to leave the scene. She ran back to Pete and stripped off his armor and grabbed the shotgun that was lying next to him.

"I'll meet you at the hospital; I have to get out of here as soon as I check on Lo-Lo!" She ran over to the smoking vehicle that she remembered Keith driving in the past and was confronted by Lo-Lo cradling Keith's head in her lap as she sobbed hysterically. Ashely noticed that Keith was still breathing slightly, but he was severely injured. Ashely urged Lo-Lo in a soothing voice.

"Loren, I have to get away from here before the police get here. You'll have help for him soon, so make sure to call and let us know where you are as soon as you get there!"

She shut the door and raced to the stolen vehicle, climbing inside as she heard sirens rapidly approaching.

CHAPTER 66

When Ashely pulled into Candace's garage, she heard a vehicle pull in front of the house and ran to a window to look out. She breathed a sigh of relief when she saw Mark Lockett's Mitsubishi parked at the curb. She straightened her business suit the best she could and casually strolled outside. She was surprised to see Candace sitting in the vehicle with him, staring intently into his face. Ashely often paused when she saw the man; she was impressed by how handsome and professional he was. Mark rolled his window down when she approached.

"Do you think it's a good idea to leave Ms. Wilson here alone? It sounded like a lot of gunshots going off nearby, and I heard that some people may even be dead. You need to be more careful with her; she's having a difficult time right now. I'm taking this beautiful lady with me to Rainbow Mental Health Center to have her evaluated. Call me later and I'll let you know what she needs. In the meantime, you should go inside until you know what's going on around the corner."

Ashely smiled and nodded her head, thinking that Mark would be singing a different tune if he noticed the gunpowder burns on her cuffs.

"Thank you very much, Mr. Lockett. I'll call Amir and let him talk to you about what Candace needs, though. He's the one that's really in control."

He looked up sharply, not missing the implication of her statement. He no doubt knew about Amir, but he was probably surprised that a sophisticated woman like Ashely would be involved with him. He eventually waved as he pulled away from the house with Amir's mother sitting in the passenger seat, smiling and muttering nonsense. Ashely pulled out her cell-phone to call Amir, anticipating the upcoming encounter with Lloyd and the Jamaicans. She felt that they would be the ones to pay for this latest attempt to assault Lo-Lo, but she silently wished that they had been successful in killing Keith.

CHAPTER 67

Arelia lay back with her legs spread wide, trembling as Tina sucked on her clitoris and fingered her sticky vagina. Her legs shook uncontrollably as she climaxed for the third time, and it turned her on more when the beautiful Russian girl moaned with her face buried into her sex. This was their second episode, and her vagina was already sore from the huge dildo that Tina had pounded her with; her backside also ached after the spanking she had received.

"Oh! Oh! That feels so good! I'm coming again! I'm cooooming!" As she climaxed, her juices sprayed onto Tina's breasts, and the petite woman pulled her body up and straddled her face. Arelia licked and sucked until Tina climaxed several times and they both finally collapsed into each other's arms.

Arelia had met Tina at a casino in Kansas City, Kansas, when she was having her lunch; it seemed as if the young bombshell had gone out of her way to flirt with her.

When Arelia eventually picked Tina up that night they had traveled to a bar in Lawrence, Kansas, and they moved on to a Lesbian bar on the Missouri side of the border. They had arrived at Arelia's house for their initial sexual encounter, but now Arelia had driven to the younger woman's home in Olathe, Kansas, for the fulfillment of her fantasies.

Arelia pulled a sheet around her slim frame as she watched Tina walk to the kitchen counter to prepare drinks. When Tina returned to the couch, she had a wicked smile on her face.

Arelia looked up at the teenager as she received her glass.

"What are you up to, girl? I know you're up to something." Tina smiled and kissed Arelia deeply with her tongue, slowly sucking on her full lips and delicate neck.

"I put a little something special in your drink; my pussy's still not satisfied." Tina dropped a capsule into her own drink and Arelia held the glass that had already been laced with the vial Ashely had given to Tina earlier in the day.

Arelia drank deeply and spread her legs wide, giving Tina a generous view of her sex. Suddenly she wore a confused look on her pretty face. Tina gave a giggle, until she was shocked to see blood pouring out of Arelia's mouth and nose as she appeared to writhe in pain and grip her neck. Tina was concerned, and she was very afraid.

"What's wrong, Arelia?" When Tina reached for the telephone, she was roughly grabbed from behind and pushed to the floor.

"Bitch! Do you want to go to prison, or what?" Ashely came out of the next room and stood over Arelia, smiling and looking down at her as if her death throes were amusing.

Tina looked at Ashely with tears streaming down her face.

"Aren't we going to help her? What was in that bottle that I gave her?"

Ashely looked at her in exasperation.

"Did you give her the whole thing? Are you crazy? You were supposed to give her half; I told you that when I gave it to you!"

Tina watched Arelia continue to writhe in agony as she remembered Ashely instructing her to empty the entire vial into Arelia's drink. She watched in horror as her lover's death throes finally came to an end with a release of urine and a loud hiss from her bowels releasing. Arelia's eyes clouded over and remained open and lifeless; Tina cried hysterically while averting her eyes and covering her nose from the sickening stench.

Ashely roughly grabbed Tina by the shoulders and looked her in the eyes while shaking her.

"They're going to give you life in prison for what you did. This was first degree murder! If you try telling anyone anything about me, just keep in mind that I'm an attorney and I represent people that will torture anyone who informs to the police. I'm going to help you because I know you made an innocent mistake; I love you, Tina. The first thing we need to do, though, is get rid of this funky bitch; I'll tell you exactly what needs to be done. Is that clear, or would you rather me dial 911 and let you take your chances?" Tina shook her head and accepted everything that Ashely was telling her. She dropped her head in defeat and looked at the body again before tossing the covers over the corpse's face.

Ashely walked out of the room and returned with a large roll of plastic, some duct tape, and a can of gasoline. Tina looked at Ashely, and the truth of the action dawned on her like being hit by a train.

"You planned this! All of this time you've been using me to set this up. You're a murderer!" She rushed toward Ashely with her hands outstretched, but she stopped in her tracks when she noticed the huge pistol pointing at her head. The tone of Ashely's voice chilled Tina.

"Bitch, let's get one thing straight right fucking now! I run this shit, and if you're smart, you won't ever think about crossing me. I just need you to do one more thing and not a soul will ever know what happened tonight. Now, get it together and help me get this stank-ass bitch out of here! I'll tell you exactly what you need to do so that we can put this behind us."

Tina moved to the other side of the room grudgingly while Ashely rolled plastic along the side of the bed. Tina decided to go along with whatever Ashely wanted, and after that she planned on leaving the Midwest for good. She couldn't think of a way out of the situation, and nothing that Ashely instructed her to do could be worse than doing life in prison or dying for a murder she didn't consciously commit.

CHAPTER 68

Amir stared down at Lo-Lo sleeping peacefully, knowing that she had been through too much in a short span of time. He looked down at the bloody gauze on her side and was relieved that all she received in the encounter was a flesh wound. He had been in Keith's room speaking with him for a while until the boy's mother entered the room and stared at him accusingly; Amir had simply left without uttering a word. Although Keith was badly injured, he had made a bold decision that ultimately saved both of their young lives. Amir could tell that Keith had been in immense pain by the strain in his voice, but he handled himself as the man he was forced into becoming.

Amir quietly closed the door to his sister's room and saw Los stepping off of the elevator with a handful of flowers and a huge teddy bear.

Amir smiled. "She's still asleep, playa; just sit the stuff down next to the bed. Pete's room is right down the hall across from Keith's." Los prepared to enter Lo-Lo's hospital room and Amir strolled down by Pete's room in deep thought.

When he heard Los talking to someone, he turned and looked in that direction. Detective Galubski was staring Los down and holding a sheaf of papers in his hand as if it were a weapon. The detective grinned when he saw the look on Amir's face.

"The famous and murderous Amir; your days are numbered, *boy*. I wouldn't be coming here to visit a Judas who snitched to the Feds; I'd be tryin' to figure out how to put the black mothafucka in a box. Pete didn't know much, but it should be enough to convince the grand jury to look at you and your wanna-be gangsta homeboy right here." The detective motioned toward Los, and Amir raised his hand to steady his friend before he responded to the detective's words. He began to respond in an even tone.

"Listen to me, you fat pig. Anything you have to say to me has to come real fucking fast; I have better things to do than to sit here and play games with a grown-ass man. Do you think that you can just tell me that my boy is a rat, and I'll just accept it? Am I supposed to take you at your word and give you the satisfaction of witnessing both our demise? I don't think so. If you have anything to say to us do it in a professional way, not in a place where we're forced to keep ourselves off your chalky ass. Do this shit in a place where I can wipe that smug-ass smile off your fat face; you'll be begging for your life if you do that." Detective Galubski stepped back as if he had been slapped; he hesitated before walking into Amir's space.

"I'm sick of you charcoal-ass coons thinking that you can do and say whatever you want!" He grabbed Amir by the collar of his starched shirt and Los began to draw his weapon.

A nurse stepped out of Pete's room with a frown on her face.

"What's going on out here? Get your filthy hands off him or I'm going to call security!" The detective released Amir with a hard shove.

"You keep getting saved by these women, punk! The next time it won't matter to me; I'll make sure we're alone." Amir straightened his tie and stared calmly at the enraged man.

"There won't be a next time, white nigga. If you approach me in an aggressive manner in the future, I promise to take that sorry-ass life out of your tiny chest." Amir turned to his best friend.

"Los, let's go, my nig. Leave this fool out here to think about if he wants to take the chance. It simply does not matter to me."

The young, sexy, Brazilian nurse listened to the exchange in wide-eyed wonder; she was pondering what was going on with these men and anticipating a serious confrontation. Amir ignored the detective and strolled into Pete's room followed by Los still clutching Lo-Lo's gifts, leaving Galubski to stare at their backs with a hateful expression. They overheard the nurse beginning to question the irate detective about the confrontation.

Pete was connected to several monitors and his left arm was wrapped in heavy gauze. He opened his eyes and smiled as Amir approached his bedside, but pain was evident in his expression.

"How are you holding up, my nig?" Amir looked at Pete as a little brother, so it hurt that the things the detective had said about Pete didn't surprise him. He had been informed about the raid on Pete's home that had landed him in jail, and Amir had been having people watching his every move.

Pete nodded. "I'm cool, man. How's Lo-Lo and that little nigga she was meeting out there? Maybe now she'll understand that when we tell her something it's for her own good." He shook his head in exasperation and Los continued to listen in silence. Amir sat down in a chair next to the hospital bed.

"A detective has been putting the word out that you have loose lips. Why would he be saying something like that?" Pete turned his eyes toward the ceiling as his face screwed up in anger, but they both noticed that he didn't deny the accusation. Los suddenly approached the bed with his weapon in his hand.

"Bitch-ass nigga! I should shoot you in yo' ugly face right now! We been treatin' you like family since we was kids, you fuckin' soft-ass nigga!" Pete averted his eyes and Amir walked over and took the weapon from Los's trembling fist.

"Los, that's not the way to go. I need you out here with me; you know we handle business smooth and silent." Amir turned and focused on Pete with loathing.

"Pete, I appreciate what you did for my sister, man, but you tried to take our lives in a different way, and I won't let that slide. I suggest you get yourself together and leave town, you fucking snake. Your police homeboys already tossed your trick-ass to the wolves." He walked out of the door without looking back, and Los followed after glaring at Pete with the promise of violence in his eyes. Detective Galubski was still in the hallway wearing a huge grin on his chubby face and a pair of handcuffs in his hand.

"It won't be long now, fellas. I'll be seeing you niggers soon."

They walked past him and eventually stepped onto the elevator with the sound of his laughter at their backs. They both rode down in silence, distracted by their own thoughts. When they stepped out in front of the hospital, Amir pulled out his cell-phone and dialed a number.

"I have a job for you. I'll let you know what it is later tonight after I handle my own business first." After he ended the call, Los asked a question.

"Who was that, my nig?"

Amir turned to his best friend with a blank expression.

"Someone Pete is going to wish he never met." He silently walked to his vehicle with a wicked smile on his face.

CHAPTER 69

Ashely walked into the nightclub and shook her head at the hungry stares coming at her from all directions, admiring the bass-filled reggae music literally shaking the walls. She had on a white form-fitting outfit with Prada heels to match, showcasing the mound of her vagina for everyone to admire. She had her hair flowing freely, but it was flipped out from her face in a stylish hairdo that caused the women in the nightclub to watch their boyfriends and husbands closely.

A blunt-smoking Jamaican rushed to offer her a seat, but she was sickened by the sour scent emanating from his long dreadlocks, and the smell of the Heineken beer he was drinking wafting from his blackened lips.

He slurred a greeting. "Come have a seat wit yo' brethren! I'm no Batti Boy, ya hear?"

Ashely pushed past him with a disgusted look on her face, and she was relieved to see Lloyd approaching with two other men. Lloyd used a fake name they had agreed on.

"Monica, come on, we over by the pool tables getting tipsy. You gwon go with drunk-ass Flip, or you gwon come wit I and me posse?

Ashely smiled and followed Lloyd and the two men with him, noticing that they wore short haircuts as opposed to the long dreadlocks that Lloyd and the other Jamaicans preferred. She pondered that if she had seen the two men from a distance, there would be no way to identify them as Jamaicans.

When they arrived at their table, Ashely looked around at men of all hues, and races. There were even a few Jamaicans with completely bald heads as well as a few with cornrows braided to the back of their necks.

Lloyd handed her a drink before making an announcement.

"Tis is me friend, Monica. I been knowing tis gal since we were youths."

All eyes were on Ashely, and she was silently relieved that Lloyd had remembered her alias; she knew that Lloyd was supposed to go by James, so she uttered the name heartily.

"Hey, Jamaican James, are you still going to teach me to play pool tonight?"

Peter walked up and gripped her around the waist and pulled her toward the game room.

"I'll teach you how to play, pretty gal, come wit I!" Ashely noticed that Peter didn't have much of an accent, and she was amazed at how young he looked. The pictures that Los had shown her of Peter were of him sitting inside of a car, so it had been difficult to get a good look at him. He had at least a carat diamond on each tooth, top and bottom. He was the main supplier to the M.O.P. and many other organizations and street gangs.

Ashely responded with a frown. "You have to be slow and careful with me, okay?"

Peter smiled wickedly as he patted her on the backside. Ashely then made a show of bending over, squatting and lowering her breasts to the billiard table they had arrived at to be certain that all eyes were focused on her. She played the role of a beginner, but in reality she played the game with more efficiency than Amir and Los combined, and they were decent at the game themselves.

Peter stood and stared at her for a moment before positioning himself behind her, making a show of teaching her how to shoot and feeling her up at the same time.

Peter slurred, "Gal, you gwon home wit me, ya hear?"

Ashely smiled and leaned forward and kissed Peter tenderly on the cheek before speaking.

"I'm going wherever Lloyd wants to go. I may stick around, though; I heard you have the best K-Town and Cush on both sides of the water."

Peter grinned. "Ya heard right! I got the baddest ganja in the area. You gonna puff on a spliff wit yo boy, Peter, uman?"

Ashely simply smiled and went back to shooting shots that didn't even come close to sinking into any of the holes. Lloyd glanced at her from time to time, but he was also speaking with Peter's brother about a deal for cocaine and heroin. Ashely knew that the conversation was only for appearances. The real plan was to shut down their operations and take any drugs and cash that were available. Peter turned to Ashely.

"Let's head to them Waffle House for some breakfast, gal. After, our can get them eyes tight with the ganja. You ridin' wit I, or driving by your lonesome?" Ashely smiled; she didn't want her vehicle seen anyway, and Peter had unwittingly solved her dilemma.

"As long as you don't drive too fast for me, Peter; I told you that I like it really slow." She looked directly into his eyes and he simply nodded his head with a grin, thinking that she had just promised him a night of steamy sex.

When they exited the establishment, the Jamaicans were entering the luxury vehicles that she had noticed on her way in. When Peter opened the door of a Maserati, Ashely knew that he had good taste and plenty of assets. She climbed in next to him and looked out as Lloyd entered the vehicle that Peter's brother, Quentin, was behind the wheel of.

Peter started the vehicle and Ashely felt strong vibrations from the heavy bass coming from the expensive stereo system. She took the punishment with a grain of salt, knowing that this would be Peter's last night among the living.

CHAPTER 70

Dick stood out in the rain, silently watching the house that held the only connections he had to finding Reese. He knew that the Black Border Brothers had drug houses in Kansas and Missouri, but he felt more comfortable stalking them from the Missouri side of the border. Besides, he thought, Detective Galubski was very good at finding ways to pursue anyone they wanted in Kansas, guilty or not. Dick had watched Amir and Los come and leave the house earlier that day, but since then it didn't appear that any business was being conducted at the "spot". He saw Slim occasionally, and he could see the resemblance the man had to Amir. Reese's best friend, Arthur, also arrived with his girlfriend, and Dick had followed them to the house where they lived. He knew that something serious was developing, and he had sacrificed two days of work to find out about it, as well as hoping they would lead him to the man that had murdered his partner. He wanted to bring in a couple of officers he knew would help him, but he didn't trust that they would keep their mouths shut when he did what he planned. He was going to kill Reese. Dick felt that the law would allow the man to escape through some mistake or loophole; this was common when the accused had access to large amounts of currency.

When he saw the lights go out in the house he climbed into his vehicle, but he stayed alert and tried not to fall asleep, and likely forfeit the opportunity to find out what was going on inside the house.

He was dozing off, but he was awakened by the sounds of several vehicles' doors slamming, and he glanced at his watch to see that it was three in the morning. He looked out to see that vehicles were parked all around the house, and some were even pulled into the yard. Dick made sure that he had a round in the chamber of his weapon and turned his radio and cell-phone off. He settled down to see what happened next.

It was not long before people began emerging from the house with large duffel bags in their hands and what looked like ski masks rolled up on their heads. Dick pulled a small pair of binoculars from his glove-box and could clearly see the eyeholes of the masks on top of their heads.

He waited until the men entered the vehicles and drove away before following. He stayed a considerable distance behind the last vehicle, noticing how the cars fanned out across the highway; casual observers would never suspect that it was a procession.

The things Dick had seen so far pointed to one thing: a hit. When he realized where the vehicles were exiting, he knew exactly where they were headed. The Wayne Manor Apartments were a haven for drug activity, prostitution, and horrific murders. Gangs infested the area, and the Jamaicans had practically taken over a section of the complex. Before the vehicles reached the entrance to the apartments, the men parked the vehicles and went into the trunks, producing the duffel bags and other items they had loaded. When the men began pulling on bullet-proof vests and produced machine guns and other weaponry, Dick knew that something horrible was going to occur.

He pulled his radio from under the seat, contemplating calling for assistance, but ultimately decided against interfering in this carefully devised felony; he realized that he wouldn't have a satisfactory reason to be present at the controversial apartments.

When one of the men casually removed his mask, Dick froze. He had not been prepared to see Arthur; the man was normally behind the scenes, especially when violent situations arose. Dick grabbed his gloves from the seat beside him and pulled on his own ski-mask, hoping he could get close enough to grab Arthur and question him about Reese's whereabouts. He would be the perfect weakness in Amir and Los's defenses.

When the killers began to pour into the complex, Dick followed from the shadows. He silently considered what would happen if he was discovered by any of the men.

CHAPTER 71

When Ashely followed Peter into the apartment, she was ready to shoot him right then. The entire time they were in the small Waffle House restaurant, the man constantly kept his hands exploring her body as if he had been given permission. She had been flirting with his friends to keep them off guard also, but Peter was behaving as if Ashely had given him sole rights to her body.

She looked around at the expensive furniture and other items inside the apartment and was amazed at the contrast to the downtrodden look of the exterior. Men and women were lounging all over the apartment, but she was not worried about the unexpected number of people inside. She planned on lacing drinks with tranquilizers in order to take their defenses down considerably.

Lloyd entered the apartment with two women in his arms, and Ashely didn't acknowledge him. They had already discussed the plan days ago, and Lloyd knew that when she left the apartment to get her "overnight bag" that the next step in the demise of Peter would be in effect. It didn't matter at that point if Peter was drugged; Ashely knew that once she promised the man sex, he wouldn't be thinking about anything else until it was too late.

She moved around the room and gave strip-tease dances to the Jamaicans, alternately slipping a fine powder into their drinks, laughing inside at their sexual vulnerabilities. Some of the women inside were even showing interest in her. It didn't matter to Ashely; she planned on drugging as many people as she could.

When Peter pulled out marijuana to smoke, Ashely realized that this would be the most difficult part of their plan. When everyone was distracted by the music and several women stripping down to their underclothes, Ashely pulled out a tiny bottle and lightly sprayed P.C.P. onto the pile of marijuana that was on the living room table. She hoped that the Jamaicans wouldn't notice the chemical scent mingling with the smell of the incense that was burning all over the apartment. Once they started producing and using cocaine, though, she knew that it didn't matter anymore; most likely their sense of smell would be affected by the white powder going up their noses. She only had crushed sleeping pills to pour into their drinks, and everyone was not drinking, so her decision on whose drinks she laced would have to be calculated. She didn't want those who were not consuming alcohol to notice anything, so she chose the tranquilizer instead of the poison they had agreed to initially. Ashely was a natural seductress, and she smiled when she looked around at the hungry stares directed at her.

Peter approached her and slurred as he spoke.

"You stayin' wit me tonight, ya hear?"

Ashely didn't show the irritation that she felt at his demand. She simply smiled and grabbed her purse.

"I just need to borrow a car to get my personal belongings since we left my car at the bar. Do you want to see me in my new panties? I also have to have my personal hygiene bag for the morning, okay?"

This last statement put Peter right where she wanted him. He ignored one of his friend's protests and tossed her his keys.

"The midnight Maxima out front. You hurry back, gal, ya hear?"

Ashely nodded, and she glanced over at Lloyd in a corner of the room with his head back; he was staring at the ceiling in deep thought. There were two women kneeling between his legs competing for the pleasure of giving the most impressive fellatio.

When she opened the door, Lloyd glanced over and winked, knowing that Ashely would be bringing death when she returned.

She glanced around the room on her way out, noticing that people were asleep and high on drugs or alcohol. She stepped outside and saw many more Jamaicans; she realized that the hit would be difficult even with the advantages she had orchestrated. She still received lusty stares and degrading catcalls, but there was also an element of suspicion written on some faces; some of the Jamaicans exhibited open hostility. From the way the men stood guard around the apartment, Ashely knew that something of value was inside. She spotted a few men with M.O.P. stenciled on their hats and across the back of their shirts. She smiled as she entered the Maxima and pulled away from the apartment; anticipating killing several birds with one large stone.

CHAPTER 72

Mecca strolled through the bridal shop with her sister, Imani, pleased that Amir had finally made his mind up to be a man and set a wedding date. Imani followed Mecca with a frown on her beautiful face, feeling that her sister was making the biggest mistake of her life. Imani really liked Amir, but she knew of the lifestyle he tried so hard to keep hidden; she felt that he was approaching devastation. She had argued with Mecca several times about Amir's not so secret life, trying to explain that there would be no smooth exit from inner-city drug trafficking. Extraction from higher levels of crime usually came with dire consequences, and Imani didn't feel that her sister should be around when the piper came around to collect his debt.

She frowned at Mecca. "Why do you insist on ignoring what is going on around you, Mecca? Amir, for the most part, is a fine man. I'm sure that there are many women that would love to be in your shoes, but I have heard many things about the man that really scares me. He's the head of The Black Border Brothers, and they are out in the streets killing people. Amir is also responsible for a lot of the drugs that are in the streets. He's friends with Carlos and Killer Reese; do I need to continue, Mecca?" Imani stood silently and stared defiantly at her sister while Mecca continued to examine wedding dresses, attempting to ignore her older sister's words.

Finally, Mecca turned around and placed her hands over her swollen abdomen before she responded.

"I realize how my man *used* to live in the past, and the two of us have had several discussions about it. I often talk to *my man* about these things that you have mentioned, and he understands that I will have absolutely nothing to do with him if he continues to live as a thug. Until then, everyone should simply give Amir a chance; none of us are perfect, and the decision he makes is ultimately between the two of us. Now, are you going to help me find a dress, or are you going to waste more time talking about something that does not concern you?"

Imani nodded her head and smiled.

"You're still a spoiled brat. I know that you're an intelligent woman, Mecca, but men like Amir sometimes have the power to make women lose their minds. Make sure that my niece comes into this world with safety and security, okay?"

Mecca nodded; she realized that her sister's words were true, and she had been afraid for Amir since she had been confronted by the detective at her doctor's office. She loved Amir, but she refused to allow him to steer her into any dangerous situations. She felt confident in his sincerity for change, and she was confident that he would keep her safe. If she was wrong, she was simply going to learn how single mothers make it in the world. She continued smiling for Imani's benefit; Mecca didn't want Imani to have any more fuel for her emotional fire by raising doubts with worry etched on her face.

Mecca suddenly spread a huge smile across her exotically beautiful features.

"After this, are we still going to Dairy Queen? I have a craving for a banana split dipped in chocolate. I've been thinking about sucking on a long, black banana all day!"

Imani looked at Mecca with amused disgust.

"Yes, we're still going, hot momma. That's why your stomach is swollen now. You're so nasty!"

They both laughed and continued to shop while Detective Galubski stayed ten paces behind, reporting to the men who employed him *outside* of the police department.

CHAPTER 73

Amir turned off James A. Reed street in Grandview, Missouri, feeling better than he had in a long time. With the violence and hypocrisy unfolding around him, the Islamic Center he attended was a sobering reminder that the life he was living did not coincide with his acceptance of Islam. His Imam was an Arab man, but he seemed to know exactly what was going on in the inner-city streets without being directly associated or connected to them. The older man didn't attempt to play the role of a priest and ask for confessions; he simply invited people into his community and reminded them that the things that were going on in the world had been occurring since man's existence.

Amir knew that he needed to get his life in order, but there were still things he felt needed to be dealt with to conclude his business in the streets. He had to find the people that were responsible for the kidnapping of his sister, as well as the murders of his friends. He also had access to more drugs than he had ever seen in his life, and he had an obligation to distribute them before he could consider severing his ties to the ruthless Border Brothers in California.

The meeting that he had with the Italians had gone better than he had expected, but there was still an underlying tension afterward. Frank was the only Italian who didn't exhibit open hostility while they were conducting business, and he had even sent Amir an invitation to his upcoming wedding. Los was being his usual self in showing contempt for the organization, but Amir knew better than to allow the men to see his emotions.

After he found Paris and Oscar, he planned on showcasing their corpses in a way that would be a constant reminder to everyone that the Black Border Brothers played for keeps. The attack on Lo-Lo was unacceptable, and the concept of turning the other cheek was not an option.

He headed toward Kansas to visit his mother at Rainbow Mental Health Center, and he hoped to give her a brief reprieve from the hell that he felt largely responsible for. He knew that Slim and Ashely would be waiting for him, but they would have to wait until he spent some time with his mother. With all of the things going wrong lately, Amir felt a dark cloud over his head, and his mother's condition weighed heavily on his mind.

He turned the crooner "Maxwell" up on his after-market stereo system and tried to relax while he traveled and thought about the good things God had given him. He glanced at a picture of Mecca mounted on his dashboard and smiled; she was his motivation to leave the streets forever. He called Slim as a frown suddenly creased his face. Pete was being released from the hospital, and Amir was going to make sure that he didn't get a chance to rat on anyone else.

CHAPTER 74

Looney listened to the stolen vehicles pull up to the house while he strapped on his bullet-proof vest and made sure every weapon was wiped down before reminding everyone to pull on latex gloves. Ashely had pulled on her black loose fitting jumpsuit, and for once was ignored by the men; it was time to get down to business.

Ashely told them as much as she could about the apartment where Peter and the other Jamaicans were, but they all realized that they had to worry more about the people watching the "spot" from the outside rather than the ones inside. Peter had people watching from several nearby apartments, and it was obvious that the one that she had been in was a store-house for either drugs, currency, or both.

Country entered the room carrying an AR-15 assault rifle, and Slim walked in with a large handgun stuffed into his belt and a 9mm carbine strapped onto his right shoulder. Looney noticed that Slim did not have his cane; he was simply walking with a slight limp- the man had obviously been working diligently to rehabilitate his recent injuries.

Lunatic and Rag entered the room with their own weapons in tow, and everyone strapped on bullet-proof vests and waited for instructions from Looney. There were eleven Black Border Brothers in the house, and ten were at Wayne Manor parked haphazardly around the apartment complex.

Looney eventually gathered everyone into one room, giving instructions to each member personally while donning his own armor, weapons, and gloves. When he was finished, he turned toward Country.

"Damu, don't get shit fucked up and think because of some gang shit I'll hesitate to treat you like my enemy if you do anything to fuck this up with some crazy shit. Do you feel me? I know some fools look at me and think that I'm some pretty-boy ass nigga, but I'm the nightmare of these streets, my nig." He turned and stared at everyone in the room before addressing everyone.

"We gotta be vicious when go up against these niggas, and we have to make it inside that apartment within ten minutes. Ashely told Lloyd to open the door when I call him, but if that damn door don't open, kick that bitch in! If mothafuckas don't follow instructions let some wind out of their bags; we don't have time to be talkin' or to be negotiating with these niggas about shit! You know that the police will be on the way real soon, trust me on that. If those bitch-ass police pull in that parking lot before we can leave, put those bitches to sleep too. Nobody is gonna fuck this shit up; are we ready?"

Everyone nodded and rose to their feet and the excitement could be felt in the room. When Looney saw the urgency in everyone's eyes and their movements, he was sure that he had chosen the right men. They heard another vehicle pull into the driveway and Looney smiled when he saw Los step out of his vehicle wearing all black, grinning from ear to ear while approaching the house.

CHAPTER 75

Looney opened the door for Los and instructed Arthur to have the vehicles running and the trunks open so they would be ready to load and move out without delay. He stepped outside and scrutinized a vehicle parked down the street suspiciously, thinking that he had seen someone inside. He eventually dismissed the thought as paranoia, and the early morning mist made him feel that the elements could be affecting his vision.

When he re-entered the house, Ashely was staring hard at Los while he explained that he wanted her to stay inside one of the getaway cars until the conclusion of the confrontation. When he finished speaking, Ashely smiled wickedly.

"Los, baby, you know that I'm *definitely* not going to wait in a damn car while these fools ruin everything we've been planning. I love you always for being concerned for my safety, daddy, so don't misunderstand, but I can teach your boys a little something about how to handle their business."

Los grinned and slapped her playfully on her ample backside. He grabbed his duffel bag and walked out of the house without another word.

Country walked over to Looney.

"I need a bitch like that, home-boy, but I wouldn't trust the hoe with anything more than settin' niggas up. If you slap the bitch, you might as well finish her off with a few slugs, cause she gonna try to kill yo' ass!"

Looney patted his friend on the back and ushered him out of the house to the idling vehicles. After the weapons were loaded, as well as the other items they would need, he instructed each driver about what route to take so that they would not be trailing each other along the way. He glanced at the vehicle up the street once more before rolling his mask to the top of his head and climbing into the vehicle with Rag and his cousin Rich. They made sure to observe the speed limits and arrived at the entrance to the Wayne Manor apartments. Everyone noticed that there were still many people out in the darkness of the approaching early morning dawn.

Ashely climbed out of one of the vehicles and pulled her mask out as she listened to the plan on the most effective route to the front door of Peter's apartment. After they were done conversing, everyone pulled on their masks, gripped their weapons, and trotted into the parking lot toward the area they were instructed to begin their assault. Looney was the first to pull the trigger.

CHAPTER 76

One of the men shooting a basketball under the streetlights looked over, noticing movements in the shadows and ran toward his duffel bag beside the court. When the rest of the men attempted to follow, Looney rained a death shower of .223 Remington rounds. He had a hundred-round drum on his AR-15, and he caught the first few men right before they made it to the group of vehicles they were approaching. Looney could see the geysers of blood where the large rounds exited their bodies, and one of the men's faces seemed to turn into a black hole as the round ruined his profile.

Some of the men abandoned their attempts at reaching their vehicles and simply attempted to take flight, but Country and Rag had cut off their exits. The men could do nothing except raise their hands in surrender, but Country was taking no prisoners. It was like lambs being led to slaughter. Country eventually stood over the prone bodies and began to look around; the Jamaicans suddenly appeared and began shooting at anything or anyone moving.

Looney glimpsed the unmistakable form of Ashely joining Country on the opposite side of the basketball court from where he crouched, and he saw her go down from a hail of bullets thwat the Jamaicans were firing. Country also noticed that she had been hit, but he could not stop to assist her; the Jamaicans had now focused their attention on him and forced him behind a stand of trees. Looney had no choice but to leave the woman; a few of his friends had made it to Peter's apartment and were forcing themselves inside.

Looney was grabbed from behind, and as he was moving his weapon in position to fire before he recognized Los's voice.

"Come on! We gotta get in that apartment before the police come. Lloyd said that most of the niggas in there are shermed out or drunk, and the rest of them are drugged up and sleep."

They entered the apartment and saw that bodies were sprawled everywhere; Lloyd was dragging one of the Jamaicans toward the rear of the apartment while hitting him in the face repeatedly with his pistol.

Los heard movement behind him and turned around to see a large form looming in the doorway, and he knew that it was Country. One of the drugged men lying on the floor began to shake his head and rose to his hands and knees. Looney realized that some of the people lying there were not dead-they were unconscious from the drugs that Ashely had given them.

Country pumped slugs into the man and did the same to a few others that were immobile.

Looney noticed Country staring down at a young woman with her skirt hiked up around her waist. He shoved him roughly.

"Come on, nigga! We don't have time for nothin' but money and findin' out where Peter's at!"

They headed down a hallway and could hear muffled voices. They spotted an open door and could see a flight of stairs going down.

CHAPTER 77

The two men slowly descended the staircase and saw Los, Rag, Arthur, and a man they all knew as Lil G standing over four men on their knees with their hands on their heads; the frightened men were pleading for their lives. Looney felt that the men should have known that their begging was in vain once the killers had removed their ski-masks.

Peter's body was barely recognizable on the floor. He was missing several body parts, and it was evident from his death mask that he died while experiencing excruciating pain.

Los walked over and kicked one of the men in the face, smiling when a glittering diamond skipped across the filthy carpet.

"Nigga, you only get one chance to tell us what we need to know. Other than that, shut the fuck up, cause' you aint talkin' yo' way out of this shit!" The man still attempted to speak through his split lower lip, and Los responded by shooting the man kneeling next to him and calmly watching him squirm around on the floor; the man eventually was immobile after expelling a sickening load of defecation as he died.

"Me brudda!" The young Jamaican crawled toward the corpse and Los shot him in the back of his right leg and ignored his howl of pain. The man turned over with his hands raised in surrender.

"In da floor under the couch, mon! Take it all; Just let me and me bruddas go. Please!"

Country walked up and pulled off his mask.

"Where them M.O.P. niggas at, bitch? Tell us where they at, and let them niggas deal with this shit."

When the man told them everything they needed to know and Country saw the kilos of cocaine and cash being pulled from the floor, he and Rag began firing on the men. They left the room looking and smelling like a slaughterhouse.

They gathered up the drugs and cash and began making their exit as they continued to hear gunshots and approaching police sirens.

Los signaled everyone to pull on their masks, and they made their way through the parking lot that was now littered with corpses and covered in blood. Los shook his head when he noticed many of his friends and associates sprawled out amongst the dead Jamaicans.

They made it to the main entrance to the complex, and someone leapt from behind a truck, firing some type of assault rifle. Before they could react, the man went down, and his body was riddled with bullets. The shooter ran off to a hail of gunfire, and they all turned to the man who had just been killed. They pulled his mask free and Looney's heart sank when he saw Arthur's face that was now frozen in a painful death mask. He also had a large gaping hole where his stomach had been; intestines were hanging from his body as he lay there on the pavement.

Looney saw that everyone was climbing into the tilts and he didn't see Ashely anywhere, but he knew that they didn't have time to look for her or anyone else. The police arrived, and Looney was relieved that they were exchanging gunfire with the Jamaicans and did not notice their departure from the scene. The last thought he had before a slug slammed into his face was of Peter, and how he had died a slow excruciating death.

CHAPTER 78

Slim ended the call with Monica, wondering what could have gone wrong; she insisted on speaking with him in person. The only time she had seen him since he had gotten shot was when he had traveled to Topeka, Kansas, to surprise her at her job at the health department. He wouldn't allow her to visit Amir's home; he simply did not want her associated with their lifestyle.

He peeked into the living room at everyone getting prepared to handle their business. He decided to leave out of the back door and return before it was time to depart. He was already parked in the alley in the rear of the house, so he simply walked out of the back door, locked it behind him, and made sure things looked normal around the house.

He checked his voicemail and saw that Monica had called again; he listened to her message and could recognize that something was wrong from the tone of her voice. He climbed into his Dodge Challenger and pulled his .45 caliber Smith and Wesson out of the glove compartment, making sure that the magazine was loaded as he strained his eyes to see into the darkness of the alley. He pulled off and was eventually on the highway driving toward Kansas; it began to dawn on him how out of character Monica's behavior was. He dialed her number. After a few rings she answered; she said that she had to discuss some things with him about their son. They had no children together.

When he made it to Metcalf in Johnson County, he decided to enter through the back door of his woman's home.

CHAPTER 79

Slim parked a street over from Monica's house and turned his cell-phone off as he gripped his weapon tightly. He entered the rear door quietly, and he noticed that the lights were off on the ground floor. He had been inside the home so many times that he maneuvered his way to the staircase leading to the top floor without hesitation.

When he made it upstairs, he noticed that a light was on in her bedroom and nowhere else. He pulled his weapon from his pocket and moved down the hallway cautiously.

When he reached Monica's bedroom door, he felt something press into the back of his neck; he knew instantly that he had made the mistake of dismissing the room directly opposite the master bedroom where his woman slept.

"I knew we was gonna find yo' bitch-ass sooner or later, Slim; you shouldn't have fucked wit' the beast, or my fuckin' family!"

Slim stiffened when he heard Oscar's voice, and he had no doubt that Monica was in serious trouble or probably already dead. Oscar hit him on the side of the head with something and Slim dropped his weapon to the floor as a wave of nausea overwhelmed him.

Slim was shoved roughly through Monica's bedroom door, and he could see Monica bound and gagged on her bed; her arms were taped to the bed posts.

A man Slim did not recognize unzipped his jeans and approached the bed with his penis in hand. He sprayed Monica in the face and all over her upper body with urine. He grinned at Slim as Monica attempted to scream in anger and frustration through her gag.

Slim howled in rage as he rushed toward the man, but he was cut down by a small caliber handgun that he hadn't seen in Oscar's hand.

"Let a bitch do what she gonna do, nigga! You too damn old to be playin' Captain Save a Hoe!"

The man standing next to the bed started laughing and Slim gripped his leg in pain, looking up at Oscar with hate burning in his eyes. Oscar had bloody bandages wrapped around his abdomen, and his right arm was in a sling. The man was attempting to hide his pain without being very convincing; he was clearly suffering from the fresh wounds.

There were three other men silently watching from the corner of the room, and it was obvious what Monica had been enduring. She was naked, and she had bite marks on her neck and chest. Her face was also red and swollen from the obvious beating she had endured. There was the smell of vaginal and anal sex in the air, and blood and feces stained the white sheets.

Slim looked down at where Monica's vagina had been and was sickened to see an open, bloody, burned out hole. A large pair of curling irons was on the floor next to the bed, still steaming from the burned flesh and blood that was covering it.

Monica was staring at Slim with a silent plea in her beautiful eyes, and Slim felt like killing everyone in the room, including Monica; he wanted to take her out of the misery she was experiencing. One of her arms appeared to be broken, and she was now constantly wailing- letting Slim know how much pain she was in. He turned angrily toward Oscar.

"Man, what do she have to do with any of this shit? She aint into nothin' we got goin' on!"

Oscar approached where Slim sat on the floor holding his bloody leg wounds.

"My brother didn't have nothin' to do with how you killed him either, you coward-ass nigga! Yeah, you was a big-ass man to shoot him in the damn back and leave him layin' there like a dog! Now, shut the fuck up cryin' for this nasty bitch! That pussy aint gonna be good fo' nothin' but takin' a piss now anyway; you still wanna fuck? I knew you was a damn trick, but damn, nigga!"

Slim still had his .44 caliber Desert Eagle in his shoulder holster under his jacket. When he had dropped his weapon after Oscar had shot him, they had assumed that he was unarmed.

Just when one of the men climbed onto the bed and straddled Monica's face for more fellatio, Slim made his move. He rolled away from where Oscar stood and pulled the pistol out swiftly. He felt a heavy weight hit his chest as he heard the loud crack from the weapon one of the men began to unload into his flesh.

Slim pulled his own trigger and was satisfied to see Oscar's ugly face disappear from the .44 caliber slug that passed through it and the two large holes that appeared in his chest. The last thing Slim saw was something he thought would never be welcome to his eyes. Several police officers entered the room with their weapons drawn and murder in their eyes. The other men in the room hurriedly dropped their weapons and raised their hands in cowardly surrender. Slim smiled and expelled his final breath.

CHAPTER 80

Ashely opened her eyes in confusion, looking around the filthy room while attempting to reach for her weapon.

"It's not there, Ms. Johnson." Dick pulled a cigarette from his pocket and put flame to it as he watched Ashely sit up groggily in the small bed. She was still wearing everything except her Kevlar vest and ski-mask. Once Dick saw her go down and everyone continued into the complex, he scooped her up in his arms and carried her to his vehicle. He rented a small motel room just off Van Brunt in Kansas City, Missouri, and laid her down while he rifled through her belongings; he was surprised to find her driver's license hidden in her bra. He had stared lustily at her beautiful body, but he quickly covered her, feeling like a perverted old man for his wicked thoughts.

Ashely stared hard at him and eventually recognized his face.

"You're the officer that was looking for Reese." Dick frowned and rose from his chair in anger.

"And you're the bitch that's playing both sides of the fence! If you don't tell me where he's hiding, you're dead!" Ashely smiled.

"I don't know where Reese is, so you might as well call your friends and get it over with. I have to inform you, though, that I'll be released, appearing to be a victim; do you realize that you kidnapped me when you transported me without my permission?" Dick moved forward and grabbed a handful of hair, and Ashely gave a small yelp of pain.

"Bitch, don't even attempt at your sarcasm with me! What I want to happen is at odds with what the system wants; I want that bastard dead and in a box! I don't give a flying fuck if you niggers kill each other in the streets, but that bastard murdered someone very special to me!" Ashely looked Dick over and he definitely appeared to be unhinged; there was foam in the corners of his twisted mouth. She was finally realizing how near the edge the detective had come in pursuit of Reese. He slowly eased his weapon from his holster and Ashely stiffened.

"I'm going to give you one last chance to tell me where that nigger is. If you don't cooperate, I'm going to toss your pea-shooter next to your dead body and put your bullet-proof vest back on you. They'll understand what happened to you when I give them a detailed story about your secret life of crime." When he placed his finger on the trigger and began to apply pressure, Ashely relented.

"I don't know where he is, but I can call him and have him meet with me somewhere. Give me a chance to call him." Dick pulled his cell-phone from his pocket and tossed it onto the bed.

"Tell him that you have to meet with him immediately. If you try to warn him, you die; it's as simple as that." Ashely picked up the cell-phone reluctantly; she was quickly thinking about how she could warn Reese without alerting the detective. She thought of something that would work and dialed her friend's number. He answered right after the first ring.

"Reese, I have to meet with you as soon as possible so that we can talk. Your mother called and said that your little sister didn't come home last night, and she needs to talk to you. I have to discuss something else with you also; can we meet so that we're not conducting business over the phone?" She listened to his response as well as his instructions on where to meet, and she knew that he had comprehended that she was in danger.

Reese's mother and baby sister had recently died in a violent manner, and she hated to open healing wounds, but she knew that her friend would understand the precarious situation that she was in. She disconnected the call and Dick snatched his cell-phone and pulled Ashely out of the bed where she was sitting.

"Come on! If something funny happens you're going to be the first to die!"

Ashely smiled inside because she knew that she wouldn't be the one dying. If the detective didn't have a weapon on her she would have attempted to claw his eyes out or crush his scrotum with something very heavy and preferably sharp.

Dick tossed her his keys and growled like a caged animal.

"It's the Crown Victoria. Drive straight there and be a good little girl for me. I don't have anything to lose anymore, so don't push me into a corner. All I want is the man who killed my partner."

Ashely nodded and walked out of the motel with the detective two steps behind; she realized that Reese was the man who had nothing to lose. She smiled again inside, knowing that Dick would die soon in a location that would be like poetic justice.

Chapter 81

Sheena walked into her husband's bedroom quietly, not knowing what mood Paris would be in when he heard about his father's death, but also knowing that he would need to know about the hit on Wayne Manor and his father's demise at the hands of Slim. She didn't see her husband at first, but she eventually spotted him in the corner of the room, silently sitting in his wheelchair as he stared out of their bedroom window.

She attempted to lighten her husband's dark mood.

"Hey, baby! I knew it wouldn't take long for you to be back at it. I should have known, though; my kitty cat's still throbbing from last night." Paris smiled and pushed his chair toward her, planting a kiss on his wife's mouth when she bent down.

"Sheen, what's wrong? I know you wouldn't be up this early if something wasn't wrong." Sheena lowered her head before responding.

"Peter and a lot of other people are dead, and most of the others are in jail. The police caught some of the Black Border Brothers who just hit Wayne Manor, and some of them are dead also." She paused before continuing. "Your father got killed too. He was found on the Kansas side. He killed Slim and they raped and tortured his girlfriend. The police caught the other homeboys that were there. I didn't want to be the one to tell you all of this, but I didn't want you to hear about it on the news or something."

Paris nodded with a forlorn look on his face.

"I appreciate you telling me, baby. It was only a matter of time for my pops, and I think we all knew it. Everything was personal with pops, and he didn't care about the consequences for him or anybody else. Baby, the man tried to kill his own nephew-his dead brother's son. He didn't have any boundaries; Oscar didn't care one way or another. All we can do is pray for his soul, baby. By the way, I'm sending you and Paris Jr. to your family in Oakland; there's no telling who Amir's going to hit next, but it won't be *my* damn family."

Sheena looked at her husband in astonishment.

"Are you crazy, nigga? If I'm leaving with Paris Jr., you're coming with us! What good will our son's life be if something happens to you? Just try making me, you hard-headed nigga!" She fled from the room with tears streaming down her face; Paris shook his head and reached for the telephone knowing that he would never understand women. He dialed the number in Kingston, Jamaica, and informed his connection about the things he had heard from his wife; he knew that Jamaican Tiger would be furious. The anger would not be because of the deaths of Peter and the other Jamaicans; the anger would be about the monetary losses because of the ongoing conflict. He listened to the man rage, trying to understand his words through his heavy Jamaican accent. Tiger announced that there would be no more drugs until the conflict with the Black Border Brothers came to an end and the loose ends were tied in a knot. Paris knew that this would be the kingpin's reaction, but he also thought that there would be threats of violence because of his brother Peter's demise.

Paris disconnected the call and contacted the people that were controlling his houses in Missouri. The message was the same for everyone: *We can't get money until we take care of these niggas, for good. Kill anyone associated with them, and it doesn't matter how it gets done!*

After he finished making calls and found out about his associates, he called one of the Jamaican houses in Kansas and was informed of the details of the hit. He also found out the names of the men who were with his father when he died. He planned on doing what he could for the men, but they didn't seem to have a way out of their situation. He headed into the living room to continue his conversation with Sheena and to visit with his son, knowing that he had to force them to leave before it was too late.

CHAPTER 82

Junebug tried not to show his nervousness as the highway patrolman sat in the Chevy Corvette behind him, no doubt running his license plate through the system. He was on I-35 on his way from Oklahoma, and he had two gallons of P.C.P. in the trunk of the rental car, on his way to Kansas City, Kansas. He was simply supposed to be picking his cousin Pete up from the hospital and to return to Oklahoma with him, but the temptation of making piles of money had been too great for him to play it safe. His freedom was now only a few steps from being taken away.

The officer stepped from the fancy vehicle and approached Junebug's window and ordered him to hand over his driver's license, insurance, and registration. Junebug readily complied with the officer's demands. He was surprised and relieved when the officer handed him the items back.

"One of your brake lights is out. I suggest that you pull off on the next exit, find an auto parts store, and replace the bulb before continuing to drive on this highway. Proceed in safety, sir."

The officer turned and walked back to his squad car and pulled away; Junebug was surprised to see a huge German Shepherd staring out of the back window; The man was a member of the K-9 Unit.

Junebug sat back for a moment and lit a cigarette before pulling onto the highway. He was trying to get his nerves under control while silently berating himself for his greedy decision to transport drugs from Oklahoma City. He had the drug disguised as something else inside of a large cooler in the trunk of the rental car, but he knew that experienced officers in Kansas City could figure things out and take him for a long ride.

He found an Autozone parts store in Ponca City, Oklahoma, and he welcomed their help in replacing the burned-out bulb before he continued his trip to Kansas City. He paid attention to all details along the road, being careful to remain anonymous. He knew that if he was caught, Amir would look out for his family while he was incarcerated, but he decided not to contact his friend if something happened. Junebug felt that he had put himself in the situation and he would be a man in dealing with it.

Junebug was a Crip, but his loyalty to Los and Amir was unmatched by anyone else he associated with. The organization was responsible for his recent successes in being acquitted for a capital murder that would have landed him on death row, and Oklahoma did not hesitate in carrying out their death sentences. Junebug was from Oklahoma City, Oklahoma, but he now resided in Tulsa, Oklahoma, with plenty of cash and control over a faction of the Black Border Brothers in the state. When he reached the suburbs of Johnson County in Kansas, he slowed to a fraction under the speed limit, knowing that racial profiling was alive and well in this city.

When he reached Wyandotte County, he headed straight for Arthur's house, knowing that his friend could make one call and the two gallons of P.C.P. would disappear before the day ended. As soon as he pulled in front of the house, he felt that something was wrong. There were flowers and stuffed animals all over the front lawn, and Arthur and Shonda's vehicles were missing from the driveway; the house appeared as if it were abandoned.

CHAPTER 83

Junebug dialed Amir's number to find out what was going on with Arthur, already expecting to hear something bad. When he was informed of Arthur's death, he couldn't believe his ears. Junebug, Pete, and Arthur had grown up like brothers, but Arthur was often the one that avoided trouble; he always handled his dirt in the dark. He listened patiently as Amir instructed him on what to do and where to go, and Junebug was forced to inform his friend about the drugs he had in his possession.

At this, Amir's voice took on a dangerous edge; Junebug was directed to a house that he was already familiar with. Amir even calmly told him not to worry about the sale; he would purchase the drugs himself. Junebug was aware that Amir didn't normally deal with P.C.P., but he didn't say anything else about it to Junebug; Amir realized that his friend had to get rid of the drugs before picking Pete up from the hospital. Junebug conversed with Amir for a few more minutes, offered his condolences, and informed him that he would contact him later. He knew that Amir was feeling the pain of Arthur's death more than anyone besides Shonda. Junebug wanted to be part of the retaliation that was sure to come, and he planned on discussing this fact with Amir and Los before returning to Oklahoma City. He was in Kansas City for a purpose, though, and he realized that when things settled down, he would have his opportunity.

When he pulled up to the house that Amir sent him to, the door opened immediately, so Junebug knew that he had been expected. He pulled the drugs from the trunk of the vehicle and handed them over; he drove away with a feeling of contentment and relief, satisfied that the drugs were no longer in his possession.

He called the hospital and was again surprised at how weak Pete's voice sounded. Junebug informed his cousin that he would be pulling up to the entrance of K.U. Medical Center in the next fifteen minutes so that Pete could be waiting for him in the lobby. He stopped at a gas station to buy some cigars for the K-Town marijuana he always purchased when he traveled to Kansas City, Kansas. He also made sure to purchase condoms; he was already thinking about how beautiful the women were in this part of the country.

When he arrived at the hospital he didn't recognize Pete initially. His cousin seemed to have lost at least twenty pounds. His arm was in a sling, and he moved like an elderly man. But, when Pete smiled, there was no mistaking that this man was Pete. When Junebug had heard the rumors that Pete had been cooperating with the police, he couldn't believe it. He felt that his cousin deserved to be given the benefit of the doubt.

They eventually exited the hospital and headed to Pete's house to collect some possessions that he would need; Junebug used the time as an opportunity to hear the truth.

"Cuz, people are saying that you on some 5K1 shit, homie. They said that you wasn't only snitching on strangers; they said that you said something about Amir and Los." The little dignity that Pete had left seemed to disappear as his shoulders slumped in defeat.

"Bug, I talked to Amir about this when he came to see me at the hospital. Things have been rough for me, and I can't be away from my kids for as long as they was talking about giving me. I didn't tell them anything they didn't already know, and the niggas probably would've done the same to me, you feel me?"

Junebug did not respond for a beat; he felt as if he was conversing with a stranger. When he spoke, he looked Pete straight in the eyes.

"I don't know what the fuck happened to you, and I don't give a fuck! I have a family and a lifestyle that I don't want to lose either, but we both knew the consequences when we got out here in these streets. You think it's cool to trade your life for Los or Amir's? They were the only niggas that looked out for you when your back was against the fuckin' wall! Naw peeps, I don't feel you at all, and that get down first shit you tryin' to use aint nothin' but another lame, rat-ass excuse. Let's just hurry up and grab yo' shit before them niggas change their minds and don't let you leave at all."

CHAPTER 84

Junebug pulled up in front of Pete's house and they walked up to the front door in silence; both men were occupied with their own thoughts.

Pete opened the front door and Junebug waited for him to deactivate the alarm system before following him inside. Pete walked into his bedroom to pack his belongings while Junebug headed into the kitchen for something to drink. Junebug gulped a Heineken on the way to the bedroom, tossed the bottle on the plush carpet, and slowly slipped a pair of latex gloves from his pocket and pulled them onto his shaking hands.

When Pete turned around to say something and noticed the gloves on his cousin's hands, he realized the reason Junebug had made the trip from Oklahoma.

Pete began backpedaling further into his room, but before he could get any distance between them, Junebug had his silenced .40 caliber Glock pointed at his head. Junebug shook his head sadly.

"Amir called me and said he wanted something done. When he told me what it was, I didn't look at it as a job. Killing a snitch like you will be my pleasure."

Pete's head exploded in a shower of brain matter, bone, and blood. After the smoke cleared, Junebug carved three B's into Pete's back with a switchblade, cut out his tongue, and shoved it into the back of his jeans. He took a little time to wipe down everything he had touched and climbed into the rental car that he planned on reporting stolen and driving into the Missouri river.

Junebug headed to Amir's house with a smile on his face, not regretting the decision to carry out the hit on his rat cousin, but he wondered how he would explain the violent death to the rest of his family. As a Black Border Brother, the number one rule was loyalty. Informing to the police was a one-way ticket to the graveyard, no matter who you were.

Junebug loaded his Brotha Lynch Hung album into the vehicle's system, and he listened to the stories of mass murder and mental illness, wishing that he would have had time to do more to his traitorous cousin's corpse.

CHAPTER 85

Ashely drove into the neighborhood known as Bell Crossing on the Kansas side of the border, and she felt as if she was in a time machine going in reverse when she visited the location. This had been a location for slaves to escape to, and some of the old, run-down shacks were still standing as a reminder of the past. The police avoided Bell Crossing if they could; many murders were committed in the area where the bodies sometimes were never found. Drug dealing was alive and thriving in the area. There were several new homes being built, and there were various expensive vehicles parked in front of some of the plantation-like dwellings.

She glanced over at Dick and noticed that he was shaking in anticipation; the corners of his mouth were turned up in a devilish grin. She pulled the vehicle in front of a large house that sat on several acres of land. She watched as Reese walked out of the home followed by Amir and Los, not missing the hardening of the detective's facial features.

Reese walked down the steps and approached the vehicle, but he stopped several feet away and simply stared at the crazed detective. Los and Amir strolled back into the house as if nothing out of the ordinary had occurred.

Dick suddenly grabbed Ashely by the neck.

"What the fuck is going on? Why is he just standing there like a fucking nigger statue? Tell him to come all the way to the car!"

Ashely snatched away from Dick and glared at him.

"It's over for you, cracker. You shouldn't have insisted on finding my friend."

Dick raised his weapon and began turning it toward Reese. His body jerked, and blood sprayed onto Ashely's face; she eventually heard the report from the high-powered rifle.

Dick dropped his weapon and stared down at the huge hole in his chest, attempting to breathe as blood filled his mouth and nostrils.

Los and Amir walked back outside followed by Amir's cousin, Kimani, holding the rifle that he had used to end the detective's suffering.

CHAPTER 86

The detective reeked of excrement as the corpse began to expel its interior contents. Ashely made a disgusted face before kicking the body and walking up to Los with a frown.

She glared at him. "You niggas could have done this shit another way!" She turned toward Reese. "You need to get out of town as soon as possible. This detective is going to be missed real soon, and you'll be number one on their hit list." Reese strolled over and draped his arms around her shoulders.

"You know I can't leave without you, baby-girl. I heard you got a nigga that don't know how to handle that pretty little pussy; you wanna go with me?"

Los walked up to him and smiled.

"I bet you couldn't even tickle that killer pussy, nigga! I remember when you were scared to get your little dick sucked. You need to concentrate on helping us get rid of this body and head back to Argentine before Pops finds out you're gone."

Kimani walked up with the rifle draped over his shoulder.

"We got some hogs at my place that haven't eaten in a week. They'll take care of everything but this white nigga's teeth, and we'll drop those rotten mothafuckas in Big Eleven Lake. Amir, you need to make sure this car gets out of here, though, and take the tags and melt them down or something."

Amir nodded and turned to Reese.

"Pops is expecting you to be at the youth center since it was your idea to have the hoop fest down there. The buses should be here today with the kids from California. Don't let those little boys get whipped by those kids from out of town, dawg. If they lose, Carlos Sr. will have a damn fit."

Reese nodded. "You niggas just make sure you keep an eye on those Italians. They claim they don't like drugs, but somebody gonna be upset; those bitches gonna lose a lot of money; I personally don't give a fuck!" He looked at Amir.

"You know I don't like fuckin' with those mothafuckas anyway, Meer. I don't care what those pale bitches think; talk to Frank and have him talk to his boss; we don't need them to get our shit in the city no more!"

Amir addressed Ashely. "Go clean yourself up, unless you want some type of disease. We'll talk about the Italians after we get rid of this shit over here." He motioned to the corpse that was now sweltering in the heat amidst a cloud of flies. "I have to find out what's going on with Country and Looney's bonds."

Ashely started walking to the house, but she turned around and addressed them all.

"We still have another detective to worry about. Keisha's been trying to work on him, but I may need to try something else; Galubski likes his meat dark."

Amir simply shook his head and turned to the vehicle while Los and Ashely continued to discuss plans in their twisted relationship with death.

CHAPTER 87

Lo-Lo stared down at Keith lying in the hospital bed, hoping that he would survive his more serious injuries. She had been injured also, but nothing was considered life-threatening, and she was already roaming the hallways for exercise. Lo-Lo had found out about Arthur's death by chance. She was simply being nosey and was pretending to know about the recent murders in the city. Lo-Lo was devastated by his death, and she was very upset by the news of Pete being an informant.

She viewed Amir as a good man, but she felt Pete would be foolish if he believed he would live. Amir had too much to lose to even consider allowing someone to be disloyal, and by all the events unfolding, she couldn't blame him.

She glanced down at Keith again and was surprised to see his eyes trained on her; he even had a small smile on his face.

"You have to move to Lawrence with me. I don't care what anyone thinks about that."

She nodded her head, and tears ran down her cheeks as she turned her head to listen to her boyfriend; Keith's voice was very weak.

"I know that your brother won't like it, but he'll have to live with the fact that you need to be with me. We've been through too much for me to allow anything or anyone to come between us, do you understand?" Lo-Lo nodded and put her arms around his neck, but Keith had already gone back to sleep.

CHAPTER 88

Keisha stood outside of the Kansas City, Kansas, Police Department wondering if Ashely had gone too far; she was having her meet Detective Galubski at his job, knowing that he was a married man. Ashely was waiting on the opposite side of the parking lot; she wanted her presence to be a shock.

Keisha watched the man walk out of the building, and she didn't miss the angry look on his face when he noticed her standing there. He started to walk past her as if she were a stranger, but he eventually turned and gripped her arm in anger and frustration. The detective practically growled into her ear.

"What in the fuck are you doing here?" Keisha smiled and backed away from the angry man before replying.

"I wanted to surprise you, baby! You've been distracted lately, and I wanted to treat you with something special; aren't you happy to see me, daddy?" She hated to pretend to be attracted to the overweight and very unattractive detective, but she was in a position where Ashely clearly held the cards.

Detective Galubski's face screwed up in anger.

"Look, bitch! You can surprise me anywhere but at my home or my fucking job! Do you think that I allow people to come to my place of work with bull-shit? Don't ever do this again, Keisha!" He grabbed her roughly by the arm and steered her toward the parking lot, and she felt his grip loosen as he stared at Ashely bent over into the trunk of her vehicle. She wore a skirt that rode all the way up to her curvy hips; there was a clear view of her vagina from behind because of the crotch-less panties she wore. Keisha walked over to her, squatted, and licked Ashely's vagina from behind, smiling as the woman moaned and grinded her sex into her face.

Detective Galubski approached and snatched Keisha to her feet. Her face was slick with Ashely's juices. He yelled in frustration.

"Don't do that out here for everyone to see; this is downtown, goddammit! Keisha, who is this woman?"

Keisha walked over to the passenger side of the vehicle and opened the door.

"This is the surprise I was telling you about, baby; I thought you'd appreciate a little chocolate with my cream. Do you like her?" The detective nodded, and Keisha glanced down at the obvious erection in his pants. Ashely spoke for the first time.

"Keisha told me how you be having her screaming and moaning; do you think you can handle the two of us? Never mind what you have to do today; follow us to the hotel by the airport and you can unwrap us like it's your birthday."

Galubski looked over Ashely's creamy skin, slanted eyes, and beautiful features, and he headed to his vehicle, making sure not to lose sight of the two women.

He climbed into his vehicle and immediately dialed the number to his house.

"Trish, I have a case to investigate. I'll be a little late tonight, so make sure the kids take out the trash and do their damn homework. I love you." He ended the call and followed the women to the highway ramp, knowing that they were headed to Missouri. He saw the turn signal light on the vehicle he was following close to the Main Street exit and he figured they were headed to Grand Slam Liquor Store. He began pulling into the parking lot behind them, but he decided to park on the street instead. There were many people mingling outside the store, and many men gravitated toward Keisha and Ashely as soon as they stepped from the vehicle. The detective smiled; he knew that he would soon have both beautiful women to himself.

Chapter 89

The two women entered the store, and when they exited their arms were filled with bags. Ashely waved her hand in a gesture for Detective Galubski to follow once they made it to the vehicle. He noticed that the two women completely ignored the ogling men, even though they flaunted money with their fancy vehicles and expensive jewelry. He thought to himself: *The bitches obviously have some class.*

He followed once again, and they eventually pulled into the hotel parking lot near the K.C.I. International Airport. Galubski watched Ashely hand her keys to the parking attendant, but he found his own place to park before strolling casually into the expansive lobby of the establishment. He spotted Keisha and she motioned him toward the elevator; she seemed to bypass the front desk completely.

This action put Galubski on alert, but he relaxed as soon as he spotted Ashely leaning against the elevator door. He felt that the woman looked like a mix between Halle Berry, Lucy Liu, and Beyonce. Every man's eyes always seemed to be turned in her direction. They rode the elevator up to one of the top floors, and the women ignored the detective while they made a show of tasting each other's flesh. This only heightened Galubski's arousal, giving him a gateway to fantasies he had not experienced in years. The women broke apart long enough for Ashely to swipe her card across the scanner on the door for them to enter; the detective was astonished to see what was in the room. There were various sexual toys, lubricants, and devices all over the room. There were dildos, chains, handcuffs, whips, gags; every type of sexual device imaginable was there.

Galubski was pulled to a chair beside the bed, strapped to it and gagged. The two women removed their clothing and had sex with each other in ways that amazed him.

Ashely glimpsed the detective's small penis straining against his slacks and barely restrained a giggle. Instead, she walked over and removed his restraints; Galubski immediately dropped to his knees and began lapping up her juices. Ashely was disgusted by how the man behaved. Saliva was dripping down her legs; the disgusting man seemed to be attempting to suck her clitoris off her vagina. She pulled him to his feet and forced him onto the bed as Keisha began stripping him of his clothing while devouring his miniscule penis.

Ashely walked over beside the bed and opened a dresser drawer, removing a long strand of beads and a huge black dildo. Galubski jumped to his feet when Keisha walked behind him after retrieving the toys from her sex partner.

"No way, baby. I'm not into any of that queer shit! Let's just have fun and fuck instead of playing all of these games."

Ashely frowned at him.

"If you don't like playing with me, why would I allow you to do anything to me? Does that make any sense to you?" Both women knew that the man would do anything at this point. He visibly relented before he spoke, and Ashely was disgusted by the next words he uttered.

"Just take it easy, okay? I've never done anything like this before."

While Keisha went back to administering fellatio on the man, Ashely approached, grabbed the beads and huge dildo from Keisha, and began to slowly push the beads into detective Galubski's rectum. She also attempted to push in the tip of the huge dildo. The man began panting and grunting as a sickening scent engulfed the small room. Ashely eventually tossed the sexual toys to the floor slick with blood and feces. Detective Galubski suddenly collapsed to his stomach while clutching his large stomach.

Ashely looked at him in exasperation, but she spoke soothingly to the man.

"Just take it easy and get cleaned up. I'm going to let you ram your big dick up my pussy until I can't close my legs." She lay down on her back next to him and spread her legs; Galubski embarrassingly shuffled to the bathroom with waste and blood running down the back of his chubby thighs.

CHAPTER 90

As soon as Ashely heard the water running, she trotted over and glanced inside. When she saw that he was inside of the shower, she rushed up and grabbed Keisha roughly by the arm.

"Get everything ready! Hurry up!" Keisha received bottles of liquor from her bag and placed them on the bedside table while Ashely pulled the mixture of rat poison and crushed cyanide pills from her small Michael Kors purse as she yelled into the restroom.

"Do you prefer cognac, brandy, or vodka in your glass?"

When she heard his response, she instructed Keisha to pour three glasses of Martel cognac.

Ashely realized that it would look strange for her and Keisha to be drinking something different, so they topped off their glasses with the same bottle; Ashely poured her concoction into the detective's glass before he returned to the room.

When he stepped out, Ashely could barely contain her laughter when she saw that Galubski's penis had shriveled up to the size of a Vienna sausage. Ashely's nipples were stiff from the cold air in the room, but the detective thought that she was aroused by him.

He grinned wolfishly.

"Don't worry, baby, after we have these drinks, you're going to be getting plenty of this meat." Keisha walked up behind him and draped her arms over his shoulders.

"Let's just have a drink and get back to sucking and fucking!" Keisha didn't notice that Galubski had switched glasses with her; the detective assumed that his drink had been laced with some type of tranquilizer so that he could be robbed as he slept. He leaned forward and pulled one of Ashely's nipples into his mouth.

"Let us all drink to pussy, and all of the trouble that comes with it!"

They all lifted their glasses and took long gulps of the liquor. It wasn't long before Keisha began blinking rapidly and was clawing at her throat.

Detective Galubski laughed.

"That shit tastes funny, right bitch? Yeah, *you're* the one that's going to get taken advantage of while you sleep! I don't want your little money; I'm going to stick my dick in your tight little white ass-hole and try to shoot my seed out of your filthy mouth!"

When he saw the vessels burst in Keisha's eyes, and the filth streaming from her mouth, he finally realized what the two women had attempted to do to him. He looked around frantically for his pants where he knew his cell-phone was located, spotted them, and made a dash toward them in order to call paramedics while Ashely calmly pulled her red dress over her head.

After he dialed 911, Galubski looked up and saw the bedroom door closing, but when he ran into the living area, Ashely was long gone.

After the detective spoke with the dispatcher and gave him the information, he pulled on his clothes, already forming a story in his mind for why he was present inside of the hotel where he had possibly witnessed a young woman's death.

He looked around at the sex toys and glanced down at the bed that was covered with his blood and excrement. He went to work in erasing himself from the scene, knowing that he must find the evil woman that had attempted to take his life.

CHAPTER 91

Amir, Los, and Reese stood outside one of the buses that had arrived, watching the young kids stretch their legs after the long trip from California; they all seemed eager to hit the basketball courts. Carlos Sr. had organized the youth events, but Reese had come up with the idea to bring something positive to the most needed parts of the city.

The Border Brothers who had traveled to Kansas City, Kansas, were speaking with Carlos Sr. and his two brothers, Jorge and Felix. They were standing next to one of the buses while smoking marijuana and considering the near future.

Amir turned to Reese after releasing a mouthful of smoke into the air.

"We need to get you away from here before you get caught up in the middle of this drama." Reese reached for the blunt and took a puff before responding.

"How shit is going right now, you niggas might *need* me around to sleep some more of those M.O.P. mothafuckas. They ain't hella deep, but they ain't duckin' either. We gonna have to smash them niggas all the way out for this shit to be over. At least we don't have to worry about fuckin' with those Italians no more; If you niggas keep fuckin with me we can take over the damn Bottoms. Fuck those pale mothafuckas!"

Los frowned. "What is this lame-ass plan you came up with to bring the dope into the city? I keep hearing about the shit getting' here another way, but it's just a damn rumor until we can get back in the lab to get this bread." Reese smiled and leaned back onto the bus.

"The shit is already here, my nig. When Carlos Sr. gets finished taking care of business, I'll show you that my words were backed up before they came across these playa-ass lips!" They all laughed and continued to smoke and relax while they watched the young basketball team mingling with the young girls in the neighborhood.

Carlos Sr. and another man walked over to them laughing and patting each other on the backs; two older men ignored them and walked onto the bus. Reese rushed in right behind them while Amir and Reese looked at each other in confusion.

Amir walked up the steps of the bus and could see Reese and the two strangers squatted on the floor in the rear of the bus. Carlos Sr. appeared, standing in the aisle watching them while smoking a cigar.

When Reese rose to his feet holding two plastic-wrapped bundles, Amir and Los understood. The sporting events were going to be the method to bring the drugs into the city inside the buses. It was a plan they had never considered, and it was very risky, but they all knew that it would be doubtful that anyone would suspect anything.

Reese tossed one of the packages he was holding to Los and walked toward them with a huge grin on his face.

"I told you niggas a long time ago that we didn't need those spaghetti eating Italians. We already be giving those mothafuckas our gambling money, but they won't get another dime off our dope!" Amir draped an arm across Reese's shoulders as they stepped off the bus.

"Reese, you know that Carlos Sr. and the rest of the Border Brothers are going to appreciate this and so do we. If you didn't have this bull-shit hanging over your head, I'd make sure that you get rich just by being around to secure the drops. Anyway, we're still going to make sure you're set up to live comfortably, regardless, but we need you away from here for now."

Chapter 92

Carlos Sr. was talking into his cell-phone as he and the other men exited the bus.

"Jorge! Get everyone down here to start unloading this shit. Yes, everything looks fine. We need to get this done immediately." He shook his head in exasperation before continuing. "Leave the bitch there for all I care! You need to get your fucking priorities in order, carnal!" He ended the connection and angrily pushed the cell-phone into his pocket.

"That's my brother; he's always thinking from between his legs. You boys always remember that the vagina always comes easiest to the man that handles his business first and comes home with loaded pockets." They all nodded their heads and Amir spoke to Carlos Sr.

"Sir, I'm going to set up a meeting with Frank sometime next week to discuss our parting ways. The border has always benefitted us because of certain situations, but we will not give away our cash for something we no longer need. Frank is the only Italian I have dealt with that is reasonable and has a level head, so I'll explain everything to him, and we can prepare to get this money without having to pay an unnecessary expense."

Carlos Sr. nodded, and Jorge walked up with a group of men to retrieve the drugs from the various locations inside the buses; they were told to store everything inside a nearby van for transport to the safehouses.

Amir started heading to his vehicle, but he remembered something important and turned to Los.

"Bro, we have to get together soon. I have something to tell you; it is very important and you're definitely the first one I want to know about it." He turned toward his other friend.

"Reese, you need to keep a low profile until it's time for you to leave. We can't risk your freedom or ours with any more of this drama; you're too important to us for that." Reese smiled crookedly.

"I appreciate it, dawg, but if them M.O. P. niggas get out there, I'm gonna be the first one to straighten them out. It's best just to kill em' all so we don't have to look over our damn shoulders. Just call a nigga like me when you feel it's a good day for them niggas to die; you know I'm those niggas' worst nightmare."

They all laughed while Carlos Sr. and the other men stared in confusion. Reese and Los performed their personal handshake, but Amir stared at them with a hard expression when they were finished. Reese looked at his friend and turned serious before speaking.

"Alright, dawg, I feel you on that. Anyway, you niggas need to remember this shit when you hit my line to straighten those fools out."

Amir simply turned and walked to his vehicle without saying another word, knowing that Mecca would be upset because he had been purposely ignoring her calls. He knew that she probably wanted something important, but he had to handle his business in the streets first. He made it a point not to intermingle his family life with what he was doing in the streets. As beautiful as Mecca was, Amir still couldn't alter that rule for her or anyone else.

CHAPTER 93

Mecca stared out in fear at the vehicles sitting in front of her house. She wondered who the people were, and she was frustrated that Amir was not answering or returning her calls. There were two white men standing on her porch, and when she asked them what they wanted through the window, they simply stated that they needed to speak with Amir. That was the only reason she hadn't called the police right then. There were also two white men smoking cigarettes while sitting on a government-looking vehicle and two other men were conversing with each other on the sidewalk. Mecca couldn't understand what these people wanted, but she doubted that anything positive would come from their presence.

Since she had been calling Amir, some of the people had been openly drinking beer and other alcohol and casually throwing the empty bottles on her lawn as they stared aggressively toward the house. One of the men even urinated onto her roses in plain view and turned to shake his penis, grinning at her as she turned her head in disgust and shock. Mecca held one of Amir's pistols in her hand now, not knowing what the men wanted, hoping that Amir would at least call her back. Just when she dialed his number for what seemed like the hundredth time, she spotted his GMC Denali. Amir soon appeared, approaching the small group with a brandished firearm in his hand. Mecca thanked God that nothing had happened to her and their baby, and she cursed Amir for once again allowing his street life to intrude into her security. She placed her hand on her swollen stomach and felt a slight kick; she smiled and headed to the shower because she knew that Amir could handle himself. She glanced out of the window on the way, though, pondering her sister's last warning to her about Amir; she prayed that her man would prove everyone wrong.

CHAPTER 94

Amir noticed people and vehicles in front of his home and immediately gripped his 9mm Beretta as he pulled into the driveway. He instantly regretted not answering Mecca's calls all day; he felt he should have known something was wrong, but Mecca's pregnancy had made her very unpredictable lately and she had been calling him with irritating and unreasonable requests.

The Italians were lounging around his home as if they owned it; Amir felt a burning anger, but he refused to allow it to control the situation. He parked and stepped out of his vehicle with his weapon at his side; he noticed Mecca looking out of one of the windows before quickly disappearing from sight.

Amir recognized one of the Italians from their meetings in the Bottoms. He was staring at Amir with an angry expression, not bothering to conceal the weapon pushed into the front of his slacks. Amir approached the man and spoke in a slow, measured tone.

"What the fuck are you white-niggas doing hanging around my home, and who told you pale mothafuckas where I live?" Amir rarely used profanity or lapsed into Ebonics, but he was very upset at the intrusion into his personal space.

The white man's lips turned up into a crooked smile that failed to reach his eyes, but he didn't utter anything in response. Another man that Amir recognized approached and pushed the other man toward the small fleet of vehicles that was parked on the street. He spoke toward the man's back as he retreated.

"Julius, this is definitely not the time to play games. Get your ass out of sight while I speak with this young man." Amir ignored the man and turned toward his house.

"If you have something to say to me, you can catch me out in traffic. If you fucking crackers come anywhere near my home again, you're going to find out exactly what I'm made of." The man looked unconcerned at his statement.

"Amir, you disappoint me. You're standing in front of a nice home that I'm sure you own, you're driving a nice car, but your language is akin to any other nigger that chooses to be glued to the ghetto. I appreciate the other version of you; I respect the man who exudes confidence and quiet authority. I can recall you speaking as a gentleman, even to those you perceived as your enemies. Most of all, we respect the people who stay in line. This message is from the top of the food chain." He looked Amir in the eyes before continuing. "Boy". He smiled at Amir's expression. "If we don't profit from the drugs, there will be none. We've received word that you are losing interest in our agreement. We are the reason you are able to live as you do; you should be more grateful."

Amir walked up to the man and weapons began appearing in hands, but the man waved his goons off. Amir growled his response.

"We do what we want with our personal space and our money; you need not concern yourselves with either. I'll get with Frank and the two of us can discuss this situation like adults; you've just caused unnecessary friction by coming to my home and disrespecting my family." The man waved a hand in dismissal.

"This message came directly from Frank, nigger, and he wants you to know that the nice act is over! He wants you to meet with him at the Argosy Casino tomorrow night at seven. This will be your only chance to come to some type of understanding with us; if we come again it will be at night-with hostility." Amir looked at the man and smiled with confidence.

"If you come to my house again, I promise that your *hostile* ass will never leave."

He walked to his house with his weapon still hanging at his side, completely ignoring the group of men. They followed his movements with mean glares. This was something that caught Amir completely off guard. Frank had always been the one who was easy to deal with; it didn't take much for Amir to realize that it had been an act. He knew that he had to talk Mecca into leaving before it was too late; the Italians had located his home too easily and it was obvious that he was being watched; he had just recently moved into his new home.

He pulled his cell-phone from his pocket and dialed Los's number, knowing that it was time for him to know about Mecca and the child they were expecting. He also wanted his friend to know about his desire to leave the game- for good.

CHAPTER 95

Ashely strolled toward the jury box with confidence, not caring if her client was a guilty man or not.

"Ladies and gentlemen, my client is going through what many other minorities residing in this state have been going through for centuries; Mr. Davis is the victim of racial profiling and mitigating circumstances often associated with systemic racism. This man lives in the inner-city, but he owns his very own business in real estate. Mr. Davis is the sole owner of his home, several vehicles, and he chooses to wear diamond jewelry from the fruits of his hard work. From this combination of facts alone, there has arisen the assumption that Mr. Davis is a drug dealer or some other type of criminal. If my client were not a minority, people would look at his vehicles and other possessions and assume that he had been thriving from his intelligence or from hard work. Mr. Davis has ties to California and Mexico, so he has been categorized as nothing more than a mule or low-level drug…."

Ashely heard a commotion behind her and turned to a sea of blue just inside of the double doors of the courtroom. Police officers moved swiftly to bar all exits, and others approached the front of the room with detective Galubski in the lead. He approached Ashely with a frown.

"Don't believe a word that this so-called woman says. She is one of the key figures in a dangerous gang of thugs who infest this city with illegal drugs every single day. I'm sure most of you have heard of the

Black Border Brothers. She is directly connected to this group and is romantically involved with one of the leaders. She has been paid with very dirty money to defend this man who often launders large amounts of currency for them, and Ms. Johnson is actually responsible for the dirtier work that these people rely on to strike fear into the hearts of residents in the metro area." The jury members and every other individual in the courtroom stared in shock as Ashely was slammed against the Judge's bench by Detective Galubski as he yelled into her ear.

"You are under arrest for the murder of Ms. Keisha Flowers, and you are also under arrest for the attempted murder of a Kansas City, Kansas, detective: Me!" He roughly handed Ashely off to another officer and turned to the judge.

"I apologize for disrupting your courtroom, sir, but the immediate arrest of this woman could not be delayed. She looks innocent and is very beautiful, but Ms. Johnson is a seductress and a remorseless killer." Ashely began laughing as another officer gripped her handcuffed arms. Everyone turned in Ashely's direction as she screamed.

"Who do you *really* work for, detective? The Italians in this city own your sorry ass! You're the one that handed Keisha that glass. By the way, did you tell your wife how I squeezed that dildo up your funky, pale ass and made you shit yourself? No? Tell them every....."

She was pulled from the courtroom and Galubski instantly regretted opening his mouth and allowing Ashely to have a chance to speak. He already knew that he had been suspected by many for having ties to organized crime, and he had given Ashely the opportunity to bring all of the questions about him back to the surface.

He followed the other officers out of the courtroom and rushed to report to Frank; the Italians were the organization that Galubski reported to daily.

CHAPTER 96

Los finished talking to one of his workers and headed to the Argentine area to visit his son before he made his way to the address Amir had given him. His friend said that he wanted to speak with him in person about something important; Los didn't understand why Amir was being so secretive. Amir had told him about the confrontation he had had with the Italians, so Los knew better than to take the meeting with his best friend lightly. First, though, Los knew that he must see about his son and make sure that the boy's drug addicted mother was not shirking her end of the parental responsibilities.

He pulled up in front of the small two-bedroom house he had purchased and frowned at the beat-up Dodge Intrepid in the driveway; he knew that there was trash strewn throughout the woman's vehicle. If his son's mother didn't straighten up her act soon, he knew he would have to appeal to his mother or one of his many other female family members to fight for custody of Miguel.

He had to admit to himself, though, that even though Roslyn had obvious drug habits, she sacrificed a lot for their small son, and she seemed to make sure that he was happy and cared for.

Los noticed early on that his son was unwilling to speak and had a speech impediment. The boy had needed special education, and Los had concluded that Miguel's beautiful, drug abusing mother was to blame. Los kept these thoughts to himself most of the time, and he always treated his son as if there was no problem while his hatred for Roslyn simmered under the surface because of what he suspected. Miguel was doing well now, though, and the problems seemed to have retreated into non-existence.

He used his key to enter the house and smiled when he saw his son sitting on the living room floor, engrossed in some video game with a huge bowl of cereal next to him. Miguel looked up and smiled when his father sat down next to him.

"Hi, daddy, what are you doing here?" Los playfully grabbed his son around his small shoulders.

"This is still my house, little man. I'm still welcome here, right?"

Miguel giggled. "You're welcome here, daddy, but Tony acts like this is his house now that he's here all of the time." Los frowned down at his smiling son.

"Who is Tony?" Miguel had turned his attention back to his video game, but he looked up long enough to point his small finger toward the back of the house where the den was located.

Los knew that this was a place where Roslyn retreated to indulge in her drug habits and to spend personal time away from Miguel's inquisitive eyes. He patted his son on the head and made his way down the hallway, knowing that he had to reprimand Roslyn for her trifling ways. He could hear soft music playing and was surprised to find the door wide open. There was the unmistakable scent of sex in the air, so Los hurried to look into the small room.

CHAPTER 97

He couldn't believe his eyes at first as he squinted into the semi-darkness. Roslyn was sprawled atop a man in the 69 position with no clothes on; the man's penis was still inside of her mouth as the couple snored. He looked down between her legs and was sickened when he saw a string of a tampon hanging from her bloody vagina. Blood was also dried up on the man's hair and on what little of his face that could be seen. Los couldn't believe that Roslyn would be in this compromising position with the door open for his son to see. He glanced at the table in front of the couch that they lay on and spotted two crack pipes and a small pile of marijuana next to a plate that had two lines of powder on it- along with a rolled-up bill. He moved forward and snatched Roslyn awake by a handful of her long hair, satisfied as she screamed in pain.

"Ow! Stop! What the fuck?" She went mute when she noticed that Los was the one holding her. She looked around fearfully, remembering Tony's presence through the fogginess of the drugs. Her eyes widened in fear.

"Los, baby, it's not what you think. He's my man!" Tony slid from under her as he awoke, noticing another presence in the room. Los finally got a good look at his face.

"Tony? What the fuck is up with you, nigga? You a dope fiend just like this raggedy bitch? You're disrespecting my son like this up in my fuckin' house?" Tony hastily fumbled on his jeans and shirt.

"It's not like that, Los! The door was shut when we started, man! I don't know what happened! I wouldn't do nothin' that stupid, my nig, and I didn't even plan on being here this long, I swear!"

Los stared at Amir's cousin hard.

"I don't care how long you was planning on staying here, bitch nigga! Do that dope got you so fucked up that you forgot about the damn rules? There aint enough crackhead bitches around that you gotta be in here suckin' my ex's bloody, funky-ass pussy?" With his last word he slapped Roslyn so hard with his open palm that her eyes rolled back, and her jaw audibly snapped. She put her hands to her face and wailed, but when she noticed the weapon in Los's hand, she went silent immediately.

Tony rushed over and kneeled next to her and inspected her face, careful not to give Los the impression that he was being aggressive in any way.

Los glared at him.

"You better be glad that my son is in this house, or I'd kill you and this funky bitch. You shouldn't have come here and disrespected my son." He shook his head sadly before continuing. "I guess if you really care about this tramp you can help her find a place to stay; she's getting the fuck up out of here!" He shoved his weapon into his pocket, ignoring the couple while he headed to his son's room and began packing up some of his clothes and toys.

Miguel rushed into his small bedroom.

"Daddy, did you beat him up? I know you did!" Miguel ran around his room shadowboxing, and Los had to patiently calm him down.

"No, I didn't beat him up; why would I do that? Your mother can have a man; it just shouldn't be a man that I know or that's connected to me, and they should be more careful when you're in the house. Now, help me pack up some of your stuff so you can go see your grandfather and maw-maw." Tears began to well up in the boy's eyes as he looked up at his father.

"Is my mom coming with us? What about my mom?"

Los knew that this was coming, but he did not know how to respond; Miguel loved his mother and would be concerned for her. Los pulled his small son into an embrace.

"You're going to be seeing your mother, little man. You're just going to stay with my mother for a little while until me and Roslyn work some things out. Don't you want to visit with Mona?"

Miguel's face brightened immediately when Los mentioned his aunt's name. She spoiled her nephew every time she got the chance, which was rare. Los wiped tears from Miguel's eyes, seeing the mixture of the Spanish and African ancestry deep in his dark features.

"Mona moved close to your maw-maw's house, so you should be able to see her all of the time." Los could see the skepticism on his son's face, knowing that he wouldn't trade life with his mother even to visit with Mona. Miguel started packing his belongings, though, and the tears had already dried on his face. Los looked down at him again.

"Stay here."

He went toward the back room in search of Roslyn. He found her in the kitchen with a bag of ice against her face, and he noticed that Tony was nowhere in sight. She stared daggers at him, but he ignored the look and placed a hand on her face, confirming that her jaw was broken. He shook his head sadly before speaking.

"I'm taking Miguel with me. When you check into a treatment center and get yourself together you can move back in here with my son. Until that time comes, tell that nigga Tony to find you a place to stay; you're that bitch-ass nigga's responsibility now. Dial 911 when I leave so you can get your mouth taken care of. You have one week to get your raggedy shit out of here before I change the locks.

Roslyn attempted to protest, but she couldn't move her jaw in order to speak. She began to rise with her fingernails extended to scratch, but Los stopped her with a penetrating stare that she was familiar with; she sat back down before something much worse befell her.

Los silently walked back to Miguel's room and started moving his possessions to his vehicle, leading his son outside, and hoping that Roslyn didn't appear; that would only make matters worse. He noticed his son looking around, no doubt hoping to catch a glimpse of his mother, but she stayed out of sight.

As Los drove away, Miguel was silently shedding tears again, and Los was tempted to turn around and take him back to his mother. Ultimately, he realized that this form of tough love was necessary in caring for his child. He strapped Miguel into his car seat and headed to drop him off before traveling to the address Amir had given him. He wondered if Amir knew about Tony's treachery, feeling his anger begin to rise once again.

Chapter 98

Looney and Country sat at the table playing cards, waiting for Lunatic, to come back and announce the names of the three men that had just entered the jail "pod". They had been extradited to the Wyandotte County Detention Center in Kansas City, Kansas, for their previous warrants, and they were calculatingly stalking the men who had gotten caught in the act of killing Slim and torturing Monica.

Looney and his friends were like ghetto celebrities inside the jail because of their ties to the Black Border Brothers and their notoriety in the streets. Looney had already flooded their living quarters with liquor and drugs, and he also had female officers they indulged in to make incarceration more bearable.

Lunatic approached with the inmates' names that were housed in the maximum-security wing where they were located; they all sat around a metal table and scrutinized the last three additions on the document.

Country gazed into the glass-walled gym and his eyes smoldered.

"Them niggas won't even make it to court for this shit. They killed my relative and fucked up his bitch for them hoe-made M.O.P. niggas for some petty cash, and now we gotta make change!"

Lunatic gripped his arm to stop him before he could rise out of his seat; he didn't want the three men unwittingly warned before they could accomplish their goal. He calmly spoke to Country.

"My nig, let me holla at my people so they'll stay out of the way. I don't want them to think some gang shit's going down and try to come to them niggas' rescue."

Many of the people in the "pod" were Bloods, but the three new arrivals, Lunatic and many others were Crips. But, when it came to Black Border Brother business, those differences ceased to be an issue.

Looney went and spoke with the officer in charge and was admitted inside the gym with an audible click from the large lock on the door, knowing that everyone else would follow once their contraband was destroyed as he had instructed.

They watched Lunatic make his circuit around the living area, pulling people to the side and watching them closely until they had retreated to their cells. Looney was next in line to pick a team for the next basketball game.

Country and O.G. entered the gym and stood next to the rear wall and Lunatic followed, making sure the lock engaged fully after he entered.

There were also a few other men that worked for Amir and Los from time to time standing off to the side watching the game. O.G. approached their allies and nodded to them silently, satisfied at their crooked smiles and confident that they understood that something was about to go down.

When the game they had been watching ended, Looney grabbed the basketball and attempted a long-range shot and missed the hoop completely. The three newcomers glanced at each other and grinned; they suspected that they had an easy mark lined up.

Looney pointed out Country and O.G. when he was told to produce his team; the trio's smiles disappeared when they saw how huge Country was. Looney tossed one of their targets the basketball and smiled.

They were playing their game when one of the men screamed in pain. Country pulled the blade out of the man's back and grinned at the look of horror on his face. He began savagely stabbing the man and noticed Lunatic and Looney doing the same to the two other men as others blocked the window from the guard's view. There were often large groups of men in the gym daily, so the young officer didn't even glance in that direction; they had moved the three men to a blind spot where the cameras did not reach.

The man that Country had stabbed was on the floor in a puddle of his own blood, crying and begging for his life while witnessing the brutalization of his two friends. When the man saw that his pleading was to no avail, he shakily rose to his feet in a final attempt to fight back or possibly reach the door.

Country grabbed the man around the neck and plunged the thin blade into his stomach repeatedly. When the man's legs gave out and he fell onto his back, Country drove the blade into his right eye socket; he smiled in satisfaction as he watched the man's death throes and final shuddering breath.

The bodies were pulled into a corner of the gym; men began trickling out and headed for the televisions and game tables.

When one of the daily lockdowns was called, everyone went straight to their cells without hesitation.

The officer was amazed by this, and he smiled as he made his circuit of the area-until he discovered what was left for him inside of the gym.

CHAPTER 99

Looney stared out of his small window and watched the guard run out of the gym and vomit, before frantically pushing the panic button on his radio.

When several officers stormed the pod and the police were eventually called in, the tape to the cameras was being viewed by all of them on a monitor that they brought with them. The seasoned criminals knew that all they would see was who had entered and exited the gym.

Lunatic, Country, and Looney knew that they would be questioned, especially considering the murder cases they were already facing. They also knew that not a word would be spoken of the incident to anyone in law enforcement.

For the next couple of hours, the jail was locked down and word was passed around that if anyone cooperated with law enforcement, they would be visited by both Border Brother organizations. Everyone knew that if they became informants for law enforcement, their lives would end in horrible ways in or outside of incarceration.

Intercoms were inside every cell, and the inmates had learned to manipulate them to communicate throughout the jail, using items as simple as rolls of toilet paper. Word spread fast about the killings, and everyone knew that the threat from the Black Border Brothers was real.

CHAPTER 100

When Looney and his comrades were finally called, they were taken to separate rooms. Detective Galubski was in a room waiting for Looney, and the head of classification inside the detention center was also present. Both men were very familiar with Looney from cases he had fought in the past. The other man pulled on his handlebar mustache while Detective Galubski asked questions and carefully recorded the responses.

Suddenly the head of classification for the detention centre rose to his feet and moved forward.

"I know you and the other Bloods in here performed those killings, and I hope the Crips will be waiting for you when you reach prison. I honestly pray they do you exactly how you did those men in that gym." It was then that Looney was convinced that they didn't have any evidence, but he couldn't refrain from responding.

"You know the type of mothafuckas me and my relatives are; all niggas will be waiting for is to get fucked off, and you know that shit! Just take me back to the pod so I can call my damn lawyer. The next time you come, I guess I'll be getting ready for that ride to Lansing or Hutch cause' I don't know a damn thing."

Detective Galubski stood and approached Looney after slamming his chair into the wall.

"You punk-ass son-of-a bitches will be going down this time; I don't care how much money you black bastards have! Your so-called lawyer-bitch, Ashely, will be going away for a long time. It's only a matter of time for you and your home-boys; your trials won't take very long at all!" Spittle began spraying from his mouth, and his face had turned beet-red.

The other man began speaking in a condescending tone to Detective Galubski while staring hard at Looney.

"We know we will convict them, so don't waste your breath. By this afternoon, these fools will be charged with three counts of first-degree murder on top of the murder charges they are already facing in Missouri." He turned and tapped on the door they had entered. A deputy walked in and the man addressed him with a sharp tone.

"Take him back to his cell and bring the next one in."

Looney glared at the two men on the way out; when the door closed behind him the detective spoke.

"We don't have shit! If the others don't admit to anything, we won't be able to accuse them with anything more than jacking their fucking dicks at night!"

Mr. Garnier, the head of classification, had been working at the jail since Looney had first arrived as a teen; he had been tried as an adult at a very early age. He knew that Looney and his friends would never fold. The only way to charge them was by finding an informant inside of the pod that had witnessed the incident. Mr. Garnier wasn't confident that they would be successful, though. If any potential informants inside the Wyandotte County Detention Center valued their lives, they would remain silent. Looney and his friends did not have anything to lose, and they had proven that they would go to extremes to make sure that their word was the law inside correctional institutions and in the streets.

CHAPTER 101

Amir ended the call with his mother's counselor at the mental health facility feeling better than he had in weeks. His mother's condition seemed to be improving, and the counselor explained to him that Candace had been in shock; she had used the past as a refuge from the circumstances of the present.

It still surprised Amir that Mark was a psychiatrist for a major medical facility, and that he was a brother of his cousin, Mate. Amir's cousin was the perfect example of a "black sheep". He was the youngest in his immediate family, and he was the only one that had been completely engrossed into inner-city life. When he looked at Mark, the resemblance was unmistakable, but that seemed to be the only link between the brothers. Mate was a man to be reckoned with in the streets, and he was the head of a team of killers that he controlled by loyalty and respect alone.

Amir wished that his cousin was around to make things easier. Another loyal person in the city would be an advantage that would certainly lead to victory. Mate would be released soon, though, and his absence may be for the best, considering the circumstances they were facing.

Mecca entered the room with a jar of cocoa butter in her hand, sitting on his lap and kissing him tenderly on the forehead before speaking.

"Will you rub some of this on my stomach, baby? I love how it feels when you rub me." Amir rubbed between his legs with a scowl on his face.

"I'll do anything for you, Mecca, as long as you don't drop your heavy-ass on my nuts again! Damn, that ass is getting plump!"

Mecca grabbed him around the neck playfully. "If it wasn't for you and your nasty sex-drive I wouldn't be in this position, but I must admit, it was fun getting here."

Amir kissed her and wrapped his arms around Mecca's waist with affection. He felt that she was an extension of himself; her smallest gestures often made him melt inside.

Amir put a movie on, and they watched it while he carefully rubbed cocoa butter onto her stomach. He felt his cell-phone vibrating in his pocket and remembered that Los was supposed to be on his way. Amir finally wanted his best friend to know about the woman he planned on marrying. He looked at the screen on his phone, and he saw that it was indeed Los calling. He motioned to Mecca's nightgown, satisfied when she disappeared from the room to get dressed.

He answered. "What's going on, Los?"

"I think I'm outside your house; you could've left your car out so I wouldn't have to be guessing and shit!"

Amir ignored Los's sour attitude, not knowing what his friend was irritated about, but he didn't want to anger him, so he let it go.

"Just pull in the driveway; I'm on my way out right now." He watched Los pull up to the house as he stepped outside, surprised to see Miguel getting out of the vehicle.

Amir frowned as he came around the vehicle to embrace his best friend.

Los began speaking quietly.

"I'm taking Miguel to my mother's house for a while. I don't like the company that Roslyn has around him, you feel me?"

Amir nodded. "Yes, I can understand that completely, my brother."

He noticed that Los was staring hard into his face as he spoke, but he ignored him and bent down to lift Miguel into his arms.

"What's up, nephew! Are you ready for the roller coasters?" Amir interacted with Miguel in a similar fashion to how Los had been with Lo-Lo when she was young.

Miguel giggled and kicked his legs as Amir swung him through the air effortlessly while Los looked on with a blank expression. Amir had no doubt that Los had something heavy on his mind.

Amir put Miguel down and addressed his friend.

"Come inside and see my new home. Miguel can play the new video games I bought for him while we discuss the meeting we need to have with two-faced Frank."

Miguel ran into the house and Los frowned.

"You have a secret house? What happened to us being blood brothers and knowing everything about each other? How can I trust a mothafucka that keeps secrets?" Amir frowned at his friend.

"What are you talking about, Los? I told you about the detective following me around, and I let you know that I was going to relocate. Do you think that I have to tell you my every move?" Los glared at Amir.

"Roslyn is fuckin' a little skinny crackhead nigga with no honor or respect; do you know anything about that? I started to just fuck the bitch nigga off, but I really didn't know how you would've felt about the shit." Amir was incredulous.

"My nig, why would I give a fuck about a nigga your baby…"

Awareness came over Amir and he suddenly understood Los's anger. Amir's cousin, Tony, lived in Argentine and had gone to school with Roslyn. Amir had been told about the situation and had given Tony a stern warning that he should keep his distance from the woman. He had never mentioned it to Los, and he had never thought about it again. Amir had assumed that the fool had heeded his warning and relented in his pursuit of the dangerous situation. Amir could understand Los's anger; he would have felt the same if faced with a similar situation, but he also felt that his friend should have known that he had a reason for not mentioning it to him- they had always been loyal to one another.

CHAPTER 102

Los walked into the house followed by Amir and headed to the entertainment center and briefly watched his son playing a video game. He locked eyes with Amir and followed him into a spacious dining room, glaring at his best friend with scorn.

"Did you know about bitch-ass Tony fuckin' my baby's momma and hittin' the glass dick with her? If you lie I'm punchin' you right in yo' mothafuckin mouth!" Amir smiled sadly and looked Los directly in his eyes.

"If you put your hands on me, my nig, I'm going to forget that we're brothers for long enough for me to beat your yellow ass all around this room."

The two had not fought physically since they were teens, and Amir could not remember their last argument. They had had problems like any other friends, but they had dealt with situations accordingly because of their love for one another. Amir sobered and placed a hand on Los's shoulder.

"Los, I had heard about it and warned him to leave that woman alone; I swear, that shit never crossed my mind again. This crackhead shit is new to me; I didn't know a damn thing about Tony doing that." Los walked all the way up until he was inches from Amir's face.

"You know now, nigga. I caught him and that bitch in my house naked and with the door wide open for my son to see if he had walked right down the hall from his fuckin' bedroom! I'm not lettin' that shit ride, my nig. I don't give a fuck if you try to hide the mothafucka; he's about to get hit for disrespecting me!" Amir frowned.

"You're talking about my family, Los, and you're talking about killing him over a female that obviously is really the one who doesn't respect you!" Los cocked his arm back to take a swing, but he froze when Mecca entered the room wearing a maternity dress, looking fearful and confused.

"Amir, is everything alright in here? I could hear you from upstairs and that little boy in the living room was listening also. I finally stopped him from crying and convinced him that everything was okay." Amir smiled and glanced at Los before speaking.

"Everything is just fine, baby. I'm just talking things out with my brother. Los, this is my fiancé, Mecca, and this is my blood brother Carlos Jr." Mecca smiled and approached Los without fear, gripping both of his hands.

"I know everything about you and Amir. I don't know why it took him so long to introduce us, but it is a pleasure to finally meet you." Los was stunned.

"Meer, you're about to get married? Where did you find this fine-ass woman? I can see why yo' punk-ass been hiding her, though; she's a damn dime-piece for sure." Mecca blushed, and Amir beamed with pride, relieved that the evil spirits had fled the room.

Amir turned to his friend with a conciliatory tone.

"Los, this is my best-kept secret, and I love her enough to protect her at all costs. Too much has been going on for me to have let anyone know about her."

Mecca laughed, lightening the mood.

"Don't talk about me as if I'm not here. I am not a baby or anyone's property, and I definitely will not break." She turned to Los. "As much as I hear about what you two are into, you should understand why Amir didn't want me around; wouldn't you do the same for that cute little boy in there?" Los moved forward and put his arm around Amir's neck.

"We'll talk about our little situation some other time, bro." He addressed Mecca respectfully. "Baby-girl, I hope you have a sister or something for me to meet; I think a woman even close to being as beautiful as you can straighten any man out." Mecca smiled modestly, and Los was again stunned by her natural beauty.

Miguel suddenly entered the room and Mecca intercepted him; Los watched as his wild son was tamed by the woman's tenderness and exotic looks.

Los pulled Amir into the kitchen while Mecca and Miguel returned to the living room to resume playing the video game. Amir walked to a small bar and poured a shot of cognac for the two of them.

"Los, we don't ever need to get into it like this, especially behind something I have absolutely nothing to do with. I'm going to do something about Tony's trick-ass, trust me, but there is no need to kill the man. I'm sorry about what's going on between you and Roslyn, but you know her mind is fucked up with that dope; let's deal with these damn Italians and put this other nonsense behind us so we can effectively deal with the situation."

They sat drinking and discussing the meeting they were to have with Frank and what they would do about the Italians' organization. The fact that Amir's home had been disrespected had to be dealt with, and he still thought about the look on Mecca's face when he saw her looking out of the window at him. The situation with the M.O.P. was an even more serious issue.

They sat and talked as if the situation between them had never occurred, going over what they had planned for the weekend. They were playing a never ending game, and they were playing for keeps.

CHAPTER 103

Maintain stood over the large cast-iron pot, waiting for the water to boil so that he could start conducting business. He had five kilograms of cocaine dumped inside of a bucket sitting on the kituchen table, and five piles of baking soda measured for each load he would cook. There were large Pyrex bowls he used to cook cocaine for Amir and Los; he was responsible for two of their houses on the Kansas side of the border. He had shut down sales until he finished preparing the drugs, and others were busy counting cash in the basement.

Honeyboy and West Texas were gripping their assault rifles while keeping watch as Maintain placed his first Pyrex jar filled with cocaine into the pot. They all watched as the drugs slowly mixed with the baking soda it would take to transform it into crack-cocaine. They had a group of men in the next room armed with razor blades, baggies, and measuring scales to divide the drugs that would be sold out of the houses.

Maintain glanced out of the window by chance and saw two heads disappear; two sets of eyes had been gazing over the wooden privacy fence. He yelled to the others.

"We're about to get hit! Honeyboy, grab them little niggas from downstairs and get…!"

Bullets began entering the kitchen and it sounded like several semi-automatic weapons were firing from outside. Honeyboy rushed to get some reinforcements while West Texas attempted to return fire, but he was no match for the heavy assault coming their way. A bullet ricocheted off the refrigerator and Honeyboy gripped his arm in pain as a slug entered his body. Still, he picked up the rifle he had dropped and stuck it out of a shattered window, continuing to return fire regardless. He spotted a masked man climbing over the fence and shot him in the face and upper-body with 7.62mm rounds.

He yelled, "Black Border!" Honeyboy said this over and over while he fired on anyone and anything moving. Drugs were all over the floor from stray slugs destroying the bucket on the table; everyone ignored them as they concentrated on their survival.

The back door suddenly fell to the floor with a loud crash and they were forced to retreat to the living room, watching as forms appeared wielding machine guns and assault rifles; the men were firing with abandon, and they didn't seem to have a plan for their assault.

Everyone began rushing upstairs, but it was too late for them. The front door had already been kicked in and the masked men were raining death indiscriminately.

Maintain pulled Honeyboy with him when he saw him attempting to save the drugs and cash; what he was doing was tantamount to suicide. West Texas was on the floor with blood gushing out of a huge hole in his neck and a bloody hole where his right eye had been; Maintain also noticed that Honeyboy was barely moving his legs.

"Man, come the fuck on!" Maintain looked down and noticed that Honeyboy's leg was turned in an unnatural angle; Maintain allowed him to put more weight onto his shoulders while he steered him and three more Black Border Brothers into the den. There was a side door that was their only chance at survival, and there were guns hidden inside the cushions of a large sectional couch inside the room. They grabbed the pistols and made it to the door just as voices began coming their way. They exited and glanced around the side of the house before making a run for Maintain's Ford Excursion, dragging Honeyboy into the vehicle as he continued to fire at the men who were now exiting the house with loaded bags; it was the cash and drugs that the men had come for.

Maintain fired out of his window with his .45 caliber Beretta and hit two of the men that were concentrating on the bags in their hands instead of their lives. He steered while fumbling for his cell-phone to call Amir, knowing that this had not been a random act of robbery and murder.

CHAPTER 104

Lo-Lo walked behind Keith as he stubbornly refused her assistance and pushed forward in his wheelchair; he was headed for the front entrance where Steven was waiting with his vehicle.

Lo-Lo whined. "You need to stop acting like you don't need anyone's help before you end up tearing your stitches, Keith. I realize that you are getting better, but the doctor said for you to avoid too much strenuous activity until you heal more.

Keith shook his head. "I know what he said, Lo-Lo, but I don't need you to do everything for me like I'm a damn baby!"

Lo-Lo opened the door for him, and Keith smiled as Steven stared at Lo-Lo in awe, remembering the first time he had seen her. Keith was helped into the front passenger seat and Lo-Lo sat behind him. He turned around to face her.

"Lo-Lo, I really need you to get as much cash from your brother as you can now that I'm not able to work or hustle. If you can't get the other things we discussed, don't worry about it; I'll find them somewhere."

Lo-Lo knew that Keith was talking about the drugs she was supposed to steal, but he was talking in code and obviously did not want Steven to know.

Don't worry about it, Keith, Amir wants me far away from here anyway, so he'll help as much as he can."

She turned to Steven. "Let's get away from here, please; people could be watching this hospital. I don't think they'll give up until we're dead."

Steven looked at Keith with a horrified expression and hurriedly shifted the vehicle into drive and sped away from the hospital. Lo-Lo's hand stayed inside her purse, gripping the 9mm Amir had left her at the hospital. She looked at the familiar places as they left the city with regret, knowing that she would have to make a life elsewhere for the time being. Lawrence, Kansas, was not very far away, though, and it was a place that thrived in education; she planned to take advantage of any opportunities available. They were headed for a house not far from Kansas University; Steven's mother had left her home to him when she moved to California with her new husband.

Lo-Lo felt wary of Keith's persistence in asking for drugs, but she was going to make sure that he didn't get swallowed up by the streets like Amir and Los. She noticed that Keith was already drifting off to sleep; she imagined seeing the innocence disappearing from his features as she looked him over. He had been forced into manhood and had assumed the responsibility for her life as if it was his own. Keith didn't seem to have any regrets or fears. Lo-Lo realized that he would do whatever he felt was best for them, so she simply sat back and relaxed, but she glanced at every vehicle nearby with suspicion. Lo-Lo had to admit to herself that she had aged as well.

CHAPTER 105

Trig, Face, and Mack stood inside the vacant house, watching a Black Border Brother location across the street conducting business at a rapid pace. The house was disguised as a Notary Public that was thriving. The three men had been inside the downtrodden dwelling for the last two hours, waiting for the opportunity to make a hit as fast and thorough as possible.

They all looked up, hearing hail suddenly beating off the roof; it had darkened outside, and rain was falling in blinding torrents. There were loud peals of thunder and flashes of lightning. Mack took this as an opportunity, so he pulled on his ski-mask and gripped his AR-15 assault rifle. Mack was from St. Louis, Missouri, so the violence in the twin Kansas Cities was nothing new to him. He stuffed two spare magazines into his pockets and saw that Trig and Face were also masked and ready. Mack looked toward the house across the street before addressing them.

"We go straight to the house, shoot through the patio door in the back, kill anybody that gets in the fuckin' way, and take they shit! Whatever we get out of this bitch is all ours, and we still getting' paid to fuck these niggas over."

As soon as there was another barrage of thunder and lightning, the lights went out on the street, and Mack rushed out of the door without looking back to see if his boys were following. When he made it around the house and to the patio door, he knew he hadn't been seen; the cloud-hidden moon only allowed him to see a few feet in front of him. He could hear Face and Trig at his heels, so he clicked off the safety on his weapon, pointed at the glass patio door, and brought deadly light to the utter darkness of the storm with his assault rifle. The window shattered with a loud crash and he heard a grunt of pain as one of the large slugs no doubt entered someone's flesh. He stepped into the house and saw a man sprawled on the kitchen floor holding his bloody stomach and moaning.

Face casually walked over to him and fired a single round when the man looked up in surprise and fear. The lights came on and Face's profile disappeared as a slug silenced him forever as he collapsed to the floor. Mack stepped over his friend's body and peered into the living room; he noticed a man making his way down a hallway. Trig fired without hesitation and the man went down to a hail of .223 rounds from his AR-15 rifle. Mack could hear a woman screaming hysterically from one of the rooms down the hallway.

When they opened the first bedroom door, Mack could see a young woman crouching beside the bed with hands on both sides of her face, still screaming. Trig silenced her with three rounds from his weapon and looked around, noticing that the house was eerily silent. They looked around and made sure that everyone had fled the house and began searching for the drugs and money, knowing that it would not be long before the authorities arrived.

They eventually made it back to the kitchen, realizing that drug dealing had been conducted there. They opened the cabinets and saw two triple beam scales, two kilograms of what they assumed was cocaine, and two large Ziploc bags filled with currency. Although they assumed there were more items hidden inside the house, they both made a dash down the street- leaving their weapons and dead friend behind. Mack knew that there would be no fingerprints or anything else to connect them to the scene because of the latex gloves they wore.

When they entered the stolen Chevy Suburban and Mack pulled off, he turned to Trig.

"Call Paris and tell him we're on the way to Benton street; he needs to have our cash ready. We need to head back to the Lou, dirty, before these damn bodies even get cold."

Trig made the call while Mack concentrated on driving carefully so that they wouldn't be noticed by the police. Eventually Trig pulled two .45 automatics out of the glove compartment; they both knew that the inner city was too twisted to trust Paris or anyone else in Kansas City.

CHAPTER 106

Amir received a call from Maintain and more people at houses that were hit, knowing that he should have known that the M.O.P. were coming, considering the death of Oscar. He had already agreed with Los to shut everything down until they concluded their business with Frank and the Italians, so he had been furious about the hit when there should not have been any business conducted anyway. Amir was convinced that he must hit the M.O.P. so hard this time that they would not have any fight left, so he concentrated on receiving the information that he would use to his advantage. He contacted every man that he was connected to on both sides of the border. He wanted to know the locations of the M.O.P. spots, safe-houses, and places that they used for storage. He relocated Mecca to her sister's home until they could deal with the issues at hand, and he made sure that Lo-Lo was safe and well in Lawrence, Kansas. Amir knew that his sister was too young to be living with a male, but he looked at Keith as a boy that had matured considerably because of the circumstances he had overcome. Amir also knew that he could not separate the two after the pain they had been through together.

Amir finished showering and getting dressed, and he took Mecca's vehicle so that he could be incognito when he met with Los; they were having dinner with Frank in North Kansas City, Missouri that night.

He headed down I-435 and drove east toward Grandview, Missouri, enjoying the fact that he was in a vehicle that wasn't registered in his name. Messy Marv and Keisha Cole were blasting out of his stereo system as he continuously gazed into the rearview mirror to ensure that he was not being followed.

Amir arrived in Grandview, and he traveled down James A. Reed to the Islamic Center; he sat in the parking lot silently watching people file into the mosque. He was contemplating on how much he had separated himself from God with his recent deeds; he silently made a vow to spare any man or woman that was not a direct threat. Amir proudly watched the beautiful Muslim women dressed modestly and thought about Mecca, his queen; Amir hated himself for the position he had put her in. She had not accepted Islam, but he knew that she would learn what she could about the religion, help him, and make the decision on her own. He realized that there should be no compulsion in any religion. He loved that Mecca was intelligent and loving, but she would not settle for less than what she was worth.

He pulled away and drove a few miles to Carlos Sr.'s home; he smiled when he arrived and saw Mona and Miguel playing cards at a table in the front yard. He pulled into the driveway as the two watched the unfamiliar vehicle suspiciously, wondering who was inside.

He stepped out straightening his tie, and Mona ran toward him with a squeal. They hadn't seen each other in years, and Amir was surprised that she still looked the same as she did when they were youngsters; Amir had had a serious crush on her. He watched Mona coming toward him and felt good about how things had turned out between them. Ever since he and Los had made their blood pact, he had begun to view Mona as a sister; it no longer mattered how beautiful she was to him. He watched her move toward him and felt alright about how things had turned out; since Amir, Los, and Mona had matured everything had changed.

"Meer! What's up, carnal? I've been asking about you since I moved back here. Everyone talks about how busy you are, but how can this stop you from visiting your sister?"

Amir smiled and bent down to snatch Miguel into his arms as the boy stared curiously at Mona, not knowing the situation well enough to feel comfortable. Amir was surprised that Miguel stared calmly at him without showing emotion; he shook his head and lowered the boy to the ground before turning to Mona.

"Are you sure your husband is alright with a playa like me hanging around? If I was a lame, it probably wouldn't matter, but I'm a cause for concern for any man." Mona stared at him with an incredulous expression on her beautiful face.

"Don't flatter yourself, Amir. My husband is a handsome, successful doctor. Must I remind you that he is an African, by the way? He's not a Mandingo or anything, but he's definitely close enough." Amir walked to the house holding his hands over his ears playfully.

"That's too much information, baby-girl."

He called to Miguel, "Come on, little man, let's go find your daddy and make sure he's ready to go. Have you been good for your grandma?"

Miguel suddenly went on an animated tirade about how he had been behaving and bragged about how much fun he had been having at his grandparents' home. Mona stared at Miguel in wonder, amazed at how he tended to be very comfortable in Amir's presence, like everyone else was with the man. Miguel had shied away from her for weeks before he would genuinely smile in her direction; he walked into the house holding Amir's hand after not being around him consistently.

She shook her head with a smile and sat down at the table, thinking about her husband and anticipating his return from his recent trip to Atlanta, Georgia.

CHAPTER 107

Amir eventually entered the house with Miguel and was greeted by Rhonda, Los's mother, sitting in the living room having drinks with two of her friends. Amir's god-mother climbed to her feet when she saw him and Miguel.

"Amir! How are you doing, baby? Come on over here and meet my friends!" He was flirted with and groped until Los appeared and rescued him from the older African-American women. Los wore a charcoal-gray Armani suit and his hair was in a short ponytail; he had been growing his hair out for the last two months.

The women turned their attention toward Miguel, saving the two men from having to send the boy away when it was time to discuss business. They left the room and walked down into Carlos Sr.'s space in the basement.

Carlos Sr. was standing in front of the bar yelling into his telephone. When he noticed them, he retreated to his personal room and slammed the door hard. Los glanced at Amir and shrugged; they both walked behind the bar and mixed their favorite drink: Remy Martin XO and apple juice. Los took a sip and looked sternly at his friend.

"Everything is shut down until we handle all of this bullshit that's going on. There's going to be at least twenty people waiting for us after we meet up with the fake-ass Italians. Once we finish talking to Frank, it's going to be murder for those M.O.P. niggas. We know where they main spots are, but I'm personally going to that nigga Paris's house in Lee's Summit. When they fucked with Lo-Lo, they opened up all doors and deserve every fuckin' thing they got coming! I don't know what bitch-ass Frank wants, but he gonna pay for all that fake, friendly shit; he's trying to come at us like he's a straight gangsta!" Amir downed his drink before speaking.

"I don't care about Frank right now; it's obvious that he's a flunky. Manny is the one we need to be concerned with; he's calling the shots and instructing Frank on how to deal with us. We're simply going to inform them that we no longer require their assistance. If they have a problem with that, we're going to start hitting them so that they know that we're stronger than they gave us credit for; they feel that we're spread too thin because of all of the drama."

They both turned when Carlos Sr. reentered the room with an irritated expression on his face.

"Young men, we have a serious problem. The police have been raiding my brother's locations in Argentine, and your friend, Reese, barely escaped. He took my niece, Maria, on the run with him, and my brother, Jorge, is very upset. The girl is only fifteen; we both are wondering what she was doing with him in thc first place."

Amir groaned and poured himself another drink; he couldn't believe all of the drama that was occurring lately. Los saved him from having to respond.

"I'll get in touch with Reese if I can, pops, but he'll probably be getting in touch with us anyway. Reese ain't on no child molester shit, so the girl must have had a reason for being there and running away with him. Tell Uncle Jorge that after we meet with these weak-ass Italians we'll find Reese and ask him what the hell is going on." Carlos Sr. slammed the palm of his hand on the bar.

"You had better find him before we do, and he had better have a good reason for this; we have been there for him and it enrages us that it appears that he has disrespected us in the worst way!" He paused to gather himself. "That damn Galubski is the reason for this; his name was all over the damn search warrant. We need to get in touch with Ashely to find out what, if anything, she knows about this detective so that he can be eliminated before he causes any more problems."

He turned and headed up the staircase; Amir and Los followed him to the main level of the house. Los pulled out his cell and began making calls, making sure that their people were outside the restaurant in North Kansas City before they arrived.

Los eventually went to find Miguel, and Amir followed Carlos Sr. outside, relieved that Mona had disappeared.

Amir spoke. "We're going to put all of this mess behind us so that we can rock these fools to sleep and get back to the money. We have to remind everyone that the Border Brother organizations control this city, not the Italians."

Carlos Sr. ignored Amir's last words and handed him the keys to his new Chevy Silverado. Amir considered purchasing one himself as he admired the flawless interior and glossy paint. The leather seats were equipped with warmers and the dash and steering wheel was laced with tortoise shell. He climbed inside and loaded one of Carlos Sr.'s oldie disks into the player and leaned back, listening to the soulful sounds of Sam Cook. Carlos Sr. turned without another word and walked into his home.

Los eventually emerged without Miguel, but he was carrying a large duffel bag. He climbed into the passenger seat and unzipped it, removing twin .45 caliber Berettas along with four fully loaded extended magazines.

"If shit goes funny, I'm gonna shoot bitch-ass Frank in the head first. After this shit, we need to start going on a M.O.P. hunt and evaporate them niggas once and for all."

Amir pulled one of the weapons onto his lap, made sure the chamber was loaded, and placed the weapon in the console between them. He pondered Frank, and Amir felt that he should have been expecting this. He already knew what they would be up against, so he had been preparing to go against the world to save his family and everything that they had built.

He glanced over at Los and was relieved that things were back to normal between them. Los was the only man left that he felt was the blood of his blood.

CHAPTER 108

Reese stood to the side of the window in the vacant house watching the police cars speed by in search of him. Maria was standing on the other side of the room staring at him with a smile as if running for his life was amusing. Maria had been the one that found Reese's mother and little sister dead. She had arrived to braid his little sister's hair and had been nauseous for days afterward. She also had described some men she had seen suspiciously leaving the house as she approached. The killers hadn't seen her coming up the sidewalk across the street and getting a good look at their faces. She saw the men a week later when she was hanging out with her friends at Swope Park in Kansas City, Missouri. They had even followed the men to a house near Swope Parkway.

The M.O.P. members had been bragging about money and they had attempted to force themselves on the girls when they had gotten intoxicated. One of the men had attempted to rape one of Maria's friends that they had gotten high on P.C.P. laced with marijuana, but Maria and the other teenagers had stubbornly intervened. They eventually had to drag the girl out of the house with her pants around her ankles and took her to Maria's sister's house in Shawnee, Kansas. Maria hadn't told anyone about the incident until she spoke with Reese, but she specifically remembered the letters M.O.P. tattooed on the men's arms and the hate for the Black Border Brothers spewing from their lips. When she found out that Reese was staying at one of her father's homes, she had decided to give him the information, but she had unintentionally chosen the day that the authorities were raiding the house.

After she had explained everything to Reese he began fuming and pacing around the living room, until he noticed police officers running through the fence with a huge battering ram and sophisticated weaponry.

Reese climbed out of a side window and exited the house in a rush, finding his way to a vehicle that was there for him in case he was forced to make an unexpected exit.

The passenger door had been yanked open before he had an opportunity to drive away, and he groaned when Maria climbed in next to him. Reese started to tell Maria to get out, but police cars turned onto the street and he pulled her down onto the seat next to him. When he peeked out and saw F.B.I. agents on foot, he decided to exit the vehicle and enter the vacant house where they were now standing. He turned to Maria.

"Did anyone know that you were coming to the house today?"

She nodded. "My sister knew that I was coming to talk to you, and my aunt was the one who let me into the house. I just told my aunt that I was coming by to braid your hair for money. What's wrong, are you scared of girls?" Reese stared hard at Maria until she averted her eyes.

"Little girl, I just don't want Jorge or anybody else thinkin' the wrong shit about me! Your people have had my damn back, and I don't think Jorge's the kind of mothafucka to turn the other cheek when he gets disrespected; what if he thinks you're a hostage or something? Why do you keep smiling and shit? I'm wanted for murders, and the situation is real fucked up as it is, but you're thinking it's a damn game!".

Maria looked horrified; she had obviously not been informed about the nature of Reese's crimes, or why he was being hidden amongst the Latino community. Reese approached her hesitantly.

338

"When these fool as police leave, I want you to show me where those mothafuckas live that you were telling me about. After that, I need you to go directly to your father and let him know why you came to see me."

Maria looked at him flirtatiously.

"What are we going to do until then? Do you have a girlfriend, homeboy?" Reese knew that he had to be careful. Maria was obviously attracted to living dangerously, but he would not submit to her fantasies; he also could not say the wrong thing and possibly hurt her feelings.

"I have a girlfriend, but those niggas that you told me about killed her the same day that my momma and little sister were found. I haven't even thought about being with a bitch since that day."

Maria looked at him with a shocked expression and her demeanor changed. Reese felt bad about playing to the girl's sympathies, but he did not feel as if he had a choice. Maria suddenly had a determined look on her face.

"I'm going to show you where they are and pray that you don't get caught; I know what you're planning on doing to them, but I don't blame you."

Reese looked at the girl with admiration in his eyes. She was very beautiful, but she was also much too young for him to take seriously. He knew that if Maria had been in her twenties, he would have relented to her advances by now, if the authorities were nearby or not.

He walked over and draped an arm across her slender shoulders.

"When I tell you to follow me, you had better move! We need to head straight to the highway and make it over to the Missouri side. After you show me where these niggas are, do you have somewhere I can drop you off over there?"

Maria nodded, and Reese went back to looking out of the window. He wanted to distance himself as far away from Maria as possible, knowing that he would have to handle the situation before he even considered contacting Carlos Sr. or Jorge. He wanted to travel to Mexico to start a new life, but he felt that he had to separate the killers of his family from their blood in order to honor his pledge: by living eye for eye.

CHAPTER 109

Shonda passed through the metal detector and retrieved the items that she could take with her. She was inside of the Wyandotte County Detention Center visiting room. The male and female officers had finally gotten tired of gawking at her voluptuous body and had allowed her to get processed for the visit. Shonda wore a form-fitting maxi-dress, and even a glimpse of her pretty feet had most of the people inside the visiting room salivating over her looks. She sat down on a stool in front of the thick glass window and gripped the telephone as she watched Ashely approach with a female officer beside her. Ashely was looking nonchalant, as if she had been incarcerated for a driving violation or some other misdemeanor.

Ashely stopped a few feet away and stared forward with an angry expression. Shonda froze, but she turned to see another female officer walking up behind her and understood that the look was directed at the other woman. Ashely sat down and put the receiver to her mouth.

"Tell that ugly bitch to get out of here! They are not supposed to physically monitor us, and her bull-dyking ass knows it!" Shonda simply stood up and handed the deputy sheriff the receiver as she heard Ashely scream something unintelligible through the earpiece. The woman gasped and dropped the receiver with a fearful look on her face; she stormed off and Shonda watched Ashely's face transform into a wicked smile. They both sat down and picked up the receivers. Shonda looked sadly at her "friend" before speaking.

"Amir thought that it would be better if I came to see you, considering the circumstances. How are you holding up in there?" Ashely stared at her incredulously before responding with a stern voice.

"How do you think I'm *holding up*? Regardless, I'm not worried about myself; I know Arthur's death had to be difficult for you to deal with. Tell Amir that I will communicate with him through my attorney, so you don't have to come back up here pretending that we are anything more than associates." Shonda shook her head sadly.

"We don't have to get along for me to want what's best for you, Ashely. I know how long you have been with Los and Amir, so I have no choice but to respect your loyalty to them. I just don't appreciate it when you come on to me sexually; you know how I feel about that homosexual shit! Those men have burned my house to the ground, killed my lover and best friend, and they are in the streets bragging about it. I want in on whatever can be done to make them suffer; we don't have to be best friends for that."

Ashely leaned back with a smile on her face and scrutinized her new ally, knowing that Shonda was sincere. What they really needed was the detective off their backs so that they could deal with the situation effectively.

Ashely frowned. "I've heard about what happened at your house, but I didn't realize those M.O.P. fools would be stupid enough to run their mouths about it. One of their little bitches was in here yesterday talking that M.O.P. bullshit. I asked her how the group could be named money over bitches when they always fall for my pussy. When I explained how we did Marlon and the Jamaicans, the bitch froze up; she finally realized who I was. I beat that bitch until she was shitting in her pretty panties and they had to take her to the hospital to get sewed up. Don't worry, we'll come up with a way to shut them down for good real soon. You just stay out of trouble in the meantime; I need a woman out there that I can trust to move around. Tell Amir not to worry about that fat pig that is responsible for all of this shit. I have a plan for you to deal with him if you think you're ready." Shonda gazed through the glass without blinking.

"I will do anything that needs to be done for Arthur; they are not going to get away with murdering him. What does all of this have to do with the police officer?" Ashely smiled wickedly.

"Absolutely nothing, but it will be a bonus for me; it will give us more time to deal with our problems without being scrutinized. We'll simply call it poetic justice- a chance to prove that you're not just another pretty face with an even prettier pussy."

Shonda realized that she would never get used to Ashely's disgusting language, but she had already convinced herself to adopt a cold and clinical attitude if she would be of any assistance. She pondered Ashely's last comment and leaned forward, staring the woman directly in her eyes.

"You'll never know the details of how my vagina is built, but you will soon see that looks can be deceiving where I'm concerned." She slammed the receiver into its cradle with a bang and turned to walk away without hesitation.

Ashely stared at her ample backside sashaying seductively down the hallway, knowing that the M.O.P. was in serious trouble; they had created a beautiful monster.

CHAPTER 110

Amir and Los arrived in front of the plantation-style restaurant, looking around at the stretch limousines and white men with large noses standing around them. Los pulled his weapon from under the seat and pushed it into his shoulder harness before following Amir, who gave a valet attendant his keys with a smile. Black Border Brothers were already inside the restaurant dining with their ladies, and there were many more in the surrounding area in case something happened.

Two of the men at the front door approached as if to search them, but Amir glared meanly at them until they backed off. Los walked through the entrance beside Amir; one of the men they recognized from their meetings in the Bottoms approached and led them to a large table in the rear of the huge atrium. The restaurant was dim, and candles were burning on the tables; classical music was playing softly from speakers hung intermediately on the walls. The décor was extremely elegant, and they admired the crystal chandeliers that hung from the ceiling; colors were sent in all directions as the ornaments sparkled like diamonds.

Frank stood when they arrived, surrounded by a group of men that were obviously a part of his security team. Los noticed stares coming from several nearby tables and smiled inwardly; he knew that their friends and associates were also watching anxiously.

"Hey, boys, I'm happy to see the two of you! It is good for you to come and meet with me this evening. What are you fellas drinking?" Frank approached Amir with his open palm extended for a handshake, but Amir stared down at it as if it was diseased.

"We're not drinking anything with you. I have a question for you, Frank. Why did you send people to my home to disrespect me like you're Al Capone or something? You're back to grinning in our faces as if nothing has happened; what the fuck do you want?" Frank's smile vanished and was replaced by an icy stare; the friendly act had gone into remission once again. Frank glared at each of them in turn before responding.

"You fucking niggers should be grateful that I was patient with you at all; you mean no more to me than a couple of monkeys that escaped from the zoo."

Los took a step forward, but Amir restrained him with a hand to his chest, noticing people in the shadows react to the movement.

Amir smiled. "Whatever you think we are is irrelevant, white boy. All you need to know is that we no longer request your services." He paused as his smile was replaced by an angry scowl.

"We don't need you for anything. I don't know what the big deal is, anyway. Manny made it clear that he didn't want to be associated with drugs. Are you working a little side hustle or something?"

Frank sat without responding as he took a seat; it was obvious that Amir had struck a nerve. The Italian leaned back and took a sip from his drink.

"We have had a working relationship that has been beneficial to all parties, so Manny does not have to agree. I control what goes on at the border of these two cities. I will give you and your friend here two alternatives." He glanced over at Los as if he were insignificant. "One: we resume our business dealings and continue to pile up cash for our fantastic way of life. Two: You go to war with us and lose everything that you hold dear to your little nigger heart. Those are your two options; what do you say? There is really no need to become enemies." Los took a seat across from Frank and leaned forward to address him.

"Hey, bitch, we'll take the second choice! Don't a mothafucka in this world decide what the fuck we do. You think they stopped makin' guns when they made yours? While you're wasting our time trying to threaten and intimidate, you need to be thinkin' about what the fuck you can lose that's next to *your* little white-ass heart!"

Frank sat back in his chair and grinned wickedly; Amir suddenly walked over and patted Los on the shoulder.

"Come on, my man, what's going to happen is already recorded; we've been here before."

They walked toward the entrance, noticing most of the people in the room looking their way, and Amir was paying special attention to the men in the room that were awaiting his orders to strike. As they were exiting the establishment, Frank yelled after them.

"You niggers have *never* been in this position before; you've just moved to another level entirely! The bullshit that you've been having in the *ghetto* is child's play compared to what's coming!" Frank still had a smile on his face, but the evil glint in his eyes told both Amir and Los a story about what could be lying ahead.

The vehicle was brought around, and Los made calls to everyone in the vicinity, letting them know that they were safely leaving the Italians behind.

When they began to pull away, vehicles began speeding by to block traffic so that they would have a clear path if something went wrong. All of them eventually drove off into the night together while the Italians stared at their sheer numbers in disbelief. There were at least fifty vehicles in the procession, with at least three armed and masked men inside most of them. Amir looked back at Frank in his rearview mirror, staring after them and speaking into his cell-phone as his own men formed a shield around him. Amir did not know how or when the Italians would come, but he knew that they must get the M.O.P. out of the way completely; the Italians were now the number one threat to the Black Border Brothers.

CHAPTER 111

KB and Poonk were in the kitchen preparing the distribution of their favorite "K-Town" marijuana. They both turned as someone began banging on the back door. Thinking that it was a raid, Poonk headed to the bathroom where they had a bucket of m;uriatic acid waiting. They suddenly heard laughter outside of the door; when they opened it, Reese was bent over clutching his stomach with his two plaits hanging.

"You niggas was scared straight. I bet you mothafuckas wished you was anywhere else when I started bangin' on that bitch!" KB rushed forward and grabbed Reese around the neck playfully.

"Nigga, on Bloods, on the Border, don't do no bullshit like that no more! What if that nigga Poonk would've tossed our weed in the bucket?"

Reese smiled. "At least that would have taught you fools to grab a gun instead of choosin' to run like two little girls. The police bleed the same love as you niggas." Poonk stepped to the doorway and pulled his friend inside the house.

"We aint tryin' to kill no police, my nig. Come on in the house and stop standing around like this aint a damn dope spot."

348

They all sat down at the kitchen table and Reese pulled a small glass vial from his pocket and a red pack of More non-menthol cigarettes. He pulled a cigarette from the pack, loosened the tobacco, removed the filter, and dipped it inside the murky fluid in the bottle. He put flame to the "stick" and watched flame erupt from it when the ether was ignited. He took a few pulls from it and they passed it around the table until they began to move slowly, and their expressions became taught and hardened. Reese slurred his words.

"I found out where that local joker, Paris, is at. Jorge's daughter took me to those niggas house that killed my family; when I was watching the house, some bitch walked up pushin' that ho-ass nigga in a damn wheelchair. He was lookin' like a damn sucka and a sitting duck at the same time, my nigs. Are you niggas down with spilling a little more love in the streets? You fools are still my Blood relatives, right? We're on that Border shit, but we still have to be true to the game for each other."

KB stood up and slowly and walked to the kitchen sink. He bent down and opened a cabinet and came up with a Thompson submachine gun and inserted the round clip with a devilish grin.

He spoke slowly. "I got forty five caliber reasons why we should go as soon as it gets dark, playa. All hollow points; we need to meet up with Amir first, though. We're hitting those M.O.P. niggas hella hard tonight, and that nigga Paris will be a sweet bonus."

Reese replaced the cap on his bottle, not wanting to be too "shermed out" when he saw Amir. He also wasn't sure how much of the drug his friends could consume without becoming "stuck." He didn't want the P.C.P. to be an excuse for anyone when it came time to pull triggers.

He placed the bottle and cigarettes inside the freezer before going to inspect the other weapons inside the cabinet. He pulled out a Mac-11 along with two extra magazines that were lying next to it. He looked at his two friends.

"Where are the bullets?"

KB frowned. "Meer already said he got your AP9 over there with him; what do you need my Mac for?" Reese looked at him incredulously before answering.

"When we hit these niggas, guns are getting tossed into the river and down sewers. I don't have no damn bodies on the A.P. yet, but there most likely will be tonight. If you want me to pay for the cheap mothafucka, I will." KB shook his head.

"Keep your money, dawg, just make sure you get rid of that one too. You can help us with this bud, though; As soon as we finish bagging, we're meeting up with Amir. We have all the masks we'll need; all we have to do is stop at QuickTrip or 7-Eleven to get a bunch of gloves."

Reese nodded and grabbed one of the pounds of marijuana off the table to break down for bagging. He could imagine his finger throbbing to pull the trigger on Paris and the rest of the M.O.P., but he wanted the death of those that had raped and killed his mother and little sister to be drawn out and excruciating. Revenge is a dish that he wanted to serve cold, like the old-school gangsters did that he had revered growing up. He felt that the death of these men would finally halt the visions he had about the rape and murder of the only family he cared about.

Reese grinned as he began packaging the drugs, and Poonk glanced over at him nervously; he couldn't imagine why Reese was smiling as if he was having the time of his life. Poonk hoped that his friend would come back to reality, at least while they handled their business in the streets. He had heard about some of the things Reese had done, and Poonk felt that he had lost his mind. He would watch him closely; a man who had nothing to lose did not have friends for long. He began filling bags with marijuana after making sure his 9mm was riding on his hip. The P.C.P. was beginning to work overtime on his paranoia, and he knew he would have to purchase some milk when they went to purchase the gloves. Poonk also felt fear for his younger brother's life. Danny had grown up on the Missouri side with his father, and he was a member of Paris's M.O.P. organization. Poonk wanted to warn his brother, but he didn't know how to do it without being a disloyal Judas. He eventually planned to slip away before they headed to meet Amir. He was determined to make sure his brother wasn't around when they attacked. Poonk knew that if Reese found out, though, one of them would be dead before the night was over.

CHAPTER 112

Detective Galubski watched the beautiful woman's head bobbing up and down between his legs, and he savored the sensations before leaning back to close his eyes. He had parked at the "Lookout Point" in Kansas City, Missouri, so that he could remain anonymous alongside the many others that visited the large parking lot daily. He couldn't believe how lucky he had been to meet the woman in the small restaurant on the Kansas side where police officers primarily dined. He had been eating alone when he noticed her, and she had frequently glanced at him, watching him boldly at times as he devoured his meal. He could not believe how beautiful and innocent the woman looked. She was a light-skinned African-American woman with slanted eyes and a voluptuous figure stuffed inside of a business dress. When she walked sexily out of the diner, he rushed to make his move. Her innocent act disappeared swiftly as she caressed his crotch after he asked her out.

He stopped reminiscing as he ejaculated into the woman's pouty mouth as she began to suck and pull with vigor; she drained his semen and swallowed with a gorgeous grin on her face.

He lay back and pulled on his pants with a sigh.

"Damn, you're special! You're not in a rush, are you? I want to fuck you when I get a little energy back." He was shocked when he looked at her and she was pointing a pistol at his face; he realized just how naïve he had been. As he attempted to snatch the weapon from the woman, a part of his face disappeared in a shower of red before Shonda unloaded the .40 caliber Smith and Wesson into his face and torso.

Shonda dropped the gun into his lap like Amir had instructed, and she made sure there were no holes in the latex gloves that she was wearing. She removed her wig and stuffed it inside of her purse and tousled her long hair around her face before exiting the vehicle.

She stepped out and sprinted to the S.U.V. that Los had left for her, locating the keys beneath the driver's side floor mat. Shonda shivered in fear as she inserted the keys into the ignition, but she composed herself, knowing that she was being watched from the other vehicles in the parking lot. She also knew that the police were on their way after the people heard the explosive rounds from the small cannon. Shonda didn't feel the pleasure she had expected from the killing, but she knew that she would eventually. She grinned as she calmly drove away.

CHAPTER 113

Amir sat watching the security cameras as vehicles continued to pull in front of his home and one of his loyal henchmen ushered them inside. The youngster stood on crutches because his leg had been broken in a shootout at one of their houses, but he demanded to have some role in the conflict until he could get back on his feet. He had given a stray bullet story to the authorities and had not said another word.

Carlos Sr. and Jorge had just left; they had been relieved that Maria had been returned to them unharmed, but they now worried about Reese and how far he would go to avenge his loved ones. They could fully understand the man's rage, but they hoped that he considered what he was already up against before he roamed the streets in a rage.

Amir looked around the room at the weapons and ammunition and shook his head, knowing that many lives would be lost by morning. He walked into his study, pleased that everyone had donned dark clothing and seemed to be equipped with everything they needed. He looked toward the opposite side of the room and was surprised to see Shonda nursing a drink and staring at the ceiling in silence. He walked over and kneeled in front of her as he gripped her hands firmly.

"What are you doing here, baby-girl? You've already done your part in this madness; do you want to go into one of the rooms to rest?" She looked at Amir with tears in her eyes.

"No, I don't want to lay down, Meer. I know that you're only trying to help, but I just can't stop thinking about how my baby died. I also can't stop thinking about what I did for and to that man last night; I allowed him to treat me like a whore." Amir kissed her hands and pulled her to her feet.

"We have to do things we disagree with sometimes, baby. Trust me, I don't like many of the things I have done either, but if I keep dwelling on them without moving on, I'm as good as dead. Arthur wouldn't want you doing hits with his friends, so I'll have to insist that you stay out of the way."

He watched her exit the room, and he greeted each person in the house, making sure there was no identification on them and that all distinguishable marks were concealed. The people with gold or diamonds inside their mouths were given football mouthpieces, and the individuals with long hair had it tied with rubber bands and tucked away. He had seen many people get convicted because of simple mistakes, so they were also told to eliminate any potential witnesses to improve their chances of success.

"Look at this pretty-boy ass nigga!" Amir turned to see Reese's diamond and gold teeth shimmering from the lights as he displayed his signature smile. K.B. and Poonk were with him; they moved forward and shook Amir's hand after he and Reese broke their brief embrace.

Amir frowned. "What are you doing here, Reese? I know that you're out for revenge and I can understand your position, but do you think it's wise right now? The police are at your heels and your face has been all over the news all week." Reese walked over and sat down on a couch.

"I don't give a fuck if the whole fuckin' army is out there looking for me! I know where bitch-ass Paris is; I'm killing him and as many of his

355

bitch-ass homeboys as I can! You know how I get down, my nig, and I know you would do the same if you was in my shoes. I was thinking that me, you, and Los would handle that nigga personally. I want to hit these fools so hard that they get out of the way and go back to corner serving." Amir nodded and pulled out his cell-phone and dialed a number, talking calmly and sternly when the call was connected.

"Is everyone here yet? Okay, they all need to come downstairs. Anyone that's late can be the drivers and lookouts for the niggas that are on time and took my words seriously." He hung up and pulled Reese off of the couch before turning to the room full of men; people were still coming downstairs into the large room. Amir began speaking to the crowd of his loyal henchmen.

"We have one reason for going out into the streets tonight: shutting the fake-ass M.O.P. down and letting everyone else know that we're the only ones that matter out in these streets. We're not taking any prisoners or negotiating; they didn't give Slim or anyone else that option. We'll worry about the Italians later, but we all know that that situation is going to be more difficult, but we will shut that shit down also! We need to get these M.O.P. clowns out of the way right now, though." He paused and looked around the room. "Each team will have a driver and a leader for their hit. If anyone bitches out on their team don't come back here. If you do, you're going to die. If any leader feels that he can't handle the responsibility, speak up now; we need to do this the right way." Everyone glanced around the room, but not a word was uttered in response. Amir continued. "Me and Los run this machine, but we're not like those cowards who hide behind money and pay others to do their dirty work. Me and my homeboy will be out in those streets right with you spilling blood; we're risking more than anyone in this room. Have a few drinks to relax; remember to leave the celebrating for when we all make it home safe, though."

Everyone nodded and tried to get hyped for the bloody night that everyone knew was ahead. Amir nodded to Los and Reese, leading them upstairs and away from the noise. He went to his bedroom on the second floor without saying another word; he picked up Reese's AP9 off his dresser and handed it to the youngster before turning his attention toward Los.

"How about we do things like back in the day tonight? Let's burn Paris and anyone else in that mothafucka like toast!" Los grinned and they all embraced, making it clear that their friendship meant more than the organization they had formed. Los spoke with grit in his voice.

"This is for Slim, Arthur, Flip, Reese's family, and anybody else that those fools disrespected in any way." He turned away from Amir. "Reese, you keep your head up, my nig, and let's kill these niggas with no consequences." Reese replied with tears on his cheeks.

"I aint new to this shit, playa, but you niggas need to leave yo' damn fingers off the trigger when we get to those niggas that touched my mother and little sister. Those niggas are dying slow and hard, believe that!" Amir and Los nodded, and they all headed back downstairs to wait while the stolen vehicles they would need were parked on the surrounding streets.

Amir eventually walked to his prayer room in the corner, but he did not roll out his rug; he knew what evil he planned to embark on. He sat back in his leather chair and thought about what Mecca had said about the name his father had given him and he hoped to see his beautiful queen soon. He stared outside at the twinkling stars in the sky, pondering his decision to be a ruler of men, hoping that one day he would be a positive example for his seed to follow. He hoped for a true prince to be born, and not a man like him that enjoyed getting his hands dirty and risking his life alongside his goons.

CHAPTER 114

KB sat outside the Quick Trip on Kansas Avenue with B.J. riding shotgun while Poonk went inside to purchase the gloves and other things they would need. KB thought about Poonk's strange behavior since they had left the house. He turned in his seat to face B.J.

"Man, this nigga Poonk been actin' funny as fuck! I thought it was just the wet making me paranoid till I walked in the front room and saw that nigga in the corner whispering into his damn phone. When he saw me, the strange-ass nigga hung up real quick."

B.J. nudged him and they looked out of the windshield at the front of the busy store. They both saw Poonk exit a side door and disappear around the side of the building, not noticing them watching through the tinted windows. KB opened his door.

"Stay here, dawg, I'm going to see what's up with this nigga; I think he left his phone in here to try to throw us off."

He paused and grabbed his weapon off the seat and crept around the side of the building, quickly seeing Poonk animatedly speaking into an unfamiliar cell-phone. When KB moved closer, he could clearly hear the words that Poonk spoke.

"Man, I'm telling you what's real! We're on our way to one of y'alls' spots right now, and hella niggas is going all over the Missouri side to get at you niggas! I had to sneak out here to call you while they out there waiting for gloves and shit, now get the fuck up out of there!" KB walked out of the shadows and Poonk looked at him fearfully, quickly slipping the phone into his pocket.

"What's up, KB? I just had to call my girl to…" KB held up a hand to silence him.

"Why didn't you use that damn phone you left in the tilt? Why come all the way back here like you on some snake shit?" KB ignored the man's excuses, pretending that he hadn't heard the conversation, following Poonk alongside the rear of the gas station as he continued to lie.

When Poonk began to turn around with his back to him, KB grabbed him around his neck and applied pressure in a crushing headlock. He pulled Poonk to where the dumpsters were located and continued to apply pressure as he moved out of sight. The man suddenly went limp and his legs started trembling, but KB didn't release his hold on the man until he smelled urine and excrement. KB grunted as he struggled to get Poonk into one of the dumpsters, and he closed the lid so that the corpse wouldn't be easily discovered.

KB climbed back into the vehicle, and B.J. began to look around in confusion. When KB started the vehicle and pulled away, he knew what had happened. KB called Amir and tossed Poonk's phone out onto the freeway. He explained what had happened and vowed that he was careful about disposing of the body. KB had even taken Poonk's shirt and discarded it in traffic in case he had left any type of DNA from their brief encounter.

He ended the call and they headed to Kansas City, Missouri, to pick up Benji; he was the head of the Black Border Brother faction located at the Blue Hills Apartments.

CHAPTER 115

Benji was already ready when they arrived, and he even wore a Kevlar vest under a thin jacket. He carried a .44 Desert Eagle with an extended magazine.

Benji climbed inside and gave the directions to the house where the M.O.P. were located. KB informed him of Poonk's treachery and his untimely demise.

They drove past the house, noticing that it seemed to be open for business; people were moving around the "spot" frequently. KB eventually turned down the street of the house and pulled on the opposite end of the block; he watched for any sign of something out of the ordinary. He didn't know who Poonk had informed about their plans.

When they had sat watching for some time, everyone looked around before climbing out of the vehicle and donning their masks. They walked down the sidewalk on the opposite side of the street, and once a man approached and knocked on the door to the house, they all sprinted across the street. The door opened when they made it to the fence and the man that had been knocking at the door attempted to leap from the porch.

B.J. grabbed the man and KB jammed his foot inside the door so that it couldn't be forced closed. A weapon cocked and Poonk forced the door open as shots rang out repeatedly, tearing holes in the door where they had just been moments ago. KB spotted a man crouching next to the stairway and fired with his 9mm; the man clutched his chest as people yelled in fear and confusion throughout the house. Benji grabbed the "customer" and pushed him into the house with KB and Poonk close behind with their weapons ready.

Benji whispered into the man's ear. "Take us to the room where they handle business. I won't tell you again." He shot the man through the hand and ignored his howl of pain, noticing that he was already headed toward a door in the back of the living room.

KB and B.J. ran up a flight of stairs, and Benji could hear repeated gunfire from their weapons. He heard a woman scream and others begging for their lives to be spared, but all words were silenced by another volley of rounds. He pushed the man through the door and into a large kitchen. Large Pyrex bowls, beakers, baking soda, and weighing scales were all over the table and countertops. It was evident that the people that had been inside the room had made a hasty retreat. Cocaine was burning on the filthy stovetop, and the rear kitchen door was open wide. KB entered and Benji turned to him after forcing the stunned man into a chair with his weapon aimed at his head.

"These bitch-ass niggas didn't even try to fight; they just ran right out the damn door!"

B.J. entered the room carrying a large duffel bag, and he had a woman behind him with her hair gripped in his fist; she was moaning in pain and fear.

"I got the money they had stashed upstairs. This bitch tried to hide under the bed; the two niggas she was fuckin' is already dead, though. She told me that the dumb niggas be in here counting money."

B.J. had blood in his shoulder-length dreadlocks, and he absently wiped at them while the naked woman attempted to cover up portions of her body. K.B pulled the frightened man up from the chair and pushed him out of the back door. Shots rang out and they could hear the man scream in pain as his body was hit with hot slugs. Benji suddenly pushed the woman to the floor and ignored her pleas for mercy as he fired three rounds into her pretty face. He yelled to his friends.

"It aint no more bullshitting; let's get this shit over with before the police end up showing up and trappin' us in this raggedy-ass house!"

They all went to the open doorway and began firing at anything moving. After the shooting ceased, Benji turned to them with a sparkling grin from the diamonds in his mouth.

"I got one of those niggas right in the head; the other niggas ran like some bitches. There's a tall-ass wall back there, so they aint getting away."

KB yelled out of the doorway. "IF YOU NIGGAS COME OUT NOW, WE WON'T KILL YOU! THIS IS YOUR ONLY CHANCE!"

Someone yelled from the back yard. "MAN, THE MONEY IS RIGHT UNDER THE CABINETS IN THERE! TAKE IT ALL, MAN, JUST DON'T KILL ME AND MY BROTHER!"

They watched two men come into the open backyard with their hands empty and above their heads. They all walked outside, and KB grabbed one of the frightened men by his shirt.

"Are you niggas M.O.P.?" The men glanced at each other before nodding hesitantly. Benji smiled.

"You niggas chose the wrong gang. Tell them other niggas in hell that the Black Border Brothers are gonna send lots of company tonight. Take care!" They all opened fire and didn't stop till the men lay still on the grass. They all ran back inside and stripped the cash and drugs out of the cabinets, loaded it into a garbage bag, and headed for the front door. They pulled the stolen car around the corner where Benji's vehicle had been left the previous night. They had taken off their masks and gloves, tossing them into a storm drain along with the weapons. They calmly drove past police cars that were no doubt approaching the house they had just left. They all were satisfied with the hit, and they were pleased to have a bag loaded with cash and drugs to split three ways.

CHAPTER 116

Norman, Tiger, and Sampson stood inside the living room, looking at the three men that were lying face down on the floor with their hands tied behind their backs. The men could make minimal sounds with the rags stuffed into their mouths, but they could imagine the pleadings the desperate men were uttering considering the torture they were witnessing on the other side of the room.

"Ahh! Please don't hurt me no more, man, I told you everything already!" The man's lips were split, and most of his teeth were shattered and lying at his feet among pools of blood and saliva.

Tiger walked up to the man with a large pair of wire cutters, placing the blades around the man's middle finger.

"Fuck the damn money, nigga, where the fuck is that nigga Paris? We got a present for him and that fine-ass bitch he married."

He squeezed the cutters and smiled at the man's howl of pain. The sight of his finger dropping between his legs and the blood pouring from the stump caused the man to pass out. Sampson slapped him awake; he picked up a small propane torch from the floor, and began systematically burning the man's wounds to staunch the flow of blood. They continued working on the man until it was clear that he didn't know anything.

Sampson got tired of toying with the men and executed the two on the floor with rounds to the backs of their heads. Norman retrieved a large knife from the kitchen and carved two letter B's into the corpses' backs and mutilated the M.O.P. tattoos on their chests. The man strapped to the chair realized that he was the next to die. He attempted to spit a wad of mucus at Tiger from his cracked lips and was stabbed repeatedly in the face for it. He was then disemboweled by Sampson's huge kitchen knife.

They all rushed to the safe that they had forced the men to open and piled the cash onto a blanket. Tiger wrapped it up and slung it over his shoulder and headed out of the house to a waiting vehicle.

KB entered the kitchen and blew out the pilot lights on the gas stove and turned on the ranges to send deadly fumes throughout the house. Before he left, he started a small fire in one of the bedrooms before closing the door. He pulled his cell-phone out of his pocket on his way outside, hoping that everyone else was having as much fun as they were.

CHAPTER 117

Amir sat fuming inside the stolen van after ending the call with KB, knowing that Poonk had most likely alerted Paris and whoever else was with him. He looked in the back of the van as Los and Reese pulled on their masks and stuffed magazines into their pockets. Paris's home was equipped with a wrought-iron security fence with cameras covering all angles. Amir already had two stolen trucks waiting down the street in case they needed to ram any fleeing vehicles that Paris used for his escape. He decided to strike at the front gate as soon as it opened.

Amir turned toward the rear of the van. "I think they're bringing him out right now. Get up here!"

Reese and Los rushed to the front as Paris was pushed out of the large house in a wheelchair, carefully moved down a small flight of stairs, and loaded into a dark blue Chevy Suburban. Amir alerted the men in the trucks with a text message and smiled when he received a thumbs-up sign almost immediately. He pulled on his own mask and gripped his Uzi firmly.

The S.U.V.'s headlights came on before it began moving slowly toward the gate entrance behind a white Cadillac Escalade. When the Suburban began to pull onto the street, Amir sent another message.

"Go!"

He paused for a beat before texting again.

"Smash into the white S.U.V. to get them out of the way. We'll take care of the Suburban-make sure that Cadillac is taken out!"

Amir put the van in drive and grinned as one of the trucks sped down the street and smashed head-on into the Escalade. They watched as men climbed from the front and rear of the truck with weapons blazing, sending what seemed like hundreds of rounds into it.

Amir pushed the pedal to the floor and cut off the Suburban with a loud screech of his tires, shooting the first man who emerged from the vehicle and making the others duck down in their seats.

Reese and Los headed straight for the vehicle, knowing that Paris was inside. The driver suddenly climbed out of the vehicle and fired his weapon. Reese clutched his side in pain and anger, but he shot the man at least four times before going to his knees. Los bent down and inspected Reese's wound and nodded to Amir, knowing that he would be alright. Reese pulled himself up and they all cautiously approached the Suburban.

Amir stepped over the driver that Reese had killed, looking into the shattered window; he saw Paris wrapped in a blanket and trembling in fear.

Reese and Los approached, as well as J-Rock, Kimani, and Boo-Nasty who were the men who had been inside the two trucks that had assisted in the assault on Paris and his goons.

Sheena was in the passenger seat, and she began to plead with them, seeing what had happened to the men. Reese pointed his AP9 at her head.

"Bitch, I don't want to hear that fuckin' shit! Get the fuck up out of there before I kill yo' funky-ass right there in yo' seat!"

She was so frightened that she couldn't move at first, but she eventually pulled her eyes away from Paris in the backseat and grudgingly complied. When she stepped out, Reese pushed her roughly toward Los and pulled the rear door open where Paris lay sweating and in great pain. He slapped Paris viciously in the face and gripped his long braids, dragging him onto the pavement, slamming his head onto the concrete.

Sheena screamed. "He can't even walk, you bastard! Why would you do him like that when he can't even defend himself?"

Reese swung around and hit the woman in the nose with his fist, smashing it against her beautiful face.

"This bitch-ass nigga had his homeboys rape and kill a little girl and her mother, my fuckin' momma! He don't deserve shit but what he gonna fuckin' get, bitch!"

Without warning he grabbed the front of Sheena's blouse, rammed the wicked-looking AP9 into her mouth, and shot her through the back of the head several times. Los jumped back in disgust as the blood and brain matter showered on him and Boo-Nasty.

"You crazy ass nigga! The bitch could've took us to the money; I know they got some stashed around this mothafucka!"

Amir walked over to where Paris lay, watching his woman's corpse lying nearly decapitated next to him, sobbing and attempting to crawl toward her with his useless legs dragging behind him. Amir placed his foot in the middle of his enemy's back, stopping him from moving any further.

"This nigga needs to get handled right now; we don't have time to do anything else before we get the hell away from here. Half the police station will be here soon, so you need to handle your business, Reese. I have nothing but love for you and I feel your pain, but we don't have time to drag this out any further"

Reese nodded and turned and walked back to the van, returning with a blade as long as his arm. He calmly turned to Los.

"Hold this bitch up for me."

Paris attempted to get away by slowly pulling his body along the pavement, but Los and Kimani grabbed him, forcing his back onto the Suburban while he screamed in fear and begged for his life.

Reese approached the man and twisted his ear viciously, sawed it off and tossed it to the ground dismissively. He did the same to the other ear as Paris wailed inhumanly as he was held still. Reese surprised everyone as he leaned forward and clamped Paris's nose in his teeth, pulling back and leaving it hanging by a small piece of flesh. He then punched the blade through both of Paris's eye sockets. He leaned down and yelled into what was left of the man's face as he moaned and bled.

"You better be glad that we gotta go, my nig. If it was up to me, I'd cut off yo' little dick and shove it in yo' dead bitch's funky ass!"

Reese motioned for everyone to move back and unloaded the AP9 into Paris's head and body; he discarded his weapon in frustration, having wanted to do more to both of the corpses. Everyone looked at Reese with respect and a little fear. It was one thing to hear rumors about an individual, but they had witnessed the mind of a man that had gone insane because of his grief.

Everyone climbed into the van and left the other vehicles, making sure to discard everything incriminating along the way to the Kansas side-several miles from the murder scene. With Paris deceased, the head was severed from the M.O. P., but Amir knew better than to take the ones left for granted; he would keep his ears to the streets.

CHAPTER 118

Keith was in the "Ghetto" in Leavenworth, Kansas, sitting inside Lo-Lo's new Lexus and keeping an eye on the small drug dealings that were occurring around him. It didn't take much to sway the youngsters in the area to abandon their petty hustles to work for him on consignment. With the money from his savings, and the cash that Amir had given to Lo-Lo, he had purchased several ounces of cocaine and learned how to cook it for sale in the dregs of the inner-city. Keith still did not fully understand the drug business, but he was adept at counting cash and maximizing his profits. Mathematics had always been his favorite subject in school, and he simply applied this knowledge to what he was doing in the streets. Keith had attempted to establish something in Lawrence, Kansas, initially, but the authorities were much more adept at spotting crime in the college town. Also, the youngsters that were willing to work for him in Leavenworth were much more loyal; they had practically made themselves willing prisoners of a miniature section of the small city.

Keith and Lo-Lo had lost their virginities to one another, and Lo-Lo had intensified her efforts to finish high school and enroll at the University of Kansas. Keith had experienced the art of compiling fast money, and greed began to ensnare him. Keith knew that he would eventually have to talk to Amir about him choosing the streets for a refuge while living with his little sister, but he planned to continue building his own life, regardless.

Keith had already had two confrontations with men that were in the streets; they took his looks and demeanor as a weakness. The killings he had committed had flashed through his consciousness as he began to draw his weapon at times, but the men had always relented after seeing the look in his eyes. They had seen the calm detachment and chose to back off; The situations had literally resolved themselves. Keith had noticed that his young entourage were ready for battle also, proving it by relieving the men of their cash and jewelry before escorting them from the area with force. The word had spread about Keith and his group of youngsters, and he was often approached by fresh young faces that wanted to be a part of the group that they dubbed "Taliban".

Keith heard a car horn and turned to see Lo-Lo smiling through the windshield of his mother's vehicle. She stepped out drawing looks from everyone in the vicinity, wearing a skin-tight maxi dress and two-inch heels. She had her hair in two long natural plaits that hung to the middle of her back, and she wore sparkling diamonds in her ears that Los had purchased for her birthday.

She approached her man with a smile.

"Hey, baby! I thought we were going to the Legends tonight?"

Keith had already instructed Lo-Lo that they wouldn't do much traveling until they knew that the conflict that they were dealing with was behind them. He realized that his woman was simply checking up on him, but he knew that he had to put a stop to it now, or he would never have any control in their relationship. Keith didn't want Lo-Lo associated with what he was doing in the streets. He leaned right into her face, causing her smile to turn into a nervous frown.

"I told you not to come around anywhere looking for me. I feel that you're disrespecting me right now; I've told you this for the last time!" Lo-Lo's eyes welled up with tears.

"Keith, I just…" He held up a hand to silence her before continuing.

"I love you, baby, but if you do this again, we're done, and I never want to see you again. If you can't do the things I ask, you don't respect me. I can't put anyone in a position where I may harm them, especially you. I will hurt anyone that disrespects me, baby."

Lo-Lo witnessed the same look on her boyfriend's face as he had worn when he killed the men who had kidnapped her. Keith was saying something more, so she snapped out of her reverie and looked at him respectfully.

"Lo-Lo, I said do you understand me?"

She nodded and wiped away her tears, staring at him without blinking. She realized that she had to grow up and really become a woman, especially in this life she had chosen. A disloyal woman would never be complementary to a real man, and she knew that Keith had reached manhood right before her eyes. Keith pulled her close and kissed her tenderly on the lips while he smiled at her with a wink.

Lo-Lo felt contentment as she drove back to Lawrence to try enrolling in the school that she loved. She felt that she had to trust Keith; he had never given her a reason to be jealous, and she knew that he was out in the streets to benefit them both. She turned on her favorite Monica playlist and relaxed on the drive back, feeling that Keith had reminded her of a young Amir whom she loved, respected, and feared.

CHAPTER 119

Amir sipped from his glass of cognac and glanced around at his friends and associates that had returned home from the hit. T.J., A.D., and Taz were killed at one of Paris's houses and the scene was more like a wake than a celebration. Everyone was producing bags of currency and drugs that they had procured from their endeavors, dividing it between themselves without Amir or Los's interference.

Los and Reese were on the other side of the room after returning from outside having a "talk". Amir had been around P.C.P. for most of his life, and he knew, beyond a doubt, that they were both "wet". He didn't even bother confronting them about it; they already had confused, glassy-eyed stares on their faces. Amir also felt that they all deserve a break after all they had been through. He felt his cell-phone vibrating in his pocket and pulled it out to see Mecca's name displayed, deciding to answer it after considering ignoring the call.

"Hey, baby-mama, what's going on?" There was a silence that alerted him.

"Meer, do you know a man named Frank? He and three other men said that they were supposed to meet you here at my sister's house. I told them to wait outside, but they forced themselves in and refused to leave!"

Amir felt the blood turn cold in his veins, knowing that Frank's presence could only mean one thing. Amir couldn't conceal the panic he felt as he attempted to steady his voice.

"Mecca, you and your sister have to get out of there right now! I don't care how you do it!" He heard Imani screaming in the background and knew it was too late. He heard Mecca scream and plead for the life of the baby in her stomach and he froze; all Amir could feel was rage and hatred.

The line went dead, and he turned to see Los staring directly at him with a questioning look. He went into the next room and came back with two handguns, shoving one into each pocket.

"Meer, what's up, my man?" Los already had his 9mm Beretta in his hand. Amir looked at his best friend with an emotionless stare.

"They have Mecca." He headed out of the front door in a sprint. Reese grabbed his keys and ran to his vehicle, not wanting to lose sight of Amir. He followed and watched Amir get off on the I-35 exit going south, and Los knew that he was headed toward the suburbs of Johnson County. They both hoped that Amir wasn't noticed by the Highway Patrol; he was accelerating to well over 90 mph. Amir's vehicle eventually skidded into a yard and nearly ran into the side of a huge three-story house. He climbed out of his vehicle with his pistol in hand; Reese and Los quickly followed as he ran into an already open front door.

When Los reached the doorway, he could hear Amir yelling and screaming profanities as if he had gone insane. Reese rushed inside to a scene that stopped him in his tracks.

Amir was kneeling next to Mecca's lifeless corpse sprawled on the floor; her abdomen had been sliced open and the dead baby had been placed in her arms, still trailing the umbilical cord from between her legs. Imani was lying next to her with her throat slit so deep that she was nearly decapitated. Two bloody used condoms were between her legs as well as Mecca's, leaving no doubt as to what fate the women had suffered.

The Italians had sent the worst message, and Frank had backed up his threat. Los placed his hand on Amir's shoulder to comfort him, but his best friend suddenly stood with tears running down his cheeks.

"These bitches are dying tonight, playa. Get out of here before the police come; I'm going to call 911 so they can get my family off this damn floor! You're a convicted felon, so you know you can't be here when they show up." He glanced over at a stunned Reese who was obviously taken aback by the déjà-vu-like scene.

"You and Los need to take these guns out of here and I'll catch up with you later."

Amir's sudden change of attitude made them wonder about his state of mind, but Amir embraced them before they hurried out of the house. Los silently hoped that Amir would be alright; he couldn't imagine how the man felt.

1 Month Later

Los approached the visiting room glass, and Amir looked up with a smile on his handsome face, not seeming to be affected by the dire situation that he was faced with. Los picked up the visiting room receiver and placed his right palm to the glass before greeting his confidante and best friend.

"My nig, why the fuck haven't you called me? You aint fuckin' none of those punks already, are you? It aint even been thirty days, nigga!" Amir just smiled and shook his head.

"You don't ever stop, do you, bro? I've just been concentrating on my attorneys and focusing on those law books; I may have a chance at justifiable homicide considering that I was alone."

Shortly after the police finished questioning him at Imani's house, Amir headed to a bar in the bottoms and waited for Frank to arrive with his henchmen. As soon as the Italian stepped from his vehicle, Amir killed him and his two bodyguards, taking two slugs in his chest before falling unconscious in the street with the weapon still in his hand.

Los had attempted to visit Amir in the hospital, but he was already in police custody, so he had to wait until he was booked into the Wyandotte County Detention Center and could have visitors. Los considered his friend's words.

"That's cool, man, and I'll make sure to stay at them damn lawyers' throats; I'll make sure them fools are on point. You keep yo' head up in that mothafucka. By the way, that nigga Reese is out there givin' those spaghetti eatin' Italians the damn business; he layed two of em' out last night. I don't know how long he gonna be out here, though; they got my nig all over the damn news. That fool been puttin' it down for

Mecca, Imani, and that beautiful baby. We hittin' those mothafuckas again tonight."

Amir looked up at him sharply and raised his right palm in the air, dripping blood. Los looked down at his own hand, remembering when the two of them had sliced their palms when they were youngsters, shaking hands and sealing their hearts together with blood.

Los bit into the fleshy part of his hand until he tasted a salty taste in his mouth; he put his palm to the window on the other side of Amir's.

"You're the blood of my blood, my nig. Black Border Brother till they put me in a box and lower that mothafucka into the ground."

The deputy that came to end the visit looked at the bloody visiting glass window in disgust; Amir simply nodded his head at his blood brother, feeling déjà vu, but this time he was on the opposite side of the glass. They would always be there for each other; blood in and blood out.

EPILOGUE

Reese cruised down Parallel Parkway on his way to meet with Los so that he could get the address to Carlos Sr.'s new home. Things had calmed considerably, but Reese realized that his days as a free man were coming to an end; he could feel fate at his heels whenever he took a step.

He looked up just in time to see a large truck barreling toward him and cringed, knowing that there would be a terrible crash. When the impact came the driver's side air-bag hit him in the face and his door folded inward; he could feel the bones break in his shoulder and left arm. He slumped into the seat and lost consciousness.

———————————

When Reese came awake, he stared up into a dark man's grinning face, thinking that he was dreaming.

"What you doin', boi? You batty bois did not tink you could get away from killi' me brudda, did you now? This is the beginning of the fall of your Babylon, mon; you shoulda left me Peter be!"

Reese saw a shining gleam, and the last thing he remembered was seeing a group of dreadlocked men, each wielding a large machete. He felt excruciating pain as the Jamaicans chopped him to pieces as they yelled profanities in a language that he did not understand.

The End

Coming Soon: Brick Roads.